ARCHITECT OF FATE

DEATH CAME TO the *Bastion Inviolate* beneath a veil of shadow and flesh.

Castellan Lepidus outlived the command deck crew by a handful of seconds. They were asphyxiated as the machine-spirit lost control to the data-daemon and the airlocks and bulkhead doors were slammed open. The air shrieked out of the star fort, dragging many crew with it, kicking out blindly as they were thrown out into the void. Those who held on died in the next moment, blood vessels rupturing, lungs bursting, their blood coughed out into a frozen mist in the sudden cold.

A Space Marine could survive the void for a while. It was not the void that killed Lepidus.

ARCHITECT OF FATE

EDITED BY
CHRISTIAN DUNN

BLACK LIBRARY

A Black Library Publication

First published in Great Britain in 2012 by
The Black Library,
Games Workshop Ltd.,
The Black Library,
Nottingham, NG7 2WS, UK.

10 9 8 7 6 5 4 3 2 1

Cover illustration by Jon Sullivan.
Maps by Darius Hinks and Adrian Wood.

A CIP record for this book is available from the British Library.

UK ISBN 13: 978 1 84970 152 5
US ISBN 13: 978 1 84970 153 2

See the Black Library on the internet at

www.blacklibrary.com

Find out more about Games Workshop
and the world of Warhammer 40,000 at

www.games-workshop.com

Printed and bound by CPI Group (UK) Ltd, Croydon, CR0 4YY

It is the 41st millennium. For more than a hundred
centuries the Emperor has sat immobile on the Golden
Throne of Earth. He is the master of mankind by the
will of the gods, and master of a million worlds by the
might of his inexhaustible armies. He is a rotting carcass
writhing invisibly with power from the Dark Age of
Technology. He is the Carrion Lord of the Imperium for
whom a thousand souls are sacrificed every day, so that
he may never truly die.

Yet even in his deathless state, the Emperor continues
his eternal vigilance. Mighty battlefleets cross the
daemon-infested miasma of the warp, the only route
between distant stars, their way lit by the Astronomican,
the psychic manifestation of the Emperor's will. Vast
armies give battle in His name on uncounted worlds.
Greatest amongst his soldiers are the Adeptus Astartes,
the Space Marines, bio-engineered super-warriors. Their
comrades in arms are legion: the Imperial Guard and
countless planetary defence forces, the ever-vigilant
Inquisition and the tech-priests of the Adeptus
Mechanicus to name only a few. But for all their
multitudes, they are barely enough to hold off the ever-
present threat from aliens, heretics, mutants - and worse.

To be a man in such times is to be one amongst untold
billions. It is to live in the cruellest and most bloody
regime imaginable. These are the tales of those times.
Forget the power of technology and science, for so much
has been forgotten, never to be re-learned. Forget the
promise of progress and understanding, for in the grim
dark future there is only war. There is no peace amongst
the stars, only an eternity of carnage and slaughter, and
the laughter of thirsting gods.

CONTENTS

ACCURSED ETERNITY

SARAH CAWKWELL

I

+++

Amaranthine encrypted message, code Theta Gamma Four Three Nine. Captain Tanek of the Star Dragons Sixth Company, presently designated commanding officer of Containment Fleet Kappa, hear this on the order of the Ordo Malleus. I send you greetings and demand your immediate compliance. There has been a reported sighting of the vessel matching archive description of the Accursed Eternity.

By the power vested in me and through my position within the Holy Ordos, you are ordered to bring your fleet to the coordinates I will transmit following this message. This sighting warrants an immediate investigation and your fleet is the closest available. I will speak with you in person upon your arrival.

Message ends.

+++

* * *

IT DRIFTED WITHOUT direction, carried by the endless tides of space. Partially curtained by a swirling dust cloud, it loomed out of the darkness like a monstrous leviathan surfacing in a ponderous climb from the mighty deeps for a lungful of life-giving air. The analogy was not entirely without basis.

Surrounded on all sides by ruthless escort vessels, the ship was a thing of legend and myth. It may once have been a battle-barge – but since nobody had ever destroyed its companion fleet, no one had ever gotten close enough to find out exactly what it was, or who it belonged to. It responded to no hails. As soon as any fleet was sent to investigate, inexplicable warp storms blew up and the thing was gone. At most, it had only ever remained visible for five hours: barely long enough for its presence to even register. Chaos, however, inevitably followed in its wake, along with other companions: madness, corruption and death.

It had earned itself the name *Accursed Eternity* over the many years that it had been spotted. Most people dismissed it as a ghost story, a tale whispered by the ratings who toiled in the sub-levels; tales that were shared with amusement by junior officers. Veterans of the void found little laughter in such things. They knew better than to dismiss the evils of the warp so easily.

A ghost ship. The spectral echo of a vessel lost to the tides. Perhaps, the stories went, it was filled with the shackled spirits of its former crew, bound in eternal torment. Perhaps seductive sirens of ruinous powers inhabited its empty decks just waiting to lure an innocent victim to a death most unworthy.

Whatever was on board had to be a product of the warp. On that, the stories all agreed. There had to be something or someone deeply important hidden within its twisted hull to warrant the escort that it brought with it, but it was not a prize that mortal men dared attempt to reach out and snatch.

One hundred years had passed since the last time the

full fleet had been spied. One hundred years, during which the tale of its nature had had time to evolve and distort, until it became something it was not. It became a legend. It became a myth. The recovered records of the battle a century before had never been corroborated. It was believed that nobody would ever truly discover the facts of the deaths at Balanor.

In the past few decades the appearance of the lone ship itself had increased in regularity and yet it had only ever been sighted in passing, a glimpse – an *idea* – of something that may or may not have been a battle-barge. Descriptions of the ship never suggested anything physically abnormal; it was the same as any other of its kind, despite the legends surrounding it. No external markings of allegiance had been reported and the overall condition of the ship remained largely unknown.

It became synonymous with bad luck. To see the *Accursed Eternity*, even if only for a fleeting moment, was a premonition of doom and destruction.

In the wake of the fleet's sudden, unexplained appearance, the astropathic choirs of the Imperium of Mankind came to urgent life as a suitable, expedient response was sought. Increasingly frantic messages were transmitted back and forth, and were then met by a cool, calm and very deliberate response.

+++

By the command of the Ordo Malleus of the Holy Inquisition, the Balanor system and all vessels therein are deemed traitoris in extremis. In His name, we come.

This situation is now under our control.

+++

THE SITUATION WAS anything but under control. The small Ordo Malleus fleet had ripped into real space with its guns already fully charged and ready to unleash the wrath of their kind. Batteries of weapons pounded relentlessly against the encroaching Chaos fleet, constant streams of light razoring through the endless darkness. For a time, a brief and incredible moment, it seemed that they would achieve their objective. For a fleeting second it seemed that they had the upper hand. The Chaos ships looked as though they were preparing for a retreat. But they weren't.

There were five vessels in the Chaos fleet, each one unidentifiable but for a proudly displayed eight-pointed star emblem emblazoned across their prows, and as one they peeled from the ship they escorted. Turning with excruciating slowness, they broke from their prescribed path and plunged headlong into the Inquisitorial fleet. Four escort ships were destroyed instantly, caught in the path of the cruisers as they accelerated and torn to pieces. Debris, fuel and corpses dribbled from the broken vessels and briefly cluttered the path of the strike cruisers. The Chaos vessels cut a steady path through the carnage.

Not a single shot left the gunnery decks of the Chaos fleet. Every death they caused came from the fact that they rammed without hesitation into the ships of the Ordo Malleus.

Doggedly determined, the Inquisition held their ground with implacable and commendable ferocity. They re-engaged the Chaos ships and eliminated two of them with a savage and unrelenting volley of fire from their main cannons. Yet, when the ships were destroyed, there was nothing to prove that they had ever existed. No twisted, broken metal, no trails or wisps of smoke... Nothing. It was simply as though they had never been.

It was only when the Inquisition fleet had battled the enemy down to equal numbers, that they put the call out for Containment Fleet Kappa.

Mistress Kerys Jabiru, Primaris Astropath on board the Star Dragons flagship *Ladon*, was a thin woman. At one time in her life, she might have been considered slim, willowy and graceful, but the simple fact of the matter now was that she was almost painfully undernourished. The years in service to the Imperium had robbed her of any youth, beauty and vitality that might once have been admirable. Her life in servitude to the Throne of Terra had taken its toll on her, physically and mentally. But despite that, she was still able to hold herself proudly.

There was nothing even slightly womanly in her motion as she walked at great speed through the ship's dimly-lit corridors, no sensuality or feminine fluidity in her stride. She walked in a manner not unlike a strutting, long-legged water bird. Even her head bobbed slightly with every step she took. It was a gait that might have been considered comical by those whose dispositions tended towards the unkind.

Even blind as she was, her psychic senses guided her with skill and effortless ease through the sprawling vessel. Her speed only began to hint at the true sense of urgency she felt. Since she had received and relayed the message from the Inquisition, orders had begun flying back and forth, but this one was a personal missive for the captain and she was, if she would only admit it to herself, curious to see how its contents were received.

Kerys had served the Star Dragons for more than twenty years, girl and woman, and whilst she retained the proper sense of awe and respect for the Adeptus Astartes, she had, over the years, built up a comfortable rapport with the captain of Sixth Company. She was not afraid of him.

Not *too* afraid, at least.

It was hard not to like Captain Tanek. Although a fierce, stern and allegedly brutal warrior on the field of battle, when the armour came off and the other side of him was in force, there was a certain affability about him. He treated his company – and those who served them – with fairness and he actively encouraged those aboard to speak their minds. Such openness, he declared, was an important trait. His men virtually idolised him; the mortal crew component of the *Ladon* actually *did* idolise him. He found it faintly uncomfortable and did whatever he could to dissuade such adulation. Such modesty was becoming and, if anything, made the situation worse.

Kerys turned a corner and slowed her pace. The skin of her pale cheeks, papery and dry as a result of the recycled air of the *Ladon's* environment, was touched with two spots of pink from her exertions. Her greying hair, tied back in a severe knot at the back of her head, had come free and thin, wispy strands hung untidily around her pinched face. Pursing her lips tightly, she spent a few moments tucking the escaped hair back into the knot. It would not do to present herself before Captain Tanek looking so dishevelled.

The ship, which had been ripping through the warp for several hours since the receipt of the initial message, was not travelling smoothly and a sudden shifting of the floor beneath her feet made her stumble. She threw out her arms to balance herself and the ship lurched immediately in the other direction throwing her completely off-balance. Before she could fall, however, a hand reached out and caught her. A strong hand that fully encircled her upper arm with room to spare. One of the Star Dragons.

'Mistress Jabiru.' A rich, warm voice sounded and a flicker of a smile came onto her face.

'Sergeant Korydon.' She was pleased by the tone of respect and concern in the warrior's voice and she turned her blind face towards him. Her hands came up in the sign of the aquila and she bowed her head to show equal respect for the Adeptus Astartes.

'I presume you are walking to the Clutch? I would consider it an honour if you would let me escort you. The passage through the empyrean is rough and I would be deeply distressed if you were to fall.'

His manners were impeccable and she could not find it in herself to be offended. She had never seen Korydon, but she conversed with him often. He was a serious warrior with a dry, often sarcastic sense of humour that complemented Tanek's straight talking style admirably.

She had never been able to gauge the age of any of the Star Dragons, but all the clues she had pulled together from his presence at the Clutch had led her to deduce that Korydon was comparatively young. This close, she could smell the unique aroma that seemed to accompany all of the Adeptus Astartes: a mixture of gun oils and armour abrasives, and the faintest hint of sweet incense that suggested he had not long left the ship's chapel. She straightened her shoulders.

'I would be equally honoured for you to escort me, Sergeant Korydon.'

'Of course, Mistress Jabiru.'

She felt him take her hand and place it on his bare forearm so that he could guide her safely through the unsteady corridors of the *Ladon*. Although she would never openly voice the opinion, she was rather glad of his strong, steady support. The speed with which the Star Dragons and the Blood Swords were heeding the Inquisition's call was both alarming and unsettling. The news she brought now to the ears of the captain was equally disturbing.

Suddenly, she felt *very* glad for Korydon's presence. She had a deep-seated feeling that today's Clutch was going to become complicated very swiftly.

THE CLUTCH WAS the name given to the daily meeting of the *Ladon's* key personnel. During the Clutch any and all problems were brought to the table and orders shared out. It was a functional thing, rarely coloured with any sort of excitement. But a vessel the size of the strike cruiser needed to run smoothly and Tanek, whose sense of organisation was second to none, ran an exceptionally tight ship.

Led into the strategium by Korydon, Kerys paused before the statue of the Emperor. There was such a palpable aura of faith around it that it was not hard to locate it. She almost absently muttered the litany of guidance and thanked the sergeant as he led her to her given place at the table.

It was several minutes later that she heard the captain's voice. It arrived into the strategium a moment before he did and Kerys turned her head towards the sound, her ears working to gauge what her eyes never could. The years of blindness had finely tuned her other senses to be far more receptive to her surroundings. There was a measure of impatience in his voice that suggested he was fractious and annoyed, but he tempered it with customary politeness.

He was not alone as he entered; other footfalls echoed his own. Captain Khorvash of the Blood Swords, no doubt. The other captain had been on board the *Ladon* when the call had come from the Inquisition, and rather than travel back to his own vessel he had saved valuable time by remaining on board the Star Dragons craft. He had attended several Clutches over Kappa's tour of duty and had always treated Kerys with due deference, albeit with the clear distrust so many showed towards those of a psychic bent.

Her sharp thoughts almost absently brushed the minds of the two captains, and she marvelled at how two such god-like beings could project such different personalities without ever speaking a word. From what she understood, Khorvash was the younger of the two captains by several decades and it was clear, even to one as blind as she was, that he wore his youth proudly. There was arrogance in his voice and attitude that had not yet been tempered by experience. He was smart and he was eager. Yet, despite the shared rank, he obviously deferred to the older warrior. From the cadence of his voice, and the extra distance it had to travel, she sensed that he respectfully kept a step or two behind Tanek, falling into place eventually at the captain's right shoulder.

There was another presence too; Kerys could hear him walking, but he chose not to announce himself. She inhaled and coughed slightly; whereas Korydon had smelt of incense and the chapel, the other newcomer positively reeked of it. Iakodos, she deduced. The only one of the

Star Dragons she felt true fear towards.

'Thank you all for your patience,' said Tanek. He spoke in slow, almost indolent tones but offered no further explanation as to why he had arrived late. He was captain. It was his prerogative, and there was never any sense of haste or urgency about him. Kerys, who had heard many tales of Tanek's battlefield valour knew that he was a deeply thoughtful soul who ensured that he had the full measure of his enemy before he ever took up arms. It was a trait endemic amongst the Star Dragons; they were fierce, implacable fighters.

The Clutch continued as normal, each member present delivering any pertinent news. However, as Kerys had anticipated, due to their travels through the warp there was nothing that any of them could add. Korydon provided an update on the readiness of the company's squads and the state of the armoury. Kerys was sure that the rest of the Star Dragons found it compelling but she found it painfully dull. Surprised at how bored she felt and realising this was due to the earlier anxiety at the need to deliver the latest message, she allowed her attention to drift.

'Mistress Kerys? Any further communication?'

Tanek's voice had a slight hint of amusement and Kerys's cheeks flushed as she realised he had already spoken her name once. She patted the back of her hair and coughed politely to clear her throat.

'A repeat of the original request for help, my lord, perhaps sent on a relay. But, yes, there has been a further message received. It is... personal, Captain Tanek. I am under instruction to give the message to you and you alone.'

'Personal?'

Though she could not see him, Kerys suspected that the captain's eyebrow had risen.

'And who exactly is this "personal" message from?'

'He gives his name as Inquisitor Shadrach Remigius, my lord.' The sudden hiss of annoyance from the direction of

Chaplain Iakodos did little to calm the churning sea of acid that was in her gut.

'Personal. I see.' She heard him tap his fingers on the table. 'My rule has always been that there are to be no secrets on board this ship. If I cannot adhere to that myself I cannot lead by example. Please continue with the message, mistress.'

'Do you think that is wise, Tanek?' Iakodos spoke for the first time, his voice so deep that it felt to Kerys as though the floor beneath her very feet rumbled with the bass pitch of it.

'I think it is *very* wise, Chaplain.'

A flash of an unspoken battle of wills touched the edge of her psychic awareness and she knew misery. Externally, Kerys looked suddenly unsure of herself, her earlier manner of prim propriety dissolved in the sudden realisation that she was being asked to go against an inquisitor's wishes. Her senses were on fire as she became slowly aware that everyone was looking at her. She wrung her hands together anxiously and when she spoke again, her voice eked its way out as barely more than a squeak.

'He was... really quite specific, my lord. I... I'm not sure that I should... It is only very short and will take next to no time to impart to you if you would but retire to...'

'I will not. Please deliver the message, Mistress Kerys.'

His tone brooked no argument and with her expression becoming slightly more miserable, she let her voice slip into the gravelly tones of the faceless inquisitor.

'The time has come to collect my due, Tanek. I will take my payment on your arrival.'

Silence descended upon the gathering like dust settling after a flurry of wind. Kerys's hands were still wringing together miserably, her chest rising and falling swiftly.

It was Khorvash who broke the peace.

'What does that mean exactly? Tanek? Do you know this Inquisitor Remigius?'

'It is unimportant. An... existing arrangement between

the inquisitor and myself.' Tanek stared into the astropath's hollow eyes for a few moments longer, as though he could somehow discern the inquisitor's full meaning, but eventually took his piercing gaze from her. Standing up, he clasped his hands behind his back and let his gaze roam around the Clutch.

'Inquisitor Shadrach Remigius is indeed known to me, Khorvash.' He nodded abruptly. The gesture more than indicated that he had no desire to talk about it in front of the Clutch despite his earlier assertion. He tweaked his pointed beard between thumb and forefinger and considered for a moment before nodding.

'Very well. Mistress Kerys, make arrangements to respond to the good inquisitor, if you would be so kind. Tell him that his message has been received and understood. That will suffice.'

There was an undercurrent of bitter sarcasm in his voice, but Kerys decided that it would be far more prudent to keep her counsel than speak her mind. She dipped her head in a bow, her long hair falling free once again and framing her face. 'As my lord commands,' she responded, taking his order as her cue to leave.

TANEK WATCHED HER go, his expression unreadable and his consternation growing. He let none of the concern show on his face but his soul was in turmoil.

The *Accursed Eternity*. Both captains knew its name, as did many of the others present. It was a legend. A thing of myth. Yet, here they were, following the orders of the Inquisition, travelling to verify its existence.

If any of those present at the Clutch thought this was strange, none of them voiced that opinion out loud. Tanek cast a wary eye around the assembly, almost as though daring any of them to question the situation.

'Estimates put our time of arrival at less than three hours,' he said. 'Ensure that the fleet is at full battle readiness and be ready to engage as soon as we translate into the Balanor system. That is all.'

The Clutch dispersed, leaving the two captains and the Chaplain standing alone in the strategium. Khorvash studied the others with open interest. Their shared duty had formed strong bonds of friendship and loyalty.

For now, the Blood Swords and the Star Dragons travelled the wastes of space together. For centuries prior to their deployment here, they had frequently joined forces when a given situation demanded it. The proximity of their home worlds had given them great reason to remain cordial and closely allied. In the wake of the act of shame that had seen the Blood Swords torn from their home world, the Star Dragons had been there to support them. There had been no question of debt or honour. It merely *was*.

This reciprocal loyalty engendered a rare sense of genuine fraternity between the two that more commonly was confined to battle-brothers of the same Chapter. There was a pooling of similar traditions and history, and this gave rise to friendships that spanned across the two Chapters. Above and beyond this, both the Star Dragons and the Blood Swords fielded stalwart warriors with an eye for tactics that made them a terrifying force to be reckoned with when they took the field of battle together.

Khorvash had been the latest captain to take his place amongst the fleet. It was a duty that was performed on a rotational basis with each Blood Swords company captain expected to spend a preordained length of time serving aboard the Chapter's vessel *Ophidian*. As for the Star Dragons, there was nothing that commanded their presence here. They served alongside their cousins out of choice alone.

Tanek liked Khorvash. He was an eager, enthusiastic slab of pure impulse who frequently gave voice to thoughts that others might consider inappropriate or tactless. To Tanek's mind it was a refreshing honesty that served him well.

'I do not wish to pry into matters that do not concern me, Tanek,' Khorvash began after a long period of considering the others, 'but what is the meaning behind that message?'

'Allow me to share some of my greater experience with you, Brother-Captain Khorvash.' Tanek gave the younger captain a faintly benevolent smile and made a point of addressing his battle-brother in full. 'If you start a sentence by stating that you have no wish to pry, then you would be well advised not to. The details of the matter are unimportant. Suffice it to say that the inquisitor is owed a favour by my Chapter.' His eyes were clear and steady. 'Evidently he feels that the time has come to settle the debt.'

His gaze met that of Iakodos and there was concern in them. 'For now at least, that is all you need to know.'

THE RETURN TO real space from the warp was hazardous at the best of times, but to emerge straight into a void war was far more so. Manifesting from the empyrean, the small fleet was instantly caught up in the very heart of the battle that raged between the Chaos ships and those of the Inquisition. Two of Kappa's small escort vessels were incapacitated instantly by the guns of the Ordo Malleus, merely by dint of being in the wrong place at the wrong time.

Furious words from both Imperial parties were exchanged. The Inquisition had not been expecting the Containment Fleet to arrive with such alacrity, they claimed, and conversely, Kappa had not anticipated arriving into a hotly fought battle-zone. With obvious reluctance, the Inquisition ships altered their position and held fire long enough to allow the *Ladon* and the *Ophidian* to take position and lend much-needed supporting fire.

The *Ladon* opened up every gun port on her port side and unleashed a barrage of deadly fire on the traitor vessels as they traversed the void of space. As the streams of destruction burned their way towards the enemy, the Inquisition sent a security-coded message. Its contents were conveyed with all haste to the Adeptus Astartes. Tanek took the data-slate from the crewman who brought it to him and read it. His brow creased in confused irritation.

* * *

+++

Do not fire on the anomalous vessel. Inquisitor Remigius and his retinue will make their way to you with all expedience. Repeat, hold your fire.

+++

BY TANEK'S CALCULATIONS, Inquisitor Shadrach Remigius was at least in his mid to late sixties. However, the augmetics and assorted juvenat treatments that he had undergone made him seem far younger. It had been at least twenty years since Tanek had seen him last and in that time he seemed not to have aged at all.

Unless you looked directly into his eyes. Then you saw the truth of it. In the very heart of the inquisitor's cold, emerald stare was intelligence and the wisdom of his years, and the power and ability to coerce that had served him so well. But Remigius generated an aura of such inherent disdain that it shrouded his true self. People did not voluntarily meet the inquisitor's stare; they did not look into the depths of his eyes. Staring at the floor was eminently preferable to looking directly at him.

Those, like Tanek, who did possess the wherewithal to hold his gaze saw a tall, slender man with a mane of greying hair that was pulled into false order by a tattered ribbon of red cloth. His narrow face was dominated by a long, thin nose and those hard, green eyes. The right side of his face was a mass of ugly scar tissue that even the juvenat treatments had failed to disguise and his lip was drawn upwards in a permanent sneer.

One arm had long ago been severed at the elbow and its mechanical replacement was clearly the work of an artisan: beautifully made and polished to a high sheen. Not for Remigius the pretence of covering it with a sleeve. This was who he was. He was proud of it.

He wore a sword in a scabbard at his waist and as he stepped into the strategium, he kept one hand on its pommel. Tanek watched him enter and kept his voice carefully free of anything other than neutral tones.

'Greetings, inquisitor,' he rumbled. 'Welcome aboard the *Ladon*.'

'Captain Tanek. Who would have thought our paths would cross again so soon? And for such a great purpose.' His voice, when he spoke, was surprising. For such an ugly man, it was rich and almost lyrical in its quality. He turned his penetrating gaze onto Khorvash.

Before Tanek could introduce him, the inquisitor spoke again. 'You would be Captain Khorvash of the Blood Swords. You are presently serving with Containment Fleet Kappa as part of your Chapter's ongoing penitence.'

Khorvash bristled visibly and Remigius's sneer split in a parody of a smile. 'I mean no offence, of course.'

'Still yourself, brother,' murmured Tanek. He knew that Khorvash would most certainly have taken Remigius's words as a personal slur, but they could ill-afford to draw the ire of the Ordo Malleus.

'We will take this discussion to the strategium. My Chaplain awaits us.' Without further statement, Tanek spun on his heel and began marching away.

'Captain Tanek.' The inquisitor's words halted the Star Dragons captain, but he did not turn. Remigius took a few steps towards him. 'My retinue...'

'Dismiss those you do not need and retain whomever you deem necessary, inquisitor, but make it swift. My time is precious and I need a damned good explanation as to why the Containment Fleet has been denied its right to destroy that ship.' Tanek's jaw was so tight that it was aching.

'All in good time. You have nothing to fear from the *Accursed Eternity*. At least... not at this moment.'

At that statement, Tanek did turn. His dark eyes were blazing with fury.

'The Star Dragons fear *nothing*.'

'Perhaps that will change.'

The inquisitor would not be drawn any further and he

was led to the strategium in stormy silence. As he entered, Iakodos rose from his seat in a show of respect for a servant of the Inquisition. His calm gaze took in the inquisitor and his lackeys, seemingly without interest. Remigius considered Iakodos with equal attention. The Chaplain was shaven-haired and otherwise entirely unremarkable in appearance. Had it not been for the varicoloured las-tattooed dragon scales on the left side of his face and neck, he would have looked like nearly every other Adeptus Astartes Chaplain he had ever come into contact with.

'Chaplain Hetor Iakodos.' There was a reverence in the inquisitor's tone that he certainly hadn't demonstrated to either of the two captains, and Khorvash's eyebrows lifted curiously. 'The pleasure is mine, I'm sure.'

'Inquisitor.' Iakodos returned the greeting in a similarly polite manner, echoing that of his captain. 'Welcome aboard the *Ladon*.'

The formalities over, Tanek indicated all present to be seated. Remigius's retinue continued to fuss around him, but the inquisitor merely dismissed them with a wave of his hand. They retired to just outside the strategium.

The inquisitor leaned back in the oversized chair, which had been designed for a warrior more than twice his size. 'I will dispense with pleasantries and get straight to the point.' Leaning forwards on the table, he steepled his fingers beneath his chin and let his gaze wander from captain to captain, and then to the Chaplain. 'Historically, the *Accursed Eternity* has only remained visible for a few hours, enough time to sow its seeds of discord. However, this time...' His smile was unnerving. There was something reminiscent of a predator in it. 'This time, it has remained for longer than usual and we cannot possibly afford to turn down the opportunity that presents.'

'Opportunity?' It was Iakodos who asked the question and Tanek was content to let the Chaplain take the floor. 'Since we have been ordered not to destroy it, perhaps you would care to elaborate on what such an opportunity might be?'

'Of course, my dear Iakodos – you don't mind if I use your name in this way, do you? Or would you prefer to be addressed by your full title?' Iakodos tilted his head in a gesture that suggested he did not particularly care either way, so the inquisitor continued. 'I plan a mission aboard the *Accursed Eternity*. My order has come into possession of vital information concerning its origins and how to end its threat.'

'And what relevance does that have to my Containment Fleet?' Tanek asked softly.

'Containment Fleet Kappa is made up of loyal and noble warriors of the Adeptus Astartes. Fine, upstanding repre-sentations of your great brotherhood. You are… uniquely placed to give me the assistance I require.'

'You want protection.' Tanek's expression did not change one bit.

'So simple. I could not have put it better myself.' The inquisitor rubbed the palms of his hands together. 'Yes, indeed. I want protection. I must travel to the *Accursed Eternity* and deal with the threat, but I must ask for your assistance in this matter.'

'Ask?' Tanek's brow rose. 'That is not something you usu-ally do, Remigius.'

'I am pleased that you remember the tenets of my order, Captain Tanek. I have the decree here if you wish to check it?' Remigius took out a data-slate and offered it to the cap-tain, who ignored it in favour of staring at the inquisitor.

'If we do not agree?'

'I believe you will find that you are not in a position to refuse my request.' Remigius's smile could have frozen oceans. 'Or have you forgotten the terms of the agreement we made the last time we met?'

'No, inquisitor. I have not forgotten.'

There was a long pause, before Iakodos spoke. 'What is the nature of this vessel? What would we expect if we were to travel across to it with you?'

'Trials that will test the very depths of even your faith, Chaplain.'

'I will ignore that slur.'

'None was intended. My research leads me to believe that what we might face on board the *Accursed Eternity* will test and try you to the very limits of your undoubtedly considerable resolve. A challenge? Yes, I think so. But one which I am sure you are more than capable of meeting.'

Remigius got to his feet and moved down the table until he was standing before a viewport, staring out into the darkness of space. 'Agree to aid me and I will consider the debt the Star Dragons Chapter owes to the Ordo Malleus paid in full. We will wipe the slate clean, to coin an old Terran turn of phrase.'

Khorvash looked curiously at the two Star Dragons in response to this, but no explanation was forthcoming. The Blood Swords captain sensed that here was another matter into which he should not pry, so he remained silent. In the pit of his stomach, an unprecedented sense of paranoia began to squirm. It could not be denied that there was a history between the inquisitor and his cousins of the Star Dragons.

Was there more to the Star Dragons' eagerness to serve alongside the Blood Swords?

As quickly as the thought surfaced, Khorvash chased it down. He had come to like Tanek in the time the two captains had spent together. He could not imagine for one moment that the Star Dragons were acting as some kind of intermediary between a penitent Chapter and the Inquisition. Coupled with the obvious rage that the Chaplain was keeping under control, it was a foolish thought and Khorvash forced himself to purge it from his mind.

Tanek shook his head and spoke, breaking the Blood Sword's train of thought. 'No. I cannot agree to this. I would have the truth of it before I commit my forces to anything, inquisitor.'

'The truth of it. Oh, you shall have the truth of it.' Without turning to face the Space Marines at the table, the inquisitor seemed to consider his words for a while. When he did finally turn around, his expression had lost its former arrogance and there was an earnest honesty there for all to see.

'The *Accursed Eternity* is what can best be termed as a daemon-ship, though that is a crude description and not one which fully conveys its true nature...'

The admission provoked an immediate response from Khorvash, who bounded to his feet, hand on the hilt of the ceremonial sword he wore belted at the waist of his tunic. His voice boomed around the strategium, echoing against the plain walls and bouncing back to them. 'Then we should bring an end to its unholy existence! Containment Fleet Kappa is strong enough to obliterate the thing. It will take no effort at all on our part to destroy it.'

'Sit down, Captain Khorvash.' Remigius looked up at the eager warrior with an air of superiority. 'If you open fire on the *Accursed Eternity*, it will end the same way it has done for so many other servants of the Imperium across the years – in your destruction and in the ship's inevitable re-appearance once again. It is not something that can be purged through the crude and conventional methods your fleet would employ.'

Khorvash bristled and Tanek laid a hand on his forearm. The Blood Sword took his seat again, but his face was creased in a scowl.

Remigius nodded gravely. 'I'm glad that you feel so strongly about the level of threat this craft possesses, Captain Khorvash, and your enthusiasm is to be commended. Such an attitude will prove invaluable in aiding me to eliminate its threat once and for all. To defeat the *Accursed Eternity*, it will be necessary for me to exorcise the daemon bound at its heart. My order has granted me the means and the method to accomplish just that. What I do not have – and where I must look to you – is the might. Spare me a number of your warriors, ensure my safe arrival at the machine's core, and you will see this evil banished once and for all.'

Iakodos was watching the inquisitor carefully. There was complete honesty in the man's tone, in the stance he had adopted and in the words he was speaking, and yet he still sensed that the entire truth was being withheld. It was nothing he could explain beyond a gut instinct; he was no psyker.

'That is all you require of us? A bodyguard detail?'

'That is all. I do not ask for your Librarians or your Chapter champions. I ask merely for a reasonable detachment of men to ensure that I arrive alive to carry out my task.' The inquisitor looked from Khorvash to Tanek and back again. 'It can do neither of your respective Chapters any harm at all to grant me this boon. Tanek's debt will be wiped out and Khorvash will earn great respect for the Blood Swords, which will go a long way to restoring a gravely tarnished reputation. These are worthy rewards in themselves, are they not?'

'Are there not other Adeptus Astartes brothers whose skills are more suited to dealing with such situations?'

'There are, of course. However, the more – how shall we say – the more *militant* wing of my order does not have a presence in the Balanor system. The Star Dragons and Blood Swords however...' His smile would perhaps have been considered charming by some, but not by the Adeptus Astartes who saw nothing on the inquisitor's face but slyness and the half-truth that Iakodos had noted. 'The *Accursed Eternity* is a difficult problem. It comes and goes without any pattern. There is no way we can predict when it will arrive and I have to use any and all tools at my disposal when it does.'

Khorvash's scowl had not lessened any, and he traced idle patterns on the surface of the table with one finger whilst he studied Remigius. 'Our numbers are low already, Tanek,' he said after a few moments of silence. 'But if you agree to this, I would be able to spare at least one squad for such a task. Sergeant Ardashir and his men would be the perfect choice.'

'I would not ask for more from you, my friend,' came the reply. 'The Star Dragons can spare two Scales at least. The Blood Swords need to retain their numbers. All the while you are unable to recruit to your number...' He did not continue. He did not need to, and he trusted enough to their friendship that Khorvash would not take offence.

'I will go also,' interjected Iakodos. 'If this daemonic entity is truly as challenging as the inquisitor suggests, then they will need reminders of their faith.'

Tanek eyed the inquisitor. 'Thirty battle-brothers and the Chaplain. More than generous, I think you will agree. Is this acceptable?'

'More than generous.' Remigius dropped into a low bow that showed great deference, although all three Adeptus Astartes could not help but consider it slightly sarcastic.

'I tell you this now, Remigius,' Tanek said in a low and dangerous voice. 'The first hint that you have betrayed us will lead to consequences far beyond those you believe us capable of.'

'I speak only the truth, captain.'

Aye, Tanek thought. Only the truth you think we need to know, though.

II

It continued on its aimless course, drifting through the void of space, and made no attempt to attack or impede the boarding torpedoes in any way at all. Even when they connected with the *Accursed Eternity* and the grinding teeth chewed into its hull, there was no response. The ship was, to all intents and purposes, dead.

Chaplain Iakodos stepped out of the nose of the first torpedo, already wearing his distinctive skull-helm. An exquisite cloak, hand-stitched by Chapter-serfs from the skins of the reptilian *draconae* of the Chapter's home world, Draconith, fluttered behind him. As thick as chain-mail and gleaming iridescent in the half-light, the cloak was a valuable Chapter artefact and as much a mark of Iakodos's office as the crozius arcanum in his hand.

Iakodos looked around at the interior of the so-called daemon-ship. Its emergency lights were at their lowest possible ebb and the sensors in his helm adjusted accordingly. Temperature sensors registered at almost freezing.

Behind the sergeants, Inquisitor Remigius stepped out of the torpedo. A tiny figure next to the assembled Space

Marines, he was wearing a thick robe and cloak that he pulled around himself with a shiver. The rebreather mask covering most of his face rendered his expression impossible to gauge.

Sergeant Korydon of the Star Dragons Third Scale squad and his counterpart, Sergeant Evander of Ninth Scale, resplendent in their royal blue battle-plate, had been mustered for the expedition. A squad of crimson-clad Blood Swords who had been assembled under the command of Sergeant Ardashir joined them once the second boarding torpedo opened to let them out.

Iakodos watched as Korydon gathered the warriors together and further noted the way in which he eyed the inquisitor with caution. As the senior sergeant present, the overall command of the military detail had fallen to him and the Chaplain was well aware that he had been subjected to a private briefing from Captain Tanek before they had departed the *Ladon*.

THE THREE SERGEANTS had not yet put on their helms and their breath ghosted in front of their faces as they called their squads to order. Korydon considered Ardashir carefully. Whilst there was an undoubted kinship between the two Chapters, he had never personally fought alongside Ardashir and had no idea of the other's capabilities. The Blood Swords warrior had initially shown some resistance to the idea of deferring command to a sergeant of the Star Dragons, but a word from Khorvash had silenced his complaints.

Like his captain Ardashir seemed eager and energetic, a trait that both Korydon and Iakodos found pleasing. He rallied his squad with ease and they responded to his softly-voiced commands without hesitation, presenting a professional, efficient and well-ordered front. The Blood Swords had a good reputation on the field of battle. In the best possible way, Korydon fervently hoped that it would not be put to the test.

His own squad, Third Scale, and Evander's Ninth were

standing ready, their bolters slowly panning left and right to cover the gloomy corridor into which they had emerged. Iakodos walked amongst the Star Dragons first, laying his hand on shoulders and speaking words of benediction and cleansing in a clear voice.

'The Blood Swords are ready for your command, Sergeant Korydon,' Ardashir said, and there was nothing but respect in his tone. Iakodos nodded in approval. Whatever disgruntlement Ardashir had known before departure had evidently been set aside in favour of duty.

'Very good.' Pulling his helm on over his close crop of fair hair, Korydon turned to Remigius. 'Inquisitor, this is your mission. We are here to guide and support you if it is needed.'

'Oh, it will be needed, Sergeant Korydon. It's not a question of "if" but rather "when". Ensure your men are prepared to handle anything that they encounter... It will not all be corporeal.' The inquisitor's musical voice, muffled by the mask across his face, carried through the silence of the ship. 'Our targets are the enginarium and the bridge; the daemonic heart of this ship is most likely to be situated in one of these locations.'

'Most likely?' Korydon snorted. 'That is a little vague, inquisitor.'

'The activities of daemons do not conform to any sort of exact science, Sergeant Korydon. Guard your temper. Your impatience won't serve you well in this situation...'

Iakodos had watched the exchange silently, his eyes unseen behind his skull mask, but at Remigius's statement he stepped forwards, his hands raised, one palm directed at the man and another at the warrior. His face was hidden but his manner was clear.

'Peace, Brother-Sergeant Korydon. Carry yourself with decorum.' Korydon turned his face away from the Chaplain and Iakodos noted the tell-tale clenching of his fists. 'Mark my words, inquisitor.' Iakodos's gravel tones rumbled, made inhuman by the helm he wore. 'All of the battle-brothers here assembled attended me in the chapel before we were despatched. Their faith is as strong as it ever was and as their guide in all matters of a spiritual nature, I see no reason to doubt them.' He turned to the others. 'Trust in the words and the litanies we shared before we left, brothers. Trust in the Emperor and trust in the warrior beside you, and we will end this threat to the Imperium forever.'

Several of the warriors made the sign of the aquila at Iakodos's words. Korydon shrugged slightly, then shouldered his bolter and turned to Remigius. His expressionless helmet lenses fixed on the inquisitor giving away nothing of his thoughts or feelings. His voice, when he spoke, was composed and neutral.

'Lead on, inquisitor,' he said. 'We have your back.'

IT BECAME SWIFTLY apparent to all of the Space Marines and their human charge that the *Accursed Eternity* was devoid of any signs of life. There was no indication of any sort of battle that had ended lives. No bloodstains, no tell-tale scorch marks that would suggest gunfire. There was simply nothing.

'It is as though the ship just came from the shipyards,' observed Evander across the vox. 'It is... pristine. Untouched.' His words were accurate. There was a shining newness about the walls of the corridors through which they walked. The clean, desolate halls of the ship made it seem slightly unreal; something about it didn't feel right. Not one of them could fully explain what they meant but the feeling, it seemed, was universal.

Evander received no reply, but one or two of the warriors nodded agreement, Evander having merely put into words what they were all feeling. After some time, Brother Mehrak offered up a further and decidedly hesitant opinion, his words carefully chosen and tinged with doubt.

'If someone wanted to recreate the interior of an Imperial ship but did not quite know how to apply the wear and tear of age and use, it would look just like this.' He laughed without humour. 'My apologies, brothers. That is fanciful and ridiculous to even consider.'

'There is nothing to apologise for, Blood Sword. You are merely expressing your thoughts on the matter. Do not feel that you cannot do that. Do not hesitate to externalise your feelings in this place, brother,' said Iakodos without turning to look at the warrior. 'The inquisitor has suggested that this is a ship that has been taken by daemonic powers. None of us here can truly comprehend what they may or may not be capable of. Better by far to say what your concerns are than to brood upon them.'

'It feels and looks real enough. Although given its nature, it is hard to believe that is anything but an illusion. Something woven from warp-stuff. A fragment of the immaterium.' Evander gave a light chuckle. 'Fanciful, I know.'

'Be reassured, sergeant. The *Accursed Eternity* most definitely exists.' Remigius's voice cut across the vox conversations. 'Its machine spirit has been broken and compromised, but it exists nonetheless. It is solid and very real. The fact that it continues to exist despite the best efforts of the Imperium is why we are here.'

They continued down the corridor in silence, the only sounds those of the booted feet of the Space Marines ringing out on the decking, the constant hum of their energy packs and the occasional creaking of a joint of power armour. Iakodos moved down the corridor at the back of the assembled squads, his cloak billowing as he walked. He too felt the discomfort that the nature of the ship was instilling in the others.

'He does not know where he is leading us.' The Chaplain glanced sharply at Korydon who had seemingly switched to a private vox-channel. 'I am no psyker, but I sense that our charge is more than a little anxious.'

'Patience, brother. I appreciate your own need for haste, but we need to let this situation play out however it will.'

'He does not know where we will find our enemy, Chaplain. How can we believe in his claim that he knows how to deal with it?'

Iakodos was robbed of his chance to reply as, without

warning, Remigius came to an abrupt halt at a junction in the corridor. It was only because Korydon had ensured a respectful distance that the inquisitor wasn't trampled by three squads of Adeptus Astartes.

'Here is where we make a choice,' the inquisitor said, looking first one way and then another down the corridors that intersected their current path. 'The enginarium or the bridge.'

'There. You see what I mean? I rest my case.' Korydon's frustration was wearing and decidedly uncharacteristic. Iakodos scowled beneath the skull-helm and spoke aloud.

'How certain are you that we will find what we seek in either of these places, inquisitor?'

'As certain as I can be, Chaplain.'

Despite the inquisitor's confidence, Iakodos recognised tell-tale signs of uncertainty: a slight tremor to the voice, a brief clasping of the hands.

'Perhaps...' For the first time, there was genuine hesitation in Remigius's manner. 'Perhaps we could consider splitting our efforts?'

'It is not an ideal solution, inquisitor, and given what you have told us about this ship I cannot say that I approve of the idea of isolating a squad from the others.'

'It would certainly speed this process up, Chaplain.' Korydon stepped forwards. 'We can stay in constant communication and, if necessary, the squads can join back up.'

'The final say is yours, sergeant. You have command of this mission.' Iakodos stepped back again. Despite his seniority in years, he deferred easily to the sergeant's command.

Korydon raised a gauntleted hand and rubbed it against the jaw of his helm. His red lenses stared down the corridor ahead, first to the left and then the right. The same featureless white expanse met his gaze wherever he looked. He came to a decision.

'Third Scale, we will head for the bridge and make an assessment of the area. Evander, you take Ninth and Sergeant Ardashir. Stay with the inquisitor.' There was a heavy emphasis on the final command and Evander nodded his compliance.

'We will move towards the command deck,' Korydon confirmed, his tone forceful and compelling. 'We will remain in constant contact and in the event that we run into difficulties, or if you require our extra support, we will fall back to this position and reunite our forces.'

Third Scale moved apart from the others and gathered at the head of the right-hand corridor. Iakodos switched to the private channel again.

'This is a rash decision, sergeant, and one that seems ill-advised in this environment. I will come with you.'

'It is my decision to make, Chaplain. And no, you must remain with the inquisitor. I apologise for speaking so of one of the Ordo Malleus, but I do not trust him. You need to be with him. Those were Captain Tanek's express orders. He did not require the rest of us to be present, however.'

Iakodos clicked his tongue against the roof of his mouth. 'Very well, sergeant. As you command. Keep your faith strong, Brother Korydon. Keep your wits about you and heed your own warnings about falling back if you encounter difficulties.'

'I will, Chaplain. Fire and fury.'

'Fire and fury, brother.'

The two Space Marines clasped arms in a warrior's grip and, without another word, Third Scale peeled off from the main group and turned right down the corridor junction. Iakodos had no doubt that they were strong, faithful souls to a man and that they would cope with anything that might be thrown at them, but he still felt a creeping unease at their forces having been split.

'Sergeant Evander... We are now under your command, I believe.'

'Yes, Chaplain.' Evander nodded and moved ahead of the inquisitor, leading the larger of the two battle forces left towards the enginarium.

As they walked, the corridor began to take a slight slope downwards. Iakodos considered again Evander's words from earlier. There was something fundamentally unreal about the design of the ship's interior. There should have been more bulkheads, more doors barring their passage, but there was nothing but the seemingly endless white corridors. The Chaplain laid his hand against the wall and could not even feel a distant vibration from the ship's engines. The sensors in his gauntlet returned no movement, and as he passed his hand across the wall it seemed smooth and almost frictionless. No casting or welding lumps or rivets, just a stark, sterile surface.

'This vessel is dead,' he observed. 'I have never been aboard a ship that is so utterly devoid of life and soul.'

He would learn, to his great cost, that the *Accursed Eternity* was anything but dead.

KORYDON STRODE AHEAD with great purpose. He had felt the unease of his battle-brothers from the moment they had exited the boarding torpedo. It was an unease he shared and the urge to complete this duty and return to the *Ladon* was strong. He had disliked the inquisitor from the moment they had met and felt a certain sense of relief now that he was out of the man's presence. Since they had boarded, a niggling voice at the back of his skull had tried to convince him that were they to lose the inquisitor, it would be no tragedy.

'What exactly is it that we are seeking, sergeant?' Arion asked. This corridor, like the embarkation one along which they had previously been walking, was spartan and empty.

'Anything at all would be a start,' muttered Tylissus. This drew a hesitant chuckle from Third Scale and even Korydon cracked a brief smile beneath his helm.

'Have you ever known anything like this place?' Tylissus continued, the bemusement in his voice expressing what Korydon suspected all of them felt. 'When we were told this was a daemon-ship, I expected some sort of engagement the moment we set foot on the deck. Not this endless nothing. Is it possible, do you think, that the inquisitor is wrong in his assessment?'

'I do not know, Tylissus,' replied Korydon thoughtfully.

'It is more than evident that this ship is not normal. But like you, I wonder exactly what it is we should expect. I feel this sense of…' He trailed off, unable to articulate the feelings he had. It was almost like a premonition of what was to come, but that was impossible. He was a warrior. He did not have precognitive powers. 'A sense of discomfort.' It was a pitiful word compared to the depth of feeling he described, but it was the best he could manage. 'If the inquisitor asserts that this is a daemon-ship then who am I to question that?'

A *daemon-ship*. Korydon let out a soft snort of derisive laughter. He didn't know what he had been expecting either. Certainly not metre after metre of expansive, clinically white corridors. Perhaps he had been anticipating attacks from misshapen warp entities. Perhaps he had been expecting the walls of the ship to be oozing ichor and blood…

The thought dissolved into the ether and he shook himself. Fanciful, foolish thinking that had no place in the head of an Adeptus Astartes sergeant. 'Move onwards,' he ordered, waving with his bolter. Best to leave such ridiculous and fantastical imaginings to others. He could not allow such things to taint his duty.

He abandoned the thought and the Star Dragons continued forwards. In the wake of their passage, something held onto the ethereal wisp of Korydon's abandoned idea. With an inhuman appetite, it devoured what it needed to give itself the strength to take form. It had been left starving for so many years that the single thread of imagination was a veritable banquet. It was gorged upon and fed the invisible horrors of the *Accursed Eternity*. When it had finished, it wanted more.

There was a saying from Old Terra that held truth in this place. Careless talk, so the saying went, costs lives.

The future began to shape itself. In the corridor behind Third Scale, a dark and viscous fluid began to seep slowly from the walls, going entirely unnoticed by the Space Marines as they passed.

* * *

'THE CORRIDOR IS all wrong.'

The Chaplain's observation put into words what all present were thinking. They had marched for far too long down the endless white hallway and there was no sign of its end. There had been nothing but the unblemished walls and the sound of their feet on the decking. Iakodos moved ahead a few more metres and, utilising the sensors in his helm, scanned ahead down the corridor. He focused his attention on the relevant readout, but there seemed to be something preventing the runes from giving him a fixed response. The numbers flickered and changed repeatedly.

'Look, there.' Ardashir stepped forwards. There was a hint of anxiety in his voice and the Chaplain watched him sharply. He looked to see what it was that the Blood Sword indicated.

'I moved too close to the wall and made a mark just like that when we took the corridor from the crossroads,' he said. The scrape mark of red armour on the wall of the corridor was almost like a smear of blood. 'It must be a coincidence.'

'I wouldn't be too sure, sergeant,' murmured Remigius. Iakodos turned to look at him. His words sent a muttered ripple of uncertainty through the Space Marines.

'Are you suggesting that we are trapped in this corridor?' Ardashir stared down at the inquisitor. 'That we will not be able to find our way out of it?'

'I'm suggesting that there is a possibility the daemon at the heart of this ship is utilising the opportunity to play with us. Chaplain Iakodos, you need to ensure your brothers' faith remains strong. If they begin to doubt, then we will be lost.'

'We need to keep moving,' interrupted Evander. 'But to give us a clearer idea, let us be certain of what we are dealing with, shall we?' With a metallic *screech*, he dragged the forearm of his armour in a cross-stroke over the red mark, adding a blue stripe to the marking on the wall. With caution, they proceeded down the corridor.

It took them barely five minutes to return to the red and blue mark on the wall.

'It was no coincidence, then.' Ardashir slammed his balled fist into the wall in frustration. 'We are trapped.'

'Movement up ahead.' The snapped announcement from Evander drew Iakodos's attention and he brought his crozius up automatically, ready for an attack. Evander's bolter was brought to bear and he pointed directly down the tunnel. The Chaplain followed the line of the sergeant's gun and stiffened slightly as he too caught the motion. Again, his helm refused to feed him any data.

Evander took a few steps forwards, then halted, raising his bolter again. 'Moving towards us. Something... A lone figure. A huge form. Adeptus Astartes size at least.' A thought came to him and he activated his vox-bead.

'Third Scale, report in. Korydon, do you have any sort of visual contact?'

'Negative. We have found nothing at all, brother. Is there a problem?'

'Nothing we cannot handle.' Evander cut the link and ratcheted the slide on his bolter. Without needing to speak the command, the entire squad, with the Blood Swords close behind, began to move to contact.

THE ROUTE TO the bridge was remarkably uneventful for Third Scale. Apart from the single vox communication from Evander, there had been nothing to break the monotony of their investigation. They had reached a half-open bulkhead door that two of them were able to easily breach and had left the corridor behind.

Korydon's unease had not left him, however. Periodically, he had experienced the sense of shadows moving just out of the corner of his eye and had paused in his stride to turn his bolter towards something that only he could see. His behaviour was starting to cause similar actions amongst the rest of Third Scale and he silently berated himself.

On leaving the bulkhead, they had entered a darker and

much lower corridor with side rooms leading from it. Each of the Adeptus Astartes had to hunch slightly in order to fit their massive bulk into it. It was a puzzle and nothing at all like the layout of a strike cruiser that they had come to expect. The air was hazy and particles of dust twinkled in the light cast from the lumen-globes mounted on the walls.

Inhaling briefly, Korydon caught the faintest hint of an aroma carried in the air. He could not quite identify it, however, and dismissed it as nothing more than stale air of an aeons-old ship. It was a musty scent, something that reminded him of the Librarium back home on Dracolith where the precious, ancient tomes of generations long past stood in preservative stasis bubbles.

'Old books,' supplied Tylissus. Korydon turned to him, both surprised and suspicious that the warrior had just voiced the very thought he had been harbouring.

'What?'

'It smells like old books in here,' replied Tylissus, crouching low enough to peer in through one of the side rooms. It was empty but for a small cot in the corner of the room and several small piles of dust on the floor. He straightened up again and moved to look at the room radiating off on the opposite side. The same picture met him there.

'Why would it smell like old books?' It was a rhetorical question and Korydon got no response. 'More to the point, why is this ship laid out in such a bizarre way?'

'These may be the serfs' quarters. Or may once have been,' offered one of the squad, and Korydon nodded slowly. It made some sense that that might be the case; after all, the human element of a fleet's complement did not require accommodation on the same scale as the massive post-humans.

'Check all of these side rooms, then we press onwards to the bridge,' he ordered. Hunkering to a crouch, he scooped up a handful of the dust on the floor. It had a faint ochre cast to it, almost as though it was rusted metal that had simply crumbled into its component atoms.

He watched it thoughtfully as it trickled to the ground between the fingers of his gauntleted hand. It was fine and powdery and had he not been wearing his helm, which filtered the air to keep it passably breathable, he would have inhaled it with every lungful of oxygen he took.

Korydon rubbed the dust between the fingers of his gauntlet, noting how it stained the blue ceramite with its ochre shade. Tylissus, who had completed his sweep of the side room, moved to stand beside him.

'I am going to take a guess that all this dust might well be whatever is left of the former crew,' he suggested in a low tone.

The sergeant looked up at him and then back down at the dust. There was something unpleasant about the thought. He had stalked amongst the eviscerated and beheaded dead on battlefields like a spectre of death and had never felt revulsion. But to think that the very air he was breathing was filled with desiccated remains made Korydon wrinkle his nose in disgust.

He got back to his feet and absently wiped his gauntlet down the length of his thigh, leaving a red streak.

When the squad reassembled they confirmed that there was nothing to be found within the side rooms at all. Korydon had expected nothing less and so this came as no real surprise to him.

Before he could give the order to press on, something caught his attention: a strange movement from out of the corner of his left eye. He turned to face the wall and recoiled as a thick trickle of blood began to run down its length. It dribbled its way in a perfectly straight line to the floor and then, incredibly, began creeping along its length, through the dust, towards the gathered Space Marines.

He stepped back into two battle-brothers who were standing directly behind him and with a loud clatter of armour, they crashed unceremoniously into the wall.

'Sergeant?' Tylissus was alert instantly, his blade unsheathed and at the ready. 'What is it?'

'There!' Korydon pointed at the rivulet of ichor that had

been oozing towards them. Only when he looked back, there was nothing there.

Tylissus looked. He shook his head and Korydon momentarily tasted shame.

'My apologies, brothers. I thought I saw…' He shook his head and gave a gruff, humourless laugh. 'Nothing. My mistake. Something in this place is attempting to get to me. We press on.'

That was when the whispering started; and it was not just confined to the interior of Korydon's skull. Wordless noises that ranged between hissing and cackling laughter reverberated throughout the small chamber. Every weapon came to the fore and every Star Dragons warrior tensed ready for an ambush that didn't come.

The noise built to a crescendo, an almost deafening roar of sound that filled the densely packed room in which the Adeptus Astartes stood. Then the first of the figures rose from the dust on the ground. Coalescing with alarming speed, the ash flowed into a solid figure that was humanoid in shape but featureless. It wavered for a few seconds, tipping this way and that, balancing itself. Eventually it ceased its rocking motion and stopped dead.

A hideous gash split its head almost in two in a horrendous parody of a mouth. It held out a hand towards the Space Marines, a finger creating itself particle by painstaking particle. The digit extended and pointed towards Korydon.

You die now.

The words entered every battle-brother's mind though none had been spoken, and Korydon waited no longer.

'We will not,' he replied, squeezing the trigger of his bolter. The shell lodged in the torso of the dust-thing, and it dipped its head to look at it. The slit mashed itself together and with creeping horror, Korydon got the uncanny sense that it was laughing. It raised its head again.

You die now.

Seconds later, it detonated. The ash exploded outwards, showering the squad in red dust and eliminating the creature. Only now more of them were appearing, flowing upwards into the same humanoid form.

They inched forwards slowly as though movement itself was a difficult task. Korydon destroyed two more before bellowing the order to move through the chamber and leave through the other door. In short order, they were surrounded on all sides by the creeping wraiths. Bolt shells either passed through them or destroyed them in the way that Korydon's shots had with the first.

The creatures made no attempt to attack, merely continuing their slow approach towards the gathered Space Marines. They were silent but for the whispering sound that their movement generated. No more verbal threats came from them, but their very presence was menacing enough.

Arion brought his bolter up again as another creature moved towards him and let a shell loose. It disintegrated his would-be attacker and his entire suit of power armour was covered from head to foot in a layer of the fine dust. In a powdered rush, it poured through the grille of his helm. Much was instantly filtered out, but caught unaware by the suddenness of it, Arion was unable to activate the armour sealing around his grille. He swallowed a mouthful of the sediment whole.

Doubling over, he retched violently, even as his Adeptus Astartes physiology kicked in to deal with the foreign contaminant he had ingested.

Korydon cast him a sideways glance. 'Are you all right, brother?'

Arion put a hand up as though to wave away Korydon's concern and nodded his head vigorously. A few brief moments passed before he was back upright, defending himself once again.

Another creature exploded, then another... until the air of the chamber was filled with a cloying, obfuscating haze. Still the dust creatures made no apparent attempt to attack; they merely moved closer and closer. Then something inexplicable happened. Each one of the creatures threw its head back in a silent scream.

The whispering seemed to grow to a long, sibilant hiss. And then there was silence, and a huge puff of fresh dust as every last one of the creatures simply lost its animation. As one, they broke into a million specks which drifted lazily to the floor, swiftly coating it once again in an ochre carpet.

IT HAD GONE.

Whatever it was that Evander had spotted moving at the end of the corridor, it had vanished completely by the time the two squads and the inquisitor had reached the spot where it had been. It had, however, led them to a locked bulkhead, something they had not seen for the entirety of the time they had been aboard this foul vessel.

'Ninth, this is Korydon. We have just encountered–'

The vox-transmission crackled and distorted, then broke off briefly. When it came back, there was doubt in Korydon's voice. 'We have just encountered *something*. I cannot be more specific than that, but whatever it was seems to have retreated for now.'

'Any injuries, brother-sergeant?' Iakodos asked the question and received a reply in the negative.

'None, Chaplain. We will continue proceeding to the bridge, but we have received our first proof that this ship is definitely not dead. Recommend extreme caution for all. Whatever has control of this vessel must surely know of our presence. We will check in regularly. Any contacts to report?'

'I thought…' Evander began, then shook his head. 'Nothing, Kor. I will keep you appraised of the situation.'

'Understood.'

Korydon broke off the transmission. Evander released a mag-clamp that held a melta charge to his armour and made to begin setting it against the door. The Chaplain laid a hand on his arm and shook his head almost imperceptibly. Turning to the inquisitor, Iakodos stared down at the human through the red eye lenses of his skull-helm. When he spoke there was a carefully measured level of threat implicit in his tone.

'Inquisitor Remigius, it is my belief that you have been withholding vital information from us regarding the nature of this vessel. If you wish for us to offer further aid and assistance to you, then you will tell us all that you know. Should you refuse to do so, then I will open a channel to Sergeant Korydon and advise him that we are aborting this mission.'

'You don't need to fear–'

'Hold your wrath, sergeant.' Iakodos was forced to put up a restraining arm to stop Evander from reaching for Remigius. 'Inquisitor, please refrain from insulting my brothers. We are not demonstrating fear in this matter. Rather, consider that we are exercising extreme caution. You have not been truthful with us. It does not make for a conducive relationship. You can rectify that quite easily.'

'There is no need to speak to me as though I were one of your flock, Chaplain Iakodos,' countered the inquisitor in his irritatingly superior tone. 'I haven't strayed from the path of true faith. There is no need whatsoever for you to lecture me on the error of my ways and insist upon guiding me back onto the straight and narrow. I probably have more faith in my body and mind than this entire contingent has put together.'

They were near blasphemous words, and brave ones for a lone inquisitor surrounded by twenty Space Marines to utter. Perhaps it was the realisation of this fact – possibly combined with the suddenness with which the circle around him closed ever so slightly – that made Remigius snarl suddenly.

'Very well,' he snapped. 'The practical truth of the matter is this; I must get to the daemon in control of this ship so that I may speak the words and perform the rites necessary to banish it back to the darkness from whence it crawled. This sword…' He rested his hand on the hilt of the weapon poking from the finely tooled leather scabbard he wore at his waist. 'This is a weapon wrought for the destruction of the ancient evil that beats at the heart of this vessel. Hundreds have toiled in the course of its creation and hundreds more have been sacrificed to ensure its purity.'

With a flourish, he drew the sword from its scabbard and lay the flat of the blade against his forearm to show it to Iakodos. Gothic script looped its entire length, delicate and ornate. The litanies and the finely forged blade itself crackled with barely contained power. Remigius studied it with a strangely thoughtful expression on his thin face. 'Many of my own people have died so that I might stand before you now and show you the fruit of their labours. They were, in a sense, *my* battle-brothers. I owe it to the memory of their names to complete their work.'

The inquisitor looked at Iakodos, who was quietly impressed despite himself. 'You understand that, don't you, Chaplain?'

'I do, inquisitor. Very well, we will proceed. But I ask that you refrain from antagonising my brethren. There is no place for more tension on this mission.'

'Sergeant! Look at that!'

The call came from a brother of the Blood Swords squad who had been standing behind the inquisitor. He pointed with his bolter to the wall opposite. Where once there had been clinically white, featureless walls of no character, there was now a creeping, spreading line of corrosion. It began where the wall met the floor and was moving slowly but perceptibly upwards in spidery lines. Where it touched the substance of the wall, the pure white surface was visibly ageing, tarnishing before their eyes as though centuries of erosion were occurring in but a few seconds. The sterile coating of the corridor's walls flaked into little piles on the ground, and as the assembly watched the process, the lines seemed less like cracking, breaking metal and more like veins spreading across the skin of the ship.

A twisted smile flickered over Remigius's face and he sheathed the sword once again. 'Behold,' he said softly. 'The taint revealed. The presence of this weapon brings out the daemon's disquietude. Open the bulkhead, Sergeant Evander. We must hurry.'

All the earlier rage at the inquisitor seemed to be

forgotten as the sergeant, with the aid of two more Space Marines, began to prime the melta charges.

'What can we expect to deal with once we pass through this door, inquisitor? What do you know of the nature of this daemon?' Iakodos kept his voice so low and calm that he seemed to be holding nothing but a normal conversation.

Cold, hard eyes looked up at the Chaplain and Remigius shook his head. 'If I knew that, Star Dragon, I could prepare you. Simply... be prepared. It is the best I can offer you. Be assured though that once this deed is done, the name of your Chapter and that of the Blood Swords will be elevated to a position of reverence amongst the Ordo Malleus.'

Aye, Iakodos thought as the party moved back out of the detonation zone. Whether we want that dubious honour or not.

III

'ALL IS WELL here. No further incursions.'

Korydon reported back to Evander and got nothing but a burst of static in response. 'Arion,' he said without turning. 'Keep trying to raise Ninth.'

'Aye, brother.' Arion dropped back from his position at Korydon's side and quietly began repeating his sergeant's words on various vox frequencies.

Not for Third Scale the creeping repugnance of the ship's inner rot. Since their encounter with the dust creatures, they had seen nothing else. The *Accursed Eternity* had taken on a more familiar aspect and their initial tension was beginning to lessen, although none of them were off their guard.

'All is well here. No further incursions.' Arion's voice came across the vox-bead in Korydon's ear. There had still been no response from Ninth and that bothered him greatly. A warrior of great honour and resolution, Korydon was not yet quite prepared to abandon his personal mission in favour of following Evander's squad. The last contact they had received suggested that all was well with his brothers and this could simply be nothing more than a temporary communications glitch. He checked his retinal feeds for details on the current life signs of his distant brothers. That connection at least appeared to be working; all of Ninth Scale seemed to be at full health, their indicator runes green and solid. He did not have the data for the Blood Swords squad, but he felt confident enough that they would be fine.

'We should reach the bridge in a few minutes,' he said to his own squad.

There was no response.

Korydon turned around and both of his hearts leaped into his mouth. Where before there had been nine Space Marines behind him, now there was just one. Arion stood opposite him, arms hanging loosely at his side, his head tipped slightly to the right as though he were carefully considering Korydon. His posture was bizarre and for the first time Korydon feared that one of his squad had been compromised.

His squad.

'Arion, where are the rest of the squad?'

The Space Marine took a step towards the sergeant, who immediately raised his bolter, levelling it at his battle-brother. 'Do not make me do this, Arion,' Korydon said. 'We have served together for many years. But if you are compromised, you will leave me with no choice. Now answer my question. Where are Ninth Scale?'

Arion stopped and stared down at the black tunnel of the bolter's muzzle. He reached up and unclamped the seals of his helm. He removed it and it clattered to the floor. Korydon stared in disbelief. Where once his brother's battle-scarred face had been there was now nothing but shaped dust.

You die now.

Taking several steps backwards, Korydon fired his bolter at the creature that had subsumed his brother and rapidly blink-clicked through to his own squad's health readings. Arion's reading was wavering between solid green and a blinking amber. Something of his brother remained, but it would not last. He hurriedly assimilated the rest of the data; Third Scale *were* here. They were alive somewhere, but he could not see them. Repeated calls to them on the vox were returning nothing at all.

The shot he had fired had hammered into Arion's power armour, forcing the creation to take several staggering steps backwards. But just as it had somehow inhabited Arion's armour, so it had gained access to his weapons. With a whispering laugh that sounded like leaves rustling in the wind, it raised its own bolter and prepared to return fire on the sergeant.

Korydon felt the impact of the shell on his armour before it exploded, defacing the aquila that decorated his chest. The sergeant stumbled under the impact and received a second shot that scarred the Chapter badge on his shoulder and sent ceramite chips spinning in all directions. Another shell whistled through his field of vision and glanced off his helmet. His head jarred backwards with a crack and he raised his bolter to fire back.

You die now.

'You first.'

'SERGEANT EVANDER, THIS is Tylissus. Sergeant Korydon and Arion... They have disappeared.'

The explosion had rocked the two squads but had performed its designated task admirably. The bulkhead door lay in molten fragments along the corridor. That the *Accursed Eternity* was a living ship was now a moot point. The veins of daemonic life that had begun to spread from the corridor were now threaded through the floors and ceilings. Some of them pulsed as though they carried blood through them. Ardashir had hacked into one of them with his combat knife and a sticky, tar-like ichor had oozed slowly from it. The fluid had burned a hole through the floor and the Space Marines had from that point onwards made a concerted effort to keep clear of it.

They had barely gotten through the destroyed door

before Tylissus's transmission had been received.

'What do you mean they have "disappeared", brother?' Evander was already on the cusp of anger and Tylissus's words did little to assist in the calming of his mood.

'We were moving towards the bridge. Arion moved up to stand beside him and then they just vanished. As though they had never been here at all.'

Evander scrolled through his own data-feed and studied Third Scale's readings. The icons for both Arion and Korydon had winked out. 'That is impossible,' he said, more to himself than to either Tylissus or his own group.

'No,' said Inquisitor Remigius. 'No, not impossible. Highly improbable, but possible nonetheless. Daemons have abilities we can only guess at and we are deep within the realm of a powerful entity. We believe that they can create…' He paused, attempting to draw the picture in a simple manner. It was, strangely for him, not an act of condescension, but simply because the Ordo Malleus themselves had never been able to accurately describe such activity. 'They can create pockets in the immaterium. Places that exist outside of our awareness that allow them to move unhindered, unseen, until they desire otherwise. Perhaps the sergeant has been pulled into such a trap.'

'How, exactly, do we undo it? How can we bring our men back?' Evander turned on the inquisitor, his eye lenses glowing a furious red.

The inquisitor gave a helpless shrug. 'We can't,' he replied. 'If I had more of my brethren with me, perhaps we might stand a chance of performing the ritual, combining our powers with enough force to pierce this sorcery. But I don't, and with the greatest of respect, Sergeant Evander, we don't have the time. There is every chance that the pocket will tear at any moment and your missing men will return just as suddenly as they vanished, but whether they do or not, we have to move onwards. I'm sorry for your loss…'

This time, Iakodos was not anywhere near fast enough to prevent Evander from grabbing hold of the inquisitor.

The Star Dragons sergeant slammed the old man into the wall of the ship causing the pulsing veins beneath the inquisitor's back to throb slightly. A snaking tendril crept forwards and looked for a moment as though it would wrap itself around the man. With a swift move, one of the Blood Swords sliced at the tendril with a blade. More of the tar-like ichor pooled on the floor, sizzling gently.

Remigius laughed, a wheezing sound that suggested it was not something he did well; a sound his vocal cords were unused to making. His face twisted in a snarl and his cold eyes fixed on Evander.

'I am an inquisitor of the Ordo Malleus, charged by the God-Emperor of Mankind with the destruction of daemons wherever I find them. You *dare* to lay hands on me? Release me, you barbaric fool,' he said, wiping spittle from the corner of his mouth. 'What good will killing me do other than to satisfy your own primitive bloodlust? Without me, *Sergeant* Evander, you stand no chance of getting off of the *Accursed Eternity*.'

'Brother.' Iakodos moved to stand behind Evander. 'Do as he says. Let him go.'

Evander held firm for a moment longer, then he snorted in disgust and released his grip on the inquisitor's shoulders. Remigius fell to the floor and got back up, dusting himself off in an exaggerated fashion. Several more tendrils snaked out from the wall, but before any of the Space Marines could deal with the threat, the inquisitor had unsheathed his sword and sliced through them.

And the ship *screamed*. It was a horrific echo of a thousand voices shrieking in unimaginable agony. It was shrill and Iakodos felt a warm trickle from his ears beneath his helmet as blood began to drip from them. The inquisitor dropped to his knees again, doubled over with his hands clamped to his ears. The sword clattered to the floor and another vein-ridden thing reached to grasp it, but Iakodos stood on it.The screaming stopped.

'Sergeant Evander? Did you hear that?' Tylissus's alarmed tone cut into the abrupt silence.

'We move on,' Evander said. He spoke into the vox. 'Yes, we heard it, brother. Continue your investigation, Tylissus. Our... charge suggests that Sergeant Korydon may yet return. Report back to me if you find anything. Do you understand me?'

'Message received. Understood.'

The Space Marines began to move onwards and Remigius looked up at the Chaplain. He took his hands away from his ears and they were stained scarlet.

'My tha–'

'Do not give me your thanks, inquisitor,' said the Chaplain in a cold, hard tone. He leaned down until his skull mask was inches away from the inquisitor's face. 'Your deceit is something that I was prepared to make an allowance for, given the circumstances. Your repeated insults to my battle-brothers, however... Trust me when I say that I can only stay Evander's hand for so long.'

With those words, the Chaplain began to follow the others. Remigius shuddered, gathered up the sword and sloped along behind them.

BLOOD. BLOOD IN his mouth. Its coppery taste was unwelcome and yet at the same time served to remind him that he was still alive, that the creature who had murdered and possessed his brother had not won the fight. With the toe of his boot, Korydon kicked aside the crumpled pile of power armour. Not even dust remained. He was alone here – wherever *here* was.

'Korydon to Third Scale.'

His voice echoed around the corridor and went unanswered. Korydon cycled through the usual vox-channels but every single attempt to contact his brothers was met with crackling static. A further pass through the different frequencies saw no further response, but if he strained to listen, there was something. Half-heard whispers in the heart of the white noise that were indecipherable at first but which seemed then to resolve into distorted echoes of his own words repeated over and over. It was deeply unsettling.

Taking a moment to compose himself, he ran a self-analysis. The breastplate of his power armour was compromised from the bolter rounds it had withstood. Part of it had crumpled inwards, the buckled ceramite pressing against his fused ribcage. He had taken a hit to the side of the helm, much of which had been destroyed in the process and which had led to the facial injury that had put the blood into his mouth.

His retinal feed was completely broken. Not a single rune was visible and yet despite its uselessness, he could not bring himself to remove his helmet. He felt, although he could not eloquently vocalise the thought, that to expose himself fully to the air of the *Accursed Eternity* would be an open invitation to the denizens of the warp.

Keeping his bolter raised before him, Sergeant Korydon moved alone through a mirror image of the corridor where he had been, unheard and unseen. He had become another one of the daemon-ship's many ghosts.

EVANDER'S FURY WAS great. He stalked the corridor, his bolter ready to fire in a heartbeat. The disappearance of his fellow sergeant, of both of his battle-brothers, weighed heavily on his mind and the anger he harboured towards the inquisitor who had been the cause of those losses knew no bounds.

'You should have killed him when you had the chance.' The voice entered his ear via his vox-bead but he did not recognise it. Perhaps one of the Blood Swords, he thought. He did not reply and neither did he turn around.

'You could see the very lifeblood pulsing through his jugular vein when you had him held up against the wall, couldn't you, Evander? How quickly and easily you could have snuffed out his existence, like a hurricane extinguishing a candle. His very being rested in the hands of a great and mighty Star Dragon...'

'Stop that.' Evander responded into the vox. There was no reply and none of his companions gave any sign that they had even heard him. He called for a communications check and received several responses, including from Tylissus. It did little to satisfy the growing sense of unease he felt. Whose voice had it been? Which one of his brothers dared to speak in such a profoundly disrespectful way?

'Third Scale are dead.' It was the same voice, as light and insubstantial as a bubble, and it sounded delighted with the news it brought.

'What?' This time, Evander stopped and whirled around. He spoke, not through the vox, but through the mouth-grille of his helm. 'Who said that?'

'Sergeant?' Ardashir moved ahead of the group to stand before him. 'Nobody said anything.'

'Someone spoke over the vox and told me that Third Scale…' Evander stared around the assemblage.

'But they are dead. Lost to your Chapter forever and gifted to the master of the *Accursed Eternity*. Third Scale are lost.' The voice came again and he stiffened.

Ardashir noticed the strange movement and took the initiative. He spoke softly into the vox. 'Tylissus, this is Ardashir. If you witness any other unusual occurrences, be sure to let us know immediately. Received?'

'Message received. Understood.'

'See, Sergeant Evander? They are fine. Control yourself, or do you want to defer command of this group to me?' Ardashir laid a hand on Evander's shoulder. He felt great sympathy for Evander at the apparent loss of two of the Star Dragons, but he could not stand by when his brother-sergeant was starting to demonstrate such behaviour.

Their attention was snapped away from Evander's erratic mood swings, however, when a low growling noise drew their eyes ahead. A huge beast stood before them, effectively blocking the corridor. It had appeared from seemingly nowhere. It was a dark brown in colour, without fur. Beneath its thin skin muscles and sinew could be seen moving quite clearly. Eight eyes either side of its long snout burned blood-red in the glow of the Space Marines' gun-mounted lights, and its razor-sharp fangs dripped with saliva.

The daemon-beast snarled and crouched low, making ready to spring on the group.

Evander gave a single order which every Space Marine present acted upon obediently and without hesitation.

'Terminate.'

The order came a moment too late. The daemon-beast threw back its head and opened its muzzle. No sound came out, but all of the Adeptus Astartes cringed backwards as a psychic scream ripped through their minds. The inquisitor stumbled and fell, blood dribbling from his ears. The four Space Marines at the front of the group squeezed the triggers on their bolters to no avail. Even as the shells struck the creature, it vaporised. A flow of ethereal mist marked its passage as it tore between them, only to rematerialise at the back of the group where Remigius stood.

Iakodos leaned down and picked up the inquisitor bodily, flinging him backwards out of the way and to safety. Ignoring the faint sounds of protest that he heard, he raised his crozius above his head. The daemon beast shook its head, spittle flying. It bared its lethal-looking teeth again and crouched low. The muscles in its hind quarters bunched and rippled as it prepared to spring at the inquisitor.

Standing bold before the foul warp-spawned creature, Iakodos raised his skull-helmed head and crozius in defiance of its existence. He began to speak, his voice low at first but rising rapidly to a crescendo. His voice was rich and confident, carrying with it the experience of years of battle.

'I am Hetor Iakodos of the Star Dragons. I serve to live and I live to serve. With my staff of office, I mete out retribution and with my fist I deliver the justice of the Imperium. You have no place here, warp-spawn. Begone!' The eagle-headed tip of the crozius began to crackle with energy as he thumbed the stud that brought its hidden power to the fore.

There was a wet burbling sound as though the daemon laughed in response to the Chaplain's words and Iakodos wasted no more breath. Lunging forwards, he brought the crozius around in a powerful swing. It struck the daemon-beast on the flank and it let out a screech of fury before melting into nothingness again. The trail of mist flowed some way down the corridor before it reconstituted again. The beast stood there, its devil gaze locked with the Chaplain's own.

With a strange shimmering, another of the same wicked-looking creatures came into being, as thick and stocky as the first. Unless Iakodos's eyes deceived him, there was another forming into solidity behind that one. He cursed loudly. The corridor was narrow enough that no more than four battle-brothers could stand abreast, limiting the advantage conferred by their superior numbers considerably. The Chaplain considered the first daemon. A thick, sticky ichor dripped from its hindquarters where he had struck it. Beneath his helm he smiled grimly. Never worry about limitations; focus instead upon the positives.

'It bleeds, my brothers,' he said, pointing an armoured finger at the creature. 'And if it bleeds, we can kill it.'

'You cannot kill it, Chaplain.' It was Remigius's voice. 'It is a daemon. Unless you can banish it back to the warp, the best you can hope for is to… inconvenience it.'

'Then inconvenience it we shall.' At his words and with him in the lead, the Space Marines pounded down the corridor towards the beast. At the same time, the thing uncoiled its muscles and sprang at them. It struck one of the Blood Swords warriors, Kayan, in the chest with its bear-sized front paws and knocked him off balance. Before Kayan could raise his bolter and shoot, the daemon's iron jaws had closed around his leg, and with a single bite it tore the limb clean off.

Kayan's armour fizzed and popped at the thigh joint where his leg had been severed, and two other warriors grabbed him under the arms, preparing to drag him free. The daemon, however, had other plans. With a toss of its head it discarded the disembodied leg and reared up onto its hindquarters, lashing out with its front legs.

The wickedly sharp claws at the end of each massive paw gouged into Kayan's chest armour just above the midriff and cleaved through the ceramite. They pierced his rib-cage and shredded his internal organs, and with blood bubbling from his lips, Kayan died in silence, stubbornly refusing to give voice to his suffering.

'KORYDON TO EVANDER. Come in.'

Silence met his words.

'Chaplain Iakodos, can you hear me?'

Static. Nothing but static. His vox was as good as useless to him. Korydon had walked the corridors of this unreality he found himself in and he had encountered nothing. No hostility, nothing. It was as though the whole of the ship was his and his alone.

As he moved, he became painfully aware of the dull ache across his chest where his fused ribcage had splintered. The scratches and gouges he had taken during the fight with Arion were already clotted and healing, but his chest hurt with every step he took. He cursed himself softly and took a moment of respite. His body felt hot, feverish as his implants kicked in to speed his healing and, despite its damage, his power armour infused his bloodstream with fresh stimms, alleviating the pain.

After a few moments, he loaded a fresh magazine into his bolter and loosened his combat blade in its scabbard. Allowing himself to move at a pace which would grant his physiology a chance to heal his wounds, he continued onwards in the direction of the bridge. It was the only thing he could think of to do. Perhaps he would learn something if he got there.

THREE MORE TIMES the beast appeared and disappeared. The ground beneath the Adeptus Astartes was littered with the spent casings of bolter shells and their weapons were trained on the daemonic entity. The thing's torso was torn in several places, more of the tar-like ooze leaking from each wound struck by the Space Marines. It was snarling and its eyes blazed with a fury that would not be quenched. Its torso heaved, rising and falling in a bizarre parody of breathing despite it surely having no need to perform such a mortal act.

'We must press on, Chaplain,' said Remigius, pushing his way with great difficulty through the throng of Space Marines. 'I told you. You can't kill it.'

'Can you help us or not, inquisitor?' Iakodos's reply came through clenched teeth. 'Because if you have nothing practical to offer...'

As a reply, Remigius took a book from his belt. The tome was small, but thick with yellowing, dusty pages. As he flicked through it, Iakodos could feel his ire growing. Periodically, the sound of another bolter round being fired at the daemon interrupted the comparative silence.

'In your own time, inquisitor.'

The sarcasm was lost on Remigius, he was sure, but Iakodos made the comment anyway. The inquisitor seemed in no hurry as he traced a spindly finger down the reams of text on the page. Then he smiled – not a pleasant smile – and pushed to the front of the group. Unsheathing the sword, he held it up in front of him. The daemon's baleful stare moved to focus on it and once more, its powerful hind legs coiled, ready to spring.

In his musical lilt, Remigius spoke words that Iakodos could not understand and was almost entirely sure he would never *want* to understand. Stuttering syllables and guttural sounds burst forth from the inquisitor's mouth and with a howl of fury, the daemon began backing up the corridor. Striding forwards in time with its retreat, Remigius was relentless. He spoke the banishment clearly and without stumbling. He knew, as did all of his order, that one mistake could prove fatal. There was a crackling nimbus of power, faint at first but building swiftly to a crescendo, around him. Jagged lightning sparked from the palms of his hands and he thrust one towards the daemon.

With a final howl of rage, the daemon seemed to suddenly contract, and then in a rush it exploded into nothing.

No flesh, no blood... just nothing. It may as well never have been at all. Its fellows which had wavered between solid and insubstantial faded away as well.

Silence fell.

'As I said,' Remigius murmured, re-attaching the book to his belt and not even looking up, 'we must press on.'

There was nothing to say in response to that and so nobody replied, until Iakodos finally spoke, his voice low and dangerous.

'You are a psyker.' It was a statement rather than a question. 'And you did not think to tell us?'

'Think of it rather as you did not think to ask, Chaplain.'

The Blood Sword died because that whoreson did not step in sooner and banish the daemon. Third Scale are dead, Evander. Gone. Remigius could have saved the Blood Sword, but he did not. He could have done that right from the start. But he waited. Too long. Much too long.

Third Scale are dead, Evander. Soon, you will join them.

Evander walked several paces behind the inquisitor, the voice in his head filled with loathing and anger. Occasionally, he would reach up and absently tap at the side of his helmet as though he could dislodge the treacherous thoughts that way. But whenever he tried, they just came back stronger than before.

'Tylissus, this is Evander. Report.'

Static.

'Tylissus, this is Evander. Are you receiving me?' Despite himself, Evander could not help the rising tone of anxiety in his voice. 'Tylissus, report back to me, now.' Iakodos looked over at the sergeant, deeply concerned.

More static, but then, through the white noise, came the barely audible sound of Tylisuss's voice.

'...sage received. Und... ood.'

Evander drew a shuddering breath of relief but started when he felt Iakodos's hand rest lightly on his shoulder.

'Let your concerns go, brother,' said the Chaplain. 'We are all shaken by the loss of young Kayan, but we must keep our focus. We cannot afford to lose any more of our brethren due to our own distractions. What is troubling you?'

'Nothing. I am fine.' Evander shrugged off the Chaplain's touch, an action that would in other circumstances have drawn grave censure. Iakodos merely withdrew his hand and moved slightly closer to Evander than he had been, all the while murmuring soft litanies of faith in an effort to keep Evander's mind focused.

It really did very little to help, other than add to the noise that was worming its way through Evander's skull. His helm lenses bored into the inquisitor's back and he wondered what it would feel like if he were to reach out and take the man's neck in his gauntlets and wring it until he heard the satisfying sound of it snapping.

It would be the most satisfying thing you have ever heard, Evander. He has lied to you. He has kept secrets from you. He has caused the death of a brother Adeptus Astartes. And he still lives. Where is the justice in that?

Third Scale are dead, Evander.

The sergeant stopped walking and held his hands up to his ears. Iakodos immediately moved to press him against the wall, bringing his skull-helmed face in close.

'I hear voices, Chaplain!' Evander's words came out in a rushed, panicked babble of sound. 'They are telling me... suggesting that I... things I cannot let myself fall prey to. But it would be easy. So easy...'

'Pull yourself together, Sergeant Evander.' Despite the deep sympathy he felt for the unfortunate sergeant, Iakodos knew that he could not be compassionate. 'There are no voices. This is all your imagination. The enemy are picking up on your weakness, on your failure to see past the darkness and feel the warmth of the Emperor's light. See it, brother-sergeant.'

Iakodos turned his skull-helm away from Evander and reached for the strength of the God-Emperor. It came easily, as it always had. When he looked back, his voice had changed. The gently admonishing tone was gone, replaced by the hard practical Chaplain who had fought countless battles. 'Cast off the daemonic witchery that binds you, brother. Cast it off with the purity of your faith. Take it. Mould it. Control it. Use it as your shield against this foul temptation.'

'Third Scale...'

'Third Scale are well. Tylissus reported back to you. Now show your spirit! Remind your men why it is that you above any other rose to take your current rank.'

The Chaplain's words had a calming effect on Evander and he nodded slowly. He felt a faint whispering as though the voice would try to reach him again, but he used the mental image of the Emperor's light as a focus. 'Yes, Chaplain. Yes, of course. I apologise.'

'Do not apologise, brother. Merely acquit yourself with honour.'

Releasing him, Iakodos let Evander shake himself down and resume his position at the head of the group.

'We make speed for the enginarium,' announced the sergeant. 'We find this bastard daemon and we end this. For the Emperor. Fire and fury, brothers!'

IV

'EVANDER, THIS IS Korydon. Talk to me, brother.'

The futility of attempting to raise his battle-brother on the vox was beginning to exert its own pressure on the injured Space Marine. He did not understand what had happened to him but he had gone from believing he had somehow been separated from the others to believing that they had been separated from *him*. He didn't know if he was alive and they were dead or the other way around.

He had retraced his steps to the crossroads and headed in the direction the other squad and the Blood Swords had taken. He thought once that he saw them in the distance and had moved gladly towards them. They had moved towards him too, and then had simply disappeared.

His frustration was growing. Whatever had taken him, plucked him from his own existence and dropped him in this netherworld, was toying with him. Everything was tinged faintly with a soft violet glow, an unreality that he could not start to comprehend. He had considered the possibility that he was unconscious somewhere and so badly injured that he had dropped into healing stasis and was merely suffering some sort of nightmare.

It felt real enough, though.

Since Korydon, like all Adeptus Astartes, rarely required what was termed as 'True Sleep', his experiences of dreaming were extremely limited. His mind was so filled with endless reams of texts on xenos biology or weapon maintenance that simple dreams had no place in his resting thoughts. As such, it was easy enough to assume that that was what was happening to him. Simple enough, and strangely comforting. Being able to write off his situation as a dream was actually helping his focus.

For Korydon, the corridors of the *Accursed Eternity* remained empty. He encountered no more of the dust creatures. He was completely alone. It was almost as though he were the only living, breathing thing aboard the dead ship.

His footsteps resounded in a dull echo as he moved onwards towards the enginarium. Every step he took thudded through his aching body giving him a fresh reminder of the pain he would have felt had he been denied his painkilling narcotics.

A sudden movement ahead caught his eye and he looked up eagerly. But it was nothing more than his own shadow. He uttered several expletives and took a moment to check the magazine in his bolter. He had one spare left.

He cast his eyes up and down the passageway he traversed even though he had long given up hope of seeing anything or anybody else. Unsurprisingly, there was nothing to be seen. He was quite categorically alone; something he had never been in the entirety of his service to the Golden Throne. He was not afraid, but it was definitely unsettling.

Whilst his attention was thus engaged, he entirely failed to notice the strange manner in which his shadow began to coalesce and reassemble itself. It was a thing of darkness: an inky blackness into which light fell, never to return, and it was tangible. It moved slowly towards Korydon and raised its shadow weapon, bringing it to bear on the unsuspecting Space Marine.

* * *

THINGS WERE NO better for Evander and Ardashir. Their progress, impeded by the attack of the daemonic hound, or whatever it had been, was taking a turn for the extreme worse. The walls, no longer even attempting to look like a clinical ship interior, were quite literally alive. The tendrils that reached out and grasped at them were like lengths of sinewy muscle, tough and difficult to avoid. Whenever they were cut away, more of the black acid dripped from them.

Ardashir scowled beneath his helm as he hacked away yet another snaking vein and watched the pungent acid dissolve the blade of his combat knife into corroded, rusted metal. The second time he attempted to use the knife, it simply disintegrated into a thousand flakes of rust.

But the Space Marines were relentless and pressed onwards nonetheless. Every so often, one of the group would stop suddenly and turn to hack at another groping barb. Iakodos had insisted that the inquisitor walk in amongst the Space Marines rather than separately so that they could at least offer some kind of protection to him. His blessed blade was unsheathed and he had reluctantly conceded temporary ownership of it to the Chaplain. It seemed to be the only thing that made the tendrils recoil without releasing any more of their destructive bile.

The next attack came far sooner than any of them anticipated. Without warning, half a dozen figures stepped from the walls. Ardashir saw them first, and they were so repugnant and vile – such things of horror – that he hesitated before firing. As big again as the Adeptus Astartes themselves, the humanoid shapes were walking horrors. Ardashir had seen men flayed alive, skin peeling from their bodies to reveal the twitching muscle, sinew and bone beneath, but these abominations were worse. In his mind, a flash of memory came to the fore – the recollection of an anatomy chart of the human body he had seen during his earliest training. The creatures looked like that, blue veins and pulsing arteries covering them in a horrific, crawling network.

No longer insensible with disgust, Ardashir thumbed the activation stud on his chainsword and turned to face the closest creature. The tungsten teeth of his blade whirred into life at his touch and he brought the weapon down in a cross-stroke across its right shoulder. It bit into the daemon and chewed through to the breastbone. Blood and marrow spattered across Ardashir and several others who also turned to face this new threat.

'Keep going,' the Blood Swords sergeant urged across the vox. 'We will deal with this threat. No more time to waste, Evander. Get the inquisitor to the heart of the ship!'

'I hear you, brother. Join us when you are finished.'

Despite his misgivings about sanctioning another split to the group, Iakodos agreed with Ardashir. The Star Dragons set off at a swift jog and Remigius was hard pressed to keep up with the punishing pace. The Chaplain could see more of the flesh beasts forming from the walls of the ship. The foulness of them stirred his anger and hatred, not all of which was directed at the daemons. For a fleeting moment, he *hated* Remigius. He hated the inquisitor and all his kind. He loathed the fact that the Ordo Malleus had such a hold over the Star Dragons Chapter.

Hatred. It was his cardinal weapon. The Chaplain allowed the smouldering fury to raise his ire. He stoked the flames of rage that burned in his heart, fuelling his desire to deliver retribution to the enemies of mankind. Once the fire caught, it would spill over to his brothers and they too would burn with righteous anger. The familiar weight of his crozius gave him a focus as they reached yet another locked bulkhead. His fingers closed around it and he drew it close to his chest. A litany fell from his lips and several of his battle-brothers picked up the words and spoke with him.

A calmness descended. The choice had been a good one. Iakodos could feel the tension ebbing away, but the sense of readiness did not leave the assembly.

Evander shouldered his bolter as the others readied more melta charges in order to get through the next bulkhead that blocked their passage. By his reckoning, they did not have much further to go before they came to the enginarium. Once they were there, the Emperor alone knew what would be waiting for them. If what the inquisitor had hinted at was even remotely correct, it would likely be the end of them all.

'Ardashir, report.' Evander used the temporary lull in proceedings to check in with the Blood Swords sergeant.

'We are keeping them at bay,' came the strained reply. Ardashir's words were terse, his voice that of a man in the midst of battle. 'They do not regenerate, but they keep coming. It is like the *Accursed Eternity* can produce an endless supply of these things. Whatever it is that you are doing, you need to do it faster, brother.'

'Fine words, Ardashir. I am in complete agreement.'

Evander's earlier urge to grab the inquisitor by the throat and squeeze the life out of the man's body had subsided, but he still felt a gnawing hate in his gut whenever his eyes fell on Remigius.

You could snap his windpipe with no difficulty at all. The repercussions of murdering Remigius will be far less severe than what waits for you behind this door, Brother-Sergeant Evander.

He knew doubt then. Perhaps they should…

The melta charges detonated with an echoing *boom*, distracting his attention and splintering his thoughts of retreat into a million shards.

KORYDON HAD NO time to avoid the bolter shell as it thundered into the ceramite of his armour. The unexpected attack knocked him from his feet, sending him flying several metres backwards. In its already weakened state, it would not take much more to render his battle-gear entirely useless and it was this thought, more than any other that got him back to his feet again.

His breath came in a ragged, wet rasp now; the damage he had sustained to his ribcage was considerable and he intuitively knew that he had a punctured lung. His enhanced physiology was compensating, but it was at a cost to the rest of his strength. Still it wasn't enough to stop him from hurling himself with full force into his attacker.

He passed right through it, crashing into the wall. As he did so, he was sure that he heard the sound of a hollow laugh of derision.

You cannot fight what is not there, Korydon.

Had that been a voice, or his own thoughts? He no longer knew – or cared – which it was. The black shadow flickered and wavered in front of his eyes, like a poorly-crafted hololithic image. He got back to his feet again, but it was not there. The shot to his torso had been quite real. He had felt the pain of impact quite solidly and the copper taste of blood in his mouth was no illusion.

You cannot fight what is not there, Korydon.

Had his own mind been so warped and twisted by this vessel that he was now even imagining his own pain? Was it possible for him to imagine his own death? A distant memory, long forgotten, resurfaced in his skull. It was of himself as a child, before he had been given over to the recruiting sergeants of the Star Dragons. Speaking to his mother, asking her a question that she had never been able to answer.

'If I die in my dreams, does that mean I will never wake up?'

It was the type of philosophical question that his mother, a menial worker, had neither the inclination nor the education necessary to discuss. She had ruffled his hair and smiled indulgently at him. 'When you are one of the Emperor's angels,' she had said to him, 'you will find all the answers you seek.'

That had been a lie. There were still many things that Korydon questioned, and the memory of this question was now the thing that would save his life.

'Awaken, Korydon,' he said, and taking his combat blade he drove it into his own chest.

His world exploded.

* * *

I see you.

He is in some kind of trance, some sort of dream state that he cannot possibly hope to comprehend. He is at one and the same time dead, dying and alive. It is a non-state. Everything feels heavy, oppressive and stifling. His own power armour threatens to overwhelm him with its impossible weight. The agonising pain in his chest flares like fire spreading across dry grassland.

His eyes roam desperately, seeking, searching, hunting for something that will tell him what is going on, and they lock with those of another Space Marine. A matrix of exquisite crystal reaches from the gorget of his armour. A psyker.

But we brought no psykers.

His livery, whilst the blue of all witch-kin, is not the rich cobalt of the Star Dragons. It is softer, paler, more indigo than blue.

I do not know you.

He reaches out a hand as if to touch the psyker, but his gauntlet passes straight through. Another ghost. Another daemon. Not to be trusted. And yet…

You do not know me.

Are you my past? Present? Future?

Despite his misgivings, Korydon takes a step closer.

Time is irrelevant. Past, present, future… All these things are the same and yet different.

A typical psyker response. Half riddle, half philosophy and devoid of any sense at all. Korydon's fists curl in impotent fury.

Though he cannot see it, he knows that the other figure is smiling. He does not know how he knows, but he does. Perhaps it is in the stance, in the way that the shoulders shift position, or in the way that the helmeted head twists slightly. The voice, when it returns, is filled with an emotion he does not recognise and understands even less. It is pity.

For you, they are all the same, brother.

With a shudder, with a jolt of awareness, Korydon wakes. He is lying on the floor of the corridor in which he fought Arion. His brother's armour is still there; he is still naught but dust. But there is no sign of the rest of his squad.

Every movement brings fresh pain. Every shred and fibre of his being screams as he moves, but he moves anyway. What else can he do?

In the distance, there is the faintly resonating boom of an explosion. He is enough of a veteran to know the sound. It is the echo of melta charges. His brothers. His twin hearts gladdening at the thought, he hurries, as much as his battered body will allow, towards the sound.

It is then that he knows, with absolute clarity, what it is that they face behind the final door. His desperate dash to rejoin them becomes a race against time, a race that he has no hope of ever winning.

If only he realised the futility of it he would never push himself harder than he has ever pushed himself before. But then, if he knew the truth of it he would not try at all. Giving up is not in Korydon's nature. It would not end well.

Time has him in its clutches and will never willingly release him. He understands. He can grasp the concept of time immaterial without really knowing how the knowledge comes to him. This is where he has always been. This is where he will always be.

He belongs to the Accursed Eternity.

V

THIS DEEP INTO the heart of the ship, lights were flickering; fizzing and popping as though something was racing across the circuit and causing it to fail. As the Star Dragons, once more surrounding the inquisitor, passed by, the lights flared momentarily into blinding brilliance, causing the Space Marines to turn their heads away, before they faded once again to a dull and slightly pulsating ebb. The sensors in the helmets of the Star Dragons took several moments to balance the light levels out again.

Evander, still plagued by occasional whispers that suggested many glorious ends to the inquisitor's life, had fallen into a sullen silence; it was palpable, a dark mood that was now seeping through the Star Dragons like a slow poison. Evander's fingers occasionally clenched into a fist and then slowly unclenched again as he battled against the words in his mind.

'You should stay here, brother.'

The voice startled him and he looked up into the skull mask of the Chaplain. Shaking his head, Evander did not speak his reply, but in the cant of his head and the set of his shoulders, his refusal was evident.

'You are not yourself. We can all feel it. You are becoming an increasing danger to the rest of the squad, not to mention yourself. Your faith, brother. Where is your faith? Did you leave it behind in the corridor? If you are going to continue to lead this mission, then you must pull yourself together.' Iakodos struck where he knew the sergeant would hurt the most and was rewarded by the other Adeptus Astartes physically recoiling from him.

'He will bring our doom upon us, Chaplain.' The words were spoken so softly that Iakodos wondered if he had imagined them. He leaned a little closer and tapped his helmet, indicating that the sergeant should switch to a private vox-channel.

'Who will, Evander?'

'Remigius. He leads us to a fate *worse* than death. We should abort the mission.'

'We cannot do that, brother. We swore an oath to serve the Ordo Malleus...'

'Damn them!' Evander raised his voice. 'I have no idea what we owe them, but we do *not* owe them the lives of so many good men from two Chapters!'

'We are almost at the enginarium. Whatever waits for us there will soon be brought to an end. The inquisitor has the means and he has the tenacity. As to the reasons why we agreed to take this mission...' The Chaplain's hand closed around his crozius and his skull mask turned towards Remigius. 'There are some debts that cannot be ignored. In time, brother-sergeant, you will learn. For now, focus on the mission. The moment he strikes, we will withdraw. On that, you have my word.'

Evander shook his head grimly. 'It will be too late by then, Chaplain. Far too late.' He spoke the words with a grim finality and clicked off the vox-channel leaving Iakodos wondering just how prophetic the sergeant's words actually were. The next vox exchange that occurred did little to settle the uncertainty roiling in his gut.

'Evander, this is Ardashir.'

'Report.'

'The enemy are quiescent once again,' replied the Blood Sword. 'No more are attacking.' He sounded uncertain that this was actually the case and Iakodos did not blame him. There was so little they understood about this entire situation that it was next to impossible to predict what would happen next.

'Casualties?'

The pause stung and Iakodos dreaded the answer. Already they had lost one of Ardashir's squad. For a Chapter that were already dwindling, further deaths would be a harsh blow.

'One dead, three injured, but nothing that we cannot manage.'

'Hold your position there. Third Scale, begin making your way back to the corridor and head towards the enginarium. We are going to need all the back-up we can muster.'

'Message received. Understood.'

The exchange, grim though its content had been, seemed to have bolstered Evander's resolve and the sergeant's back straightened noticeably. Iakodos laid a hand briefly on his battle-brother's shoulder and nodded once.

The door to the main deck loomed before them and Remigius pushed his way through the warriors to stand before them. He raised his head up and down, then moved to place his hand on the door. He nodded vigorously.

'Yes. This is where we need to be,' said the inquisitor, speaking for the first time in a while. He retrieved the sword from Iakodos and the dormant runes that ran along its length burned ferociously. 'The daemon is waiting for us. Let's not disappoint it.'

THE DOOR OPENED easily. There was no need for melta charges or violent ingress of any sort. It simply shuddered and slid slowly apart, old hydraulics and machinery grating as though they had forgotten how to operate. Iakodos and Evander stepped up to take point, shrouding the inquisitor and his sword from view. For once, the inquisitor didn't complain. All his bluster and bravado seemed to be turned inwards. There was no sign of fear on his face, only the kind of distracted expression that suggested he was concentrating hard on the task ahead.

'Move on,' said Evander softly, and as a unit the Star Dragons crossed the threshold of the enginarium. Almost immediately, every bolter and every blade came to bear as movement caught their attention.

Ghostly figures drifted in front of their eyes, colourless things without true shape or form but with the size and build of Adeptus Astartes. They moved as though in a trance, seemingly without direction or purpose. On second, closer study, that was incorrect. There was definitely a purpose to the way they interacted. They stopped, they spoke soundlessly to one another and they continued as though uninterrupted. No markings of any kind could be made out on their largely transparent armour. And there were others, barely visible shapes that were far smaller. Servitors. Humans. They all moved around the busy deck.

Iakodos did not believe in ghosts. They had featured heavily in the tales of his childhood – a distant memory now – but his time in service to the Golden Throne had taught him that spirits and ghosts were not real. Daemons and creatures from the warp, they were tangible things that could be put down with bolter and chainsword or, at the very least, the right words from those trained to deal with them. But ghosts?

And yet here they were, right in front of his eyes. They were translucent, silvery grey and wispy things that moved endlessly around the enginarium. Not one of them took any notice of the Star Dragons and the inquisitor; they seemed intent on their task. All around him, Iakodos could hear the sounds of muttered litanies as his battle-brothers sought to reassert their faith, which had been shaken to the core so many times already during the course of this mission.

Apart from the spectres, or whatever they were, the

enginarium was as deserted and forgotten as the rest of the *Accursed Eternity* had been. Taking a few steps forwards to the top of a flight of stairs that descended to the main hub, Iakodos raised a gauntlet. It passed through the misty form of one of the ghostly Adeptus Astartes. He met no resistance as his hand scythed through. The shape simply shimmered, wavering briefly before reforming and continuing about its business as though nothing had happened.

There was no clear sign of aggression but all those present maintained a close eye on the moving figures and a tight grip on their weapons. As they descended into the central area of the enginarium, it became evident that there were still more of the ghosts, seated at stations. Here a servitor slaved to the communications terminal. There a Space Marine surveying an occulus that showed nothing at all.

'What *are* they?' Evander's words gave voice to the question that was on every set of lips. Before Iakodos could respond, Remigius spoke.

'Echoes of the past,' he said, and to Iakodos's surprise and consternation there was an audible tremble in his voice. 'We are seeing the last living moments of this ship. The Chapter who once called this vessel theirs, before it became the *Accursed Eternity*...'

'To which Chapter do they belong?' Iakodos looked more closely. There were symbols etched into the instruments but they were old, corroding and faded, and entirely illegible. The Chaplain took a few more paces and leaned forwards in an effort to make out the symbol he saw ingrained in the surface of the cogitator. He could not make it out at all.

'We have never been fully certain,' responded the inquisitor, that same tremor in his tone betraying his fear and anxiety. 'We are sure that they were loyal to the Golden Throne, however; that a series of complicated events overtook them, and that ultimately they succumbed to the warp.'

'Succumbed? Or perhaps chose to succumb. Consider that possibility, inquisitor.'

* * *

IT WAS A new voice and it was filled with venomous loathing and endless hatred. A voice so sharp it could slice through metal. Its timbre was a sonorous rumble and it was pitched at a peculiar frequency. The inquisitor shook his head as blood began to run slowly from his ears. Iakodos suspected that had he and his men not had their helmets on, they would also be suffering similarly.

Even as he watched, the walls of the enginarium began to buckle and distort, ripples passing across their unblemished surfaces as though someone had dropped a rock into a calm lake. Everything shimmered and took on a wavering unreality. The inquisitor, reaching up to wipe the blood from his ears, bellowed through the re-breather mask as loudly as it would allow. Any nervousness was gone, and despite his inherent dislike and distrust of the man, Iakodos found himself deeply impressed by the depth of conviction in the words.

'I am Shadrach Remigius, inquisitor of the Ordo Malleus by the grace of the God-Emperor, and I demand that you show yourself and meet your end at my hands.'

'In such a rush to die, inquisitor?' There was an insatiable, slavering hunger in the voice. Iakodos could not say how he knew the thing, whatever it was, thirsted for blood, but he sensed it nonetheless.

Remigius continued, seemingly undaunted. 'You are an abomination and you are cursed. I am sworn to end your existence and I will do so.'

'I will snuff you out in a heartbeat.' The amusement was gone and the daemonic voice had changed pitch. There was now an underlying growl to it that accentuated its hunger. 'You have nothing that can defeat me. Soon, the only sounds you will hear will be your own bones crunching in my grasp and the sound of your blood as it drips down to feed my master's unslakable thirst.'

The inquisitor inclined his head, then raised it again, and Iakodos could see the passion in his eyes.

'I do have something, creature. I have your name.'

VI

THE PAIN HAD stopped long ago but the memory of it still lingered. As Korydon made his way through the ship, he became aware that he was still over-compensating for the pain in his leg, despite his awareness that it was healing even as he moved. He had no other option but to continue. Despite the increasing knowledge that his efforts would get him no further, it was simply not in his nature to give up.

Occasionally, he made a concerted attempt to raise his brothers on the vox but received nothing but static for his efforts. Once, he thought he heard a voice and had answered it gladly, but he had been forced to conclude that his own mind was beginning to play tricks on him. The idea had occurred to him that this entire situation was nothing more than an elaborate hallucination, in which case there was nothing he could do but ride it to its conclusion.

Whatever that conclusion might ultimately be.

He pressed forwards. The enginarium could not be far now; but then he had been thinking that for a while.

Hours, perhaps. Or it could only have been minutes. Time ceased to have any meaning when you never seemed to get any further forwards.

His movement seemed slightly impaired now and he tried to coax himself past the memory of his injuries and into a better mental space. It was then that he noticed the first signs of corrosion on his blue armour.

Pausing in his determined stride, Korydon glanced more closely at one of his thigh plates. Sure enough, there was a hint of degradation there, as though it were old and uncared for. It was something that only happened to a warrior who neglected his armour, or to those who died in battle and whose bodies were never recovered.

But such was the design and solidity of the Adeptus Astartes' wargear such corrosion did not happen for decades, unless it were in an environment in which the process was hastened. He had not been here for decades, so he had to assume the latter.

'The sooner we get off this ship, brothers,' he muttered to the empty air beside him, 'the better.'

Korydon's armour and body were withstanding the effects of his predicament. His mind was not faring so well.

IAKODOS HAD NEVER been in such close proximity to a daemon of this power before. He had faced them on the field of battle but they had always been small and insignificant things, foul and bloodthirsty certainly, but easily defeated with faith and fire. This thing, this mighty horror that was forming in front of him, was anything but insignificant.

The first sign of its manifestation was a strong scent of coppery blood in the air, as though a body had been freshly butchered. Iakodos and the Star Dragons took up positions beside the inquisitor, ready to fire as soon as there was something to actually fire upon.

'Lower your weapons,' said the inquisitor. There was firm resolve in his stance. 'They will only stoke the daemon's wrath.'

'We are sworn to protect you,' retorted Evander, and

Iakodos noted that the words were spat rather than spoken. It was clear that the sergeant's urge to kill the inquisitor was still strong. 'And we will do that,' Evander continued, 'for the honour of our Chapter.'

Evander shifted the weight of the bolter in his grip and whether consciously or not, it ended up with the muzzle pointed directly at Remigius. Iakodos stepped forwards and nudged it discreetly away.

'There is a lust to kill in you, Adeptus Astartes.' It was the daemon's voice again and it broke the tension of the moment. 'I approve of this. My master will approve of you. You may bargain for your life with that bloodlust.'

'Show yourself, daemon,' said Remigius. 'Show yourself so that we may end this charade.' He casually shook the sword in his hand and Iakodos stared at it. The runes that had been burned into the carefully crafted blade were now glowing with a hateful red light. Eldritch lightning crackled along its edges as it responded to the presence of...

...still nothing. Only the same powerful scent of fresh blood and the images of a body-strewn battlefield it evoked. In his mind's eye, despite the urgency of the situation, Iakodos recalled his last deployment. He remembered with absolute clarity the aftermath; he had walked the ruins where the dead and dying had lain, bringing the words of the Emperor to those beyond the Apothecary's aid. It stirred his ingrained desire to fight. Yet he struggled against it. It would be too easy to fall prey to such a weakness. His judgement would be impaired.

He had little time to linger on it because with a sudden, violent shudder, the *Accursed Eternity* lurched hard to starboard. They all stumbled and the inquisitor lost his balance completely, tumbling to the ground. The sword fell from his grip and clattered to the floor.

'The blade! Recover the blade!' Remigius's scream cut through the calm resolve he had previously demonstrated.

'Why, certainly.' The daemonic voice was filled with amusement.

Iakodos did not know what he had expected from the

manifestation of such a daemon, but he had not expected the sudden, raw aura of power that filled the enginarium. He felt an overwhelming urge to turn to those around him, take out his anger on them and smite them where they stood. But Iakodos was a Chaplain. His faith in the Emperor was unshakeable and all of his years of service overrode his basic, primal urges.

'Brothers, control your emotions!' The Chaplain bellowed the order to the few brothers who had not withstood the mental assault. They were drawing their blades or aiming their bolters, turning the weapons on their own kin.

Appalled at the lack of control that his brothers were demonstrating, Iakodos strode to the closest. He pulled back his clenched fist and struck his brother squarely in the centre of his helmet. 'Orestes, stop this. Remember who you are, brother.' He flung the dazed battle-brother towards Evander who still wavered between pointing his bolter at the inquisitor and the swirling mass of particles that was taking shape before him. 'Sergeant, control your squad or I will take over the command of this mission. Get your men into a semblance of order now.'

Not waiting to see whether or not Evander complied, Iakodos strode over and dragged Remigius to his feet. The inquisitor's eyes were transfixed by the coalescing apparition. Iakodos turned his head to look up on the daemon for himself and was staggered by its immense size. What had, mere seconds before, been a swirling mass of intangibility, was now quite visible.

Twice as tall again as the largest of the Star Dragons, bigger even, perhaps, than one of the Chapter's Dreadnoughts, the daemon burst into full corporeal form as though it had torn its way into reality through nothing more substantial than paper. Its entire body was a uniform shade of blue and almost translucent, rippling as though warp tides ebbed and flowed just beneath the skin. Its lower limbs were heavily muscled and even the tiniest movement was traced in sinew beneath the surface. Its forearms ended in long and strangely delicate fingers that were tipped with lethal-looking claws. Vast wings, presently folded tightly against its back, sprang from its shoulders. Iakodos suspected that if the daemon were to unfurl them, they would be too big for the confines of the enginarium.

His eyes travelling upwards, Iakodos stared at the two heads of the creature. Avian, with a wicked beak, its eyes burned with something he could not relate to. It was not the hatred of a Space Marine for his enemy, but something unfathomably complex.

'Kill it,' the Chaplain said in a hoarse voice. 'Evander... We must kill it!'

Evander had regained control of his senses and once he had begun issuing orders the rest of the Star Dragons slowly came out of their semi-daze. As a unit, they stepped forwards and opened fire simultaneously. Every bolter shell impacted on the daemon's scaly body, but none of the direct hits seemed to have any effect.

'You humans are pathetic creatures. Always so keen to die,' the daemon said. It stepped forwards, the ground shaking beneath its tread. In a single move it swiped a clawed hand towards the closest Space Marine, impaling him on the end of one of its claws. It turned and flung the unfortunate warrior towards the wall at the far end of the enginarium. Orestes struck the wall with a sickening crack of bone and slumped to the ground, blood surging so quickly from the gouge in his chest that there seemed no way his constitution could hope to withstand it. But there was no time to check if Orestes would live or die. If he lived, he would be useless to them right now. If he was dead then there was nothing that could be done.

Another round of bolter fire sounded as the Star Dragons attempted to vanquish their enemy. Two battle-brothers pressed forwards, their chainswords roaring in hungry anticipation. They were cast back, dashed against the wall as easily as Orestes had been as soon as they got within a few metres.

'This is not your fight, sons of the Imperium. But I will never turn down such sport. If you wish to die at my hand, then I will not stop you.'

The daemon leaned down and took up the blade that the inquisitor had wielded. It sparked ferociously in its long fingers, red fire burning down the length of the weapon's blade. Though it growled as the fire curled around its flesh, the daemon seemed otherwise unaffected. There was a stench of burning meat as it raised the sword to eye level and studied the weapon closely. Its burning eyes considered the weapon's design and the runes burned into its steel.

'An amateur attempt at best, mortal,' it said, directing its comments towards the inquisitor. 'Pathetic at worst.' Without skipping a beat, without even turning its heads, it flung the sword away and it speared through Evander's torso. The sergeant cried out in pain at the sudden impact and toppled over backwards. He lay still for a few heart-stopping moments before slowly sitting back up with a groan, the sword having been stopped in its path through his body by his now-cracked ceramite plate and heavy power pack. He had sustained a severe injury, but with an Apothecary's attention he would live.

Momentarily abandoning his place at the inquisitor's side, concerned far more with Evander's wellbeing than the squeaky, stuttered rage that came from Remigius, Iakodos helped the sergeant to his feet and pulled the sword from his belly. It freed with a sickening *squish*, the blade smeared in blood. The Chaplain voxed both the Blood Swords and Third Scale to make all haste to the boarding torpedoes that had brought them to this place.

'This is Sergeant Ardashir. Message received. Understood.'

There was no response from Third Scale. Iakodos voxed them again. The Chaplain felt a sudden surge of anxiety for Korydon's squad. He had been so caught up in the unfolding drama that he had temporarily put the other sergeant's disappearance to the back of his mind.

'Third Scale, report in!'

'Message received. Understood.'

Iakodos's relief gave way to sudden doubt. He had received nothing but that response from Tylissus for some considerable time. There was no time to linger on the concern, however. They would hold this thing off for as long as possible as they made their retreat. Then he would determine Korydon and Third Scale's fate. He felt increasingly certain that it would not be a good one.

The daemon was massive, so huge that the walls of the enginarium kept it largely contained, preventing it from moving much further forwards to attack. The Space Marines used this to their advantage, peppering it with more rounds from their bolters and bolt pistols. But the shots were little more than a distraction, nothing seeming capable of penetrating whatever warp trickery protected it.

'You said that the sword would end this daemon, inquisitor.' Iakodos was long past pleasantries and cordiality. He snarled at the desperate-looking Remigius even as he turned to face the daemon, his hands gripped tightly around the haft of his crozius. 'That does not look to me like the face of defeat!'

Remigius shook his head, seemingly lost for words. His voice recovered enough to stutter out an explanation. 'It was designed to defeat the daemon at the heart of this vessel. It looks...' The inquisitor stared up at the daemon. 'Its appearance. Exactly as we had come to understand. It is everything it should be. The sword was perfect. *Perfect!* The situation is somehow wrong.'

'Well done, inquisitor. It appears that you have caught me out!' The daemon ceased its snarling at the inquisitor's words. With a *pop*, a sudden inrush of air, the creature decreased dramatically in size. One head folded in upon itself in the most hideous fashion, the other moving in a sickening way to a more central position.

'That shape was a memory,' it said. 'A guise that the former – how shall we put this – *controller* of this vessel wore. It seemed the most appropriate way to greet you.' Its sharp, intelligent eyes fixed on the inquisitor.

'The blade,' moaned Remigius, wringing his hands together in horror. 'The blade must have been forged incorrectly. Such a careful process... One error and everything is wrong. This mission–'

'This mission,' said Iakodos furiously, 'is killing my battle-brothers. We are withdrawing from this fight.' With Evander down, he had made the decision to take over command of the mission.

The Chaplain turned his head to the inquisitor, his red lenses glowing. For a fleeting moment, to the inquisitor's increasingly desperate mind, the Space Marine looked every bit as daemonic as the thing in front of them had been mere moments before. Now, it was standing there, half its previous size and apparently preening its wings in affected disinterest. No longer too big for the confines of the enginarium, it could attack at any time.

'Brothers, fall back. We are retreating.' Iakodos ordered.

'No! Wait!' Remigius leaped forwards and grasped the Chaplain's arm. 'Let me at least try the banishment. It is a daemon of the Chaos god of change! This could be a double-bluff. Give me a few moments more. Just hold it at bay for as long as it takes me to perform the necessary rites to invoke the power of its name! Let me try that one last thing, then we can retreat! It is your *duty*, Chaplain!'

The heads of the rest of the squad turned to Iakodos, awaiting his orders. Evander was stumbling, but on his feet. The injury had clearly injected sense back into him because his bolter was very firmly trained on the daemon. He flipped the weapon to semi-automatic and opened fire. As before, every shell impacted harmlessly against the daemon, but this time instead of clattering uselessly to the ground, they were repelled by the thing's invisible defences. Several shells were fired straight back in Evander's direction and only by throwing himself to the floor did he escape their impact. They struck the wall behind him, detonating one after the other. The damage to the walls of the ship repaired itself even as the Space Marines watched.

'How is that possible?' Evander voiced his disbelief.

'This is my ship,' said the daemon, its tone almost conversational. 'I can shape it as I wish. I can shape myself as I wish and that extends beyond my body to the vessel I inhabit.'

Its attention seemed largely focused on the inquisitor now. Remigius had dropped to the floor and was drawing a number of incomprehensible runic shapes on the floor with the tip of his blade. The runes were being drawn in Evander's own blood and the arterial red sigils stood out on the hard, metal deck.

'What are you doing, inquisitor?'

Remigius didn't answer and the daemon advanced, pausing as it encountered another round of covering fire from the Space Marines. It stared at them in irritation and thrust out a hand. Instantly, the walls of the enginarium came to life in much the same way as they had done in the corridor. But no corpses tore free from the walls this time. Instead, disembodied arms stretched from the skin of the daemon-ship and grasped blindly for them. For the first time, Iakodos noted that the ghosts on the deck had stopped moving. They were still, as though someone had paused a hololith in the middle of playback. Perhaps, he thought wildly as he struck at the reaching limbs with his crozius, the daemon only has strength enough to manifest one aspect of this madness at a time.

'What are you *doing*, inquisitor?' There was a strange catch in the daemon's voice and it stepped closer again to Remigius who was scribbling frantically. All the while, inaudible to human ears but perfectly clear to the enhanced aural sense of the Space Marines, he was muttering words in an unfamiliar language.

'Your time is at an end, daemon of Tzeentch,' said the inquisitor as he finished his work. 'With this sword, I could not defeat you. But with this weapon and with the one true word I have at my command, I can banish you back to the heart of the warp.'

With that said, he began to speak the guttural words he had been uttering before. He used the sword to help him back to his feet and raised his head to stare the daemon directly in the face. Iakodos felt an ethereal wind whipping up in the enginarium and despite the distraction of his own battle could not help but watch the unfolding events.

'I name you, daemon,' said Remigius, his voice barely a whisper. 'Mortal man may know you by the name Fateweaver, but now I invoke the true power of the name which binds you.'

He slammed the blade of the sword down in the centre of the runes he had hastily drawn. A glaring white light spewed forth from the tip of the weapon, boiling around the wards on the deck and around the inquisitor.

It was so bright that Iakodos had to turn his eyes from it. The wind rose to a crescendo of howling and he could not hear the rest of the words that the inquisitor spoke. Then, with a primal scream of terrible rage and agony the daemon dropped to its knees. It buried its bestial head in its claws and roared its terrible fury. It was a sound that caused every hair on Iakodos's body beneath his armour to stand on end. It was horrific. Yet again, the Chaplain felt blood trickling from his ears. The power of a daemonic name to harm extended far beyond its bearer, it seemed.

The old inquisitor for his part was channelling every last shred of his psychic power through the force sword. The light still roiled from the runes on its blade although it was no longer blinding. Iakodos could see, from the way that Remigius's body was shaking that he could not possibly support himself for very much longer. But the grasping hands had stopped and been absorbed back into the walls, and the daemon seemed far too concerned with its own horrific and impending demise.

'This is our chance, Chaplain.' Evander's voice whilst wracked with pain was clear and firm. 'We should leave. Now.'

'The inquisitor has to finish the ritual. We cannot just walk away.'

'That thing said that this was not our fight. We cannot harm it. What good can we do by staying here? Look at him, brother. The inquisitor is giving his life for this. He cannot survive that much power. We have done our duty. We should go whilst we still can.'

Evander was right. The inquisitor's face was a vision of

exquisite pain, his psychic power tearing the very essence of his being free. The daemon had stopped screaming now which was a blessed, merciful relief, but its face was contorted in a silent agony. The Chaplain considered his options, then he nodded to Evander.

'Take the squad and make your way back to the boarding torpedo. Do what you can to establish the fate of Third Scale.'

'Chaplain Iakodos?'

'I will cover your retreat. Remigius may be a bastard, I do not dispute that. But he is giving his life to rid the Imperium of this creature. We owe it to the Inquisition to return his body.'

'I will not accept this.'

'You are presently unfit for command and Sergeant Korydon is absent. I am therefore in charge of the mission and I am giving you a direct order. Take Orestes and the squad. Get out of here now. If you locate Korydon on the way, then bring him too.' The Chaplain paused for a heartbeat. 'Do not linger in your search, though.' Iakodos spoke softly but with such command in his voice that the only thing Evander could do was nod in acquiescence.

The inquisitor was slowly sinking to his knees, his shaking legs unable to support him any more, and he stared up at Iakodos as the Chaplain came towards him. Weakly, he put a hand up to stop him coming any closer.

'It's still wrong,' he said, his voice barely a whisper. 'It's… not working how it should.'

The daemon was furled in a foetal ball, its back to the inquisitor and the Chaplain. It suddenly stopped moving, but an instant later bounded to its feet, a cackling screech of gloating laughter emanating from its beak-like mouth.

'*Twice* wrong, inquisitor! Your words have no power over me, for I am not the Oracle of Tzeentch!'

'No… This cannot be.' Remigius's voice was a croak. 'Years of research. You are Fateweaver. You must be. How can you be ano–'

'Enough of this. What has taken place on this ship is not

the business of pathetic fleshlings. Accept the simple truth of the matter. Your precious "research" has led you to your demise. You are *wrong*. And now you die.' It prowled sinuously towards the weakened inquisitor.

Iakodos closed his grip tightly around his crozius and placed himself squarely in its path.

'Out of my way, Adeptus Astartes warrior. I told you before that my fight was not with you.'

'Regardless, you will have to go through me to get to him.'

'A noble intention. But really?' With an almost idle wave of its hand, the daemon caused Iakodos to fly backwards into the wall. Undeterred, the Chaplain got to his feet once again and calling upon every ounce of his strength began to charge towards the daemon.

The creature let out some foul epithet in its besmirched guttural language, which took on warp-fuelled substance and crawled over the Chaplain's armour, peeling away the ceramite and crippling him with agonising seizures. He watched, helpless to move or act as the daemon reached Remigius. It looked down on him almost as though it pitied him, then took the failing man up in its vicious grasp. Its clawed hands closed around the inquisitor's throat.

'I have a gift for you, Shadrach Remigius,' it said to the stricken man who, unable to respond, stared back at the daemon in horror. 'Since you have gone to so much trouble to track me down, I will give you what you seek. You desire my name? You shall have it. A tragedy that this lesson will be your last. The power of a true name works both ways...'

These last words were spoken in no more than a whisper, but even from the distance he was presently at, Iakodos could feel the raw warp power that came with them.

The inquisitor tried to turn his face away from the shards of sorcery in the daemon's breath as it spoke, but he was held tight and could not move. Iakodos watched with a mixture of disgust and fury as the skin on the old man's face began to peel away. Strips of raw meat that had once been the inquisitor's visage blended with chunks of metal from his implants. His eyes bubbled and melted and eventually all that remained of Shadrach Remigius was a bloodied skull attached to a ruined body.

With arrogant indifference, the daemon crushed the skull in its grasp until it was dust. Then it dropped the corpse to the floor and turned to Iakodos.

'You had a chance to leave and you did not take it. You sealed your fate with that lack of foresight. The others you sent to investigate elsewhere in the ship – their unknowing sacrifice gave me quite a taste for your kind's flesh.' Its eyes narrowed sardonically. 'Message received,' it said in a disturbingly passable impression of Tylissus's voice. 'Understood.'

A soft groan escaped Iakodos's lips. Now that the fate of Third Scale had been revealed, his desire to exact revenge on this thing grew. But still caught in the coruscating power of the creature's sorcery, his armour smoking, he remained helpless.

Whether to enrage him further or merely out of a sadistic desire to reveal its dark nature, the daemon continued.

'It was their presence which awoke my consciousness. I've been alone on this accursed ship for an eternity. But their minds... were sharp. They were delicious. And their imaginations! They expected bleeding walls, creatures of the warp, and I was all too glad to oblige.'

A sickening knot tightened in Iakodos's gut as he realised that it had been their very thoughts which had brought about the demise of Third Scale and the deaths of the Blood Swords. He fervently hoped that Evander was heeding his order.

His demise was imminent and he faced it stoically. The daemon considered him for a moment and took a step towards him. Then it stopped short, its eyes narrowing as it looked over Iakodos's shoulder to a point just beyond him.

'What do you mean?' the daemon said, to Iakodos's surprise.

* * *

KORYDON HAD REACHED the enginarium just in time to see the daemon crush Remigius's skull. He had stared at the unfolding scene. His battle-brothers seemed hazy and pale: flickering images that had no substance. Only the inquisitor and the daemon seemed real to him. Iakodos was a pale, shimmering ghost that only the daemon seemed able to communicate with.

The Star Dragons sergeant had stared down at his old, scuffed armour. It was corroded with age and wear. He knew with absolute certainty that he had witnessed this exchange before. It was how he had known what his battle-brothers would find behind the door of the enginarium. Korydon had fathomed with absolute clarity the nature of the *Accursed Eternity* and that, combined with all the hypno-doctrination that had shaped his early years, had led him to a simple conclusion.

'You will not kill him,' he repeated to the daemon. It was not a threat, not a plea. It was merely a statement.

'How do you know?' The reply was filled with deep curiosity. And then the daemon smiled nastily, understanding in an instant what Korydon had taken a lifetime to realise.

Iakodos was released from the trap that had snared him and he fell to the ground with a thud. He paused for a few moments, catching his breath. He gripped his crozius and stood, ready to fight for what he knew and believed was right.

The daemon was distracted by something, though what it was Iakodos could not understand. It seemed to be staring directly at one of the white figures that had bustled around the deck previously. This one, however, was different. Its armour was far from pristine, old and uncared for. The insignia had long been erased. And yet there was something hauntingly familiar about it. It was as still and unmoving as the others, but the daemon's attention seemed intent upon it. Considering his options carefully, the Chaplain reached the conclusion that a tactical withdrawal was rapidly becoming the best course of action.

'You will not kill him.' Korydon squared his shoulders.

'It is not something that you have ever done and you will not do it this time. You are trapped in this course of events just as much as I have been. I have seen that you will not kill him.' Korydon took a breath. 'Ergo, you will not.'

'A self-fulfilling prophecy. Clever.' The daemon flexed its powerful shoulders and shifted its gaze to linger on Iakodos. The hunger that lay within the infinite depths of its oil-black eyes was palpable and for several brief moments tension crackled between the two, Adeptus Astartes and daemon-spawn of the warp.

'Why are you still here, mortal?'

It was all Iakodos needed. He did not understand what it was that had transpired. All he knew was that he had been given an opportunity to withdraw, possibly even the chance to get back to his ship alive, although he was not prepared to trust the daemon in the slightest. Nonetheless, he made his way to the exit leaving the corpse of the inquisitor lying on the floor.

The daemon watched him go, then turned its attention back to Korydon. The Star Dragon's armour was corroded, where it still held together. The sergeant showed all the signs of having spent decades, maybe centuries, in the same wargear. The warp taint that infused the vessel created things that even the daemon did not fully understand. It had seen this before, though. Mortals caught in pockets of time.

Tricked many thousands of years ago by the daemon Fateweaver, the creature now bound at the heart of the *Accursed Eternity* lived a cursed existence, doomed to live the same sequence of events in endless repetition. Yet every time history repeated itself, something changed. Sometimes it was something small and seemingly insignificant: a word spoken out of place, a head of hair where previously a warrior had borne a shorn scalp. Other times something more important had altered, but the daemon could not quite fathom the nuances of its prison. It was not the warp creature's nature to understand – or even care – about the nature of causality.

'You said I would not kill him,' the daemon said to Korydon eventually. A slow, cruel smile raised its peculiar mouth in a sadistic twist. 'But the ship itself may have other ideas.'

VII

THE FIRST OF the boarding torpedoes was already loaded with Adeptus Astartes by the time Iakodos sighted the landing zone. His eyes sought eagerly for Third Scale only to realise disappointment and sorrow at their continued absence. With that came the memory of the dead Blood Swords. He took some comfort from the fact that some of their fallen had been recovered, at least. The daemon's words regarding the fate of his brothers had been truth, he suspected. He slowed from a run to a steady walk and Evander raised a head, nodding at him curtly. The sergeant was clearly feeling the pain of his injury, but he lived.

'Get the first torpedo out,' he was saying to those aboard. 'We will follow as soon as we can. I want to do a final sweep for Third Scale...'

'They are gone, brother. We have to retreat ourselves.'

Evander stared at the Chaplain and his face showed a moment of grief. 'You are sure of this?'

'I am positive. And there is no time to investigate the daemon's claim any further. You know as well as I do. Here.' The Chaplain clapped a hand against his breastplate.

The sergeant nodded abruptly and leaned into the boarding torpedo. 'As soon as you are in communications range, tell the *Ladon* that once we are clear, they should open fire on this cursed ship.'

The battle-brother closest to the open end of the boarding torpedo acknowledged the order and reached for the lever that would seal it closed and begin the retraction process. Gears ground back into life and slowly the tube began to scrape back through the hull of the ship. Whatever it was that passed for intelligence aboard the *Accursed Eternity* acted instinctively, the ship sealing the gaping hole in its hull like skin closing over an open wound.

The first torpedo had barely completed inching its way into the void of space when the howling began: a low, keening wail that set hair and teeth on edge, and brought with it the banshee promise of certain death. The remaining Space Marines, most of Ninth Scale and three of the remaining Blood Swords, watched in a state of horrified disbelief as the remaining rent in the hull of the *Accursed Eternity* began to warp. It shifted and distorted impossibly before their eyes becoming a fanged maw that closed tightly around the second boarding torpedo.

'It will tear it apart!' The Blood Sword who had spoken merely voiced what they were all thinking. But it was nothing so simple. The malformed mouth, a circular series of razor-sharp fangs, merely clamped itself down on the boarding torpedo, locking it in place.

The blood-curdling wail sounded again, accompanied by the sound of many scurrying feet as though the entire corridor was filled with rats or other rodent-like creatures. So vivid was the sound that Evander and several others turned the muzzles of their guns to the floor.

Iakodos held his crozius aloft. With the unswerving devotion and loyalty that had earned him his rank and title, he spoke in a steady voice that fuelled the faith and fire of his battle-brothers. The Litany of Devotion was one of the first things that he had committed to memory as a young novitiate and never had its words felt more true and meaningful than they did right now.

'Where there is uncertainty, I shall bring light. Where there is doubt, I shall sow faith. Where there is shame, I shall point atonement...'

His voice never changed pitch and never wavered, even as he caught sight of the daemonic pack-beasts thundering at full speed down the corridor towards him. He could hear Evander barking out commands to set melta charges around the sides of the torpedo in an effort to free it, but he focused on the words he was speaking.

'Where there is rage, I shall show its course... My word in the soul shall be as my bolter in the field.'

The Litany complete, he held his crozius out in front of him and spoke a final time. 'All of this I say and all of this I am. Die!'

In an effort to buy some of his companions time to blast the torpedo free from the infernal grip of the daemon, Iakodos led a counter-charge against the creatures. Spent shell casings hit the floor like rain as bolters spat out one round after another. When the magazines were spent, the Space Marines resorted to blades and pistols. Every shot that was fired and every blow which was landed was a singular strike against the dark forces that contrived to keep them prisoner and to overwhelm them.

THE FIRST OF the two boarding torpedoes had achieved a perfect exit and had cleared the hull. The Space Marines within took a moment to check their weapons. They might have retreated successfully from the ship, but that did not mean by any stretch that they considered the mission to be at an end.

Ardashir switched vox-channel and hailed the *Ladon*. He had his orders from Evander, who had once again taken command in Korydon's absence.

'Boarding party first vessel returning. Complement...' Looking around the interior of the torpedo, Ardashir felt a sting of loss. They had travelled across with three full squads as well as the Chaplain and the inquisitor. Thirty

Adeptus Astartes. They had lost the entirety of Third Scale and several others to boot. 'Complement twelve souls,' he finished, his voice heavy. 'Five remaining on board the *Accursed Eternity*. Once they are in transit, unleash hell. Tear that ship from the void.'

Silence followed his report but for a few bursts of crackling static. Ardashir repeated his report, and then the vox officer's voice came timorously across the distance that separated them from the *Ladon*.

'Ship's chronometers have your insertion at less than an hour past, sergeant.'

An hour? They had been trapped in the horror of the daemon-ship for what had felt like an eternity. Had it really been only an hour? For a moment, Ardashir doubted himself. Perhaps he had simply lost his mind. But the gravely injured form of Orestes, slumped in the corner, reminded him that his experience had been anything but based in imagination.

'We will debrief fully when we get back on board. Repeat message. Once Sergeant Evander and his remaining warriors are extracted, destroy the *Accursed Eternity*.'

'Message received. Understood.'

The words, the same that Third Scale had repeatedly responded with across the vox, sent a chill down Ardashir's spine.

THERE WAS NO way that the melta charges could be placed any faster than Evander was managing. He moved as swiftly as he could, his ears ringing with the jumbled sounds of his remaining four battle-brothers fighting the daemonic creatures. Their snarls and shrieks of bitter hatred cut through everything and Evander longed more than anything for Iakodos to end the monsters' existence. Ammunition was running low, but the sheer ferocity of the combined force of Star Dragons and Blood Swords was at least keeping the horde at bay.

'Charges set,' Evander said finally, speaking the words that Iakodos was longing to hear.

Pressing forwards, the Chaplain renewed his attack on the daemon-beasts, every one of his brothers, including Evander, joining him. They forced their attack, pushing the daemons back a little further down the corridor but not so far that they were putting themselves out of the range of their escape route. When the charges blew, the hull of the ship would be torn open to space and they would have to move swiftly.

With tremendous force, the melta-bombs detonated, the sound and reverberation shaking the very ground beneath the Space Marines' feet. The hull of the *Accursed Eternity* ripped apart and the torpedo was freed.

Bellowing the retreat as loudly as he could, Evander called the five Space Marines to the boarding torpedo. Four of them dived in leaving only Iakodos facing down the daemons. With a final roar of defiance, the Chaplain turned, ran and dived into the torpedo. Evander slammed the release lever and the tube closed up even as the creatures hurled themselves at them.

They could feel them scrabbling against the smooth surface of the torpedo but they all held tightly to their faith. They had come too far and endured too much to give up the belief that they would make their way to freedom and that they would see this foul ship destroyed.

A scream of daemonic fury reached them even through the armour-plated hull of the boarding torpedo as it made its way slowly out of the *Accursed Eternity*. Then the scream was joined in a sinister harmony by an answering shriek, then another, and then another. Within scant moments the sound of multiple screaming daemons could be heard as the monstrous host of the vessel threw everything it had at its escaping prey.

It was too little too late. The boarding torpedo dropped into the void and moved agonisingly slowly away.

'This is Evander. We are clear. Repeat, we are clear of the hull. Fire on my mark.'

'Received, Sergeant Evander.'

Timing would be critical. If they were too close when the

fleet fired, they would be vaporised along with its target. The viewing aperture in the torpedo was little more than a slit and it was difficult to gauge the distance between them and the *Accursed Eternity*...

Far enough. Evander let out the breath he'd not realised he was holding and spoke a single word.

'Mark.'

Both of the strike cruisers, as well as their escort fleet of destroyers and frigates, opened fire simultaneously and a relentless stream of ordnance razored across space, striking the daemon-ship with unerring accuracy. Light flared brightly through the viewport of the torpedo and Evander was forced to turn his face away. Their vox crackled and spat in relation to the proximity of the various weapon discharges, until finally there was nothing but silence.

And in the silence there was nothing. The *Accursed Eternity* was no more. But to Evander, staring over at Iakodos who was knelt in fervent prayer, simple destruction was not nearly enough. He voiced this concern to the Chaplain who looked up at him and reached up to remove his skull-helm.

Iakodos ran his gauntleted hand across his shorn head. 'You may be right, my brother,' he acknowledged. 'But thank the Emperor that it is no longer there.'

THE MEETING WITH Remigius's retinue lasted long after the *Accursed Eternity* had disappeared. Nobody could comment upon the veracity of the claim that it had been destroyed, but then nobody could prove that it hadn't been. Careful scrutiny of the augury returns suggested conflicting answers. There were all the signs that there had been a plasma core breach but there was no debris to support this.

Iakodos had taken the burden of relaying the news of Remigius's actions to his followers and had been met with cold anger, the rage of those in denial at news they had half-expected but had never fully prepared to hear.

Shock had turned to disbelief, and that in turn had led

to anger. Iakodos had stood patiently through the tears and the pleas and then the barrage of accusations, until there was nothing left to say. He had not lied to the inquisitor's retinue; he had given them a full and frank account of what had occurred there.

It had taken one man to raise a single question for the conversation to come finally to an end.

'What of the Star Dragons' debt to the Ordo Malleus?'

Tanek, who had sat in silence throughout Iakodos's debriefing had stood abruptly at this question. He had leaned across the table that had separated him from the servant. It was that and the captain's exceptional self-control that ensured the man wasn't throttled where he stood.

'My men did everything Inquisitor Remigius asked of them. As a result of this mission, my company has been decimated. I suggest that you learn from your errors. In future, you should think very long and very hard about the sense of asking a captain of the Adeptus Astartes a question like that.'

An icy look crossed the captain's face and he turned his back on the gathering. His voice, when he spoke again, was low and measured. Iakodos knew his captain well enough to recognise that tone. 'The Star Dragons have more than paid back their debt to the Ordo Malleus. You have precisely two hours to get off of the *Ladon* and to remove yourselves from the vicinity of my vessels. As one of the commanders of the Containment Fleet, I suggest that your foolishness in this engagement has generated enough risk for us to consider you a threat.'

'And if we don't leave?' Remigius's elderly adviser attempted a moment of bravado.

His unfortunately chosen and highly facetious comment was quelled instantly when Tanek turned around. The genial and affable face that they had come to know was replaced with the mask of a tyrant.

'Then you will be disobeying a direct order of Containment Fleet Kappa. And I would heartily suggest that you do not test me to see where that path leads.'

It was a threat, plain and simple. Had the inquisitor still been alive, there would have been resistance to the suggestion but, perhaps fortunately for the demoralised remains of Remigius's followers, he was not. Picking up on the barely shrouded threat, they left with such alarming haste it seemed as though all the daemons of the warp were hot on their tail.

'There will be questions, captain, possibly censure,' Iakodos finally took a seat at the table. 'The Ordo Malleus will not let this go. You appreciate that, I am sure.'

Tanek nodded. 'Let the questions come,' he replied. 'I will answer them honestly and truthfully. We were summoned here to aid the inquisitor and we have done that. I propose we remain in the area for a while. Continue to give support to our brothers in the Blood Swords and monitor for any sign of that ship returning.'

'You do not believe it is destroyed?'

'I simply do not know, Chaplain.' Tanek sighed. 'Our Chapter has taken a great loss today and I have to hold on to the hope that the *Accursed Eternity* was destroyed. Otherwise, what was the point of our Chapter's sacrifice? I cannot allow myself to walk that dark path of thought. Its end is not a good one.'

The Chaplain laid his crozius on the table. 'Brother-Sergeant Evander may be a concern for a while,' he said softly. 'His mind was weaker than I had hoped. He fell easily to the whispers of the daemon. We should watch him closely for a while.'

'What of the Blood Swords?' Ardashir and his men had travelled back to their own vessel for debriefing and to undergo care at the hands of their own Apothecary.

'Exemplary,' replied Iakodos without hesitation. 'Those who whisper in the shadows against them, those who scorn them for their penitence should watch their words in future. They are well on the path to redemption.'

'And you, Chaplain?' Tanek turned his attentions to Iakodos. He had been through many campaigns with the Chaplain's words of faith powering him forwards. But he had learned long ago that it did no harm to assess the spirituality of the most spiritual of them all.

'I am...' Iakodos sought for the words to describe how he felt. 'I am cautious. Do I think that the *Accursed Eternity* is destroyed? I do not know either. If I were to speak plainly I would have to say that I do not believe it is the last we – or others of our kind – will see of that daemon-ship. The inquisitor believed he knew its name and its nature, but he was wrong. Those mistakes cost him his life and cost us even more dearly. But if we have banished the vessel, even if only for a time, we must look upon it as a success, high though the cost has been.'

His words held conviction, even if his eyes did not.

'Aye,' replied Tanek. 'For the good of the Imperium. Ours is not to question why, Chaplain. Ours is merely to serve. We have to pick ourselves up from this blow and move forward with renewed purpose. It is our purpose.'

HE WAS LOST.

Not in space, but in time. Whatever foul warp magic had seen him step sideways into an entirely different causality had effectively ended any hope he might ever have had of returning to real space.

Staring around the enginarium of the *Accursed Eternity*, Korydon finally understood the reason for the ship's name. In time, he came to know all that there was to know about it. After all, he had lived within its confines for centuries, maybe even millennia. His armour was old and corroded, and he had witnessed its history over and over. He had been here before. He would be here again. Of that, he was certain.

Without the life blood of the Star Dragons and Blood Swords on board the ship to sustain its physical presence, the daemon had faded back to the warp, trapped within its prison until the next time it was woken. Korydon was alone on board the cursed ship, but for the ever-present shifting ghosts of those who had once called this place home. They seemed unaware of his presence.

He was lost and he was alone. But he was not without hope. Just as the daemon had, Korydon had come to learn that every time events replayed themselves, every time the endless loop repeated, something changed. And one day, the change would come that would mean he could step from the shadows and once again take his place alongside his brothers.

When that day comes, I will exact revenge. Not even knowing if his prayers would be heard by the distant God-Emperor, Korydon swore himself to the moment.

He waited. He was faced with an eternity. It was all that he could do.

+++

Amaranthine encrypted message, code Theta Gamma Four Three Nine. Captain Tanek of the Star Dragons Third Company, presently designated commanding officer of Containment Fleet Kappa, hear this on the order of the Ordo Malleus. I send you greetings and demand your immediate compliance. There has been a reported sighting of the vessel matching archive description of the Accursed Eternity.

By the power vested in me and through my position within the holy Ordos, you are ordered to bring your fleet to the co-ordinates I will transmit following this message. This sighting warrants an immediate investigation and your fleet is the closest available. I will speak with you in person on your arrival.

MESSAGE ENDS.

+++

SANCTUS

DARIUS HINKS

I AM BETRAYED, thinks Sergeant Halser. *Betrayed*.

'Comus is down!' howls Brother Volter over the vox. 'Dead, maybe... I-I can't be sure. They've taken the infirmary. I'm pulling back. What are your orders? Sergeant?' His voice is broken, his words half-buried beneath the sound of artillery. 'Are you there? Sergeant Halser?'

Halser keeps his gun pressed to the prophet's head and gives no reply. The pilgrims scream at him from the shadows, but he keeps his gaze fixed on a pair of grotesque, fathomless eyes.

The prophet stares back.

Halser places his finger on the trigger.

'I can save both of us,' says the prophet. His head lolls inside his bowl-shaped helmet, suspended by a pale, thin neck and a gloop of viscous liquid. The solution distorts his voice, but he tries to contort his vowels into something more human, enunciating each word carefully, as though speaking to a child. He points a long, webbed finger at the man in the doorway. 'They've lied to you. They have murdered us both. They knew *exactly* what would happen. They have *always* known.'

Halser follows his gaze and sees to his horror that Gideon Pylcrafte is laughing. No mouth is visible beneath his black hood, just a quivering mass of cables, but his amusement is clear. Halser's resolve evaporates. His hand falters. If Pylcrafte saw this coming, the whole mission was a lie. Halser tries to marshal his thoughts. He tries to pray, but the sound of Brother Volter's pain knifes into him, merged with the wailing of the pilgrims. The artillery grows louder until it seems the whole valley is groaning. The noise is unbearable and too loud to be just heavy guns. As the blasts ring around his head, Halser is forced to accept the truth.

The orbital bombardment *has* already begun.

Without Comus's protection, his mind edges quickly towards collapse. The temporal distortion has reached its zenith and the pilgrims' voices claw at his thoughts like blades across metal. He cannot be sure what is now and what was then. Simultaneously, he is leading the squad through the catacombs, slaughtering the pilgrims at the city gates and reaching the inner temple, but he knows that has already been. He stares deeper into the prophet's misshapen eyes, trying to anchor himself.

'Comus is down!' howls Brother Volter over the vox. 'Dead, maybe... I–I can't be sure. They have taken the infirmary. I'm pulling back. What are your orders? Sergeant?'

Halser curses and looks back at the doorway. Time is collapsing. He has heard those words before, but how many times?

'I will *not* let you live,' he snaps, turning back to the prophet. The metallic ring of his amplified voice booms around the chamber. 'You're an abomination.'

The prophet's bloated skull drifts to one side and splits open in a grin. 'You have a ship and I have vision. The clouds are no barrier to me.' He waves at Pylcrafte. 'He's wronged us both. Why should we accept our fate? We are the elect few. We have great work ahead of us. Great deeds.'

Halser shakes his head, but there is doubt kindling in his

eyes. To shoot the prophet means death. Worse than that, it means failure. But what is the alternative? After everything he has seen, how could he let such a man live?

The prophet brushes his elongated fingers against Halser's power armour. They trace around a filigreed skull and he narrows his eyes. 'Why did you come to Madrepore, *Relictor*?'

The chamber lurches and the ground shifts. The enemy fire is closing in. Centuries-old marble tumbles from the vaulted ceiling. Ten-metre eagles splinter and crack, covering the floor with vast, broken wings.

'Behold, the immutable will of the Emperor!' cries Pylcrafte from the doorway, raising his voice over the cacophony. 'You're a proud fool, Sergeant Halser. This is all on your head. This is the price you pay for all your lowly, creeping misbelief and your repeated use of xenos–'

Halser silences him with a shot to the head. The blast echoes around the chamber and Pylcrafte crumples in a plume of blood. The cables in his hood twitch for a few seconds longer, then he lies still.

Halser turns away and presses his bolt pistol back against the prophet's helmet. 'You're a mutant.'

'And what are you, Relictor?' The prophet's glass helmet is now splattered with Pylcrafte's blood but his voice remains defiant. He waves at the network of passageways that lead off from his throne room. 'There are weapons here. Weapons we could *use*.' His voice grows softer. 'They lied to you, Relictor. All of them. Your fidelity is misplaced, don't you see?'

Halser grimaces as the agonised chorus grows louder: Brother Volter's desperate requests for orders, the chanting of the pilgrims, the groaning of the earth, the pounding of the guns. But worse than the noise is the doubt. How could Mortmain have tricked him? As the question torments Halser, the doubt turns to rage. Even his oldest friend does not believe in him, does not believe in his Chapter. He and his men have been sent to their deaths. Perhaps the braver act would be to listen to the prophet?

'I will prove you wrong, Mortmain,' he spits. 'I will make you *pay*.'

As his fury grows, the déjà vu becomes unbearable. The prophet's words loop around the chamber, growing louder with each repetition. Halser's indecision grows and lights blossom in his head, merging with the crystals in the walls and the glyphs rolling across his visor. He sees a corona of sunlight around Ilissus, shimmering like spun gold as he breaks orbit and drops down into the storm.

CHAPTER ONE

'ILISSUS IV. SHRINE World.' Pylcrafte speaks in the awed tones of a supplicant. 'Until the enemy seized control, this was one of the holiest sites in the galaxy. Before the dark days of the Heresy, the Emperor Himself trod its hallowed earth.'

As they fall from the heavens, the curvature of the planet vanishes, obscured by a tormented mass of thunderheads and tornadoes. The gunship begins to rattle and shake, but Sergeant Halser is distracted by the strangeness of the storms: strands of gilded vapour, rising from bottomless valleys of cloud. The whole planet is shrouded. It looks like a ghost.

'And the clouds?' he asks.

Pylcrafte lowers his voice. 'A sign of the infernal transgressions that have doomed Ilissus, a badge of its utter corruption. This is the witchcraft Inquisitor Mortmain spoke of. The tempest is not natural, Sergeant Halser. It is the most profane manifestation of Chaos. The clouds appeared after the arrival of the Black Legion, three centuries ago, and they *bleed* heresy. They are sentient.

Malevolent. A metamorphic likeness of nature. A cheap glamour, constructed to hide the face of the enemy. And their reach is growing longer.'

Halser is a bull-necked lump of rage. His slab-like features are flushed and trembling and his lips are curled back in a sneer. The glare he turns on Brother-Librarian Comus would shrivel a normal man.

Comus scowls back, undaunted, his eyes full of the same bitter fury.

'What do you sense?' growls Halser.

Comus shrugs his broad, armoured shoulders and looks down at something in the palm of his right hand. 'Sorcery, yes, the libellus is clear on that, but in the clouds...?' His scowl deepens as he turns towards Pylcrafte. 'I'm sure Inquisitor Mortmain's servant is correct.'

The gunship lurches again as the golden storm envelops its hull. Servitors scurry back and forth trying to silence alarms and steady flickering lights.

Halser punches the comms panel as though imagining it is someone's face. 'Thunderhawk Five, this is Thunderhawk Four. Brother Silvius, state your position.'

There is a burst of static, followed by a staccato, inhuman voice. '... Five... Navigation difficult... Unsure of altitude... Extreme turbulence...' There is another burst of static, followed by: 'Sergeant, I'm not sure if we can hold our–'

The connection dies, leaving a thin screech of feedback in its wake. Halser silences the machine and glares at it for a few seconds. Then he looks over at Pylcrafte. The turbulence has thrown him into his seat and his hood has fallen from his tonsured head, revealing the oily knot of cables where his face should be. Each coiled flex ends in a glistening, brass-rimmed lens, and as he turns towards Halser they focus on him with a series of whirring clicks.

'Inquisitor Mortmain warned that landing would be difficult,' says the inquisitor's acolyte, 'but as long as your men follow his counsel exactly, they will only be on the surface briefly. The planet is riddled with tunnels. They were wrought thousands of years ago by mendicants, before they yielded to the malign dominion of the Inferior Powers. The corruption in the air is clearly of no concern to heretics, but to us it could mean death, or even worse: transmutation. We must spend as little time in the open as possible.'

'Mortmain mentioned the priests. He said they were connected to the original invasion.'

Pylcrafte nods. 'They were confounded by the Ruinous Powers, and then they were butchered by the Black Legion.' His voice trembles slightly. 'And, to the eternal shame of the Ecclesiarchy, they brought it all on themselves. A group of senior priests were responsible for Ilissus. Who else could watch over a world where the Emperor once walked? But their deceit brought ignominy on their blessed brotherhood. The priests left in charge of the infamous Zeuxis Scriptorium became enamoured of certain artefacts, certain *magic* charms enshrined during the days of the Great Crusade.' Pylcrafte pulls his hood back into place and withdraws his optical cables. He looks like a snail, retreating into its shell. 'It's a tale as old as the Imperium. What began as innocent research ended in loathsome idolatry. The doomed priests summoned the most vile, unspeakable malefactors into their temples. They handed over their souls to the Black Legion as a gift. It would seem that whatever they found in the scriptorium was too much for their simple faith to overcome. They were the architects of their own miserable fate.'

Comus clenches his fists and mutters to the floor. 'And here we are, following in their footsteps.'

The spasms in Halser's face grow more noticeable as he struggles to keep his voice low. 'Mortmain sent us. Why would he do that if he thought we were insufficient for the task?'

Pylcrafte raises a slender, ivory cane and waves it at the distant fleet. 'I would remind you, Sergeant Halser, that my master did not *send* you anywhere. He merely pointed out the tragedy of losing such an ancient site in the impending Exterminatus.'

'He said more than that.'

The inquisitor's acolyte shrugs. 'He gave you no orders, Sergeant Halser. He learned of your esoteric interests and, by the providence of our Most Venerable Emperor, he was able to offer you a chance for elucidation – an opportunity to explore the scriptoria before they are destroyed. You are here of your own volition.'

Halser's lips curl back further from his teeth into a terrifying smile. 'Don't worry. I learned long ago not to expect any official endorsements.'

The gunship banks hard and Pylcrafte's cane slips from his grip, clattering harmlessly off Comus's armour and bouncing into a corner. As the gunship plunges through the clouds, the lights fail for a few seconds. In the darkness Halser sees Pylcrafte's cluster of eyes, watching him closely from within his hood. He remembers something odd that Comus said about him and leans forwards with a question. Then the sound of the turbulence becomes deafening and he leans back.

The question is forgotten.

'WE NEED TO find shelter!' yells Pylcrafte. He is cowering behind the armoured bulk of Halser with his cane wedged in the dust, struggling to stay on his feet.

Comus and the rest of the squad are spread out around the downed gunship with their bolters trained on the storm, as motionless as statues. Their pewter-coloured armour matches the smoke pouring from the ship's damaged hull; if not for the white skulls painted on their pauldrons they would be nearly invisible.

Halser ignores Pylcrafte, fascinated by the view. Even his enhanced vision cannot pierce the clouds, but as they whirl and heave around him, he catches glimpses of Ilissus's strange landscape: soaring limbs of rock, wrenched from the earth by forces he can only imagine, creating a bewildering web of ruddy stone towers, almost indistinguishable from the storm. The rock is so contorted it resembles a great coral reef, dragged from beneath the ground. As the clouds rush between the columns they howl, and it seems to Halser as though they are trying to speak. He even holds his breath for a second, trying to catch a meaning in the sound; then he gives a short bark of laughter, amused by his own ridiculousness.

Remembering the pain in his leg, he looks down at the jagged hole in his armour. The Larraman cells have already done their work – the wound scabbed over in seconds – but he will be left with yet another ugly scar. He mutters a prayer of thanks. Every jagged line only serves to remind him of his proud burden. A lesser man would not have survived such a disastrous landing.

He stoops to wipe the blood from his damaged armour then turns to the others. They are still scanning the horizon for signs of attack. A few of them have injuries of their own but, to a man, they are straight-backed and alert. He feels a swell of pride. Even now, after all the lies and slander, they are unbroken: as determined as he is to prove their worth – even if only to themselves.

'Which way to the scriptoria?' he calls, ignoring the cowled figure standing next to him.

Pylcrafte flinches at the sergeant's words. The crash has left him badly shaken. His floor-length robes are torn, and as he looks back at the Librarian his head twitches with fear.

Comus nods in reply and unclasps a book from his power armour. It is small, leather-bound, sealed with gold clasps and foiled with symbols that are far too bizarre to be of human design. It could be mistaken for a harmless piece of arcana, but Halser knows the truth. He knows what he is asking of his old friend.

Comus unlocks the clasps and flips open the cover, frowning with concentration as he handles the tiny book. There are no pages inside, just a hinged, steel case covered with dials, runes and a glass screen. The Librarian inserts a cable into a socket on the side of the device, closes his eyes and winces in pain. Then he begins to mouth words that are lost to the wind.

As he watches Comus praying, Pylcrafte's terrified expression becomes a sneer of disgust. 'How can you allow him to handle such a *talisman*?' he asks, looking up at the sergeant.

Halser gives no answer, but he knows the question is a fair one.

'According to the libellus, the Zeuxis Scriptorium was five kilometres north of this spot.' Comus's voice is taut with pain. 'If I understand the xenos text correctly, the storm has not thrown us too far off target.'

'Five kilometres away?' cries Pylcrafte, looking afraid again. 'Then we must move fast. We've already spent too long above ground. I told you – the only safe way to cross this planet is underground. We must find a tunnel before we do anything else.'

Halser nods. 'Once we've located Brother Silvius's ship.'

Pylcrafte reels as though slapped. His voice shrieks even higher. 'Your battle-brothers could be scattered across the continent. They could all be dead. You've heard no word from them.' He jabs his cane into the dusty ground. 'We need to find cover *now*.'

Rage is ever-present in Sergeant Halser's eyes, but for a moment it seems on the verge of boiling over into violence. His huge jaw tightens and his voice fills with disbelief. 'Are you *ordering* me?'

A little colour creeps into Pylcrafte's pallid face. 'Of course not, but you've tried to contact your men and there's no response.' He lowers his nest of eyes. 'You may have to consider that they have fallen. Why would they ignore your signal?'

Halser thumps the lifeless auspex at his belt. 'Since that storm spat us out, we *have* no signal.' He looks again at the towering clouds. 'Nothing. We are alone.' He lifts his helmet and snaps it into place. When he speaks again, his voice is an inhuman growl. 'But I will not abandon my brothers.'

Pylcrafte cringes pitifully and clutches his cane to his chest. 'Of course not, Sergeant Halser. But you must understand, if we don't head below the surface now, we might encounter the enemy.'

Halser studies him through the featureless visor of his helmet. Then he raises his bolt pistol and clangs it against the battered grey ceramite of his chest armour. 'I hope so, Pylcrafte, I really do.'

CHAPTER TWO

INQUISITOR MORTMAIN SITS quietly in the cathedral, head bowed and weary, relishing the solitude. Even here, deep within the bewildering network of cloisters and buttressed towers he cannot fully escape the sounds of the ship: the rumble of engines, the grinding of weapons batteries and the droning hum of power circuits; but it is the closest thing the *Domitus* has to a haven. Vast, lancet windows watch over him, flooding the cathedral with coloured light and painting his face a lurid green. Mortmain could never be considered handsome. His features are as angular and harsh as the statues that line the nave, but there is a fierceness to his blunt, crooked nose; a sense of purpose beneath his low, heavy brow, that would mark him out in a crowded room, even without the badge of office that hangs around his neck.

As he studies the windows Mortmain finds it hard to meet his master's eye. Despite the horrors the ship has endured the Emperor's gaze has not faded. The stained glass was crafted on Terra, countless centuries ago, but the scale of the artist's vision is undimmed: the Emperor glares down resplendent from the backlit glass, still sure of His purpose, still blazing with unshakeable faith.

The inquisitor grimaces and steers his thoughts beyond the glass, beyond the cathedral, beyond even the rest of the *Domitus*. He pictures Fleet Sanctus, trailing after him through the void. The Emperor's might, turned aside from its purpose, redirected at his command. Mortmain pulls his thick leather cloak a little tighter, suddenly conscious of the cold. His shoulders slump as he considers the weight of his choices. In his left hand he grips a vellum scroll, beautifully illuminated, clasped with silver and covered with wax purity seals. It bears the mark of governors, company commanders, captains and bishops: everyone who could possibly question his decision. The Concordat of Zeuxis they named it, in recognition of Ilissus's famed scriptorium, but Mortmain is under no illusions: it is a death warrant. The fate of an entire world is in his hands. Maybe more. He draws a deep breath. Compared to such weighty matters, what concern is a friendship? Is he risking too much?

A polite cough interrupts his thoughts. He looks up and sees a hooded priest watching him from the far end of the nave.

'Is the Novator here?' Mortmain has not spoken for several hours and his voice is a hesitant croak, but the acoustics of the cathedral are such that his words are amplified, echoing around the vaulted ceilings and sculpted columns.

The distant figure nods. 'Should I show him in, Inquisitor Mortmain?'

Mortmain clears his throat and rises to his feet, flinging back his floor-length cloak. There is a flash of silver as the light plays across his etched breastplate. The intricate designs in the metal are worked around a central device: the letter I, crossed with three bars and studded with a single, blood-red stone.

Mortmain has a black, serrated billhook tucked into his belt and as he stands he grips the hilt in his right hand, soothed by the feel of its cool, pitted ebony against his skin.

He nods, and when he speaks again the doubt has gone from his voice. 'Bring him to me.'

The priest bows and shuffles back into the shadows.

After a few minutes a man approaches. He is stooped low to the floor and moving backwards in a series of strange, lurching hops. Mortmain realises that he is dusting the floor, furiously wiping the stones to save the shoes of his master.

This must be van Tol, thinks Mortmain as another man appears. The second man walks upright, with a confident stride and his shoulders thrown back. He is immaculately dressed in a starched military uniform. Every centimetre of his tall, elegant frame is braided and adorned, and there is an ornate, gilt-handled sabre at his side. As he catches sight of Mortmain, his waxed moustache quivers over a glib smirk. 'Inquisitor,' he drawls. 'Have I interrupted your prayers? You must forgive me.' His face is the complete antithesis of Mortmain's, with a small, receding chin, creamy, flawless complexion and features so delicate they are almost pretty.

Mortmain gives a stiff bow and steps away from the altar, filling the cathedral with noise as his iron-shod boots clang across the flagstones. 'Not at all, baron. I have been looking forward to meeting you again.' As he approaches his guest, the inquisitor notices other men waiting in the shadows: the baron has brought his guards. This is no social call, he thinks, gripping the billhook a little tighter.

Baron van Tol holds out a limp, white-gloved hand. It is unclear whether he expects it to be shaken or kissed.

Mortmain grasps it firmly in his own. 'Your chambers are sufficient, I hope?'

The baron continues to smirk. 'Sufficient, yes.' The words merge into one another, as though he can barely find the energy to separate vowels from consonants. He is unusually tall and studies Inquisitor Mortmain down the length of a long, aquiline nose, his eyes half-lidded and full of disdain, like those of a basking lizard waiting idly to be fed. 'Not a single dissenter,' he says.

Mortmain frowns, confused.

The baron nods at the scroll in Mortmain's hand. 'The concordat.' There is an unmistakable note of mockery in his voice. 'Your word is law, Inquisitor Mortmain. Your doubts were unfounded. There are few, even here, who would question the will of the Imperial Inquisition.'

Mortmain shrugs, ignoring the baron's sneering tone. 'I claim no credit. We are all just vessels for the Emperor's will. And, besides, your evidence was persuasive. What hope do we have of containing anything with corruption left unchecked at our backs?'

'*Exactly.*'

The two men stand in silence for a few seconds, still clutching each other's hands. Finally, Mortmain withdraws his grip and waves to one of the pews.

'Tell me,' says the inquisitor, once they are seated, 'what has brought you to the *Domitus*? The concordat is signed. I thought you would be eager to return home. I understand that being in such close proximity to the Eye of Terror is particularly unpleasant for someone with your talents.' At the word 'talents' he gazes briefly at the baron's forehead. Van Tol is wearing a peaked cap, pulled low, and there is no sign of anything strange; beyond a vaguely translucent quality to his skin, he might be a normal man.

The baron shrugs. 'I will return to Terra as soon as possible, of course, but I...' He hesitates, as though doubting the inquisitor's ability to understand. 'I have complete confidence in your abilities, Inquisitor Mortmain. Let me make that clear. I have nothing but respect for men who drag themselves up from the...' a look of distaste crosses his face, '*lower* orders of society. I'm sure that you're a very *competent* individual.' He seems unwilling to meet Mortmain's gaze. 'But I will not be able to rest until this situation has been resolved.'

Mortmain raises his eyebrows and leans back in the pew. 'Ilissus will be destroyed, Baron van Tol.'

'Of course it will, Inquisitor Mortmain, I have no doubt of that. No doubt at all.' The baron laughs. It is a shrill, mirthless sound and his eyes remain fixed on the floor. 'But it would set an old man's heart at ease to witness the deed first-hand.'

Mortmain opens his mouth to reply, but before he can speak one of the baron's attendants steps out of the shadows. He is a double of the baron, with the same feminine features and languid bearing. The only difference is a little less grey in his moustache and a few less medals on his uniform.

'Why is there no action?' demands the younger noble, his face flushed with emotion. 'Every minute sees the contagion spreading. While we–'

'Silence, my dear Palchus!' The baron's voice is soft, but full of venom. 'How dare you interrupt? Stand down.'

The young man's eyes glitter with rage, but he does as ordered and steps back into the darkness.

The baron turns back to Mortmain, clearly embarrassed. 'You must forgive my son's appalling manners. We are all very concerned about the situation.' He shifts awkwardly in the pew. 'In his clumsy way, though, he has asked the question that is on my own mind: when exactly will the bombardment begin? Your ships are in place, are they not?'

Mortmain studies the baron in silence for a few seconds, struggling to keep his expression neutral. 'Ilissus will be destroyed.' He chooses his words carefully. 'The nobles of House van Tol have played an important part in bringing this situation to light, but the matter is now in the hands of the Inquisition.'

The baron briefly meets the inquisitor's gaze, his eyes still hooded with mirth. 'Of course. I merely came to offer my assistance. You must understand…' The baron's words trail off as he notices how closely Mortmain is studying him. The smirk finally vanishes, as abruptly as a light being extinguished. 'Has the defence of Ilissus *definitely* been abandoned?'

Mortmain stares at van Tol, unused to having his actions questioned.

'I just wondered,' continues the baron, 'about the two gunships that launched a few hours ago.'

Mortmain continues to stare.

The baron waits for an answer that never comes. Eventually he rises to his feet, uncomfortable under Mortmain's intense gaze. 'I sense I've annoyed you Inquisitor Mortmain, and that was not my intention.' He steps back with a slight bow. The smirk returns. 'I will be in my chambers if you need anything.'

Mortmain narrows his eyes, but says nothing as he watches the baron saunter down the nave, whispering to his lackeys as they vanish into the long shadows. Once their footfalls have faded, the inquisitor looks up into the benevolent gaze of the Emperor. 'They're hiding something,' he mutters, keeping his eyes fixed on the glass.

A voice replies from the darkness. The words are moist and distorted, as though spoken through a bundle of wet rags. The language is impenetrable and revolting.

Mortmain nods in agreement and purses his lips. 'Exterminatus can wait a little longer. I will not consign millions to their deaths without knowing *every* relevant fact.'

Another stream of gurgled vowels answers him.

Mortmain massages his shaven head and slips back into silent reverie. 'The young one,' he says finally, 'the baron's son. I think the Novator called him Palchus. He is clearly unstable. I'm sure we could use that to our advantage. The *Domitus* is a large ship, after all. I imagine he might easily get lost.'

There is a rumble of laughter, accompanied by the sound of chains, scraping across stone.

Mortmain's voice is full of distaste. 'Be gentle, Cerbalus. I will soon have the death of a world on my conscience. Do not add to my burden.'

CHAPTER THREE

EVEN THROUGH THE howling wind, the sound of bolter fire is unmistakable as Brother Thymus spins backwards through the storm, a blackened hole in his breastplate.

'Down,' snaps Sergeant Halser over the vox, and the Relictors vanish from sight.

Pylcrafte moans pitifully as he cowers between the sergeant and Brother-Librarian Comus. 'We must be steadfast,' he whimpers, trembling violently. 'The dominion of the idolaters is–'

Comus clamps a hand over his mouth and shoves him unceremoniously to the ground.

Their cover is a narrow gulley, no more than four metres wide.

'The next ridge,' mutters Comus.

Halser nods and looks back through the swirling dust clouds. Brother Thymus is lying on his side, convulsing. Blood and hydraulic fluid is spraying from his punctured chest armour and he seems unable to rise. He has fallen above the gulley and is completely exposed, but it is useless to think of saving him. The sound of his laboured breathing is terrible to hear. He will not survive.

The sergeant is so furious that for a few seconds he cannot speak. How could he be so foolish as to lead his men into an ambush? Brother Thymus has served at his side in countless engagements. Inside Halser's helmet, his cheeks flush purple with rage and he spits a prayer. 'Everything that happens is the Emperor's will.' The words bring him no solace. He shakes his head and raises his hand, preparing to give an order.

Before he can speak, two objects clatter across the rocks.

The Space Marines react instantly, recognising the frag grenades before they even settle, but it is no use: the grenades are primed to detonate on impact.

The gulley fills with sound and light.

Halser lands heavily on his back behind a narrow limb of rock, his ears ringing from the blast. Great plumes of dust mingle with the storm as he strains to see the others. Bulky, grey shadows dash through the smoke but he cannot see who, if anyone, has fallen. He repeats his prayer, sounding even less convinced. 'Everything that happens is the Emperor's will.'

The limb of rock explodes as a round of bolter fire slams into it. The sergeant rolls clear, dropping into another gulley and glimpsing muzzle flare above a distant crest of rock. He marks the position.

The smoke dances away in the storm and Halser spots Brother-Librarian Comus, crouching a few metres away. He looks uninjured, but he is clutching the ornate mantle that surrounds his gorget, grimacing in pain. The cables that connect the metal hood to his skull are pulsing with inner fire.

Halser catches his eye, nods to the location of the enemy and mimes a throwing movement; then he taps his bolt pistol and waves it down the gulley.

Comus nods in reply, but the grimace remains on his face and as he unclips a grenade from his belt he clutches his head with his other hand, furiously massaging his temples.

There is another deafening blast as Comus's grenade finds its mark.

At the same moment, Sergeant Halser emerges from the far end of the gulley, sprinting towards the crest of rock. As he knifes through the clouds, a black-armoured figure rises and tumbles away from him, thrown back by the grenade blast.

Halser fires as he runs, unloading several rounds into the reeling figure and drawing his chainsword. As he vaults over the lip of rock, the sergeant's blade is already rattling and spitting oil.

The enemy tries to return fire, but before he can level his pistol at Halser, the sergeant's chainsword slices through his forearm in a shower of sparks, blood and splintered bone.

As his opponent staggers back, clutching countless wounds, Halser gets a clear look at him.

The Traitor Marine is clad in ancient, black armour, twisted and sculpted into a baroque mess of curves and spikes, and trimmed with golden, razor-sharp edges. The mouth grille of his helmet has been wrenched into a bestial leer and his breastplate is emblazoned with a pus-yellow eye.

The sergeant howls. The sound could either be rage or ecstasy, it is impossible to tell. He raises his chainsword to strike again.

The Traitor Marine is too fast. He blocks Halser's chainsword with his own and the air fills with sparks and the sound of grinding gears.

Halser lifts his bolt pistol but, before he can fire, pain explodes in his side. He is lifted from his feet, spun around and sent crashing to the ground. Before landing he glimpses a second Traitor Marine, looming out of the storm and lifting his bolter for another shot.

Halser rolls to one side as the ground explodes around him.

Then there is a screech of grinding metal and the gunfire stops.

He rises from the ground and sees the second Traitor Marine drop his bolter and clutch his chest, howling in pain. The blade of a sword has emerged from his chest armour and is slicing up towards his throat. The sword shimmers with unnatural light as it rips the enemy warrior in two, emitting a final, blinding pulse as it wrenches free in a fountain of blood and sparks.

Brother-Librarian Comus steps around his victim as he topples, lifeless, to the ground. His force sword is still blazing with psychic energy as he turns towards the other Traitor Marine but, before he can strike, he clutches his head in agony and stumbles, the tip of his sword clattering uselessly against the rocks.

The remaining Traitor Marine turns his gun on the Librarian but the left side of his helmet evaporates before he can pull the trigger, leaving a smouldering pulp of ruptured armour and charred brains.

He drops to the floor with a whistling gurgle.

Sergeant Halser steps over him and fires a second shot into his mouth grille. Then another. He keeps firing until the traitor's head is nothing but a bloody stain on the rock. Then he crouches low and spins around, peering down the barrel of his gun. The rattle of bolter fire echoes around the valley, but the sound is distorted and muffled by the clouds, making it impossible to pinpoint anything.

'Squad Elicius,' he grunts into his vox-bead, 'state your condition.'

Voices crackle over the comm-net. The fighting has been brief. Only Brother Thymus has fallen.

Halser shakes his head, suspicious at the ease of their victory. 'Hold your positions. The enemy don't usually attack in such small numbers.' He turns to see that Comus has dropped to his knees and is still clutching his head.

He rushes to the Librarian's side. 'Are you wounded?'

As Comus looks up, his face is ashen and his eyes are blazing. 'Is the device sending me mad? Can't you hear it?'

Halser shakes his head in confusion. 'Hear what?'

'The clouds,' groans Comus, his voice filled with horror. 'They're talking to us.'

CHAPTER FOUR

MONKS AND SERVITORS melt into the shadows, scattering like vermin before the approaching Navigator. A servo-skull drifts ahead of him, trailing smoke-shrouded censers and bearing a tall, guttering candle. As the light flickers across rows of gloomy alcoves, it picks out the *Domitus's* cowering denizens. They peer suspiciously at the slender noble and mutter prayers into their hoods. Even the ship's most ill-omened wretches breathe a sigh of relief as Palchus van Tol passes them by.

At the end of a long, vaulted passageway stands his father, peering through a leaded viewport. It is hard see anything through the metre-thick panes, clouded as they are by ash and cobwebs, but as Palchus approaches he can just make out the vague, spectral presence of Ilissus.

'They were Relictors,' he mutters.

'Who were?' asks the baron, turning towards him.

'The Adeptus Astartes sent down onto the planet. I spoke to some of the stevedores. Mortmain himself had sworn them to secrecy.' He grimaces. 'It was not easy to extract the truth.'

133

'Oh yes, I know who's down there.' Baron van Tol fixes his half-lidded eyes on his nephew. 'You're not the only one here with sight.' He raps his knuckles against the glass. 'What do you see now, though?'

Palchus looks out at the ghostly planet and shakes his head. 'Nothing. Nothing beyond the warp storms, that is. I've never seen such power.'

The baron sneers. 'It's a dirty, crude form of sorcery, but yes, it's certainly powerful.' He looks around, noting the hooded figures flitting through the shadows, and leans closer to his nephew, lowering his voice. 'If Mortmain doesn't act soon the corruption will spread.' He plucks an object from his braided ceremonial jacket and lifts it up into the candlelight. It is a tiny hourglass, housed within a frame of intricately engraved finger bones.

Palchus grimaces at the sight of it. The sand has gathered in the centre, refusing to fall either way. He grabs his father's wrist, pulls the hourglass closer and shakes it, to no effect. 'What does it mean?'

The baron shrugs. 'Time is on the run, Palchus. The storm on Ilissus is spreading.' He lowers his voice even further. 'The concordat has only bought us a brief reprieve. If Ilissus isn't destroyed soon, the other Houses will smell a rat. They have a little more insight than these plebeians.' He looks back at the planet. 'They won't believe this rubbish about the Black Legion. They will see the storms for what they truly are. We will be ruined.'

'Then what do we do?' Palchus's voice is edged with panic. 'The inquisitor is obviously lying to us. Why would he send Space Marines onto a planet scheduled for Exterminatus?'

The baron shakes his head and puts the hourglass back into his pocket. 'The Relictors are scavengers. They're famed for it. They're vile magpies, always peering beneath stones that ought to be left unturned. Everyone knows they're just a step away from heresy, but Inquisitor Mortmain must have allowed them one last chance to explore the planet for some reason. Before–' He pauses and curls his lip with displeasure. 'Before the problems arose, Ilissus was famed for its scriptoria. One in particular is said to house documents and relics older than the Imperium itself.'

'The Zeuxis Scriptorium.'

The baron nods. 'The Zeuxis Scriptorium is *particularly* infamous. The priests in charge had similar interests to the Relictors, interests that most reputable people would consider heretical. It has been lost for centuries, but the Relictors have a knack of unearthing things.' He pulls back his shoulders and raises his chin. 'I must think. Meet me in my chambers in an hour.' As he ambles off down the passageway, another servo-skull drifts down from the rafters and trails after him, lighting the way. 'Do nothing,' he says, sneering at Palchus as he disappears around a corner.

Palchus drums his fingers against the viewport. What's Mortmain thinking? Why would he delay even a second when so much is at risk? Why would he ignore the concordat? Someone must know. He stands there for a few minutes, muttering to himself, until an idea hits him. It seems to arrive fully formed, as though the ship itself has answered his question. 'Of course,' he mutters. 'There are other Relictors on board. They must know what's going on.'

He strides over to an empty alcove. It is a shrine of some kind, but he pays no attention to the hunched, winged statue crouched in the darkness, as he sits on a stone bench and closes his eyes. He places his fingers beneath the peak of his cap, resting them on a swelling in the middle of his forehead. Then he whispers an incantation under his breath and, after a few minutes, his breathing begins to quicken and beads of sweat appear on his face. Numb pain spreads from his forehead and he moans softly. Images tumble through his mind. He sees engines: vast, oil-black behemoths, thundering and belching far below him in the belly of the *Domitus*. Then he sees miles of featureless hab blocks, housing legions of crewmen and priests and whole regiments of Guardsmen. Many of the Guardsmen are wounded and as Palchus's mind touches theirs, he feels agony and fear. He moves on, holding his breath as he looks through flight decks, chapels, cloisters and hangars, searching desperately until he senses something quite different from the Guardsmen: a sliver of cool, hard arrogance. 'Yes,' he whispers. The minds of the Adeptus Astartes are unmistakable. He removes his fingers from his forehead, pulls his cap back into place and finally exhales. 'Just a few kilometres away.' To find his targets so easily seems a little odd, but Palchus is so anxious he does not pause to consider the odds of stumbling across the Relictors so quickly.

He rises and looks out into the passageway. The baron's light has faded from view. 'I'm sorry father,' he says, his voice trembling with emotion, 'I won't just sit around as our name is thrown to the dogs.' With that, he turns and hurries in the opposite direction, quickly disappearing into the endless maze of corridors.

After a few seconds the large, winged shape crouched in the shrine climbs down from the wall. As it steps out into the passage, the outline of the thing is hard to discern, but as it slips quietly after Palchus, one of the hooded onlookers is unfortunate enough to catch a brief glimpse. He stumbles back against the wall with a curse, left with an image of torn, ruptured flesh and battered, jagged iron. As the onlooker drops to his knees, pressing his palms over his eyes, he hears the rattle of chains, scraping into the distance.

AFTER HALF AN hour, Palchus notices that the passageways are growing narrower and less well-kept. There is no sign of any servitors and piles of waste lie uncleared in the corners. The air grows thick with the smell of engine oil and faeces, and the Navigator hides his face behind a silk, perfumed handkerchief. Are these really suitable quarters for Adeptus Astartes, he wonders? Then he remembers which Chapter he is looking for: the Relictors. Their fall from grace is almost laughable. An open sewer is the perfect place to house men with so many accusations of heresy hanging over them.

Eventually, the ceiling falls so low that the servo-skull is unable to follow and Palchus curses, stumbling to a halt in the darkness. 'What *is* this place?' he mutters, pulling a small light from his jacket pocket. As the thin beam washes over the walls ahead, he sees the passageway is no longer made of stone: it is a jumble of corrugated iron, rusted heating vents and gurgling, hissing pipes.

'Perhaps this isn't right,' he mutters, stooping and edging slowly forwards.

Then he hears a sound from behind him and turns around, levelling his light at the shadows. The darkness ripples and slides but he can see nothing clearly. A feeling of dread grips him.

Palchus draws his sword and considers turning back, but barely has the thought formed in his mind when the door behind rattles free of its supports and slams down onto the stone floor. The resultant *clang* causes the Navigator to flinch so violently that his light slips from his fingers and bounces away into the shadows, extinguishing itself as it goes.

Palchus curses as pitch dark descends. 'Is anyone there?' he calls, his words echoing weirdly through the narrow passageway.

There is no reply.

Palchus drops to his knees and reaches through the darkness. He is sure he can pinpoint where the light fell, but as his fingers brush over the cold stone, they find no trace of the metal cylinder.

'Where is it?' he hisses, with a rising sense of panic.

As the Navigator's fingers stretch further, they brush against something soft and warm.

He yelps in horror, scrabbling back towards the wall.

Terror grips him as he climbs to his feet and backs away as fast as he can. The darkness is so complete that he is forced to feel his way along the cold, sticky metal of the walls, cursing under his breath as his fingers catch on jagged edges and broken screws.

Despite the pain he gradually picks up speed, gaining

confidence as his eyes start to adjust to the dark. He realises that there is an opening up ahead and breaks into a
sprint, holding his sword out in front of him as he runs.

As Palchus nears the doorway, he glimpses movement
up ahead: a hunched, glistening shape, too fast to make
out clearly.

Seconds before he reaches the opening, the door clangs
shut.

Palchus slams into it with a grunt. His sword buckles
and twists painfully in his grip.

As he slides to the floor, holding his hands up in front of
his face, he senses something in the darkness.

A shape is approaching.

CHAPTER FIVE

As the rest of squad Elicius clamber awkwardly over the rocks, Sergeant Halser pauses on an outcrop and waits for Brother-Librarian Comus to catch up. As he watches his old friend approaching he feels a painful mixture of anger and guilt. Comus's power armour is cloaked in dust and as he stumbles over the weird terrain his face remains locked in a grimace, but he still has the libellus clasped firmly in his grip. 'I had no choice,' growls Halser to himself. 'This is our last chance.'

He wipes his visor and scours the horizon for signs of the enemy. The sun has already slipped lower in the sky, trimming the clouds with bronze and making it even harder to see. Halser grabs the auspex from his belt but it is still dead. They have heard nothing from Brother Silvius since the crash. More worryingly, they have not been able to contact Fleet Sanctus or the *Domitus*. They are utterly alone. As his gaze falls back on the stooped figure of Comus, Halser keeps thinking the same thought. This is our last chance.

Comus is only a few metres away when Halser notices something odd. As the Librarian enters a narrow defile, he vanishes briefly from view, before re-emerging and giving the sergeant a wave of his sword. Sergeant Halser nods in reply, but then frowns. A bank of dust drifts between the two Space Marines and when it clears, Comus has vanished. Halser prepares to call out, but before he can, Comus reappears, climbing into view exactly as before. He even gives Halser the same wave, as though nothing has happened. Halser feels a chill of alarm. Something is wrong, but he is unable to say exactly what. Comus could have stumbled back into the defile, but there was something strange about the way he signalled. His second wave was identical to his first. Halser shakes his head and rises to greet the Librarian. Déjà vu, he thinks, but the sense of alarm stays with him as he helps Comus up the rocks to his side.

'Are you fit for duty?' he asks, hiding his concern behind a scowl. He realises that there are tears of blood welling in the Librarian's eyes.

Comus nods, but is too short of breath to reply.

'Is it the presence of the Traitor Marines?' asks Halser. 'Is that what's causing you such pain?'

Comus frowns and shakes his head. 'No,' he manages to grunt after a few minutes. As he speaks, small flecks of blood glisten on his lips. He nods at the libellus. 'It is the xenos device – and something else. There is something else here.'

Halser waves at the columns of rock and the rolling clouds. 'This is the work of heretics, though, surely?'

Comus follows his gaze and looks up at the tormented sunset. 'Something else,' he repeats.

Halser realises that he has never seen his battle-brother in such pain. 'Should you head back to the gunship, Comus? We don't have time for passengers. Perhaps you could help the tech-priests? They seemed to think the repairs would take a while, but an extra pair of hands might speed things up.' He hesitates. 'Perhaps you could show me how to use the xenos device.'

Comus grips the sergeant's arm. 'No. I must continue.

I'm shielding you from something.' He waves at the clouds. 'That's why...' His words trail off and he grimaces again. 'The pain is not just from the libellus. It's because I'm holding back the prayers.'

'Prayers?' Halser shakes his head in confusion. 'Whose prayers?'

'There are prayers on the wind. And they are filled with such power they would flay you to the bone if I let them.'

'Power? You mean witchcraft?'

Comus closes his eyes and presses a hand against one of the dozens of purity seals that adorn his power armour. His fingers press deep into the lump of wax and crumpled parchment, and when he opens his eyes they are a little clearer. 'No, not witchcraft. At least, not the sort you mean. I hear catechisms and the names of saints. I hear prayers that speak of obedience to the Immortal Emperor.' He massages his scalp. 'But there is a power in them like nothing I've ever...' His voice trails off and his eyes fill with confusion. Then he turns to Halser. 'I do not believe Ilissus has fallen to the Black Legion. Some great power is in control here, but it has no love of Chaos.'

Halser shakes his head furiously. 'Of course the planet has fallen to Chaos. Inquisitor Mortmain was certain. Exterminatus is only hours away.' He looks at the rest of the squad, picking their way across the brutalised landscape. The inquisitor's acolyte is tiny in comparison, leaning heavily on his cane as he stumbles after the Space Marines. 'Pylcrafte said the clouds were a mark of Chaos. He said they arrived with the Black Legion.'

Comus locks his gaze on the sergeant. 'I do not place much faith in the words of that man. I sense he is holding something from us.'

Halser shrugs off the Librarian's grip and nods at the horizon. 'Well, we will find out the truth soon enough if we keep moving. We only have six hours. Then Inquisitor Mortmain will begin the bombardment, Chaos or not.'

* * *

THEY HAVE NOT travelled far when shots ring out again.

The squad vanishes silently into the storm.

Sergeant Halser drops behind a trunk of rock. 'Brother Vortimer,' he hisses into his vox-bead, 'Is anyone hit? What do you see?'

The reply is a burst of white noise.

'Brother Vortimer?'

There is another hiss of static, but this time words are audible beneath the distortion. 'Bolter fire. The shots went wide. They are holed up in some kind of building. Half a kilometre east. It might be a tower but I can't be–'

The signal dies.

Halser feels his pulse quicken. He will not lose another man. He opens up the comm-net to include the whole squad. 'Brothers Vortimer, Borellus and Sabine: circle around, approach from the rear. The rest of you hold your positions. Wait for my signal.'

He turns to face Comus. 'Is this the power you felt?'

The Librarian shakes his head. 'This *is* Traitor Marines.' He frowns. 'They are in such terrible pain.'

Halser looks at his auspex and curses the blank screen. Then, as a particularly fierce dust cloud twists past, he risks a glance around the stone. Brother Vortimer is right; there is some kind of building to the east. As the clouds roll past he sees it quite clearly: a fluted spiral of rock, topped with crumbling, teeth-like projections that resemble the merlons of a castle. It looks to be part of a larger building, but before he can make out anything else he sees movement behind the jagged stone. As he ducks out of view he glimpses a flash of light.

A fizzing whine cuts through the storm and, a few metres to the left of Halser, the ground dissolves into a cloud of dust and spinning rock. As stone pings off his armour the sergeant curses. 'Lascannon.' He looks back at Comus. 'They're not in too much pain to fire their weapons.'

Comus shakes his head. 'Something is badly wrong with them, though. Why do you think their aim is so bad?'

Halser nods at a narrow trench a few feet back, and as

they drop heavily into it he opens up the comm-net. 'Vor-timer, Borellus, Sabine – are you in position? What do you see?'

Halser receives his answer in the form of gunfire: a whole volley of rattling shots that ring out from the tower.

'Move in!' he cries, leaping from the trench and racing in the direction of the gunfire.

CHAPTER SIX

PALCHUS AWAKES TO darkness and the sound of rattling chains.

He tries to move but an awful, wrenching pain explodes in his stomach. 'Who's there?' he gasps, trying to stand. To his horror, he realises he is trapped. Thick, leather straps are wrapped around him, binding him to some kind of metal chair. Terror grips him. 'You don't realise what you're doing!' he cries, peering into the shifting shadows. 'I belong to the House of van Tol.'

The sound of scraping metal continues, but there is no reply.

Palchus raises his voice into something approaching a scream. 'I am Navis Nobilite! You may *not* treat me like this!' He strains to free himself from the chair and feels the awful pain in his stomach again. Something is embedded in his flesh and he realises his jacket is drenched with blood. 'What have you done to me?'

Finally there is a reply: a liquid gurgle that comes from somewhere behind him. The words make no sense whatsoever but, simultaneously, Palchus becomes aware of something else. As the vile belching sound fills the darkness, the Navigator feels words forming in his mind. He realises, to his amazement, that the small, hard eye embedded in his forehead is processing the gibberish into a language he can understand. It is as though the warp itself is speaking to him. Every syllable adds to his pain, like needles being pressed into his brain.

'You did that to yourself, actually.' The words appear as thoughts, rather than sound, and the thoughts are full of hate. The sense of malice is so great that the Navigator lets out an involuntary whine.

'Did what?' he manages to gasp eventually.

'You have quite literally fallen on your sword, Palchus.'

The Navigator peers down at his stomach. It is too dark to see anything clearly, but he can just about make out a glimmer of twisted steel, jammed into his belly. 'I need help then!' he cries. 'You can't just leave me like this.' His fear starts to mingle with rage. 'Who *are* you?'

The burbled reply makes no sense but, as before, words appear in Palchus's head. 'I have more names than I care to remember. Some of them might make sense to you, I suppose, but none of them come close to the truth. My current master calls me Cerbalus. That will suffice for one such as you.'

Palchus latches desperately on to these shreds of information. 'Your master? Who is your master? Let me speak with him. As soon as he realises who I am, you will find–'

'Oh, Inquisitor Mortmain knows very well who you are, Palchus van Tol. You are here on his instructions, in fact.'

Despite his agony, Palchus lets out an incredulous laugh. 'Mortmain? He would not dare!'

The darkness fills with the sound of scraping metal and a face appears directly in front of Palchus. It is the most terrifying thing the Navigator has ever seen. It must once have belonged to a mortal, living man, but now it is a fleshy casket, straining to contain a writhing, unspeakable horror. The shaven scalp has split in several places, revealing cherry-coloured coils of bone and a faint, shimmering light. The eyes have been scorched away, leaving two blackened pits, with cold blue fire shimmering in their centres. The whole head is torn and misshapen. Only one thing seems to be holding the mangled lump together: a mass of rusty chains snake in and out of the face, embedded deep in the bones and glinting dully as the mouth opens in a wide, toothless grin. 'Oh, you would be surprised at what he dares.'

As the ruptured flesh talks, Palchus sees the reason for the gurgling, moist quality of its voice. The thing's throat is torn and ruined, and its vocal cords are clearly exposed, rattling loosely in a nest of glistening muscle.

Palchus tries to pull back from the monster. Terrible as its appearance is, the thing that really appals him is the voice in his head. The words are so unnatural and malignant he can feel his mind buckling under the strain. This is no mortal creature leaning over him. Something unholy has been bound into the flesh of man. The word 'daemon' drifts into his thoughts, but he tries to squash it before madness overwhelms him. 'You have to help me,' he gasps.

'Of course I do,' answers the pile of gore and chain. 'Mortmain was most concerned for your safety. I cannot leave you in this awkward condition.'

Palchus screams. The monster has placed a hand on the sword in his belly and is tugging it up towards his ribcage.

'Of course,' it continues when the Navigator is quiet again, 'I can remove this blade quickly or slowly. I can remove it with care, or less care.'

'What do you want of me?' moans the Navigator, as fresh blood pools in his lap.

'I want you to talk, Palchus, that is all. There is no need for any more unpleasantness. I just need to know why you and your family have come to the *Domitus*.'

Palchus sees a glimmer of hope, then sighs as he realises the truth of his situation. Strangely, he feels his fear diminishing slightly as he accepts his fate. 'You could never let me live. Not now you've told me who your master is.'

There is another rattle of shifting chains and something

appears in front of Palchus's face. It is the monster's hand. The fingers are grey and crooked. Gleaming patches of bone are visible beneath lines of jagged, crudely sewn skin. The nails are purple and torn. But it is not the ruined flesh that Palchus notices, it is the long, metal syringe in its grip.

'You're quite wrong,' explains the voice in Palchus's head. 'If you would just talk to me, I can wipe away all memory of this encounter. My master has an endearing propensity for mercy, you see. He has specifically requested that I try to help you. You will be found slumped in a gutter, near the slaves' quarters, wounded but alive, and your father will reprimand you for nearly getting yourself killed.' The monster brings the needle closer to Palchus's face so that he can see the liquid dripping from its tip. 'All you need to do is explain why you have not left for Terra. What is your family's particular interest in this planet? What links you to Ilissus?'

Palchus's heart begins to race again as he sees that he might be able to survive after all. All he need do is tell the monster about the true cause of Ilissus's storms.

The ravaged face moves closer, sensing that the Navigator is about to speak.

Then Palchus closes his eyes and bites down hard on his lip. To his surprise, he realises that something means more to him than his own precious life. How could he confide in this creature? If the truth about Ilissus were revealed, it would be the end of everything; the end of House van Tol. Their long, distinguished history would be stricken from Imperial records. His glorious lineage would be made worthless. Their properties would be taken and, worst of all, they would be disgraced. The whole of Terra would think that Palchus van Tol was the son of a traitor.

Palchus groans in torment. 'I won't tell you anything,' he whispers, unable to believe what he is saying.

The monster leans on the broken sword and sends another bolt of agony through Palchus's stomach. 'Are you sure?' A long, rusty knife appears in front of Palchus's face. 'I'm more than happy to extract the information from you, but people don't generally enjoy my methods.'

Palchus knows all too well the methods that are likely to be employed by an Inquisitorial lackey, but there is a new sensation mixed with his abject terror: a surety that he cannot let this dreadful being discover the truth. 'Some things are worth dying for,' he says quietly.

The thing laughs. 'Oh, you won't die, Palchus, I will make sure of that.' The blade presses against the Navigator's trembling throat. 'I'm very skilled at my craft. I've had millennia to perfect it.'

Palchus's voice remains oddly calm as he replies. 'My father had doubts about coming to the *Domitus*. He knew it would be disastrous if one of us spoke out of turn. His great fear was that Mortmain might discover the truth.'

'The truth, Palchus? What *is* the truth?'

Palchus lifts his chin and flares his nostrils. 'The truth is that you will get nothing from me. My father foresaw just this kind of eventuality. He made us take precautions.'

The voice in Palchus's head sounds excited, as though trying to contain laughter. 'Precautions? What do you mean? What kind of–'

The sentence goes unfinished as Palchus stamps his right foot on the stone floor with all his strength. The heel of his boot collapses and the explosive charge contained within fills the chamber with blinding light.

The blast is so powerful that the sound travels several kilometres, to a small, dingy chamber, where Palchus's father looks up in alarm.

CHAPTER SEVEN

THE GROUND SPLITS and churns as Halser races towards the tower. Rocks and bolter shells rattle against his helmet as he weaves through the enemy blasts. At the foot of the building he launches his power-armoured bulk against a rotten door and it implodes in spectacular fashion, sending him tumbling into a small courtyard. The gunfire grows even more frenzied, but the sergeant turns his tumble into a roll and clatters across the exploding flagstones, scraping to a halt behind a ruined well and raising his bolt pistol to return fire.

He sees a row of Traitor Marines, slumped against the undulating parapet at the top of the strange tower. One of them is carrying a twisted, horned lump of metal. At first Halser cannot recognise it, but as a beam of crackling blue light erupts from the thing's barrel, he realises it is a lascannon.

The well disintegrates and Halser is thrown back across the courtyard. The impact would have killed a mortal man, but the sergeant's power armour softens the blast with a wheeze of hydraulics, allowing him to roll clear, unharmed. As a second Traitor Marine opens fire with an equally grotesque bolt pistol, Halser stands and calmly fires back. Shots ring out from several directions at once, filling the courtyard with light, sound and smoke, and making it impossible to see anything. Power-armoured boots pound back and forth, and metallic voices ring out through the din.

Halser cannot be sure if he has hit anything. He tries to aim at the traitor with the lascannon, but the drifting smoke makes it impossible to be sure what he is seeing. Twice he almost fires and then lowers his weapon, afraid of hitting one of his own men. He sees a flash of sparking metal to his left. Comus is jamming his force sword into someone Halser cannot see. There is a screech of grinding metal as the Librarian wrenches his blade free, painting the clouds red as he staggers back and prepares to swing again. 'Their shots are wild!' he cries, levelling his sword at the walls. 'Someone else is attacking them!'

Someone else? Halser pounds through the smoke to get a better view. As he nears the wall he sees the Chaos Marines lined up on the battlements. Comus is right. All of them are being twisted into bizarre positions: dragged awkwardly to one side or wrenched back over the wall. One of them manages to aim his bolter at Halser, but the shot whines past his head, missing by a metre as the traitor struggles to hang on to his gun.

Halser sprints through the whirling clouds, calling for the squad to advance as he spies a staircase at the foot of the circular wall. As he pounds up the crumbling steps, he sees the reason for the Chaos Marines' odd poses. The clouds of smoke and dust have taken hold of them, wrapping around their misshapen power armour in hazy, shifting columns.

The traitor with the lascannon hefts it round to face the oncoming sergeant, but as he tries to aim he slumps forwards onto his knees, weighed down by the storm.

Halser raises his bolt pistol to fire and pauses in shock. His opponent's leg is now encased in stone, stone that merges seamlessly with the clouds. The limbs of smoke are solidifying as they envelop the Chaos Marines, and morphing into rock. 'By the Throne,' gasps Halser, stumbling to a halt. He does not have long to consider the strangeness of the scene. The parapet behind him explodes as another shot goes wide. Halser puts aside his amazement and charges at the beleaguered enemy, jamming his rattling chainsword into the first breastplate he reaches and howling a battle-cry as he disappears in a shower of blood and shredded armour.

The others race up after him, firing calm, precise shots into the heaving mass. The enemy outnumber them two to one, but there is no contest. As the Relictors blast them apart, the Chaos Marines are wrenched to the ground by vast, animated banks of smoke. As they drop to the flagstones, the smoke forms spines of rock – just like all the other twisted pillars that cover the planet's surface.

For a few minutes the clouds pulse with light as Halser and the others unleash a sustained volley at their howling foes. Then, as it become clear that there are no shots being fired in return, Halser wrenches his rattling chainsword from a limp body and staggers back, raising the bloody weapon over his head and turning to face his men.

The gunfire ceases and the Relictors lower their guns, surveying the carnage they have wrought. The walls of the tower are scorched and peppered with holes, and the mangled remains of Chaos Marines lie sprawled across the blood-slick masonry. The Relictors watch in amazement as the columns lose their last shreds of smoke and settle into solid, fixed limbs of rock, enveloping the fallen like a shroud. Horned, groaning helmets adorn the towers like onyx studs in a vast piece of jewellery.

Halser counts the Space Marines gathered on the wall. Only seven have climbed up with him. There is no sign of Comus. He looks down into the courtyard and sees the Librarian's distinctive blue power armour, spread-eagled across the flagstones, surrounded by blood. A man is backing away from him, quickly disappearing into the rolling dust clouds.

The sergeant's pulse pounds in his ears, still charged with bloodlust and, without a second thought, he raises his pistol and guns down the receding figure. Only as he climbs down the steps does he see that the fallen man is unarmed and his robes are embroidered with Imperial insignia. Halser curses and turns the man over with his boot. He is still alive but gasping for breath and clutching feebly at the ragged hole in his shoulder. His robes must have originally been white, but they are quickly turning red. The wound looks bad but not fatal and Halser cannot decide whether that is a good or bad thing. The Imperial aquila is emblazoned across the man's chest, but there is something about him that reeks of heresy: both his eyes have been surgically removed, replaced by a two lines of ragged stitching, and a lump of crystal in the shape of a star has been hammered into his forehead.

The man tries to speak, but his words are muffled by the blood welling up in his mouth.

Halser crouches down next to him and raises him into a sitting position. 'What did you say?'

The wounded man spits a gobbet of blood onto his chest and tries again. 'Stay away. Stay away from the prophet,' he gurgles, before being wracked by a terrible cough that dislodges even more blood.

'What?' asks Halser, looking anxiously at the slumped form of Comus, lying a couple of metres away. 'What prophet? Who are you talking about?'

'Astraeus,' he gasps, grasping Halser by the shoulders. 'You must allow him to complete his trials. You must not ruin his great work.'

'Astraeus?' Halser shakes his head. 'What great work?'

The man pulls himself closer and Halser has the unnerving sensation that he is looking at him through the crystal star. As he turns his head from side to side, the failing light refracts through the prism to reveal the grey, knotted brain beneath. 'Ilissus is just the beginning. He will purge the entire galaxy.' He turns towards the columns of rock that have enveloped the Chaos Marines. 'The elements are now his to command. Soon, the Dark Powers will learn to crawl. The Great Enemy will grovel before him like a cur.' The man's voice grows shrill. 'But you must leave Ilissus! You will ruin everything–'

The man stiffens and lets out a hoarse croak as a smouldering hole appears in his chest. Blood fountains from his nose and he slumps back in the sergeant's arms.

Halser drops him and whirls around.

'Filthy idolator,' hisses Pylcrafte, lowering his laspistol and withdrawing his optical cables back into his hood.

Halser leaps to his feet and grabs Inquisitor Mortmain's acolyte by the throat, lifting him up from the ground and slamming him against the shattered wall. 'You do *not* make the decisions here!' His words are so loud that they emerge from his helmet as a distorted blast of noise.

Pylcrafte whines with a mixture of terror and outrage. 'This planet is damned! We cannot preserve the life of transgressors! The unsparing severity of the Emperor's wrath must be as swift as a–'

His words end in an explosion of air as Halser slams Pylcrafte onto the ground and aims his pistol at his undulating hood. 'Silence!' he howls, his whole body trembling with anger.

Pylcrafte looks up at the circle of Space Marines who have gathered around him. Every one of them has levelled a weapon at him. He mutters under his breath but says nothing more.

Halser looses him and turns away, waving his men over to the fallen Librarian. 'Comus,' he says, kneeling down beside him. 'Are you shot?'

The Librarian shakes his head and grimaces at the clouds undulating over their heads. 'No, I can continue.' He nods at the dead stranger. 'I'm starting to understand. The pilgrims never left Ilissus. They never died. They are still here, after all these centuries, but their worship has become confused.' He waves at the clouds again. 'The prophet he mentioned is somehow connected to all this. He is the one who has doomed Ilissus.' He clutches his head and groans in pain and confusion. 'But he is *not* a follower of the Ruinous Powers.'

Pylcrafte cannot hold his tongue. 'Then why have they defiled a shrine of the Immortal Emperor! What does it matter who their leader is? They are the worst kind of–'

At a nod from Halser, one of the Relictors steps forwards and clamps a gauntleted hand over Pylcrafte's face.

'Whoever this prophet is, we are very close to him,' continues Comus as he sits up and looks around the courtyard. 'Either by chance or his design we have stumbled across one of the routes to his home.' He taps his finger against the small leather-bound book. 'According to the libellus, if we find the Zeuxis Scriptorium, we will find the prophet.'

Halser turns to look through the ruined walls of the tower. The sinking sun flashes crimson across the visor of his helmet. 'Come nightfall, Mortmain will begin the orbital bombardment. We have less than four hours left to find the scriptorium.' He lowers his voice. 'Brother Silvius and the others must manage without us.'

Comus shakes his head as Halser helps him to his feet. 'But what really is the use in finding the scriptorium, without any guidance from the *Domitus*?'

There is a hiss of escaping air as Halser removes his helmet. His brutal features are as red as the sky. 'This is our last chance, Comus, don't you understand? Mortmain is our only friend and our enemies are legion. We have to convince them all. We have to show them that our willingness to learn is not heresy, but the Imperium's last hope. We have the courage to go where the other Chapters will not. We are the only ones who–'

'You do not have to explain any of this to me,' interrupts the Librarian with a look of disbelief. He leads Halser a few paces away from the others and speaks in an urgent whisper. 'But how will we get off the planet before Mortmain begins dropping his bombs? If we cannot navigate the clouds, how will we make it off the planet alive? We have four hours left. Perhaps we should return to the gunship and see if we can help the tech-priests?'

A network of throbbing veins spreads across Halser's face and he hisses through gritted teeth. 'If we return empty handed we are dead anyway. You remember Captain Asamon's orders: find a weapon powerful enough to cleanse every world in the system. Only if the Inquisition sees our true potential will we have any hope of redemption. If we return now, with nothing, the Relictors are doomed. Every last one of us.' He clutches his hands together as though praying. 'But if we can show the strength of our faith, show them that we can wield even the most powerful artefacts, they will *have* to accept us once more as true servants of the Emperor.' As the sergeant looks around at the shattered tower there is an edge of mania to his voice. 'And anyway, what use do you think it would be returning to the gunship?' He waves at the dust clouds. 'We have no signal. How would we fly? I doubt we would make ten kilometres before hitting a mountain.'

Comus narrows his eyes, unnerved by the sergeant's odd tone, but he cannot deny his logic. It was a miracle that they managed to land as well as they did. And since then the weather has become even more violent.

Halser pounds his chest armour. 'We're not done yet, Comus. I will not allow it!' He stamps one of his boots on the ground, surrounding them both in a cloud of dust. 'The Zeuxis Scriptorium is the best known of Ilissus's reliquaries. Think what treasures might be there.' He nods at the bloodstained flagstones. 'And you say it is also the source of all this,' he waves at the sky, 'sorcery. Why should we head back to the gunship without at least investigating this so-called prophet? I do not doubt he is a charlatan, but who knows what kinds of artefacts he is hoarding. Alone, without any Imperial support, he has outwitted the Black Legion. Think what that might mean! He has surrounded the whole planet with clouds that turn men to stone. How could he achieve such things? Perhaps by harnessing a forbidden text? Perhaps by uncovering a relic from the days when the Emperor Himself walked here?'

Comus shakes his head. 'I don't understand. You want

us to head towards the man who has corrupted the whole planet?'

'Why not?' Halser's voice is a ragged snarl. 'By the Throne, Comus, can't you see? Maybe we *are* doomed, but at least we might end our days covered in glory. At least we might put an end to whatever monster is plaguing this wretched planet. And perhaps...' A trace of smile appears on his face. 'Perhaps we could find something that truly makes the trip worthwhile.'

The Librarian turns to look at the other Space Marines. They are waiting patiently for orders, as proud and noble as ever. He sighs and shakes his head. They do not deserve to die in Mortmain's firestorm, but he knows Halser is right: they are doomed anyway. For decades now, the Inquisition has been working towards their destruction. Perhaps this *would* be a more fitting end: death in battle, at the hands of the Imperium's foes, rather than excommunication and disgrace at the hands of a shadowy cabal. He looks back at the sergeant and falls quiet, unsure what to say. All the options seem black. Then he looks into Halser's eyes and sees how fiercely they are burning. If they have any hope at all, he decides, it is here – in the fury of Sergeant Halser.

Comus takes out the strange little book and attaches another cable to it. The others wait patiently as he prays. Even Pylcrafte ceases his struggles.

'I see another group of towers,' says the Librarian in a hoarse voice. 'Two kilometres south of this one. They are on the exact location of the underground temple network that once housed various scriptoria, including Zeuxis. If we can make it that far, I believe we will find the man who is in control of Ilissus. What we would do then, I cannot imagine.'

Halser grabs the Librarian by both arms. 'Have faith, Comus.' He looks south and watches the spirals of wind, whipping across the desolate landscape. 'We will be heroes again, I promise you.'

CHAPTER EIGHT

INQUISITOR MORTMAIN PICKS his way through chunks of glowing metal and smouldering flesh. The space where the interrogation chamber once stood is now a blackened wound. The blast was so fierce that several walls have buckled and fallen, creating an oddly liquid scene: girders, doors and coving lie draped over each other in a surreal slump of melted steel and shattered stone. Mortmain wrinkles his nose in distaste; the air is thick with the smell of charred meat. 'Oh, Palchus,' he breathes, kneeling to examine a pile of ash, 'What did you do?'

A towering figure watches from the darkness: a hulking giant, clad in gleaming bare ceramite. As he steps closer, the light of Mortmain's torch washes across the giant's power armour, revealing rows of intricate letters engraved into every available space. When he speaks, his voice peals from his helmet like a sword being drawn. 'Does it live?'

The inquisitor lifts a piece of broken chain from the rubble and holds it to his chest, muttering a prayer. 'Emperor save us, Justicar Lyctus, it might.' He looks up at the silver-clad Space Marine and shakes his head. 'I've been a fool. Cerbalus must have seen this coming. Whatever the Navigator used to do this has broken the wards and bonds we used to bind the daemon. If it managed to latch on to any other living thing, it will now be loose on the *Domitus*.' He rises and turns to face the Space Marine looming over him, his face utterly drained of colour. 'Cerbalus knows everything. It knows that Ilissus is on the verge of plunging the whole sector into madness. If it lives, it will attempt to stop the Exterminatus.'

Justicar Lyctus seems unimpressed by the urgency in Mortmain's voice. His glittering gauntlets remain draped calmly over the hilt of his halberd; if not for the faint light, flickering across the weapon's blade, Lyctus could be mistaken for a statue. 'What do you intend to do, inquisitor?' he asks, in the same ringing tones.

Mortmain clutches his shaven scalp in both hands and mutters another curse. 'I have no choice.' He looks out through a misshapen viewport at the wraith-like planet below. 'I can wait no longer. Baron van Tol's wretched secrets will have to wait. I must destroy Ilissus now.' He looks back at the Space Marine and shakes his head in disbelief. 'Damn it all. If Cerbalus lives, I may already be too late. It will tear the *Domitus* apart.' He looks past Justicar Lyctus into the shattered remains of the corridor. The light of his torch reveals more glittering, statuesque figures. 'You and your squad must do what you can.' Mortmain places a hand on the cover of a metal book, hung around the Space Marine's cuirass. 'I will pray for you.'

Lyctus nods and envelops the inquisitor's hand in his own massive, silver gauntlet. 'If it lives, we will bring it to heel, Inquisitor Mortmain.'

Mortmain shakes his head and withdraws his hand. 'No, you will not, justicar. Not this one. Even you will be unable to destroy a horror such as Cerbalus.'

There is a hint of emotion in the Space Marine's reply that is either disbelief or injured pride. 'Then what are you asking?'

Mortmain looks up at him. 'If Cerbalus is free, we are

already dead. But Ilissus must still be destroyed. Too much is at stake.' He looks out at the planet again. 'You must buy me whatever time you can. Find Cerbalus and throw yourself against it with all the fury you can muster. You cannot win against such a being, but you must try anyway. If you can keep the thing at bay long enough, I will be able to begin the bombardment of Ilissus.'

'And what about Sergeant Halser?'

Mortmain lowers his head. 'I will pray for him too.'

CHAPTER NINE

BARON CORNELIUS VAN Tol stumbles awkwardly to the door of his chamber, clumsy with fear. The dry, ironic tone is entirely absent from his voice as he calls for his guards. 'Something is approaching,' he cries as ranks of soldiers, wearing peaked caps and epaulettes, hurry towards him. 'The inquisitor has sent some kind of…' His words trail off and he seems unsure how to continue. He shakes his head. 'No, not Mortmain, this is something else. Something worse. Man the doors!'

Rows of polished lasguns line the passageway as he emerges, peering anxiously into the dark. 'Something is on the ship,' he mutters, drawing a gold-plated pistol and training it on the rippling shadows. 'The *Domitus* has been breached.'

A captain arrives, hastily fastening the collar of his uniform as he bows to the baron. 'My lord, what has happened?'

Van Tol looks back at him, his eyes wild with fear. 'Thayer. Didn't you hear the explosion?'

The officer's aristocratic features are identical to the

baron's, and as he sees van Tol's fear his skin pales to the same shade of grey. He has never seen the baron show such emotion before. 'I heard a noise, uncle, but I assumed it was just an engine fault. The *Domitus* is as ancient as the stars. Perhaps it was just–'

'Palchus is dead!' whispers the baron, clutching the officer by the shoulder. 'I can feel his absence.'

'Dead?' Thayer's mouth drops open. 'How? Was it the inquisitor?'

The baron shakes his head and looks back at the darkened corridor. The night sights attached to his men's guns send flickering red lines across the vaulted masonry, creating an unnerving sense of movement. 'No. This is not Mortmain's doing. Why would he attack his own flagship?' He lowers his voice and pulls his nephew closer. 'I can *see* something.' He taps the front of his cap. 'It's as though the immaterium has come after us and breached the hull.' He shakes his head in disbelief and looks at the floor. 'Palchus is *dead*.'

Captain Thayer frowns. 'The warp has entered the ship? What do you mean? How could that happen now? We're in real space.'

The baron gives a vague nod and starts to reply, but his words are lost beneath the whining screech of las-fire.

The two officers turn to find that the corridor has erupted with crackling energy as the soldiers fire wildly into the darkness.

They both raise their pistols and crouch next to the other soldiers.

'What is it?' cries the baron to the man next to him, struggling to be heard over the noise. 'What did you see?'

The soldier shakes his head, clearly terrified. 'I saw nothing,' he admits, 'but the others–'

'Hold your fire!' cries the baron, realising that his men are jumping at shadows, infected by his panic.

The shots continue for a few more seconds, until the baron manages to make himself heard. Then, one by one, the soldiers lower their guns and look towards him.

'My lord,' cries a man at the front of the group. 'There was something there. I couldn't see exactly, but it was moving quickly.'

'And what if it was one of our own sentries?' asks the baron, rising to his feet and peering into the dark.

The soldier's mouth flaps wordlessly as he fails to think of a suitable answer.

'Perhaps you should go and see what you've been incinerating?' The baron's voice is sharp with grief. 'If you're so certain you saw something.'

The soldier's eyes widen in fear. Then he regains a semblance of self-control and rises to his feet, adjusting his cap and giving a stiff salute before stepping away from the rest of the men. He keeps his lasgun levelled at the oily shadows as he edges forwards. The others watch in anxious silence as he approaches a gloom-shrouded fork in the passageway.

'I might have been mistaken,' says the soldier, looking up and down the corridors. He peers down the barrel of his gun, scoping the shadows for movement, but sees nothing. The relief on his face is visible, even in the half-light. Then his eyes narrow as he spots a darker shadow slip across the floor towards him. He mutters something, but the words are too quiet for the others to hear.

'What was that?' calls Captain Thayer, leaning around his uncle for a better look.

'Nothing,' replies the soldier, raising his voice. 'I think it's just a rat.'

'A rat?' Thayer looks at his uncle in disbelief.

'That's not it,' hisses the baron, fixing Captain Thayer with a wild stare. 'There *is* something out there.'

'Kaleb?' cries one of the soldiers. 'What's the matter?'

The baron and the captain look back down the corridor and see that the soldier has started acting strangely. His body has been gripped by some kind of spasm. 'A rat!' he cries in an odd-sounding voice. The words sound as though they are echoing in a vast cavern and as he cries out again the sound draws out into a long, rolling bellow.

'Kaleb?' calls out another voice, but the soldier's fit is growing rapidly worse. His head is jerking from side to side, spraying spit and curses as his legs collapse beneath him.

A few of the soldiers start moving towards him, but the baron halts them with a barked order: 'Halt! Hold your positions, damn you!'

The soldiers' desire to aid their fallen comrade is short-lived. As they watch in horror, his flesh starts to ripple and bulge, like a sheet caught in the wind.

'I knew it,' breathes the baron as the soldier's arms and legs begin to elongate, forming a teetering, arachnid frenzy of limbs, lashing violently back and forth across the stone floor and filling the air with a horrible, wet thumping sound.

'Kill it,' he whispers, but nobody hears.

The writhing mass lurches up from the shadows and the soldiers back away in horror. The thing that was Kaleb is now a five-metre nest of twitching limbs, surrounding a yellow, egg-shaped sack that quivers with revolting, subcutaneous shapes.

'Kill it!' repeats the baron. His voice is now a scream and before his men have a chance to respond, he begins firing his laspistol at the nightmarish vision.

Gunfire throws back the darkness for a second time, as the soldiers unleash a desperate volley of las-fire at the approaching colossus. The light is dazzling. It is impossible to see anything clearly so the soldiers fire blind, screaming as they register the full horror of what they have seen. The onslaught continues for several minutes, until finally the baron calls a halt.

As the echoes and smoke drift away the soldiers peer at the distant, hulking shape blocking the far end of the corridor.

Someone screams.

The monster has absorbed every shot as a welcome, nourishing feast. The featureless sack that passes for its head is now pulsing with inner fire and its jumble of spider limbs has swelled to three times the size, completely filling the passageway.

A few of the men begin firing again. A few drop to their knees and clutch their heads, their minds splintered. The rest turn and flee, dropping their guns as they race past the baron and disappear into the dark.

'Uncle,' gasps Captain Thayer, pulling at the baron's arm. 'Run.' To his horror, he realises that his uncle's face has gone slack and his eyes are fixed in an unblinking stare, locked on the undulating mass squeezing down the passageway. He tries again to drag the baron after his fleeing men, but van Tol will not move. Thayer keeps his gaze averted from the approaching mass, sure his mind will break if he looks at it even briefly, but he senses that the featureless sack is turned towards his uncle, as though the monster has singled him out amongst the crowd of terrified soldiers. 'Uncle,' he repeats in a tremulous wail, barely recognisable as speech. Finally, as he sees the forest of limbs in the corner of his vision, slithering across the ground towards him, he lets go of the baron's arm and bolts, sprinting after the others.

The baron is not conscious of his nephew's departure. He is not conscious of the figures dashing past him. He is not even conscious of his own being. All he sees is the vast, pallid, featureless head looming out of the darkness, fixed determinedly on him.

The creature heaves its awkward, pulsating bulk the last few metres to the baron, then reaches out with several of its triple jointed limbs. It grasps the baron in a delicate embrace and picks him carefully from the ground, lifting him towards its trembling, bloated head. For a second it holds him there, just a few centimetres away from the gleaming expanse of skin, then it shoves him through the membrane with a liquid *plop* and he vanishes from view.

The baron finds himself drowning in a saffron-coloured sea. The liquid fills his ears and rushes down his throat but, despite the absurd horror of his situation, van Tol feels a part of his mind step back, calmly removing itself from the agony of his death throes. This fragment of sentience is not even surprised to hear a voice, drifting through the yellow fluid.

'Baron van Tol,' it says in a perfectly reasonable tone.

The baron feels an inexplicable swell of pride that his murderer should know his name.

'What is down there, baron, on Ilissus?'

The baron's lungs are already full of the creature's fluid and there is no way he can form speech, but as life slips away from him, he answers with his mind, delighted to be able to answer the god-like being that is digesting him.

He feels sure his answer will come as a surprise.

CHAPTER TEN

GIDEON PYLCRAFTE KNEELS in the dust and mutters a prayer. The towers rising up ahead of him defy all logic. They resemble the fossil of a tornado, preserved at its most destructive: frozen, twisted spirals of rock, ten times taller than anything they have yet seen. They lean and bulge in a way that should send them toppling to the ground, but instead of falling they weave several kilometres up into the churning sky, towering over everything. 'Sweet, merciful Emperor,' moans Pylcrafte, shaking his mass of cables, 'save us from this place.'

Sergeant Halser lets out a bitter laugh. 'I think we will have to save ourselves.'

Halser, Comus and the rest of the squad are stood behind Pylcrafte on a lip of rock, also surveying the mountainous towers. If they feel any of Pylcrafte's horror, it is hidden behind their expressionless helmets. Only the Librarian has his face exposed to the needling dust and he is poring over the book chained to his power armour.

'According to the libellus,' he says, tracing a finger over the murky screen, 'the Emperor once paused here to rest.

169

In those days the planet was a verdant haven, full of life. The natives flooded the towns and cities, showering their saviour with rose petals and chanting His name. It must have been something to see.' Comus looks up and his face is a mask of pain. Blood is flowing freely from his eyes and his skin is as grey as the lifeless rocks. He closes the book. 'Whoever rules this place now is a saviour of a different kind.'

Sergeant Halser nods. Even through the grille of his helmet his voice betrays his excitement. 'But a saviour nonetheless.' He nods at Pylcrafte. 'Inquisitor Mortmain believed this place was crawling with the Black Legion. And what have we seen? A few pitiful stragglers at most. This prophet clearly has great weapons at his command.'

Pylcrafte climbs to his feet and points his cane in the direction of the towering peaks. 'How can you say such things? Look at that! It *reeks* of sorcery! My master gave you license to investigate ruins, not to consort with magicians and apostates!'

Halser grips the hilt of his chainsword and speaks in a series of explosive barks. 'Keep. Your. Mouth. Shut.'

Mortmain's acolyte clutches an I-shaped medallion as though it will ward off the sergeant's fury. 'I am my master's eyes and ears, Sergeant Halser, you would do well to remember that.'

Halser lets out an incoherent howl and rises up over him, but Comus steps forwards and places a hand on his arm, looking at him with pain-filled eyes.

Halser backs away with a curse and waves his men towards the towering shapes. 'Don't just stand there, move!'

The Relictors climb down from the lip of rock and start making their way across a featureless plain towards the warped peaks. The scene resembles a clearing in a forest of stone, and as the Space Marines lurch and stumble through the knee-deep dust, they keep their guns trained on the horizon, conscious of how exposed they are, even in the golden, hazy dusk. As they near the columns of rock they realise they are the beginnings of a bizarre mountain range. As they climb a gradual incline, they see dozens more of the teetering spires stretching away across the horizon.

'Are you sure this is the right place?' calls Sergeant Halser through the swirling dust.

Comus nods. His chin and neck are slick with blood and his face is white with pain. He is leaning heavily on one of the other Relictors. 'The xenos device is pointing here. The Zeuxis Scriptorium is hidden somewhere in these mountains. And the air is so thick with prayers, I can hardly breathe.' He waves weakly over the sergeant's shoulder. 'They are coming to greet you.'

Halser peers through the clouds and sees a group of tiny silhouettes rippling through the storm. He signals for his men to fan out and keep their guns on the approaching figures.

Even in their servo-powered suits, the Space Marines find it almost impossible to walk through the shifting terrain and it takes another fifteen minutes to reach the men. There are three of them: skeletal, shaven-headed wretches dressed in white, priestly robes. As they bow in greeting, light flickers across the star-shaped crystals embedded in their foreheads. Each of them has a line of thick, black stitches where their eyes should be.

'Heretics,' mutters Pylcrafte inside his hood, quietly enough that Sergeant Halser does not hear. 'How can they see without eyes? Unless they have witch-sight.'

'Friends!' cries one of the men in heavily accented Low Gothic, holding up his hands in greeting.

Sergeant Halser notices that none of them are carrying weapons but keeps his gun raised just the same. 'Who are you?'

The man beams back at him, delighted by the question. 'We're the Sons of Astraeus.' He signals for the two men behind him to approach. 'I'm Frater Gortyn. This is Frater Eusebius. And this is Frater Carmina. We are Pilgrims of the Sacred Light.' He points at the tower behind them. 'It is by our will, and the will of Astraeus himself that you have been allowed to find your way here.'

Sergeant Halser feels his hackles rising at the word 'allowed' but manages to keep his reply reasonably civil. 'And where is "here"?'

Frater Gortyn steps towards him with his hands still outstretched in greeting and Halser notices that they are wrapped in a silken mesh that stretches around his fingers, giving them a webbed appearance.

The pilgrim's smile grows even wider. 'You have found that which the enemy never could.' He looks past the Space Marines to the rocky outcrop at the edge of the plain. 'But we should talk once we are safely through the catacombs. Even now, the Great Enemy has not completely withdrawn from Ilissus. Astraeus has recently turned his thoughts to the celestial bodies. He cannot devote as much time to material concerns as he once did.' The pilgrim waves at the mountains. 'We can relax once we are in the city.'

Sergeant Halser gives Comus a questioning glance, but the Librarian's only reply is a shrug.

At the sight of Halser's hesitation, Frater Gortyn's smile falters. 'Is something wrong?'

'We have travelled a long way,' replies Halser. 'We have come from the celestial bodies that you mentioned, in search of an ancient scriptorium. Have you heard of such a thing? It was once known as the Zeuxis Scriptorium.'

The pilgrim smiles again and makes a strange little gesture with his hands, as though scattering light from the crystal in his head. 'Astraeus knows everything.' His voice is a droning chant. 'All questions shall be answered. All truths shall be revealed.'

Halser studies the white-clad figures for a moment, taking in their thin, wasted bodies, gangly, feeble limbs and gaunt, eyeless faces. Despite the eagle designs daubed on their robes, everything about them screams heretic. He has seen the same vacant, blissful smile countless times before, on a hundred worlds, and it has only ever meant one thing: corruption. Without looking back he can sense

Inquisitor Mortmain's lackey staring at him, willing him to execute them, and for once he is not sure that Pylcrafte's puritanism is misplaced. Doubt grips him and quickly morphs into anger. He feels as though he is teetering on the brink of something without knowing which way to fall. He scowls at his men as they wait patiently for his next move; their faith in him is as complete as it is unquestioning. Even Comus is staring at him, his eyes as full of hope as they are of blood. Halser looks past him at the sunset. The knotted branches of cloud are taking on a crimson sheen as the day's light slips from the sky. Only a few more hours, he thinks.

He turns back to the mutilated pilgrims. 'I am Sergeant Halser. We are the Emperor's Adeptus Astartes. Lead on.'

CHAPTER ELEVEN

CAPTAIN THAYER VAN Tol weeps as he runs, sprinting past crowds of wailing crewmen, Imperial Navy officers and his own, whimpering guards.

Behind him the *Domitus* is being devoured.

The battleship screams along with its crew as a monster tears into its brittle flesh.

The captain flings open a door and pounds up a flight of stairs, struggling to maintain his balance as a series of violent spasms rock the corridor, tearing support struts from the walls and firing rivets across the splintering floor. He slices through the carnage and bolts into a vast, open space. The ceiling disappears into cavernous darkness, only interrupted by the occasional winged saint, peering down sadly at the crowds flooding into one of the *Domitus's* launch bays.

As he joins the terrified throng, Captain Thayer sees he was not the first to think of abandoning the doomed battleship. Thousands of desperate souls are clawing over each other in an attempt to reach the hulking rows of frigates and cruisers.

'Make way for House van Tol!' he cries, but his voice is lost, drowned beneath the general clamour. 'Let me through!' he demands, but nobody hears.

The chorus of screams grows as a vast shape tears through the wall on one side of the hangar. As the dust and debris settles, it becomes clear that Cerbalus has grown to surreal proportions. As its limbs unfold from the shadows, they dwarf even the beleaguered spacecraft, crumpling armoured hulls like tinfoil as they carry the daemon into the chamber. Then the egg-like head swings into view, hanging over the shrieking crowds like a sloshing, glistening moon.

Once more, Captain Thayer manages to look away before he takes in the full horror of the thing. He feels his mind tremble on the edge of collapse, but manages not to plunge fully into the abyss. Others are less lucky. All around him rows of hardened crewmen drop to their knees, howling and clawing at their own eyes in an attempt to remove the vision that has ruined their minds.

The Navigator shouts prayers as he turns and flees back the way he came, vaulting over the toppling, drooling ranks of crewmen. He is conscious that the impossible monster is ploughing through the crowds towards him. The screams leap in pitch again as the thing stuffs hundreds of pitiful souls into its quivering head, spilling yellow fluid onto the crowds as it attempts to satisfy a dreadful, centuries-old hunger.

Thayer makes it back to the doorway, but sees to his horror that the stairs have collapsed. 'Emperor preserve us,' he gasps, looking around for another exit.

Those still sane enough to control their limbs are now flooding back out of the hangar and Captain Thayer finds himself barged and jostled into a corner. Terror overcomes him and he draws his laspistol. 'Stand back!' he screams, levelling the gun at rows of ashen faces. Nobody hears him and after a glimpse of the creature's teetering, spider-like limbs, a pistol does not make much of an impression.

As the crowds press closer Thayer loses control and

begins firing indiscriminately into the crowd. Men, women and children are indistinguishable to him as he attempts to blast a path to another door. As quickly as the bodies tumble to the floor, more rush into the gaps they create. However desperately he fires, the captain only manages to move at a snail's pace, and all the while he senses the huge shape looming closer – smashing through the remaining ships and tearing statues from the balconies overhead.

'Let me through!' he screams again and, this time, to his amazement, the figures ahead of him *do* actually move to one side. Captain Thayer can barely believe his luck as he rushes towards the door.

He has only taken a few steps when he sees the reason for the gap in the crowd. A towering, glittering figure is striding towards him: a Space Marine, wearing flashing plates of unpainted power armour and carrying a halberd that shimmers with blue light. As he smashes effortlessly though the crowd, the Space Marine makes a formidable sight. The sheer bulk of him is incredible and every inch of the warrior is clad in thick, gleaming plate.

'Wait!' cries Captain Thayer, reaching out to the Space Marine, but he finds himself barged unceremoniously to one side as the warrior ploughs through the crowds towards the still-growing monster.

The captain scrambles back to his feet and manages to climb onto the pedestal of a broken statue. As he looks out over the heaving throng, he catches other glimpses of silver, appearing at various points in the vast, shifting darkness. It seems almost as though they are arriving from nowhere. As Thayer watches in disbelief seven of the glittering figures materialise from the shadows and begin charging towards the mountain of thrashing limbs.

Thayer looks back at the door and sees that he has a chance to escape, but he finds he cannot leave. The scene unfolding before him is like a tale from the oldest legends: a giant creature from the warp, surrounded by glittering, armour-clad knights. The captain forgets his terror for a moment as he watches the Space Marines charge towards the thing that is devouring the ship.

The monster lifts its mountainous pile of limbs, severing a cluster of fuel pipes and spilling gouts of blue flame across the hangar. Whole swathes of the crowd ignite and their agonised shadows begin to dance and writhe across the walls.

The fire does not slow the Space Marines and as they race towards the writhing monster they raise their halberds with mute synchronicity, levelling the pulsing blades at its huge, arachnoid limbs.

At the last minute, Captain Thayer looks away, unwilling to watch the creature feed on its silver-clad attackers. Then, rather than the sounds of messy consumption he was expecting, he hears a new sound: a thin, piercing whistle, so loud he has to clamp his hands over his ears. He looks back and sees to his amazement that the vile creature is rearing up in pain. The Space Marines' weapons are embedded deep in its legs and their power has spread across its flesh in a network of glittering, sapphire veins.

As he follows the lines of light, Thayer sees that they are racing towards the warp creature's featureless, sack-like head. The captain howls in fear, realising too late that he has made a terrible mistake: in his excitement he has looked directly at the thing. His mind recoils from the insanity of it. 'Mercy,' he groans, sliding down the pedestal onto the trembling floor. No mercy is forthcoming as his thoughts race down avenues best left unexplored. In a fraction of a second the captain perceives all the dreadful, pitiless lunacy of the universe. 'Mercy, mercy, mercy,' he repeats as screaming, burning figures barge past him. His shattered thoughts present him with a variety of disturbing images, one of which might be reality. He sees the monster lash out with its countless limbs, sending a Space Marine spinning through the air like a child's toy. The warrior flies up towards the gloomy, vaulted ceiling of the hangar, then plummets back down into the hellish inferno.

The vast hangar is quickly filling with flames and the

temperature is rocketing. As Captain Thayer lies gibbering against the pedestal, the rows of faces racing past him begin to shimmer in the heat. Then he starts to question even that; is it really the heat making their features undulate and slide? There is something fierce and bestial about their expressions.

He looks back at the warp being and sees that, incredibly, most of the Space Marines are still attacking it. The light spreading from their halberds is blazing even brighter and the monster is recoiling in pain. Captain Thayer realises that the thin squealing sound is coming from its yellow, membranous head. 'Mercy,' he says again, but this time his tone is one of awed respect. Even from the depths of his growing madness, he realises the immensity of what they are doing. How can they be so calm, he wonders, in the face of such a mind-bending horror?

As the creature attempts to wrench its limbs free, its impossible bulk topples back against the wall of the chamber. The whole edifice teeters and as the wall gives way, so does a large section of the ceiling. Marble saints topple from the shadows: gleaming goliaths the size of houses explode as they slam down on the raging fires.

Still the Space Marines endure, climbing, mountaineer-like, up the monster's heaving bulk. Another one dies, pulped against the wall as a twitching, kilometre-long limb breaks free. But the rest simply thrust their blades deeper. The blue light is now so bright that the warp creature's innards are visible – pulsing like the flames below.

Captain Thayer realises that however hard they fight, the Space Marines have no hope. With every second that passes, the monster continues to grow in size and fury. Thayer starts to laugh. It is a wild, shrill sound, almost in tune with the monster's screams. As he laughs he places the muzzle of his pistol against his head and makes a final plea for mercy.

CHAPTER TWELVE

As THEY ENTER the catacombs, Frater Gortyn plucks a torch from the walls and waves it around his head, pushing back the darkness to reveal a jumbled mess of broken headstones and shattered sarcophagi.

'These old stones mark the heroism of a glorious age,' he says, dusting down one of the inscriptions with his silk-clad hand.

Sergeant Halser's eyes glitter hungrily in the flames. The names carved into the stones have long since faded, but their power still hangs heavy in the air. This is clearly the resting place of legendary figures. Rows of alcoves lead off into the darkness, each one filled with tall, pillared tombs, grandiose winged sculptures and faded murals. 'Who were these champions?' he asks, taking another torch from the wall and holding it over a tomb.

The gaunt-faced pilgrim still has the same, inane grin frozen on his face, even as he discusses the dead. 'Forgotten heroes, Sergeant Halser, of the highest order. These men and women fought beside the Holy Emperor as He carved a great empire in the stars. Only the bravest and most loyal of His servants were interred in the sacred earth of Ilissus. For many decades they were brought here, as defiant and noble in death as they were in life. As the Emperor's wars grew in ambition, the number of casualties grew too. But we cared for them all, placing their remains in the most beautiful caskets we could build and storing the spoils of their crusade in our most secret reliquaries.'

Brother-Librarian Comus is still hesitating at the entrance, but Frater Gortyn waves him in and hurries off down the aisles of gloomy alcoves. 'But the Emperor never forgot his loyal comrades. He visited Ilissus several times in his star chariot. Many records from those days are still held in the scriptoria. They describe how the Emperor did not just come here to pay His respects, He came seeking solace and even advice when He was most sorely pressed. The Zeuxis chamber contains several portraits of Him, kneeling at these very tombs.'

Most of the Relictors look around in awe, shocked by the idea that they might be treading in the Emperor's footsteps, but Halser rushes after the pilgrims, lifting his torch higher. 'Then the scriptorium *does* still exist!'

Frater Gortyn turns his grin back on the sergeant. 'The Pilgrims of the Sacred Light have endured on Ilissus since the days of the Holy Emperor, guarding and waiting. When the Emperor's fallen heroes came to us laden with strange, dangerous treasures, we swore to protect not just their memories, but their power. Our centuries of vigilance are recorded in great detail.' His smile falters. 'There were many dark years, of course.' He waves at the dozens of smaller passageways that lead off from the main artery of the catacombs. 'The Emperor's visits ceased without explanation and we were forced to hide ourselves down here as the Great Enemy ran unchallenged, razing our forests and farms to the ground.' Then the smile returns to his face and he makes the strange gesture again, flicking his fingers away from the crystal. 'But finally the Emperor sent us a sign that He still lived. A star fell from the sky. And that star was His prophet, Astraeus.'

As the Relictors squeeze their armoured bulk past the mounds of shattered stone, the smaller, hooded shape of Pylcrafte hurries after them, eyeing the group of pilgrims with undisguised hate. 'And just how did you survive all those "dark years"?' He points his cane at the ceiling. 'Hiding under a few rocks is not usually enough to avoid the snares of the Ruinous Powers.'

The bile in Pylcrafte's voice is obvious to everyone except Frater Gortyn, who smiles cheerfully back at him. 'You are quite right, friend. Over the years the black knights hunted us down without mercy. Our numbers dwindled and many priceless treasures had to be destroyed, lest they fall into the enemy's hands.'

Pylcrafte shakes his head, but keeps his optical cables fixed on the grinning pilgrim. 'And I suppose you had no option but to lay your hands on those "priceless treasures" and turn them against your foes? After all, why would you let your fraternity fail, when you had access to items of unnatural power?' He shivers in disgust. 'Whatever the source of that power might be.'

Frater Gortyn stumbles to a halt and shakes his head in speechless denial. The smile drops from his face.

One of the other pilgrims steps from the shadows, looking equally dismayed. 'Oh, no. You don't understand. We cannot *use* the objects left in our care. They are for the hands of the Emperor alone.' He shrugs. 'And the hands of His prophet, of course.'

Pylcrafte sounds unconvinced, and Sergeant Halser makes no move to silence him, keen to hear more detail about the relics left in the scriptorium. 'So how have you survived?' demands Pycrafte in a peevish tone. 'It is a matter of Imperial record that the Black Legion landed on Ilissus in large numbers. How can your order have survived intact, unless...' He draws himself erect and places a hand on the medallion swinging beneath his hood. 'Unless you are in league with them?'

Frater Gortyn steps closer to Pylcrafte, oblivious to the revulsion his nearness induces in Inquisitor Mortmain's acolyte. Despite his lack of eyes, the pilgrim reaches unerr-ingly for Pylcrafte's arm and grips it with his silk-bound fingers. 'Some of us fell, it is true. Mephitis and Axum and many other places failed in their duty, overcome by fear, but who can really blame them?'

Pylcrafte snatches his arm free and jabs a finger at the pilgrim. 'You do not even condemn their heresy, then?' The cables under his hood flick out like snakes and focus on the Space Marines towering over them. 'Did you hear that? He who excuses heresy must himself be a brother of the damned. He just said that they have survived down here for years, but we know that in recent times the planet has been utterly overrun by Chaos. How can they have survived? Answer me that?'

He draws his laspistol and levels it at Frater Gortyn. His voice is verging on a scream. 'There is blatant her-esy here, Sergeant Halser. Are you really willing to let it go unpunished? By the Emperor – they don't even have eyes! How do they see? Will you really endorse such repugnant sin?'

'Brother Volter,' says the sergeant, with a nod to one of his men.

As the Space Marine steps towards him, Pylcrafte backs away, cursing, and holsters his gun.

Halser's jaw ripples with muscle as he glares at the hooded figure. Then he turns to Frater Gortyn. 'How *did* you survive?'

The pilgrim steps away from Pylcrafte and raises his hands in a gesture of bemused innocence. 'Astraeus, of course.' He frowns at the sergeant. 'If you have travelled from the heavenly bodies surely you must know of the Emperor's prophet? Have you never heard of Astraeus?'

Halser shakes his head and looks back at Comus. 'Does the name mean anything to you? Is it recorded in the libellus?'

The Librarian is clutching his temples again, clearly in pain, but he manages to shake his head.

'Well,' exclaims Frater Gortyn, grinning at his fellow

pilgrims. 'It looks like we are going to spread a lot of happiness this day!'

They grin back at him, nodding eagerly.

'The prophet is both father and shield,' he continues, turning his crystal star in the direction of Pylcrafte. 'He is one with Ilissus. He is one with the earth and the air. He blinds the eyes that would wish us harm.'

'And this prophet,' asks Halser, 'is he here somewhere? We have very little time.'

'Of course!' beams Frater Gortyn. 'He knows everything about you. He's dying to meet you. He's waiting for you in the City of Stars.'

CHAPTER THIRTEEN

INQUISITOR MORTMAIN STANDS in the doorway for a moment, silhouetted by the inferno raging behind him. His leather cloak is lined with smoke and his shaven head is caked in blood. His eyes are as flat and lifeless as those of a corpse.

'My lord?' cries a young Naval officer, rushing towards him. 'Are you injured?'

Mortmain gives no reply as he slams the door shut. He turns, aims his laspistol at the lock and fires repeatedly, turning the mechanism into a molten lump. Then he stands there in silence, staring at the door as the officer watches him anxiously.

'The ship is lost,' he announces after a few moments, without turning to face the officer.

The officer laughs nervously and looks around. They are standing at the end of a long antechamber that leads onto the bridge of the *Domitus*. Ranks of limbless, hooded servitors line the walls, grafted onto flickering control panels. Their pallid, slack-jawed faces show no sign of recognition but the officer hurries to the inquisitor's side and lowers his voice. 'Perhaps you should speak to the captain, I'm sure he can reassure you.'

Mortmain finally looks at the officer and sees that he is little more than a boy. The inquisitor shakes his head sadly, then says: 'Lead me to him, son.'

CAPTAIN SEVERINUS IS a ruddy-faced bear of a man, with a wispy crown of red hair and a barrel chest that his braided jacket cannot quite hold in check. His reply is a deep bellow of laughter. 'I do not think we should write off an Imperial battleship quite so easily, Inquisitor Mortmain. Do you realise what kind of manpower we have on board?'

Mortmain gives no reply, and the captain looks to his officers for an explanation. They look as confused as he does.

'What have you seen, Inquisitor Mortmain?' The captain cannot entirely hide the fear in his voice. Whole sections of his ship are imploding without any sane explanation. The only information that *has* made its way back to him is the kind of lunatic gibberish that he would rather not consider.

The inquisitor looks at the hunched rows of servitors. 'We don't have much time. We will have to begin sooner than I thought.' He grabs the captain by the arm and drags him back to his chair. 'Give the order to drop into orbit. Alert the rest of the fleet. We must prepare the missiles for launch.'

Captain Severinus wrenches his arm free and his cheeks shift from red to purple. 'I'm not a navvy!' he roars, drawing back his shoulders. 'This is my ship, Inquisitor Mortmain. Show some bloody respect! *I* give the orders on this bridge. Even the Ordo Malleus can manage a little–'

Inquisitor Mortmain rounds on him with a snarl. 'We're going to die.' His voice is low and dangerous. 'Very soon.'

The captain shakes his head and opens his mouth to reply, but the inquisitor is too fast.

'*Listen* to me!' he roars. 'We are going to die. All of us.

But if you can shut up and listen for a second we may still be able to save the rest of the sector.'

Captain Severinus's jaw drops. He has never heard the inquisitor's voice raised before.

When he is sure he has the captain's full attention, Mortmain gives a nod of satisfaction. 'Good,' he says, in a softer voice.

'What is it? What has happened?' asks the young officer.

Mortmain runs a hand over his blistered scalp and looks back at the door. The sounds of destruction are growing louder with every second that passes. Deep, rumbling explosions rock through the hull and the rattle of gunfire rings up through the mesh floor. It feels as though the ship is already in its death throes. 'The immaterium has taken physical form. And it is hungry.'

'What do you mean?' The captain regains a little of his anger. 'We left warp space weeks ago. How could such a thing happen?'

Mortmain looks at the floor for a moment, unsure how to reply. 'There is no time to explain, captain. It is enough for you to understand that we are carrying a daemon. A *daemon*. It is making its way towards us, but it wants more than just our souls. I believe it will attempt to stop the Exterminatus.'

Captain Severinus drops heavily into his chair, looking dazed. 'A daemon from the warp?' He clutches his head. 'How could that happen?'

'What interest would such a thing have in Ilissus?' asks one of the other officers, his face draining of colour. 'The planet has already fallen to the Ruinous Powers.'

Mortmain looks out at the vaporous planet. 'The daemon knows of our mission. It knows the strange nature of the weather that has been spreading from Ilissus. I believe it will attempt to save the planet and then feed the disturbance with its own life-force. No one entirely understands what is happening down there, but one thing is clear: if the disturbance is not curtailed immediately, we could be looking at a catastrophe of unimaginable proportions.' He taps the tube of parchment clasped to his belt. 'All these pretty signatures will be meaningless if the daemon manages to stoke whatever strange fire is burning down there. The temporal disturbances that have been plaguing this system could spread to the whole sector.' He looks at the officer. 'Even I cannot predict what would happen then.' His voice drops even lower. 'We must destroy the planet now, while our souls are still intact.'

Captain Severinus lifts his head from his hands. 'But we've just sent men down there. And not just any men: Adeptus Astartes.' His jabs a finger at the viewports. 'One of them is your friend!'

Mortmain nods and closes his eyes for a second, but gives no other reply.

Severinus shakes his head. 'There has to be a way to stop this thing. Even a daemon must have a weakness. Surely the Ordo Malleus has faced such things before?' He narrows his eyes. 'I hear that you have Space Marines in your own entourage, Inquisitor Mortmain. Adeptus Astartes who travel with an inquisitor? What horrors must they have seen? Surely they can do something to help?'

Mortmain scowls. The captain has been prying into things that do not concern him. Then he shrugs. What difference does it make now? He waves his hand at the door. 'If you listen carefully, Captain Severinus, you can hear them dying.'

They all listen to the distant sounds of battle, the wailing of sirens and the groaning of the damaged ship.

Mortmain closes his eyes. 'Their heroism is beyond reckoning, but it will not be enough.'

The captain's cheeks flush darker. He places a hand on the hilt of his sabre and glares at Mortmain. 'And what if you're wrong? What if it's our close proximity to Ilissus that's causing the problems? If we enter attack formation we might open ourselves up to even greater danger. What if–'

Inquisitor Mortmain moves with unnerving speed. Before the captain can finish his sentence he steps forwards, draws his laspistol and clubs him to the ground.

There is a loud *thud* as Captain Severinus slams onto the floor.

Mortmain calmly wipes a splash of blood from his cheek and looks around the circle of officers. His expression is a sharp contrast to their looks of shocked disbelief. 'I apologise for my rough manners, gentlemen,' he says, holstering his pistol, 'but we really don't have time for a debate. Does anyone else wish to question my authority?'

The officers shake their heads and back away, looking anxiously at the pool of blood spreading around their captain's head.

'See to him,' mutters the inquisitor, turning to the young officer.

As the youth kneels to examine the captain's injury, Mortmain addresses the others. 'Inform the rest of Fleet Sanctus. Prepare for bombardment.'

CHAPTER FOURTEEN

As THEY LEAVE the catacombs Frater Gortyn steps proudly to one side so that the Relictors can enjoy the view.

Sergeant Halser is the first to emerge, taking a deep, grateful breath of evening air as he steps out onto a rocky promontory. He immediately staggers back and mutters an oath, stunned by the unexpected scene spread out before him. They have come out at one end of a long, steep-sided valley. The strange, convoluted mountains rear up on either side of them, dripping with scarlet fire, robed by the setting sun. It is not the sheer-sided peaks that cause Sergeant Halser to gasp, though. At the heart of the hidden valley lies a beautiful, glittering secret.

'Welcome to Madrepore,' sighs Frater Gortyn, his voice trembling. 'The City of Stars.'

As the other Relictors climb up out of the shadows, they are as stunned as their sergeant. Madrepore is a small, walled city, designed in the shape of a five-pointed star and even in the fading light it sparkles like a polished jewel. The towering walls are as organic and coral-like as their surroundings, but they are also bedecked with countless shimmering lights. The whole structure has a shifting, pearlescent quality quite unlike anything the Space Marines have ever seen. It seems as though a portion of the heavens has fallen to earth and is slumbering amongst the mountains of Ilissus.

Halser steps further onto the ledge. 'What is this place?' He shakes his head. 'That's not Imperial architecture.' He grabs the hilt of his chainsword and glares at the grinning pilgrims. 'Where have you brought us? Is this a xenos city?'

'Far from it. This is our home.' The pilgrim laughs and points to a single tower that reaches even higher than the city's outer walls. 'Astraeus lifted these stones from beneath the ground with nothing but the power of prayer. His father, the Emperor of Terra, bequeathed him the merest scintilla of his eternal light, but that was enough to create this blessed, beautiful haven.' He waves at the surrounding mountains. 'For decades we hid ourselves down here in this valley, guarding the ruins of the old scriptoria in the knowledge that one day, inevitably, the Great Enemy would find us. But then, when the prophet came, his prayers did more than build us a city – they also shrouded the valley from sight. Nobody can see over these peaks. If Astraeus had not willed it, even you could never have found this place.'

Sergeant Halser looks back at Brother-Librarian Comus with a raised eyebrow.

Comus nods in reply but is too weak to make comment. He has clasped the libellus back onto his belt, but there is no sign of his pain lessening. If not for the firm grip of Brother Volter, he would not have made it through the catacombs.

Halser looks down at the sparkling city walls. 'What are the lights in the rock?'

Frater Gortyn's smile becomes a giggle and he does not seem to have heard the question. 'The prophet's vision goes far beyond mortal sight. His mind is alive with countless images. He sees the movements of the heavens and the changing of the weather. In fact, he *is* the weather.'

Gortyn waves at the tumultuous clouds, merging seamlessly with the spirals of rock that cover the landscape. 'What you see here is only a fraction of his power. The spirit of the Immortal Emperor has been harnessed and refracted through the prophet's flesh. The towers you see out there are the fingers of Astraeus, reaching up and dragging us to salvation.'

Pylcrafte mutters under his hood and even Halser clenches his jaw. He has heard this kind of deluded cant before. He feels a growing sense of dread as the pilgrims lead the way down a narrow, stone stair, chuckling merrily to themselves as they go.

UNLIKE THE REST of Ilissus, the land around Madrepore is flat and verdant. For several kilometres in every direction, well-tilled fields and herds of grazing cattle skirt the City of Stars. Clusters of adobe huts run alongside wide, tree-lined tracks, bustling with white-robed figures. After the desolation that preceded it, the Relictors struggle to comprehend the orderly scene spread out below them. Stranger still is the greeting they receive as they reach the valley floor and begin marching towards the city gates. The sound of power-armoured boots crunching down the road should cause a commotion, regardless of the pilgrims' mutilated eyes. But as the Relictors march past, the groups labouring in the fields pay them no attention, as though the arrival of Space Marines is a daily occurrence.

'Do they not wonder who we are?' asks Sergeant Halser, turning to Frater Gortyn.

'They know who you are,' replies the pilgrim. 'We are all one with the mind of our father. Everything he sees, we see.'

Halser grimaces. Every minute he spends in the company of the pilgrims confirms his doubts. He looks around at the blind, toiling figures and mutters under his breath, horrified to see how confidently they swing their scythes and leap onto the back of moving carts. He decides to ask Gortyn about the star-shaped crystals in their foreheads but, before he can speak, he feels a tap on his shoulder and turns to see Comus. The Librarian is holding up the xenos device and tapping its screen. The casing is smeared with blood, but he has discerned something in the glyphs pulsing beneath the glass.

'I was right,' he gasps. 'The Zeuxis Scriptorium *is* here.' As he struggles to speak, energy arcs from the mantle of his power armour and crackles across his furrowed brow. 'Whoever this prophet is, he has built his city right over the top of one of the Ecclesiarchy's most ancient reliquaries.'

Halser pauses for a moment to let the pilgrims move ahead. 'Then we must gain entry to the scriptorium, by whatever means, and see what it is they're guarding. If the objects stored there are as powerful as they think, we may even find a way to navigate a way back through the storms.' He grabs the Librarian by the shoulder. 'Do you still have the strength to contact the others, back at the gunship? Could you summon them to this spot?'

Comus grimaces and nods at the blood-drenched book. 'This xenos filth is killing me.' He closes his eyes for a second. 'But yes, contacting them should still be possible.'

Sergeant Halser nods. 'Good. The repairs to the ship should be complete by now. It would take them minutes to reach us. We might be able to salvage a victory yet. If we can find something to help us see through these wretched storms, we could empty the scriptorium and be out of here before the bombs start falling.' He looks at the chrono-meter attached to his weapons belt. 'Inquisitor Mortmain has promised me another two hours.' He waves at the crowds of eyeless pilgrims shuffling through the fields. 'Then these dupes will receive their heavenly reward.'

Comus looks at the glittering walls looming ahead of them. 'And what if we are unable to gain access to the scriptorium? What if we can't leave Ilissus before the Exterminatus begins?'

Halser's habitual sneer grows even more pronounced. 'Then we all burn together.'

CHAPTER FIFTEEN

JUSTICAR LYCTUS CRAWLS along the shattered remains of a girder, clutching his glimmering halberd to his chest while beneath him the hangar disintegrates. As the daemon continues to grow it has begun tearing holes through the ship's hull, its colossal, viscous mass growing more frenzied with every second. As the rest of Lyctus's squad struggle to hold it in place, the nest of segmented limbs jerk back and forth, wrenching machinery and support struts free from the walls and sending screaming crewmen sailing through the air. As Lyctus clings determinedly onto the girder, the *Domitus* is spilling its innards to the void, but he keeps his gaze locked on the heaving yellow sack at the centre of the mayhem.

As he nears the daemon, the justicar's armour begins to ripple with light. Countless inscriptions flash and shimmer, straining to protect Lyctus from the unholy power washing over him.

'Brothers,' he breathes into his vox-bead, 'just a few more minutes. Then lend me your faith. I'm almost overhead. I'm going to drop straight–'

Lyctus's words are cut short as a new sound is added to the cacophony: a barking claxon that cuts through the sound of grinding metal. At the same moment, in the areas of the hangar that are still intact, rows of red lights blink into life.

Justicar Lyctus curses as the daemon lurches back towards the gore-splattered hole in the wall.

From the furthest reaches of the *Domitus* comes the deep rumble of heavy munitions roaring into life.

'Justicar?' crackles a voice in Lyctus's helmet. 'Is it withdrawing?'

As the screaming crowds continue to charge past the Space Marines, the daemon heaves its revolting flesh upright and pauses for a moment, like a dog that has caught a scent. The only movement is a slight trembling of its egg-like membrane.

Justicar Lyctus nods his head. 'Inquisitor Mortmain must have reached the bridge. He is preparing the Exterminatus.' Then, as the daemon starts to swing its bulk around, Lyctus realises they are about to miss their opportunity.

'Brother Gallus,' he snaps into the vox-bead. 'Your incinerator!'

The darkness is torn open by a column of flame. It leaps up from one of the Space Marines and envelops the featureless head of the daemon. The air fills with the smell of burning scented oil as the daemon jerks back, flinging its attackers across the hangar and emitting another high-pitched scream.

The thing thrashes in pain and Justicar Lyctus spots his chance, charging across the girder and leaping off the end, diving headlong at the daemon with his halberd held before him like a lance.

There is an explosion of pus, flame and psychic energy as he bursts through the wall of membrane and disappears from view.

Down below, on the blood-slick floor of the hangar, the rest of the Space Marines climb awkwardly to their feet. Some of them have wide, bloody gashes in their power armour and some topple back onto the mounds of corpses, gasping in pain, but one of them, Brother Gallus, swings his heavy, two-handed weapon around for a second shot, lighting up the vast chamber with another dripping arch of fire.

Justicar Lyctus sinks through the daemon's flesh, feeling its ancient malice clawing at his soul. Every liturgy and prayer inscribed into his armour burns with the strain of upholding his sanity. The Emperor preserves, thinks Lyctus, drawing on his bottomless, inviolable well of faith. Three centuries of devotion shield him, even as he feels his armour warp and crack. 'I rebuke you, Cerbalus,' he whispers, knowing that the daemon can hear. 'I forbid you to exist.'

As Gallus struggles to hold his bucking, thrashing incinerator, he senses his injured battle-brothers lining up beside him. As the column of flame forces the daemon back into a corner of the hangar, the other Space Marines begin firing their own psychically-charged weapons. A blinding volley of fire, metal and faith tears into the lurching daemon.

'Advance!' orders Brother Gallus, his voice calm and sure.

As they approach the daemon, its head begins to pulse with light, becoming a kaleidoscope of different colours as it jerks from side to side. At the heart of the display is a silvery core: Justicar Lyctus's shape is recognisable as he spins in the daemon's mind. Then, with another explosion of energy and gunk, the justicar's halberd bursts from the flame-shrouded sack.

The daemon's head begins to split open, vomiting brains across its hideous legs and changing its piercing cry to a moist, popping gurgle.

The daemon's head collapses and Justicar Lyctus tumbles into view, spewed out on a virulent, yellow wave. He clatters to the hangar floor, shrouded in smoke and sparks and then lurches to his feet, stepping clear seconds before a tree-sized limb slams down where he landed.

There is no victory cry from Lyctus's men as they surround the collapsing daemon. They simply maintain their unrelenting volley of blessed promethium and bolter shells, forcing it back into the corner.

Justicar Lyctus staggers drunkenly towards his men, still clutching his blazing halberd. His armour has been scorched and wrenched out of shape and his bloody chin is visible through a rent in his helmet, but as he joins the other ranks of Space Marines he raises his fist and fires a screaming volley of shells from the storm bolter mounted on his wrist. As he shoots he repeats his cry: 'I rebuke you, Cerbalus!'

The daemon collapses into a wall of billowing flames and disappears from view.

After firing a few more rounds, Justicar Lyctus opens his raised fist, signalling for his men to hold their fire.

For a second the daemon falls quiet, but the hangar is still a riot of noise and colour: the claxons are blaring; crowds of crewmen and servitors are crushed against the various exits, screaming desperately as others are sucked out into the void. Banks of blue flame are still gushing from the severed fuel pipes and the *Domitus* itself is howling as its infrastructure gives way, wrenched out of the holes torn by the daemon's violence.

Lyctus keeps his hand raised as he edges closer to the rolling flames.

There is a flash of light and a shape flies towards him. A lean, red, humanoid figure that towers over the Space Marines as it crashes through them and bolts towards one of the exits.

Lyctus and the others fire wildly after it, but the blood-red figure carves straight through the crowds and dashes through the exit, disappearing from view.

Justicar Lyctus rises painfully to his feet. His armour is ruined and bloody, and half his men are dead. He nods calmly as he surveys the carnage. Then he speaks, not to his groaning men but to Inquisitor Mortmain, on the far side of the ship. 'You were right. It will be with you in minutes.

We will attempt to pursue.' He pauses and kneels, trying to stem the blood rushing from one of his men's throats. 'Our prayers are with you, inquisitor.'

The reply that crackles in his helmet is just as composed. 'Thank you, Justicar Lyctus. It has been an honour serving with you. The Emperor protects.'

CHAPTER SIXTEEN

TWO VAST, ETCHED iron gates loom over Sergeant Halser as he reaches the city walls. He looks up at the strange designs and sees stars, planets and galaxies whirling in a stylised storm. Far above, at the top of the walls he sees rows of pilgrims surveying the valley as it sinks into darkness, as uninterested in the Relictors as all the other pilgrims they have passed.

Frater Gortyn and their other guides reach the foot of the gate and wait without knocking. After a few seconds, the doors begin to swing slowly inwards, revealing a glimpse of bustling crowds and a wide, sweeping road.

The rest of the squad are still half a kilometre away. Sergeant Halser curses under his breath as he sees how slowly they are moving. Only the hunched, cowled figure of Pylcrafte has managed to keep up with him and he is staring at the city in abject horror. Brother Librarian Comus can barely walk and the others are matching their pace to his agonised steps. In an attempt to distract himself, Halser steps to the side of the road to examine Madrepore's soaring, rippling walls. The dusk is reflected in the countless rows of gems, embedded in the contorted rock. It is these crystals that give Madrepore its sparkle and, as he waits for the rest of the squad to arrive, Halser leans closer to examine one of them.

'By the Throne!' he grunts, turning to Pylcrafte. 'What *is* this?'

What he had mistaken for crystals are actually eyes. As Halser and Pylcrafte stagger back in disgust, they creak in their jagged sockets, rolling to watch them. Every one of them shimmers with an inner light, but they are unmistakably human. Halser looks over at Gortyn's scarred, empty sockets and howls. 'What sorcery is this? What have you done?'

Frater Gortyn's drawn features remain fixed in a vacant smile. 'There is no sorcery, Sergeant Halser. We have merely lent our vision to the prophet.' He taps the star-shaped crystal lodged in his forehead. 'We see so much further now.'

Sergeant Halser groans as he looks back at the banks of rolling, blinking eyes. He can bear this no longer. He draws his bolt pistol and levels it at Frater Gortyn. 'This is unspeakable. If I had known–'

Halser's words are drowned out by an explosion. The blast is so violent that the whole valley shakes, jolting the sergeant sideways and sending his gun clattering across the road.

Pylcrafte lets out a stream of curses as he topples backwards into a ditch.

Ignoring his cries for help, Halser and the pilgrims look back down the road in confusion. A huge plume of smoke is rolling down into the valley from the entrance to the catacombs and distant shapes are visible, moving quickly through the haze.

Frater Gortyn's grin finally drops from his face. As a line of black-armoured figures begins pouring down into the valley, he slumps heavily against the city gates. 'The enemy,' he groans, turning to his fellow pilgrims. 'How? How can they have found Madrepore?'

Sergeant Halser curses and snatches his gun from the road. 'I thought you said your prophet kept them blind to this place?'

Frater Gortyn clutches his head in his hands as his brethren begin whining in fear. 'He does. They are.' He pauses and turns his head towards the sergeant. 'Or, at least, they always have been.' His voice becomes a hideous shriek. '*You've* led them to us! How else can this be?'

The other two pilgrims cease their whining and turn around, shaking their heads in shock. 'It's the only explanation,' gasps one of them, pointing at Halser. 'You're in league with the Black Knights. You must be! You've betrayed Astraeus!' He looks up at the faces looking out from the battlements. 'We're betrayed!' he cries, pressing his mouth to the gap opening between the gates.

Halser backs away, keeping his gun trained on the wailing pilgrims. 'How many?' he breathes into his vox-bead, snatching a brief glimpse at the distant line of figures.

Brother Volter is the first to reply, his voice full of disbelief. 'Sergeant, they must have been toying with us. Those small attacks must have been a feint.'

'What do you mean?' snaps Halser, still unable to take his eyes off the raving pilgrims.

'There are hundreds of them, sergeant. I can't even count the–'

The exchange is interrupted by another huge explosion and this time it is much closer. Halser staggers again and the pilgrims launch themselves at him. He moves to shrug them off, but to his fury he feels a blinding pain in his forehead and words echoing beneath his scalp. 'Betrayal!' drone the voices, so loud that Halser cries out in pain.

'Get out of my head!' he roars, but the voices swell in volume, chanting the word 'betrayal' like a prayer as Halser drops, groaning, to his knees.

Blood erupts from his nose as the pilgrims continue their furious assault on his mind. He is vaguely aware that they are also thrashing uselessly against his power armour with their fists, but the external world is quickly slipping away from him as their prayers clamp around his agonised brain.

'Comus,' he manages to gasp as the pain overwhelms him.

Immediately he feels another presence in his thoughts, enveloping the wailing voices and easing the pain in his head. Before the agony has a chance to overpower him again, Halser rises to his feet and fires his bolt pistol, tearing a ragged hole through Frater Gortyn's chest and sending him spinning across the road.

The other two pilgrims scramble for cover but he guns them down too, killing them before they can reach the gate and sending a fan of bright blood across the hammered iron.

Halser spins around and stares back down the road. The mountain looks as though it has sprung a black, glistening leak. Countless ranks of Traitor Marines are flooding down across the foothills and gathering on the road. He sees the gold trim on their spiked power armour, glinting as they charge towards the city.

'The barn!' he cries, waving to a low, stone building at the side of the road near his men. 'Take cover! Volter, buy them time.'

The Relictors finally move with some speed. Two of them lift Comus from his feet and charge from the road with him while the rest dive for cover. At the same time, Brother Volter drops to one knee and brings his lascannon to bear on the approaching hordes. The far end of the road erupts in blue flames as he finds his mark. Tiny, black-clad figures spin into the air and for a moment the advance falters. Before they have chance to return fire, Brother Volter rolls across the road and drops into the roadside ditch.

Seconds later, the road where he knelt explodes like a lake in a hailstorm. Stone and shrapnel whines through the air as the enemy guns tear up the landscape.

As the Black Legion continue to race down the road, the Relictors hunker down by the barn and open fire. The enemy make no attempt to find cover and the air shimmers with the heat of the Relictors' bolter fire.

The evening lights up again as Brother Volter fires a second shot with his lascannon, cutting another great hole in the advancing ranks.

As the wall behind him starts shattering under the enemy fire, Sergeant Halser clamps his helmet into place and looks from his men to the gates behind him. Through the gap he sees a stampede of white-robed figures as the pilgrims empty the streets and rush to defend the walls. 'What can they do?' he wonders aloud. Then he remembers the pain of Frater Gortyn's prayers, clawing at his thoughts.

'Comus,' he snaps, dragging the still cursing Pylcrafte from the ditch. 'I think I have a chance of reaching the scriptorium. The pilgrims will focus their attention on the Traitor Marines. Can you lend me your support if they try and stop me?'

The reply through the vox-bead is a hoarse, indecipherable grunt, but a clearer voice appears in the sergeant's thoughts. 'Be quick. There are too many of them for us to hold.'

'I think you may have help,' replies Halser, watching the pilgrims rushing to man Madrepore's battlements. He turns and addresses Pylcrafte. 'I'm going in. Stay and fight, or help me find the scriptorium.' Then, as the enemy fire grows in ferocity, he leans on one of the iron gates and shoves it back a few more centimetres, allowing himself enough room to squeeze thorough and enter the city.

The sight that greets him is bewildering. At the heart of the city is a huge fortified temple with a thick, hexagonal tower at its centre. Nestled around it are hundreds of other buildings, all constructed of the same, writhing, coral-like rock, and all glittering with rows of crystalline eyes. As the eyes roll and blink, the buildings shimmer, so that the city seems to be undulating with light, and the whole scene is shrouded in vast, drifting columns of moonlit cloud. The storms Halser saw from orbit seem to be emanating from this single point. The combination of glimmering eyes and writhing clouds is overwhelming. It looks as though

Madrepore is carved from shifting, moonlit water.

Halser pauses for a second, trying to see a way through the pulsing clouds and milling, panic-stricken crowds. He hisses into his vox-bead: 'Which way, Comus? What do I do?'

'Head for the centre of the city,' comes a reply in his mind. 'The prophet has built his temple directly over the scriptorium. If anyone knows what happened to its contents, it will be him.' There is a pause, then Comus speaks through the vox-bead, his voice a ragged growl. 'I don't know how long I can keep them out of your head, sergeant.'

Halser nods, but still hesitates, unsure how to proceed through the incredible display. Most of the pilgrims are charging to the walls, but hundreds are also racing down the wide road that leads from the gate to the temple.

'So many of them, and all damned,' mutters a trembling voice at Halser's side and he remembers the inquisitor's acolyte is still with him. Pylcrafte is waving his cane at the shifting clouds, as though he can ward off the corruption surrounding him.

The sergeant turns to speak, but before he can, a huge section of wall explodes just above the gate. The air fills with screams and spinning chunks of masonry and, to Halser's delight, the road ahead clears, as the pilgrims scramble for cover.

'Keep close,' he cries, charging down the road.

As he approaches the temple walls he sees a long building to his left, topped with a huge stone star and crowded with pilgrims. Many of them have stopped to watch him and, even with Comus shielding his thoughts, he starts to feel their furious prayers battering against his mind. He tries to ignore them and focus on reaching the doors to the temple, but as he does so, he stumbles to a halt.

He is back at the city gates, looking down at Pylcrafte.

'So many of them, and all damned,' says the hooded figure, waving his cane.

Halser curses and shakes his head, trying to rid himself

of his confusion. 'What is happening?' he cries. 'I keep seeing the same thing, over and over.'

He hears the voice of Comus in his head again. 'Sergeant. The power of this Astraeus is like nothing I've ever felt. I think time itself is bending to his will.' He pauses. 'Or maybe not even that. It feels almost as though time is collapsing.'

Halser groans in frustration. 'By the Throne, Comus. What are you talking about?'

There is no reply and Halser vents his frustration on the city wall, slamming his armoured fist into the rock and shattering a cluster of blinking eyes. Then he tries again, racing off towards the temple with Pylcrafte stumbling after him, still cursing and muttering into his hood.

BROTHER-LIBRARIAN COMUS LIES bleeding in a ditch. Bolter fire rattles and whines overhead but he is only vaguely aware of it. All his attention is fixed on the small, metal-bound book clutched in his hand. He remembers the first time he handled the xenos device, given to him by Inquisitor Mortmain, all those years ago. It took months of fierce, uninterrupted prayer before he would even consider opening his mind to such unholy, alien sentience. He was sure of his purpose then: to glean what he could whilst keeping his mind intact. But now what does he feel? The thing is killing him, he is sure of that. Every time he allows those luminous characters to flood his mind, he feels a little more of his soul being torn away. Even on a purely psychical level the effect is obvious: he has been bleeding heavily from his nose and mouth since they arrived on Ilissus and, without the aid of his battle-brothers, he can barely stand. However, that is not the worst of it. The thing that fills him with dread is that the libellus no longer feels so alien. It no longer feels wrong. It is becoming part of him. Comus draws himself upright and closes the book with a shudder. What is he becoming?

He turns to the Relictor crouched next to him in the ditch. Brother Borellus has his bolter balanced on the scorched earth and his shoulder is jerking back as he fires round after round down the road, picking off the advancing traitors with medical precision. For a second, Comus cannot recall exactly how they got there.

'Where are the others?' he groans, wiping the blood from his eyes.

Brother Borellus holds fire for a second but does not turn around. 'Brothers Sabine and Thaler are just behind you, further down the ditch. Strasser, Vortimer and Brunman are holed up in the barn, although they've taken some heavy hits. Volter is on the far side of the road.' A note of pride enters his voice. 'His lascannon is giving them pause for thought.' He fires off another few rounds, muttering happily to himself as more of the traitors spin back into the clouds. 'And Sergeant Halser has entered the city, with Inquisitor Mortmain's servant, but...' He looks down at the Librarian briefly, his voice hesitant. '...you know that.'

Comus nods, relieved that Borellus's words make sense. He cannot help but notice, though, that his battle-brother's Low Gothic seems unusually crude and clumsy. He realises, to his horror, that he is comparing it unfavourably to the alien language that has embedded itself in his thoughts. Anger knots his stomach. Why should they have to endure this? Why should they have to prove themselves after so many long centuries of service and so many sacrifices in the Emperor's name? He shakes his head and looks back along the ditch. As Borellus stated, there are another two Relictors crouched behind him firing steadily into the oncoming ranks. Above them, further down the road, rise the walls of Madrepore and its shimmering, hexagonal tower. Prove them wrong, Sergeant Halser, he thinks, grasping one of the religious texts chained to his power armour. Show them what we are worth.

CHAPTER SEVENTEEN

As Inquisitor Mortmain marches through the *Domitus*, he draws the billhook from his belt. The black metal blinks red under the flashing lights as he strides through the corridors, swinging it back and forth, testing the weight of the blade in his hand. Crude script runs down its centre: words too vile for even an inquisitor to study. As he reaches a shattered door he pauses, listening to what he hopes is the sound of vast, thermonuclear weapons powering up. But the ship is shaking so violently he cannot be sure if he is hearing the result of his orders or the sound of the approaching daemon.

'Cerbalus,' he breathes, wondering if he has the strength to face the coming encounter. He is an old man, and all the faith in the galaxy cannot match the fury of youth. The officers on the bridge have their orders and they will work fast, but he will still need to buy them time. The inquisitor casts his mind back through the decades to the day he bound Cerbalus to his will. On the scorched earth of Azoras he and his brothers faced the monster down, armed with powerful, ancient wards and a bitter chorus of litanies. But the cabal that saved Azoras is no more. Inquisitors Medeon, Orium and Shaaraim are long dead. This time he must face the beast alone. Even his old friend Sergeant Halser will soon be gone: torn apart by a firestorm of Mortmain's own creation.

Mortmain looks down at the capital 'I' emblazoned across his breastplate. Youth is gone. Friendship is gone. Faith will have to suffice. He kicks the broken door, scattering the blackened metal across the heaving corridor and strides into the next chamber. He enters a pillar-lined cloister, so wide and tall it seems as though he has stepped out into a stormy, summer's evening. The air is cloying, thick and sulphurous. Ancient, beautiful mosaics are tumbling from the walls, exploding across the flagstones like brittle, enamelled rain.

At the far end of the central colonnade there is a shape. It is no more than a shadow amongst shadows, but Mortmain knows his prey. Evil seeps from it like smoke. The inquisitor peers through the darkness, straining to make out details, but the shadow shifts and ripples across the floor, liquid and supple.

There is still hope, thinks Mortmain. The idea surprises him, but once loosed from his subconscious it grows in certainty. 'There *is* hope,' he breathes, realising that the daemon is bodiless; it has no host. Its vile presence has been set loose by Justicar Lyctus and his Grey Knights, and without a physical home it will soon be dragged into the immaterium, folded back into the shifting hell that spawned it.

The shadow elongates and drifts down the colonnade, assuming a fixed shape only when it is a few metres away. It adopts the form of a man; or, at least, something resembling a man. It towers over Mortmain, three metres tall and topped by the head of a diseased, slick-feathered carrion crow. As the daemon steps closer, it spreads a pair of ink-black wings and two scrawny arms, delighting in the destruction it has wrought. 'Do you think, master,' it asks in an amiable tone, 'that, after all these years of service, I might request something in return?'

Mortmain gives no reply, stepping sideways between the columns, passing the billhook from hand to hand. He knows his pistol would only feed the thing's strength, but the blade has secrets even Cerbalus does not share.

'Come now,' laughs the daemon. 'Is it so much to ask?' Its form breaks apart and reassembles itself behind Mortmain, causing him to whirl around and adopt a fighting stance. 'Think of the squalid deeds I have performed at your request. Think of the blood on my hands that should have been on yours. Surely I deserve a little thanks? A little recompense?'

Mortmain backs carefully away. There *is* hope, he thinks again as he notices an edge to the daemon's voice. Despite its attempt to sound calm, he senses an undercurrent of emotion. Decades of interrogation have honed his senses until he can discern even the subtlest hints of fear, or anger. As he circles the daemon, Mortmain realises that he has one final weapon: the daemon hates him, hates him with a passion that could even blind it to anything else.

'You think I would let your vile presence pollute the body of an Imperial inquisitor?' Mortmain's voice is as calm and even as the daemon's. Suddenly he feels as though his entire life has been building to this moment, this single test of his will. Can he keep the daemon distracted long enough for the crew to launch the attack on Ilissus? Can he play one final trick on a servant of the greatest trickster of them all? 'Try me, Cerbalus!' he roars, relishing the look of shock in the daemon's avian eyes. 'I will take you down, daemon! Send you back to the pit you crawled out of!'

Cerbalus's huge, ragged wings droop and it tilts its head to one side, surprised to find the old man in such a defiant mood.

Before the daemon has chance to reply, Mortmain snaps a syllable so coarse and guttural he has to spit it out with a grimace. As he speaks, the first of the glyphs carved into his billhook blazes with light and he attacks with surprising speed, slashing the blade through the daemon's leg before it has chance to recoil.

Cerbalus screeches. The sound slices through the cacophony, shrill and hideous as it echoes around the towering columns. 'How?' it whines, scrabbling back into the darkness, tearing up flagstones with its clawed feet.

'How?' cries Mortmain. 'How can I hurt you like that?' He swings the billhook from side to side, flinging inky blood into the shadows as he advances on the huge, cowering shape. The first character on the blade is still aflame with the force of his oath, and as he advances he spits out another contorted syllable. As the sound leaves his lips, a second glyph pulses into life and Mortmain leaps forwards, hacking another chunk out of the daemon's leg.

Cerbalus wails in pain and shock and, with a beat of its enormous wings, hurls itself up towards the distant, ribbed vaults of the ceiling.

'Your name, daemon!' Mortmain's voice is a deep, victorious howl. 'I did not share everything with you! Do you think I have been idle all these long decades? Do you think I never foresaw this moment?' The inquisitor climbs on the shattered stump of a marble column and levels the billhook at the shape hovering overhead. 'Face me, abomination! Or are you afraid?'

Cerbalus swoops across the chamber and wraps its shifting form around one of the pillars, several metres above Mortmain. At the word 'afraid' its bird-like head snaps around and glares at the inquisitor. 'Afraid?' it screeches. Its rage is so great that its form shifts through dozens of shapes, trembling and flickering in and out of view. 'You are nothing! You are the lapdog of a puppet corpse. How can you even look at me? You are an insect!'

The lights in the chamber dim as a grinding, deafening hum rumbles through the walls.

The daemon snaps its head in the other direction, peering at the broken door. 'You have already begun,' it whispers. 'Exterminatus.'

The chamber lurches to one side and Mortmain is forced to grab a pillar to steady himself. 'Go, then, daemon,' he cries. 'You will find nothing but pain here.'

Cerbalus looks back at the inquisitor, its eyes full of dark fire. 'What would you know of pain?' The daemon launches itself from the pillar, ripples through the darkness and materialises next to Mortmain.

Before the inquisitor can raise his billhook, a ragged, filthy claw slices through his leather cloak and sends him flying across the room in a spray of blood. He slams into a pillar with a howl of pain and scrambles away into the darkness, cursing under his breath.

Cerbalus spins on the spot, spreading its wings and arching its long neck as it laughs with pleasure, forgetting everything but the ecstasy of revenge.

Mortmain staggers from pillar to pillar, his head spinning. Once he reaches the far side of the chamber he pulls back the shreds of his cloak to reveal an arm that is equally torn. His left bicep is completely ruined, hanging from his tattered flesh like raw steak. As the daemon continues spinning through the shadows, laughing to itself, Mortmain tears a strip of leather from his cloak and ties a quick tourniquet. He still has the glowing billhook in his right hand, and as he taps it against his breastplate he is relieved to feel that it is still intact. Without the prayers and sigils worked into its ornate metal, the mere presence of the daemon would split his mind as thoroughly as his ruined arm.

Suddenly the laughter is right next to him, but this time Mortmain is ready. He rolls clear of the daemon's claws and chants a third, potent syllable, lighting up another character on his weapon.

Cerbalus cringes at the sound, but before it can withdraw its claw, Mortmain chops down with the billhook, slicing another piece of the daemon and causing it to screech in pain and frustration.

This time it does not flee, though. Before Mortmain can draw breath for another letter, the daemon stoops low over him and a talon rips open his thigh, sending him toppling to the ground. The pain is like nothing he has ever experienced but, as he slams onto the floor, he manages to gasp another syllable and lash out with the billhook.

Cerbalus croaks and gurgles as the blade rips open its throat.

By now the inquisitor's black weapon is alive with flaming characters. 'I have your name!' howls Mortmain, attempting to disguise the lie by screaming it with all the force he can muster. 'I will banish you, Cerbalus! You have no place here!'

The daemon's twisted, stooping form backs away from him, clutching at the wound in its throat, unable to comprehend how the inquisitor's weapon could sever flesh that does not even exist. 'My name? How could you?'

The lights dip again as another deafening rumble fills the chamber.

Almost there, thinks Mortmain. Just a few more minutes.

The daemon looks at the doorway, its head twitching with indecision. It looks in the direction of the *Domitus's* bridge, then back at the gore-splattered man writhing at its feet. It peers suspiciously at the short, curved blade pulsing in Mortmain's grip, trying to make out the characters that have yet to ignite. 'You do not have the power to wield such a thing. If my name were really held in that piece of metal it would tear your mind open.'

Knowing that he only has to maintain the lie for a few more minutes, Mortmain screams another syllable and attempts to stab Cerbalus again.

The daemon beats its wings and disappears.

Mortmain's broken body floods with adrenaline at the thought that the daemon has given up on him and made for the bridge. Then he sees it reappear, crouched like a gargoyle on the broken pillar where he was standing a few minutes earlier.

'My flesh is not for one such as you!' he cries, spraying blood across his breasplate. He tries to stand, but his leg collapses beneath him and he sprawls across the flagstones like a drunk. 'Try me, Cerbalus. Just a few more characters and you will be in my power once more.'

Cerbalus lets out a scream that even drowns out the

klaxons. It launches itself from the pillar, smashing head-long into the inquisitor and sending them both tumbling across the bloody flagstones.

As they roll, Mortmain continues crying out the foul syllables and hacking into the daemon's shifting flesh, even as Cerbalus's frenzied claws tear his body apart.

Finally, they come to a halt against the feet of a statue and Mortmain begins to laugh.

'You are mine!' screams the daemon, lifting the inquisitor up into the air by the throat and shaking him like a broken toy.

Mortmain continues to laugh even as his innards spill to the floor. The chamber is shaking more violently than ever as the *Domitus's* weapons silos finally launch their missiles at Ilissus.

'Perhaps you will have me after all, Cerbalus,' he laughs, vaguely aware that silver-clad figures are emerging from the shadows, their weapons trained on the daemon. 'But you will never have Ilissus.'

Far below, the planet's surface flashes red, then purple, then a beautiful opalescent white as it begins to die.

CHAPTER EIGHTEEN

THE TEMPLE OF Astraeus is the grandest of follies. As Halser races through the great hall its walls swoop and bulge around him like the sails of a ship. Every inch of the place – floor, ceiling and walls – is studded with thousands of eyes, all of which follow the sergeant as he pounds towards the archway at the far end. The windows have been constructed in such a way that stars appear to hang in the air, and the dervish-like eddies of dust and cloud are even more fierce inside the building: waltzing and swaying like dancers across the floor, merging seamlessly with the undulating walls. It seems to Halser that he has been cut adrift in the heavens, and as he runs he weaves drunkenly from side to side, disorientated by the extraordinary display.

'Heresy!' whines Pylcrafte, stumbling after him and firing shots at the walls with his laspistol, shattering as many of the blinking eyes as he can. 'Heresy, heresy, heresy, heresy, heresy!' He has his cane in his other hand and he tries to stab the rolling clouds, hacking and lunging like a deranged swordsman.

Halser ignores him and keeps running towards the archway.

'He's going to unfetter us.' Comus's pain is clear to Halser, even over the vox. 'Whatever he's doing, it's going to unhinge time.'

'I don't understand!' cries Halser, reaching the archway and leaning against the stone to catch his breath.

'Ilissus is heading towards some kind of time loop. Maybe even the whole sector. Whoever this prophet is, you need to stop him.' There is an uncharacteristic note of fear in the Librarian's voice. 'You have to kill him, sergeant. The Black Legion want him to succeed. They have only attacked now to stop us hindering him. They could have struck at any time. He is *dangerous*, Halser. More than I guessed. Maybe he doesn't even realise it himself.'

Halser shakes his head and stumbles into the next chamber. 'A time loop? I don't understand.' The room he has entered is a vast, glass-roofed atrium, surrounding the hexagonal tower at the heart of the temple. Most of the pilgrims have fled to the walls to launch whatever strange defence they can manage, but a few are leaving the tower as Halser approaches. They drop to their knees and start screaming, horrified by his presence in their inner sanctum. The sergeant gasps and reels backwards. Their screamed prayers fill his head like a sickness. The pain snatches his breath and he stumbles, gasping inside his helmet, unable to breathe. He drops to his knees, feeling unconsciousness looming. Before he blacks out, he fires his bolt pistol. The shots are wild and frenzied, but one of the pilgrims crumples to the floor and the pain lessens. Feeling stronger, Halser manages to stand and fire off a few more shots. The pilgrims make no attempt to flee and it takes seconds to kill them. Then he staggers on, feeling his mouth filling with blood.

Pylcrafte staggers after him, waving his cane at nothing as he goes, trying to strike the prayers that fill the air.

Halser does not pause as he passes the pilgrims' corpses and enters the tower. He sees a wide, serpentine, spiral staircase and begins to climb. His mind is numb with pain. He can barely remember his purpose, beyond a fierce drive to reach the architect who summoned this nightmarish temple into being. As he climbs the stairs more of the pilgrims launch attacks on his mind, but he guns them down without even pausing, haunted by Comus's ominous term: 'time loop'.

'PULL BACK TO the city!' cries Comus, staggering through the shrapnel and smoke, and pointing his force sword at the walls of Madrepore. 'We have to buy Halser some time. We can hold them at the gates!'

The barn has become a smouldering crater. Brothers Strasser, Vortimer and Brunman are dead. The remnants of their power armour is scattered throughout the rubble, torn open by the enemy's heavy artillery. There are five Relictors left to make the run. Brothers Sabine and Thaler help Comus while Borellus and Volter give them covering fire.

After a few minutes, Volter lowers his lascannon and races down the road after them, but Borellus remains crouched in a ditch, firing blast after blast with his bolter.

'Borellus!' snaps Comus as he reaches the relative safety of the city. 'Move!'

Brother Borellus shakes his head and continues firing.

Volter reaches the gates and rolls clear as a storm of bolter fire follows him into the city.

Comus jerks to one side as a hole explodes in the wall next to him. Then he peers briefly through it and sees that Borellus is still in the ditch, firing as calmly as ever, despite the fact that the enemy ranks are almost on him.

'Borellus,' he repeats, but there is no command in his voice now, only respect.

Borellus nods calmly in reply, then vanishes from view as the black-clad figures swarm over the ditch.

Comus hears a brief cough of pain over the vox as the Traitor Marines tear Borellus apart, and he lowers his head in prayer. Then he looks around the city. Hundreds, if not thousands of pilgrims are gathered on the city walls. He can feel the weight of their prayers as they try to repel the attacking army. And he can also feel their panic as they realise their words are having no effect.

'They could have killed you at any time,' he mutters, his voice full of disgust. 'But they wanted your prophet to complete his work as much as you did.' Then he notices a low, flat-roofed building to the left of the gates, with thick walls and small windows. He waves his force sword at the building and staggers towards it, ignoring the sound of enemy fire pulverising the city walls.

The other three Relictors sprint after him.

BY THE TIME Halser reaches the top of the stairs his mind is like that of an animal closing in on its prey, blind to everything but the chase. The City of Stars is collapsing but all he can think of is the prophet. He can barely remember why, but he knows he must stop Astraeus, even if it means his life.

Ahead of him is a tall, white door, studded with the same rolling eyes that line the walls. He pauses for a second and looks at them; blue, grey and brown irises look back, filled with terror and hate. *Hate.* Suddenly Halser remembers something other than the prophet of Ilissus. He remembers every doubt, rumour and lie that has been levelled at his beloved Chapter. An involuntary growl rolls deep in his chest and he shoves the door open, entering the central chamber.

The scene that greets him is strange enough to halt him in his steps. Pilgrims line the walls, kneeling in the five corners of a room built in the shape of a star, and the object of their genuflection is even more peculiar than they are. The man that Halser assumes is the prophet is as tall as a Space Marine, but where Halser is an armour-clad hulk of muscle, the prophet is a grey, emaciated wraith of a man, draped in voluminous black robes that hide most of his skeletal frame. His flesh is the colour of rain clouds and his limbs and hands are oddly elongated. The fingers clutching the arms of his ornate throne resemble pale spider's legs; they are also webbed, like those of a lizard and end in long, crimson talons. Strangest of all is his head. It is swollen to three times the size of a normal skull and it is contained within a spherical, liquid-filled bowl. His eyes are barely visible behind thick, tinted goggles that also cover most of his forehead, and his pallid skull is pierced by a forest of thick wires that emerge from the glass helmet and connect to a bewildering collection of measuring devices: brass sextants, compasses and spinning, ticking depth gauges are all piled on the glass bowl like a rusty crown.

Despite everything he has seen on Ilissus, the sight of the prophet leaves Halser speechless. Everything strange about the planet clearly emanates from this one, bizarre figure. The coils of cloud that spread from the temple to the heavens are all trailing from his swollen, smiling face.

It takes Pylcrafte, stumbling into the room a few moments later, to state the undeniable truth. 'You–you're a Navigator,' he stammers, as his nest of cables snake from his hood to focus on the prophet.

Astraeus smiles, eliciting a chorus of sighs from his subjects. 'I used to be.' His voice sounds odd and distant, muffled by the liquid in his helmet, and as he speaks the air in the chamber ripples like heat haze. 'I was once Iarbonel van Tol, the first son of Baron Cornelius van Tol. But that was a long time ago, and I have a suspicion I might have been disinherited. The Emperor has a better name for me now, though, and a far greater purpose.' He fixes his gaze on Halser. As the light in the chamber swells, his eyes become visible behind the lenses of his goggles.

Halser forgets his purpose for a moment, hypnotised by the prophet's stare, then he shakes his head and recalls the words of Comus. 'What are you doing here?' he snaps, waving his gun at the rolling clouds and the banks of eyes. 'What sorcery is this?'

The prophet's smile falters. He frowns, clearly surprised by the accusation of sorcery. 'I have watched you from afar, Space Marine,' he says. 'I thought you at least would understand.'

Halser continues shaking his head, too confused to answer.

'When the Emperor cast me down onto Ilissus I thought He had abandoned me.' The prophet waves at the ceiling. 'My beloved ship was utterly destroyed.'

Halser looks up and notices Imperial designs, warped into the strange architecture, as though the whole place has been grown from the carcass of a battleship.

'My injuries were horrendous,' he turns his head slightly revealing the signs of crude, brutal surgery on the back of his skull, 'but my children kept me safe.' He smiles at the adoring pilgrims. 'Over time, I realised the damage to my brain had untapped my true potential. That is all you are seeing here, sergeant: the *true* potential of a loyal subject.' He flexes his fingers and the air ripples visibly, like water. 'Soon I will have the power to crush those who would oppose us.' His voice grows higher in pitch. 'I will be invincible.'

Halser grips his bolt pistol tighter as he remembers his goal. He must stop this deluded monster before he tears the whole galaxy apart with his witchcraft. He raises his gun and mutters a prayer, but before he can fire, the temple lurches to one side.

The pilgrims' prayers become a scream of terror as the walls start to bulge and sag.

'It is beginning,' smiles the prophet, leaning his head forwards so that the glass bowl touches Halser's gun with a *clink*. 'Your friends have sent you to your death. They want us to die together.'

Halser gasps. 'You're a liar!' he cries, but as he speaks he recognises the scale of the explosions. He snatches the chronograph at his belt. 'I still have time!' He looks at the crumbling walls in disbelief. 'Mortmain would not do this to me!'

The prophet nods. 'They fear courage more than anything. My own father has sent them to kill me. And you...' He pauses. 'They sent you here to die, my friend. Your death, by my side, will be their final proof. Now they will speak openly the word they have long whispered against you: heretic.'

EYE OF TERROR CONTAINMENT

FORCE DISPOSITIONS

COMPILER'S NOTE: This is a partial list of the Imperial military strength forming the containment force around the *Occularis Terribus*. Communications difficulties and the secrecy of some Adeptus Astartes Chapters mean that this should be considered little more than conjecture.

ADEPTUS ASTARTES
'PRAESES' CHAPTERS

These are the Space Marine Chapters founded to guard the regions surrounding the Eye of Terror. The entire strength of each of these Chapters is devoted to this purpose.

ANGELS ERADICANT	+++DATA CORRUPTED+++
BLACK CONSULS*	MARINES EXEMPLAR
BROTHERS PENITENT	NIGHT WATCH
CRIMSON SCYTHES	RELICTORS
+++DATA CORRUPTED+++	+++DATA CORRUPTED+++
EXCORIATORS	SUBJUGATORS
+++DATA CORRUPTED+++	+++DATA CORRUPTED+++
+++DATA CORRUPTED+++	+++DATA CORRUPTED+++
IRON TALONS	VIPER LEGION
KNIGHTS UNYIELDING	WHITE CONSULS

*Reported destroyed 455.M41. Current status unknown.

OTHER ADEPTUS ASTARTES

BLOOD SWORDS	(8 Companies)	IMPERIAL FISTS	(4 Companies)
BRAZEN CLAWS	(6 Companies)	IRON HANDS	(3 Clans)
DARK ANGELS	(+UNKNOWN+)	IRON KNIGHTS	(4 Companies)
DARK SONS	(7 Companies)	STAR DRAGONS	(5 Companies)
DOOM EAGLES	(5 Companies)	SPACE WOLVES	(1 Great Company)
EXORCISTS	(4 Companies)	WHITE TEMPLARS	(2 Companies)

++CONTINUED IN FILE RTB01++

NOTABLE IMPERIAL GUARD UNITS

BAR-EL PENAL LEGIONS	(4 Legions)	DROOKIAN FEN GUARD	(12 Companies)
CADIAN KASRKIN	(486 Companies)	GUDRUNITE RIFLES	(47 Regiments)
CADIAN SHOCK TROOPS	(612 Regiments)	KNOVIAN GHARKAS	(14 Regiments)

++CONTINUED IN FILE RIG86++

INQUISITORIAL TASK FORCES

+++CLASSIFIED. Insufficient clearance to access files.+++
+++Access attempt has been reported to Adeptus Arbites precinct 27/alpha/332/gold.+++

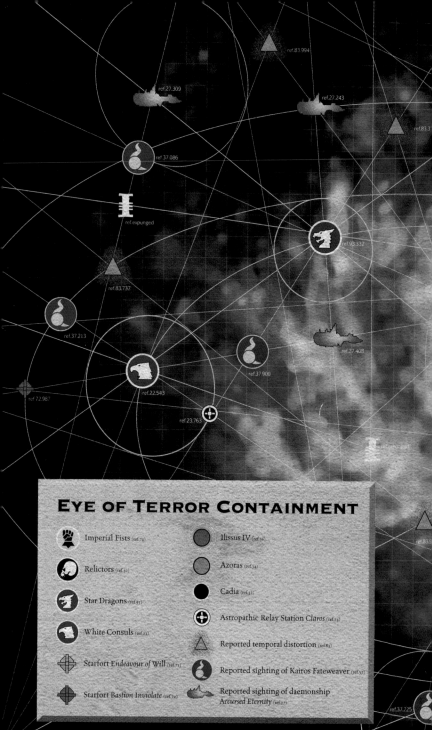

ref.83.994

ref.27.309

ref.27.243

ref.83.3

ref.37.086

ref.expunged

ref.93.332

ref.83.737

ref.37.213

ref.27.408

ref.37.900

ref.72.987

ref.22.543

ref.23.763

ref.83.5

ref.37.725

EYE OF TERROR CONTAINMENT

Imperial Fists (ref.74)

Relictors (ref.52)

Star Dragons (ref.93)

White Consuls (ref.11)

Starfort *Endeavour of Will* (ref.71)

Starfort *Bastion Inviolate* (ref.74)

Ilissus IV (ref.36)

Azoras (ref.34)

Cadia (ref.32)

Astropathic Relay Station *Claros* (ref.23)

Reported temporal distortion (ref.83)

Reported sighting of Kairos Fateweaver (ref.37)

Reported sighting of daemonship *Accursed Eternity* (ref.27)

ref.27.102

ref.expunged

ref.37.453

ref.71.274

ref.83.226

ref.27.410

ref.27.032

ref.37.556

ref.83.624

ref.52.745

ref.expunged

ref.32.936

ref.36.066

ref.27.903

ref.83.273

ref.27.202

ref.34.294

ref.expunged

ref.74.863

ref.27.455

ref.37.482

ref.83.634

ref.83.587

MADREPORE : CITY OF STAR

A TEMPLE OF ASTRAEUS
B CENTRAL KEEP
C CATHEDRAL
D DORMITORIES
E CLOISTER
F LIVESTOCK
G INFIRMARY
H HOMESTEADS

N

0 200
metres

I AM BETRAYED, thinks Sergeant Halser. *Betrayed.*

'Comus is down!' howls Brother Volter over the vox. 'Dead, maybe... I–I can't be sure. They've taken the infirmary. I'm pulling back. What are your orders? Sergeant?' His voice is broken, his words half-buried beneath the sound of artillery. 'Are you there? Sergeant Halser?'

Halser keeps his gun pressed to the prophet's head and gives no reply. The pilgrims scream at him from the shadows, but he keeps his gaze fixed on a pair of grotesque, fathomless eyes.

The prophet stares back.

Halser places his finger on the trigger.

'I can save both of us,' says the prophet. His head lolls inside his bowl-shaped helmet, suspended by a pale, thin neck and a gloop of viscous liquid. The solution distorts his voice, but he tries to contort his vowels into something more human, enunciating each word carefully as though speaking to a child. He points a long, webbed finger at the man in the doorway. 'They've lied to you. They have murdered us both. They knew *exactly*

DARIUS HINKS

what would happen. They have *always* known.'

Halser follows his gaze and sees to his horror that Gideon Pylcrafte is laughing. No mouth is visible beneath his black hood, just a quivering mass of cables, but his amusement is clear. Halser's resolve evaporates. His hand falters. If Pylcrafte saw this coming, the whole mission was a lie. Halser tries to marshal his thoughts. He tries to pray, but the sound of Brother Volter's pain knifes into him, merged with the wailing of the pilgrims. The artillery grows louder until it seems the whole valley is groaning. The noise is unbearable and too loud to be just heavy guns. As the blasts ring around his head, Halser is forced to accept the truth.

The orbital bombardment *has* already begun.

Without Comus's protection, his mind edges quickly towards collapse. The temporal distortion has reached its zenith and the pilgrims' voices claw at his thoughts like blades across metal. He cannot be sure what is now and what was then. Simultaneously, he is leading the squad through the catacombs, slaughtering the pilgrims at the city gates and reaching the inner temple, but he knows that has already been. He stares deeper into the prophet's misshapen eyes, trying to anchor himself.

'Comus is down!' howls Brother Volter over the vox. 'Dead, maybe... I–I can't be sure. They've taken the infirmary. I'm pulling back. What are your orders? Sergeant?'

Halser curses and looks back at the doorway. Time is collapsing. He has heard those words before, but how many times?

'I will *not* let you live,' he snaps, turning back to the prophet. The metallic ring of his amplified voice booms around the chamber. 'You're an abomination.'

The prophet's bloated skull drifts to one side and splits open in a grin. 'You have a ship and I have vision. The clouds are no barrier to me.' He waves at Pylcrafte. 'He's wronged us both. Why should we accept our fate? We are the elect few. We have great work ahead of us. Great deeds.'

Halser shakes his head, but there is doubt kindling in his

eyes. To shoot the prophet means death. Worse than that, it means failure. But what is the alternative? After everything he has seen, how could he let such a man live?

The prophet brushes his elongated fingers against Halser's power armour. They trace around a filigreed skull and he narrows his eyes. 'Why did you come to Madrepore, *Relictor*?'

The chamber lurches and the ground shifts. The enemy fire is closing in. Centuries-old marble tumbles from the vaulted ceiling. Ten-metre eagles splinter and crack, covering the floor with vast, broken wings.

'Behold, the immutable will of the Emperor!' cries Pylcrafte from the doorway, raising his voice over the cacophony. 'You're a proud fool, Sergeant Halser. This is all on your head. This is the price you pay for all your lowly, creeping misbelief and your repeated use of xenos–'

Halser silences him with a shot to the head. The blast echoes around the chamber and Pylcrafte crumples in a plume of blood. The cables in his hood twitch for a few seconds longer, then he lies still.

Halser turns away and presses his bolt pistol back against the prophet's helmet. 'You're a mutant.'

'And what are you, Relictor?' The prophet's glass helmet is now splattered with Pylcrafte's blood but his voice remains defiant. He waves at the network of passageways that lead off from his throne room. 'There are weapons here. Weapons we could *use*.' His voice grows softer. 'They lied to you, Relictor. All of them. Your fidelity is misplaced, don't you see?'

Halser grimaces as the agonised chorus grows louder: Brother Volter's desperate requests for orders, the chanting of the pilgrims, the groaning of the earth, the pounding of the guns. But worse than the noise is the doubt. How could Mortmain have tricked him? As the question torments Halser, the doubt turns to rage. Even his oldest friend does not believe in him, does not believe in his Chapter. He and his men have been sent to their deaths. Perhaps the braver act would be to listen to the prophet?

'I will prove you wrong, Mortmain,' he spits. 'I will make you *pay.*'

As his fury grows, the déjà vu becomes unbearable. The prophet's words loop around the chamber, growing louder with each repetition. Halser's indecision grows and lights blossom in his head, merging with the crystals in the walls and the glyphs rolling across his visor. He sees a corona of sunlight around Ilissus, shimmering like spun gold as he breaks orbit and drops down into the storm.

ENDEAVOUR OF WILL

BEN COUNTER

PART 1

LOCHOS WAS A beautiful city.

Steel spires burned silver in the sun of Olympia. Rivers of mercury ran through the streets, winding between the forges and the temples of that warrior-world's oldest ancestors. Minarets and steeples competed to reach the sky. Mosaiced streets glittered and hearth-fires glowed deep red in the shadows between the foundries. From mountainside to seashore the city stretched, encompassing a thousand generations of Olympia's past, and a million dreams of her future.

Statues of mighty armoured men of war stood atop every important building. The new gods of Lochos, the icons of a pious world, they were emblematic of the new galaxy and the Great Crusade that was to unite it. They were exemplars of what humanity could one day become. They were the Iron Warriors.

This was the sight that beamed down on Shon'tu as he knelt upon the sacrificial stone. The warsmith had never knelt to any man, but he knelt now, because it was in deference to something more than a man. The vision of Lochos, the lost capital of Olympia, filled him with something that might have been emotion. He could not properly remember it, because it had been ten thousand years since he had last felt joy, or sadness, or anything so petty as that. Iron within, he had told himself then. Iron without. Never again will there be anything in this soul but the iron of purpose and the steel of fury.

Perhaps it was regret he felt. It might have been longing that flickered across Shon'tu's barely-human features, the few fleshy parts of his face almost crowded out by the steel jaw and the studded metal cranium. The man that later became Shon'tu had been born in Lochos. That man's memory remained in Shon'tu. He remembered when he left it to join the Great Crusade of the wretch he would later know as the False Emperor, the Corpse-God. He remembered when he returned. He remembered when it fell.

Lochos was dead. Olympia was dead. But its spirit still lived.

'I kneel,' said Shon'tu.

'Stand,' replied the Spirit of Lochos.

Shon'tu stood up, armour clanking and whining, letting off jets of steam from its archaic motors. The Spirit of Lochos filled the whole ritual chamber, giving the impression that the chamber carried on for dozens of miles in every direction. In truth it was a small patch of holy ground set aside within the confines of the *Ferrous Malice*, consecrated with battlefield trophies offered up by the Iron Warriors. The ship was a relic of a previous age, pitted and scarred by the millennia, as gnarled and vicious as the Iron Warriors who rode in it. It was more than a machine or a weapon – it was cruel and self-aware like an animal trained to attack. Every piece of it was consecrated in battle, but the ritual chamber had been set aside solely for Shon'tu. The sacrificial stone was one pried from the streets of Lochos and bathed in the blood of its people long ago. Shon'tu had poured his own blood – though little enough remained in his body – onto it.

'I was born in the streets of your city,' continued the Spirit. 'My birth pangs were the screams of its people. In the deeds of the Iron Warriors alone I live on. To you alone I grant my presence.'

'The dying words of a hundred oracles brought us here,' said Shon'tu, 'to this place beside the Eye of Terror. They spoke of havoc and bloodshed to be wrought.'

'They did not lie, warsmith.'

'Then how shall we find it?'

Battles were raging in the streets of Lochos now. Citizens and soldiers facing the Space Marines of the Iron Warriors. Each Warrior was like a walking bastion, invulnerable to the fire and blades of his enemies, blazing death from his guns. The Purging of Lochos was a time of horror and betrayal, but it was also the time when the Iron Warriors had realised the weakness of the Emperor and his new order. It was the birth of Shon'tu's Legion, a sacred time, a forging in fire. The vision of the city reddened as the streets ran with blood.

'The Eye has opened,' said the Spirit, 'and Chaos pours forth. Many of the Corpse-God's lackeys are isolated and alone, though they do not yet know it. Two star forts guard a gateway into the Eye. The *Bastion Inviolate* and the *Endeavour of Will*. If they are attacked, there are none to help them save a few. Their loss will strike a grievous blow, for deprived of them the Imperium will not recapture the region without a crusade of a magnitude beyond its capacity to mount. But this concerns you less than those who hold them now.'

'Who?' said Shon'tu.

The bodies were being heaped up now in the squares and crossroads of Lochos. Good men and women, portrayed as rebels and traitors by the Emperor, whose deaths were demanded to prove the loyalty of the Iron Warriors. Instead, the betrayal compelled loyalty only to the powers of the warp, the Gods of Chaos, of whom the Spirit of Lochos was a messenger.

'The Sons of Dorn,' replied the Spirit of Lochos. 'The Imperial Fists.'

Warsmith Shon'tu was silent for a moment, watching the carnage in the city. He remembered being there. He remembered taking part in it. Somewhere he was there in the vision, striding from house to house, killing everything that dared move. The same bolter that hung at his waist had shed blood that day. The same combat knife sheathed on his chest. The same hands.

Then, Warsmith Shon'tu began to laugh.

'IT'S THE FERROUS MALICE.'

The man who had spoken, Cartographer Skune, was dwarfed by the Space Marines who stood beside him. In the gloom of the *Bastion Inviolate's* command deck, wearing the golden armour of his Chapter, Castellan Lepidus looked more like a statue carved from amber than anything that had once been a man.

'You are certain?' said Lepidus.

'As certain as can be,' replied the Cartographer. His rank was high among the unaugmented humans who crewed the star fort, but his deference to the Space Marine was clear. He could not look Lepidus in the eye, as if Lepidus were some holy relic and Skune's eyes were unworthy to look upon him. 'The ship profile is very old and somewhat corrupt, but the correlation is clear.'

Lepidus stood at the head of the command table, which took up the centre of the deck. The deck resembled the interior of a castle on some feudal-level world, with shields and swords hung on the stone-clad walls beside tapestries of the star fort's battles, the holo-projectors and station controls hidden within the huge hardwood table. Around the edge of the chamber sat the crew, their dark blue uniforms and golden fist emblems marking them out as unaugmented men and women who served the Imperial Fists Chapter.

'Prepare the machine-spirit for war and bring all weapons on-line,' said Lepidus. A smile crept onto his face. 'And alert the astropath. Send a communication to Strike Fleet Helios informing them of our position. Include a note for Captain Lysander. Let him know that if he is quick, he might have the chance to pick over the corpses we shall leave in our wake.'

Castellan Lepidus had earned his role in command of the *Bastion Inviolate* with several episodes of intense violence levelled against the Chapter's foes. His armour was in the form of a fortress, the ceramite collar worked into ornate battlements and his greaves buttressed like foundations. It was hung with trophies of the enemies whose lives he had taken – ears from a greenskin warlord, delicate wraithbone trinkets from a farseer of the eldar, teeth and vertebrae from a host of malformed aliens. He clapped a fist to his chestplate.

'I have a space kept here,' he said, 'for a part of the heretic who helms the *Ferrous Malice*. Many of us have sworn to take him down, and I shall be the one to keep that oath. Some finger or jawbone, a rib or a hand, it does not matter! Some piece of Warsmith Shon'tu shall hang here.' He turned to the crew already working at the various command helms, bringing up the many weapons systems of the star fort. 'Rejoice, you sons and daughters of mankind! This day you shall serve your Emperor by giving him the head of an Iron Warrior! The head of Shon'tu!'

DEEP IN THE heart of the star fort, infernally hot and lit by the winking green lights that studded the menhirs of black datamedium, Techmarine Korgon waited for the machine-spirit of the *Bastion Inviolate* to unfurl. The intelligence was encoded in the millions of sheets of datamedium, untold trillions of calculations in every fraction of a second weaving together to create a sentience as old as the Imperium. Forged in the age before the Emperor had united humanity, the *Bastion Inviolate* had accumulated more battle-wisdom than a whole Chapter of Space Marines could boast.

From a well lined with black crystal a swarm of flickering motes rose, glowing blue and green. They coalesced into a shape that could have represented something alive, perhaps a serpent squirming in knots or a colony of polyps. Or it could have been an expression of something mathematical, a fractal constantly splitting and turning in on itself.

'Bastion!' called out Techmarine Korgon. 'We are at war!'

'Who,' demanded the machine-spirit, 'is the enemy?' Its synthesised voice filled the datacore of the *Bastion Inviolate*. The spirit was known to be curt and crude, constantly angry about something.

'The Iron Warriors,' replied the Techmarine. The servo-arm on his armour's backpack inserted a dataprobe into a socket on the crystal wall behind Korgon, inputting the data the star fort's sensorium had collected on the enemy ship. 'The *Ferrous Malice*, known to be the flagship of Warsmith Shon'tu. Less than half an hour ago it emerged into real space within striking distance of us.'

'Filth-licking dogs!' spat the machine-spirit. 'Would that I had hands to wring their necks! Would that I had bowels that I might void them on their corpses!'

There was a reason Techmarine Korgon tended to converse with the machine-spirit alone. He was used to its temperament, but the same could not be said of the other Imperial Fists and Chapter crew who staffed the *Bastion Inviolate*. 'You echo our own sentiments,' he said. 'The *Ferrous Malice* is a Castigation-class grand cruiser and is a formidable foe. We ask that you lend your wisdom to the battle sure to come.'

'My wisdom?' snapped the machine-spirit. 'Wisdom counts for nothing against such a foe! No, it is hatred that will count! Rage! They stew in their filth and imagine our heads on spikes. But I'll split their hull open with my lance fire and turn them into frozen mist! My servitors will string their entrails on my battlements! Whatever foetid data festers in their systems, I'll delete it zero by one and scrape that ship bare! Long ago the *Ferrous Malice* opened its machine-spirit up to traitors and daemons! Whatever's left, I'll kill. You'll be lucky if there are any Iron Warriors left on whom to practise your aim.'

'Then I shall cede the primary weapons to you, machine-spirit,' continued Korgon. 'And retain the defensive systems under the command of my crew that you might focus on the enemy. I have ordered them to make ranging shots at–'

'Quiet!' bellowed the machine-spirit. The fractal of light flattened and spread out, the holo-image rippling over the Techmarine's armoured form and up the crystalline walls. 'I can hear them.'

'Hear them?' said Korgon. 'They are still beyond medium sensorium range. We can barely pick up any comms at all.'

'They are here,' said the spirit. 'I can taste them. I can smell their filth! Filling the radio spectrum with their ordure! Flooding the data network with seething rot! Techmarine, this is no physical assault! I am... I am besieged!'

The fractal darkened. Flecks of yellowish light flickered like fireworks in the datacore. A tendril of fractal spilled against the edge of the well, like a weary hand steadying a battered fighter.

'Bastion!' said Korgon in alarm. 'Speak! What ails you?'

'Witchcraft!' spat the machine-spirit. 'Daemon-magic! Flee this place, Techmarine! Flee! These rancid frag-holes, these rot-belching vermin, they have undone me! Ten thousand years, an entire age of Imperium, and now by these cowards I am undone!'

The whole datacore shook. Shards of black crystal fell as the stacks of datamedium fractured. The floor tilted and split, crevasses opening around Korgon's feet.

'What must I do?' shouted Korgon over the din of tearing metal.

'Go! Now! Run! Take my guns and blast them from the void!'

'I cannot leave you! I have my duty!'

'Your duty is the destruction of our foes!'

Tendrils of yellow-green light were writhing through the steel of the deck and the crystal of the datamedium now, like snakes squirming beneath the surface of black ice. Korgon fell, the deck breaking under him, and he grabbed at the shards of metal to keep himself from sliding into the well.

The fractal was shimmering between black and sickly yellow-green, a semblance of tormented features shuddering across it. There was something else in in there with it, too, something dark and sinuous, smoky coils wrapping around the machine-spirit to strangle and constrain it.

Korgon scrabbled to his feet and backed away from the struggle. The daemon-coils snagged around his feet and arms but he broke them, breaking into a run as he headed for the exit that would take him into the maintenance sections of the *Bastion Inviolate*. A hand half composed of greenish light and half seething darkness grabbed the dataprobe on the end of the Techmarine's servo-arm and wrenched it towards one of the datamedium stacks. The probe stabbed into the black crystal and the servo-arm glowed bright as a torrent of data stormed through it.

Korgon's back arched as his muscles convulsed. Bones cracked. His lips peeled back from his teeth and his eyes rolled back, his body shuddering. Foam flecked around his mouth.

'Techmarine!' yelled the machine-spirit. 'My brother!'

Korgon's body deformed under the convulsions of his own muscles. The ceramite of his armour buckled. Where it split, blood flowed.

Where the armour was torn, eyes bulged, veined and filmy, staring madly. Korgon the man disintegrated, replaced with something awful and inhuman.

The machine-spirit of the *Bastion Inviolate* bellowed in anguish and pain. As one the stacks of datamedium shattered, shards of crystal howling on a gale of shredded information. The daemon-shadow slithered over everything and a well of darkness erupted in the heart of the star fort.

DEATH CAME TO the *Bastion Inviolate* beneath a veil of shadow and flesh.

Castellan Lepidus outlived the command deck crew by a handful of seconds. They were asphyxiated as the machine-spirit lost control to the data-daemon and the airlocks and bulkhead doors were slammed open. The air shrieked out of the star fort, dragging many crew with it, kicking out blindly as they were thrown out into the void. Those who held on died in the next moment, blood vessels rupturing, lungs bursting, their blood coughed out into a frozen mist in the sudden cold.

A Space Marine could survive the void for a while. It was not the void that killed Lepidus. It was the face that bulged up from the deck under his feet, its lines carved hard from the steel, huge glassy black eyes unblinking as Lepidus was dragged down into its yawning mouth by hands of data-shadow. The Castellan was drawn into a pit of gnashing blades, the throat of a steel serpent lined with jagged teeth, and swallowed whole by the abomination conjured from the substance of the *Bastion Inviolate*. His shouts of defiance were swallowed by the vacuum and his life winked out as his body was shredded and crushed down there beneath the deck.

The scene was repeated all across the star fort. The fort's small detail of Imperial Fists were ground to paste or impaled on fingernails of steel from hands that unfolded from the machinery around them. Others followed the crew out of the airlocks, tumbling through space, alive for the moment but certain to die as their armour's air supplies ran out. They had the last sight of the *Bastion Inviolate*, of the way its ornate arches and buttresses folded in on themselves to form huge faces, of the enormous filmy eyes that stared from the wounds opening up in the star fort's hull.

As they died, they saw the *Bastion Inviolate* die too. In its place was created something much, much worse.

SOMETIMES, CAPTAIN LYSANDER'S thoughts turned to sacrifice.

The first lesson he had learned as a Space Marine was sacrifice. The man who had begun his training under the Chaplains of the Imperial Fists was long gone now, replaced by someone who was more a legacy, an embodiment of his Chapter, than a human being; but Lysander still remembered what he had learned. In battle, nothing can be won without sacrifice. Be it the expenditure of a single bullet or the death of a whole world, victory had to be paid for somehow.

Sacrifice was foremost in his mind now as he regarded the tactical map of the region surrounding the Eye of Terror. In the immediate vicinity of the Eye, grey icons marked worlds which had been sacrificed to the tide of Chaos that had flooded from the Eye. There were the graveyards of vast armies and planetary populations, billions fallen to the Chaos-worshipping heretics who called themselves the soldiers of the Black Crusade. Prominent battles and naval actions shone bright in the holo-display, all of them marking mass sacrifices to the possibility of victory by Imperial commanders. Some had been successful. Most had not, and the campaign around the Eye was one of containment. The Chaos spearhead had to be blunted. If it burst through in force from the Eye and crashed through the cordons the Imperial Navy had thrown around it, the Black Crusade would make for Terra herself.

That would not happen. The Imperium would sacrifice everything it had to keep it from happening. The Imperial Guardsman or Naval crewman might not understand that. He might equate victory with survival, in the way that the small-minded Imperial citizen had to just to stay sane. But Lysander understood.

Lysander contemplated this in the tactical orrery of the strike cruiser *Siege of Malebruk*. The ship had been sent from Fleet Helios, the Imperial Fists fleet guarding one of the approaches from the Eye. It was all the fleet could spare. Any moment now the fleets of Chaos could approach and force the Imperial Fists to a naval battle. Lysander himself was an asset that the Imperial Fists could ill afford to have anywhere but in the heart of battle – but his task was more important even than to lead his brother Space Marines of Fleet Helios.

His task was to confirm that Warsmith Shon'tu really was dead.

Lysander's vox-link chirped behind his ear.

'Speak,' he said.

'Captain,' came the voice of the ship's commander, Chrystis. 'We are exiting the warp. All indicators green.'

'Contact the *Bastion Inviolate* and the *Endeavour of Will* as soon as we are in real space,' said Lysander. 'Have us battle-ready. The fight will have been joined and may still be going on. We must be ready to lend our guns.'

'Yes, captain,' replied Chrystis. 'Breaching real space now. The Emperor protects.'

The tactical orrery, clad in brass and inscribed with the cogs and stylised enginework of the Adeptus Mechanicus, shuddered as the *Siege* tore through the veil between the warp and reality. For a split-second the architecture of the orrery shifted; impossible angles ghosted across its architecture as reality protested at the intrusion. Then the moment was over and the *Siege* was back in reality.

The holo-display winked out and was replaced, the ship's immediate vicinity being picked out in light. The *Endeavour of Will* was surrounded by flickering icons representing its small garrison of Imperial Fists. A star a handful of light hours away, with dead moonlets and a band of asteroids. Long-defunct explorator platforms.

There was no *Bastion Inviolate*.

'Comms coming in,' came Chrystis's voice over the vox. 'It's garbled. Distress beacons everywhere from the *Endeavour*.'

'What of the *Bastion*?' demanded Lysander.

'Nothing,' said Chrystis. 'We're searching for it. It's not putting out anything, not even static beacons.'

'Find it,' said Lysander.

'Yes, captain. Should we hold position?'

'No,' said Lysander. 'Bring us in to the *Endeavour of Will*.'

DAEMON VIRUS, THE last message had said. In the arcane code of the astropath, it had flickered across from one star fort to the other at the speed of thought. *Witchcraft. Moral threat. We are undone.*

The words ran through Techmarine Hestion's mind as he

241

shouldered his way through the bulkhead door, forging a path through a maintenance passage not built for a Space Marine in armour. From somewhere deep in the engine and power sections of the *Endeavour of Will*, warning klaxons were blaring and synthesised voices were issuing dire warnings in a confused babble of sound.

Hestion pulled himself through a hatch into a vast, cold vault. The arched ceiling high above was obscured with freezing mist, and the polished metal of the walls was caked in ice. The vault housed a roughly spherical mass of archeotech, a biomechanical mass woven together from dozens of human forms, swathed in cabling and steel casings. The machine-spirit of the *Endeavour of Will* was housed here, the rhythms of a hundred human bodies regulating its functions and a hundred human brains containing the architecture of its mind. Just as the servitors that maintained the star fort's systems were built around the bodies of deceased crew, so this machine was composed of the bodies of the various tech-adepts and magi who had maintained it over the millennia. Their final honour had been to join the machine-spirit, their own minds mingled with it, their own wisdom added to the vast knowledge fillings its memory banks.

'I can see them,' said the *Endeavour of Will*, its voice issuing from its hundred mouths. 'They are between the seventh and eighth moons. They watch us.'

'The enemy ship is not the biggest threat,' said Hestion. 'The last communication from the *Bastion Inviolate* spoke of witchcraft. Of a tech-virus, born of daemon magic.'

'Then the *Bastion* is lost,' said the *Endeavour of Will*. 'I felt an emptiness in the realm of information, and I feared my friend was gone. For ten thousand years we have been brothers, forged in the same age, fighting alongside one another in the age that followed. So does time rob us even of that which cannot die.'

'They will assault us next,' said Hestion. 'Shon'tu and his Iron Warriors will not be satisfied with one prize. He will want to take us too.'

'He cannot have us,' said the *Endeavour of Will*. 'You and I, we are forewarned. We will fend off this daemon-scourge. Shon'tu will have to pursue his victory with gun and blade, not witchcraft.'

'This I swear too,' said Hestion.

A Space Marine's lifespan far eclipsed that of an unaugmented human, but even by a Space Marine's standards Hestion was old. His long, mournful face seemed out of place in the red and gold armour of an Imperial Fists Techmarine. He lacked none of the size and presence of a Space Marine, but somehow still looked more like he should be bent over a scholar's desk instead of bringing fire and bloodshed to the Emperor's enemies. Sure enough, bundles of scrolls and books hung from his armour, containing the various tech-rites with which he honoured the spirits of the machines and wargear he maintained for the Chapter.

Hestion took one of the thickest books and his servo-arm unfolded down over his shoulder, the manipulator at its tip unlocking the clasp holding the book's cover closed. Hestion flipped rapidly through the pages and found the ritual he was looking for.

The pages were covered in blocks of zeroes and ones, separated by complicated algebra. Hestion ran his finger down the page, the bionics behind his eyes whirring as they parsed the phrases of machine-code and sent them to the logic circuits in the back of his skull.

'Omnissiah,' read Hestion. 'You whose knowledge builds a fortress of understanding in the realm of information. You whose domain is everything forged and wrought. The dark powers look upon your servant with jealousy. Protect him and snatch his sacred knowledge back from the jaws of sin.'

The mouths of the many bodies opened. The machine-spirit inside coordinated their vocal cords to create a harmony of machine-code, a white noise of clicking and buzzing that echoed Hestion's words in a language that an unaltered human mind could not comprehend. Fingers twitched as their nervous systems, long unused to movement, stuttered into life.

'Ah, they are here,' growled the *Endeavour of Will*. Warning lights flickered across the casing, sending red-edged shadows flitting across the columns and arches of the vault. 'An edifice of such profane knowledge, crashing through the sea of understanding like a ship crewed by the dead and hung with the trophies of violation. Would that you could see them, Imperial Fist! Even your vaunted hate would be inflamed to a new height!'

Warning icons ghosted over Hestion's vision, projected onto his retina. They told him that an unknown vessel had breached the sensorium range of the *Endeavour of Will* and was approaching fast, cloaked in all manner of sensor-fooling effects that rendered it a shadow on the void. The Imperial Fists garrison and the human crew, already on the highest of alerts after the death rattle of the *Bastion Inviolate*, were powering up the star fort's weapons.

'But it was not guns or torpedoes that took down my brother star fort,' continued the machine-spirit. 'That is something he could have fought on his own terms! Fire with fire! No, it was the very soul of deceit that brought him low. But I will not follow him into the depths of ignorance! I will not be lied to! By the holy truth shall I be shielded!'

Hestion's servo-arm reconfigured and seared a complicated pentagrammic symbol on the floor of the vault with a cutting laser. The steel of the floor seethed and bubbled around it, and not just with heat.

The shadows were darkening. The bodies of the machine-spirit's casing were ageing rapidly, skin turning grey and flaking away, muscle and organ sinking into skeletal hollows. Faces decayed into bare teeth and black eye sockets.

'Omnissiah, grant us your aid!' shouted Hestion. 'Delete not this ancient soul! Permit not this corruption!'

Crackles of red lightning played across the high ceiling forming blood-coloured fingers along the columns and walls. Distant voices chanted and gabbled, competing with Hestion's lone voice. One section of the wall bowed in and split, becoming the lids of a huge bloodshot eye that rolled madly. Hestion yelled and threw a handful of pure carbon into the circle, and the eye withdrew.

The vault was shuddering. Voices were flitting across the star fort's vox-net, carrying information about the enemy drawing closer. It was a grand cruiser, its shape well-known by the tactical histories accessed from the valley of datamedium in which the machine-spirit kept its immense reserves of knowledge. It was a flagship of the Iron Warriors, servants of Chaos. If Hestion did not fend off their daemonic attack, the Imperial Fists would never have the chance to look this enemy in the face.

Thick reddish veins blistered up from the floor and up the side of the machine-spirit's casing. Withered bodies broke and flopped aside, revealing the tangle of circuitry and cabling inside.

'Back! Back to the warp with you!' came the machine-spirit's voice, distorted to an atonal bray. 'You will not have this soul! For ten thousand years I have wrought a grim end for your kind! I will not die now! Not now!'

Hestion looked around him. Corruption was flooding through the vault. Eyes were opening above him. The circle, the focus for his ritual, was distorting, new symbols appearing among the sigils of protection and warding.

'Flee!' said Hestion. 'Move your spirit to your datamedium vault! Abandon this place!

'I cannot,' replied the *Endeavour of Will*, synthesised voice distorted. 'It will follow me. There all my knowledge is vulnerable.'

'They will not follow you,' said Hestion. 'I swear. I cannot hold it back here. I will not lose you. Flee, *Endeavour of Will!* Let this fight be mine!'

'Then Emperor's speed upon you, Techmarine,' said the *Endeavour of Will*. 'What you have done for me will never be deleted.'

The lights on the casing turned dark. The bodies remaining fell limp, the cacophony of their machine-code silent and replaced by the wrenching of metal as the vault was warped and distorted by the daemonic virus seeking out a way to the machine-spirit.

Hestion extended his servo-arm and plunged it into the machine-spirit's casing. 'In a few seconds you will reach this machine,' he said aloud, knowing that whatever was attacking the star fort could hear him. 'And nothing I can do will stop that. But you will find no way to the machine-spirit. Your virus will follow the only path it can, the only one open to it, and that is me! My body! You will never reach it, because you have to go through me first!'

All the mass of profane knowledge that made up the daemon-virus, all the vastness of its hate and the torrent of its blasphemy, poured through Techmarine Hestion's body. Hestion jerked and spasmed as if in the throes of electric shock, fire spitting from the extremities of his armour. The edges of his battle-plate glowed red and the skin around his collar scorched as he cooked in the heat. Blood ran from his eyes and ears. He slumped to his knees but did not fall, muscles held rigid by the force of the current.

The daemon virus coalesced into a pair of triangular red eyes, blistering down from the ceiling of the machine-spirit vault. Monstrous features pushed against the steel of the vault from the other side of reality, gnashing mandibles twisted with anger, pseudopods bowing up the floor and pushing in the walls. The daemon's roar echoed through the chamber, competing with the howl of twisting metal and the crackle of the power coursing through Hestion.

Hestion ripped the dataprobe from the machine-spirit casing. The link was snapped. Its information spine broken, the daemon screamed, an impossible sound that was both loud and distant, a thunder from another dimension booming through the star fort. The whole vault was suddenly twisted as if wrenched in two opposite direction by a pair of gigantic hands, and shards of torn metal fell from the broken columns.

Hestion fell to the floor, smoke rising from him, blood dribbling from his face. He dragged himself half a pace and slumped again, all his energy drained away by the task of standing against the virus. He doubled up in pain as the vault collapsed around him. The whole ceiling loomed down as the fabric of the vault failed.

Hestion waited to die. He would be crushed as the machine-spirit vault collapsed on top of him. He had saved the *Endeavour of Will*. To die fulfilling such a duty was no bad death.

He was moving now. He thought the floor had partly collapsed into the maintenance deck below and was tilting, and that he was sliding towards a crevasse opening up. But what little of his sight remained caught a glimpse of a gold-armoured hand grabbing one wrist and dragging him away from the collapse, towards the vault entrance. Behind him the machine-spirit casing disappeared in a torrent of torn metal where he had been lying a moment before.

Hestion forced his head to turn. Skin tore away where it had been welded to his collar armour. But what he saw took enough of the pain away.

He was looking up at Captain Lysander.

VELTHINAR SILVERSPINE RECOILED in anger, shuddering the jewel-encrusted pillars of its temple. Slabs of silver fell from the wall, and the lesser abominations that attended on it, misshapen things like mosquitoes crossed with many-armed humans, squealed and flitted around in fear. One of Velthinar's many limbs swatted a couple from the air, slamming them against the temple walls.

Around the temple, which took up a good portion of the midsection of the *Ferrous Malice*, ran a gallery where supplicants and sacrifices could walk around the temple at Velthinar's eye level. At intervals along this gallery were statues looted from benighted, primitive worlds where the gods of the warp were worshipped, and their sacred power helped keep Velthinar manifest while the *Ferrous Malice* was in real space. Onto this gallery emerged Warsmith Shon'tu, the only man on the ship who could walk into the presence of Velthinar when it was angry and not rile it up further.

Velthinar, if anything, sank down a little at the sight of the warsmith. It was here on the sufferance of the Iron Warriors leader, whether it liked it or not.

'You failed,' said Shon'tu.

It was not an accusation. It was just a statement of fact.

'I was betrayed!' replied the daemon. 'Betrayed by ignorance! One of them was armed with the knowledge of their false machine-idol. That pitiful god of stupidity and rust! That its teachings should befuddle me so! Had I known I would have stripped that information from their minds and left them grass-eating imbeciles.'

'But you did not,' said Shon'tu. 'Your virus form could not break the *Endeavour of Will*.'

'It will,' said Velthinar. 'It will! The next time I will decorate the walls with the liquid mush I leave of their brains! I will–'

'There will not be a next time.'

The daemon Velthinar Silverspine resembled an enormous bloated insect, something that might be found clinging to a leaf on a poisonous jungle world but expanded to a titanic size. Its fleshy bulk could not be contained within its exoskeleton and bulged between the carapace plates in pallid hanging folds. It had legs, many of them, but its size was such that it could not hope to move normally, and it lay on its back with its head curled up over its thorax. Its carapace was iridescent and jewelled, like a suit of alien armour created by the finest craftsmen, with fine silver filigree over plates of deep blue that shimmered to purple. Its head was a mass of eyes and mouthparts, its mandibles sheathed in silver and decorative rings and jewels hanging from every piece of exposed flesh. Its eyes were orbs of red and blue, misty and swirling inside like a soothsayer's crystal ball. Its lack of apparent mobility was irrelevant given its role – its shadow form, the shape it took when shifted into the realm of information, was the form it used to do all its damage. It was the techno-virus that had destroyed the *Bastion Inviolate*, just as it was the insectoid horror that lurked inside the *Ferrous Malice* like a parasite in a hollowed-out organ.

'But… to me was promised the spirit of the star forts!' Velthinar's voice, issued from several sets of mouthparts, sounded like several chittering, sibilant voices clamouring at once.

'And you promised that you would cripple their machine-spirits and deliver them to us!' snapped Shon'tu. Velthinar's flesh rippled as it recoiled a little. 'You will devour the *Bastion Inviolate*. That you have earned. But you did not deliver on your side of the bargain where the *Endeavour of Will* is concerned. The Iron Warriors will do with that star fort as we wish.'

Velthinar's many eyes narrowed. 'If you think, warsmith, that a lord of the Silver Towers will be cowed by your anger…'

'Anger?' replied Shon'tu. 'Why do you think I am angry?'

It was normally impossible to read expressions from the daemon's alien face, but the waggling of its mandibles and flexing of its forelimbs might well have indicated confusion.

'The lords of my Legion care only that a blow is struck against the sons of Dorn,' continued Shon'tu. 'But what glory is there in watching their corpses tumble through the void? What pleasure can be gained from giving the kill to a creature such as you? Now, the Iron Warriors can face the Imperial Fists as it should be, face to face! The iron within us, and the iron without, will crush their entreaties to their Corpse-Emperor, and prove with whom the strength of the warp lies! Perhaps we need some humanity in us, daemon, to understand. Whatever I now am, I was once a human being, a man, and still I possess the jealousy and rage of a man faced with an enemy whose inferiority he cannot demonstrate. Now I can sate that anger with the blood of Imperial Fists! I give thanks to all the gods that you have failed, Velthinar. It is a gift from the warp! I am not here to remonstrate with you. I am here to tell you to stay out of our way until the killing is done.'

Velthinar was silent for a moment, limbs folding and unfolding as its various eyes came to focus on the Iron Warrior. 'I begin to understand,' said the daemon, 'why this task was given to you.'

THE APOTHECARION OF the *Endeavour of Will* was kept dark, the patients illuminated by the spotglobes that trained their lights on the prayer book over each bed. Automated manipulators turned each page at regular intervals, to make sure that if no one else was reading a prayer over the wounded, the eyes of the Emperor at least were looking on their words of devotion.

The *Endeavour of Will* had an apothecarion large enough for the wounded of an army. Now, however, it only had one patient – Techmarine Hestion, stripped of his armour and surrounded by medical servitors patiently weaving artificial skin over the wet red expanses of his burnt body.

Lysander watched the servitors work. Hestion was unconscious, kept in an induced coma by the autosurgeon pumping chemicals into his system. He could die then and there, or he could hold on for a long time. But Hestion was most certainly dying.

'His sacrifice will be remembered,' came a voice behind Lysander. Lysander turned to see another Imperial Fist in the doorway of the apothecarion. He walked into the ward, the dim light revealing him to be a lot younger than either Lysander or Hestion, a sergeant by his markings of rank, fresh-faced and relatively unscarred by the years of battle a Space Marine veteran endured. Young, thought Lysander, to have his own squad. Five Imperial Fists, wearing the same squad markings, followed him in.

'It is our duty,' replied Lysander, 'to see that someone lives to remember.'

The sergeant held out a gauntlet. 'Sergeant Rigalto,' he said. 'It is an honour, First Captain.'

Lysander remembered the name. Every Space Marine in a Chapter at least knew of every other. Lysander remembered

Rigalto as a line trooper, bright and respected, but not an officer.

'Those campaign badges,' said Lysander. 'Agripinaa subsector.'

'You are correct, captain. Storming of the Basilica Pestilax.'

'Then that explains it,' said Lysander.

'Explains it?'

'Heavy losses at the Basilica. Your sergeant died and you took his place. Am I correct?'

'You are,' said Rigalto. 'My honour and my despair. I saw him die, and could not stop it. One day he will be avenged.'

'Such things must be known by a captain of the Chapter without asking,' said Lysander. 'We are spread so thin, we can die without our brothers knowing of it.'

'They will all be remembered, just like Techmarine Hestion,' said Rigalto. 'In time, their names will be written down, when the enemy is driven back into the Eye.'

Lysander nodded. 'That at least I can promise. Well, we have you and your squad, and myself. Who else holds the *Endeavour of Will*?'

'Scout squad Menander,' replied Rigalto. 'They are on their tour of service, in preparation for elevation to full brotherhood. The station crew under Enginseer Selicron, and Astropath Vaynce.'

'And my command squad,' said Lysander. 'Seventeen Imperial Fists, including myself. Quite the army, is it not?'

'And the *Siege of Malebruk*,' said Rigalto. 'And the weapons of the star fort. Thanks to Hestion, the machine-spirit still has some of the weapons on-line.'

'Enough to kill Shon'tu,' said Lysander. 'He banked on us being slain by his virus attack without his traitors having to raise their guns. Now he must give us a fight that we can win.'

'I have heard tell,' said Rigalto, 'of the *Shield of Valour*. Of Malodrax. To us, those who were recruited after the event, it is told like a parable. But to you, it was real. It is memory. To fight alongside one who–'

'Malodrax is in the past,' said Lysander, holding up a hand to silence Rigalto. 'A battle is to be fought now, and it is to the present that I would have us turn our thoughts.'

'Then it is enough to say that we shall help you make the Iron Warriors pay for the *Shield of Valour*, and all that followed.'

Lysander's vox-link chirped. 'Chrystis here,' came the transmission from the *Siege of Malebruk*.

'Speak,' said Lysander.

'Captain, we are under attack.'

FROM THE GLARE of the system's sun, the waning red star Kholestus, the *Ferrous Malice* dived through sensor-baffling bands of solar radiation.

The *Siege of Malebruk* turned to face it, presenting a broadside which brought as many of its guns to bear as possible. In its tactical orrery, Chrystis and the ship's battle-cartographers used holographic void-maps, and rulers and compasses alike, to build up an arsenal of manoeuvres the *Siege* could execute depending on the actions of their enemy. On the *Ferrous Malice* far less natural things, crewmen possessed with daemons of cunning and corrupted machine-spirits, were doing the same.

Naval battle proceeded at its own pace, as if time meant something different when it came to ship-to-ship murder in the void. Torpedoes and broadside shells proceeded not at the speed of gunfire, but lazily, spiralling through space to intersect with the likely locations of the enemy. It was war in which geometry and helmsmanship counted for more than aggression and fearlessness, cold-blooded and removed compared to the thunder of face-to-face battle.

That cool detachment broke as the first shells hit home. The barrage from the *Ferrous Malice's* nose cannons speck-led the hull of the *Siege* with silvery explosions, and inside, crewmen were shredded as metal deformed into bursts of jagged blades. Air shrieked out of hull breaches and damage control teams stationed beyond the inner hull died as the void boomed in to strangle and freeze them. Fires broke out, cutting off teams of crewmen with walls of flame.

The return fire from the *Siege* took its toll, hammering into the armoured prow of the enemy ship. Hull plates were torn free, and ribbons of frozen blood billowed out as the strange, half-living physiology of the ship was breached. The *Ferrous Malice* passed under the *Siege*, both ships battered by the first exchange of fire.

The *Ferrous Malice* was the larger ship, a grand cruiser of a design long forgotten by the shipyards of the Imperial Navy, and it sported more firepower covering every angle of attack. But the *Siege of Malebruk* was a Space Marine strike cruiser, with far greater agility and a quick-witted machine-spirit that calculated thousands of attack solutions every moment at the same time as fending off the virus attacks from the mind of Velthinar Silverspine. The two spiralled around one another, the Chaos vessel in one moment seeming lumbering and slow, and in the next making the strike cruiser seem massively outgunned and outclassed.

But this was just the overture. In a plume of purple black flame, alchemical rockets flared along the spine of the *Ferrous Malice* and slowed it down suddenly, twisting it into a reverse manoeuvre far beyond any Imperial-built ships of its size. At the same time its prow split open, revealing folds and tendons of vulnerable muscle, already torn and bleeding from the opening fire. From this biomechanical mass emerged the snout of a nova cannon. Few Imperial shipyards could forge such a weapon now, and none knew the secrets of creating the nuclear flame that now flared around the barrel as the weapon charged.

The crew of the *Siege of Malebruk* responded to this unexpected change in the battlefield by turning every effort towards evasion. The machine-spirit charted a crazed, jinking path that wrapped itself around the *Ferrous Malice*, too far for defensive turrets to open up against the strike cruiser but too close for the nova cannon to be brought to bear.

The nova cannon stayed silent. The *Siege of Malebruk* moved out of its arc of fire, even as the Chaos ship's alchemical rockets fired again to turn it back on itself again.

The *Ferrous Malice* had no machine-spirit. In place of an artificial intelligence roosted a host of data-daemons, insubstantial warp creatures that flocked to serve their master, Velthinar. They squabbled and fought faster than the speed of thought and, through the sheer bedlam that went through their inhuman minds, wove battle plans that no enemy could predict. Their pronouncements were passed on to the crew and the strange unwholesome creatures that writhed through the oil sumps of the engine decks. The insane command structure of the ship, with the Iron Warriors overseeing multiple castes of mind-slaves, possessees, daemons and mutants, should never have permitted anything so complicated as a warship to function – but the *Ferrous Malice* was a construct of Chaos, transformed into a voidbound asylum by millennia in the warp, and by some incomprehensible process all the madness produced a ship that could think and act faster than should have been possible for its size.

And so the *Ferrous Malice* rolled on its side, presenting a scarred expanse of hull to the enemy. The broadside guns mounted there did not fire, and the crew of the *Siege of Malebruk* took advantage of this unusual good luck to hammer out a broadside of their own, stripping away hull plating and ripping charred craters along the length of the enemy. Fires billowed out into the void as ammunition and fuel stores cooked off. The wounding was terrible, with laser turrets boring holes decks deep and vast areas of the *Ferrous Malice* depressurising and throwing struggling handfuls of crew into space.

Then the hull peeled away of its own accord. Coils of muscle unravelled, whipping across the closing gap between the two ships and wrapping around the extremities of the *Siege of Malebruk*. The tentacles reeled in the strike cruiser, even as armoured beaks, like the mouthparts of some sea-dwelling kraken, emerged from the ruination of torn flesh and metal inside the *Ferrous Malice*.

The machine-spirit of the *Siege of Malebruk* had not factored in this turn of events. The ship had nothing to fight off the grand cruiser's predations. Up close it had its defensive turret fire, which was designed to shoot down approaching torpedoes and bombers, and would have scarcely any impact on the mass of the *Ferrous Malice*. It had the option to board, but aside from the few spare crewmen it could arm it had only the single command squad who had accompanied Captain Lysander to the star fort. The *Ferrous Malice*, meanwhile, was guaranteed to be brimming with mutants, psychopaths and worse.

The Imperial Fists on board, offensive as the presence of the *Ferrous Malice* was, would not throw their lives away boarding it and accepting certain death. They would do more good opposing the ship's undoubted intention to take on the *Endeavour of Will*. The order was given for the *Siege of Malebruk's* crew to abandon ship.

The *Ferrous Malice* had no intention of letting all those fleshy morsels go. Tendrils snapped out from its ruptured hull, snaring saviour pods and shuttle craft as they fled the *Siege*. Dozens of men and women died as their escape craft were smashed open, or were forced alive down one of the gullets that opened up within the biological mass beneath the hull of the *Ferrous Malice*. The armoured shuttle carrying the Imperial Fists weaved between spinning wrecks and the biological growths trying to ensnare it, the survival of five of the Imperium's finest warriors now down to nothing more than the encoded skills of a servitor-pilot and a hefty dose of fate.

The *Ferrous Malice* reeled the *Siege of Malebruk* into a close embrace. Beaks armoured with bone crunched into the strike cruiser's hull, ripping through decks and shearing off one of the ship's engine sections. Plasma coolant billowed silver-black into the vacuum, and the reactors discharged their power load in a storm of blue lightning. The shockwaves tore apart more escape craft, or shredded their guidance systems to send them tumbling without power in all directions.

The Chaos ship dismembered the strike cruiser, forcing massive chunks of spaceship into its many jaws. The machine-spirit of the *Siege of Malebruk* survived until the last, moving from one stack of datamedium to the next as parts of the ship were crushed or torn away. The strike cruiser was a gutted shell by the time it ran out of places to hide, and its existence winked out in the closing maw of the Chaos ship.

The *Ferrous Malice* let the remains of the *Siege of Malebruk* drift away. One side of the strike cruiser was gone completely, the rest hollowed out like a carcass abandoned by scavengers. The Chaos ship had a bloated appearance, an insect gorged on blood, squatting in a haze of debris. Only a few silvery specks remained of the *Siege's* crew. The *Ferrous Malice*, sated for now, ignored the fleeing escape craft, and the escapees clung to life for a few hours more as their craft headed for the relative safety of the *Endeavour of Will*. Among them were the five members of the Imperial Fists First Company, seething with eagerness to get to grips with the enemy who had just handed them such a total defeat.

PART 2

Shon'tu stepped through the door of the Dreadclaw, and breathed in the ancient, stale air of a dying empire.

Behind him, a squad of Iron Warriors followed him out of the Dreadclaw's jaws and into the interior of the *Endeavour of Will*. The Dreadclaw was a make of hull-boring assault capsule that the Imperium had long since forgotten how to make, but which still hung in their dozens over the assault decks of the *Ferrous Malice*. Its bronze-cased beak had torn through the star fort's outer layers and come to rest in a maze of maintenance passages and superstructure supports, into which the Iron Warriors emerged already prepared for a fight.

Shon'tu went helmetless, for even a sudden vacuum could do little harm to his artificial skin and bionic lungs. 'Dust and desolation,' he said. 'Like the inside of a tomb. Such a lifeless place.'

'And we shall make it literally so,' said Brother Ku'Van, one of the veterans accompanying Shon'tu.

'As we have done so many times before, my brethren,' replied the warsmith. 'We shall leave this voidbound coffin as empty as the souls of those we kill. For they have no iron within!'

'Iron within!' shouted the squad in response. 'Iron without!'

'Warsmith!' came a vox from somewhere nearby, among the webs of dark iron and cramped maintenance spaces that soared in every direction. The rune on Shon'tu's retina told him it was Steelwatcher Mhul speaking. 'My coven has made safe breach.'

'As has the Choir,' came another vox from Forge-Chaplain Koultus. Koultus's voice was unmistakable, a brash growl of amplified bass and churning sub-tones. It had to be, or the Choir couldn't have heard the prayers with which he drove them forwards.

'Then converge on me, brothers,' replied Shon'tu. 'To you has been given the honour of accompanying me in this boarding action. Prove to me that you deserve my favour. Drive on, strike hard and without pause, and we will drive a spear of iron into the heart of this place!'

'WELL MET, CAPTAIN,' said Brother-Sergeant Laocos, clapping a hand to the enormous ceramite barrel of his chest.

'Well met, my brother,' replied Lysander.

The star fort's archive, a high-ceilinged room lined with cases of books and scroll tubes, was one of the few places Lysander and the Imperial Fists of his command squad could gather without being cramped. Like Lysander, the five-strong squad wore Terminator armour, a mark of the esteem in which the Chapter held the First Company, and the rarest and most advanced piece of wargear in the Chapter's armouries. Each man was closer to a walking tank than a single soldier, close to three metres tall and not much less across. Most other suitable places on the *Endeavour of Will* were too small to accommodate them all comfortably. It was the first time Lysander had seen the men of his command squad since he had left the *Siege of Malebruk* to see to the star fort's situation in person.

'I so nearly lost you,' continued Lysander. 'The Emperor's shield was on you.'

'Perhaps,' said Laocos. 'But the *Siege* did not have such good fortune.'

'I saw only via the tactical sensors here,' said Lysander. 'It looked bad enough from there.'

'It was a horror such as I have rarely witnessed,' replied Laocos. 'All we knew of Shon'tu and the *Ferrous Malice* is but a fragment of the truth. We were–'

'We were caught out,' said Lysander grimly. 'This is not an act of opportunism by the Iron Warriors. Scavengers they may be at heart, but Shon'tu knew the disposition of the star forts and the fact we could spare but few to defend them if their own weaponry failed. He had exactly the tools he needed to destroy them, and but for the valour of Techmarine Hestion he would have done just that. He made sure to bring a ship the equal of the best we could afford to spare from the front line. What we know – what I know – of Shon'tu is enough to tell me that he will have brought the means to destroy the *Endeavour of Will* now, even when his assault on the machine-spirit failed.'

'Then what will he do next?' said Brother-Scholar Demosthor. Demosthor, in training to attend the Reclusiam of the Chapter's Chaplains, had passages of Dorn's philosophy pinned to his armour, and to the casing of the squad's assault cannon, which he carried.

'The Iron Warriors are creatures of directness,' said Lysander. 'Not for Shon'tu another round of deceit and trickery. He will take the path that leads most clearly to victory, though it may be the hardest.' He looked from face to face, noting the features of men who had served their Chapter for the better part of centuries even before they had been assigned to Lysander's own squad. 'Shon'tu is going to board us. Against any other enemy, any other Chapter, he might pause. But not against us. He wants to fight us. He wants our blood on him, he wants to see us die.'

'If he wants battle,' said Laocos, 'should we give it to him?'

His words were answered with an explosion from somewhere far off in the body of the star fort, and the equally distant blaring of alarms and klaxons. A cogitator console near the door of the archive lit up with warning icons.

'We will,' said Lysander. 'To arms, Fists of Dorn.'

THE STAR FORT'S six segments radiated around its core. The core, heavily armoured and covered by the defensive weapons the machine-spirit still controlled, housed the datamedia vault and other essential command systems, along with the power plant. The six segments housed all the other structures needed for a battle station – barracks, now almost completely empty, supplies and ammunition stores, fighter decks silent without crew to fly the fighters and bombers stored there, fuel tanks, sensorium stations and mountings for weapons now lost to the machine-spirit. Here could also be found the places of worship used by the station's crew, chapels to many faces of the Emperor and shrines to Rogal Dorn for the use of the Imperial Fists.

One of these sacred places was consecrated to the hero of the Chapter who was entombed there. In death, he still watched out on the void for the enemies of mankind, for his sarcophagus had been installed on the *Endeavour of Will* some two and a half thousand years before.

It was at the Tomb of Ionis that the Imperial Fists drew the battle lines.

SCOUT SERGEANT MENANDER peered across the expanse of the Tomb of Ionis, his magnoculars sweeping past the fluted columns and scrollwork. It was a forest of stonework, as dense as a death world jungle. With little need to conserve space on the huge star fort, the tomb had grown with successive generations of masons and artisans, so the sarcophagus sat at the centre of a labyrinth of statuary and decoration. The sarcophagus itself rose like a granite mesa in the centre of the tomb, crowned with an outsized carving of Ionis himself lying in state.

Menander's squad crouched around him among the coils of stone. Their cameleoline cloaks had turned speckled grey to match their surroundings, and they were adept at clinging to the shadows and breaking up lines of sight. Menander's four Imperial Fists Scouts carried sniper rifles, draped in cameleoline strips to diffuse the outlines of the weapons.

'Brother Moltos,' said Menander softly. 'Bless us.'

Brother Moltos made the sign of the aquila, and clapped a hand silently to his chest in the salute of Dorn. 'Emperor most high, and Omnissiah who knows all, bless this battle-gear that will so sorely be tested. Keep our lenses bright and focused, and fill them with the sight of the enemy. Let our bullets fly true. Let the armour of the enemy crumble before them. Let them find nothing but the hearts of traitors.'

'Amen,' said Menander, echoed by the other three Scouts. 'Spread out. Intel pattern. Do not engage.'

The Scouts split up and moved quietly through the tomb, heading on different winding paths towards the sarcophagus. Menander glanced behind him and could see the glint of golden ceramite between the columns lining the near edge of the tomb. Captain Lysander and Sergeant Rigalto's squads were mustering there, ready to act.

And somewhere up ahead were the enemy.

'I have movement,' came a subvocalised vox message from Menander's right. Scout-Brother Tisiphon's rune winked. 'Three hundred metres, approaching. Two of the clock.'

Menander looked in the direction Tisiphon had indicated. He thought he could see movement, black against black. He held up his magnoculars and could make out, clearly now, the dark shape advancing towards the Imperial Fists.

It moved without concern to stealth. Menander could even hear it now, crunching through granite carvings. It was taller than a Space Marine and far more broad, and the oily gunmetal of the Iron Warriors' armour was deformed by red, weeping bands of corded muscle.

'Captain,' voxed Menander. 'I have sighted the enemy.'

'Is Shon'tu among them?' came Captain Lysander's reply.

'I cannot tell,' said Menander. 'They have sent in the Obliterators.'

SHON'TU WATCHED AS the Obliterators forged ahead. The five sons of the Coven, marshalled by the relatively normal Steelwatcher Mhul. Each Obliterator had once been an Iron Warrior, just like Shon'tu or Mhul himself. But the fates had seen fit to infect them with a warp-born tech-virus that had melded their flesh and armour into one, and turned them into machines of Chaos.

The Obliterators were twice the size of a Space Marine, and crashed through the statuary towards the high ground of the sarcophagus. Their limbs, wrapped in clubbing masses of muscle, opened up into dozens of orifices from which emerged gun barrels and chainblades. Each one was a walking arsenal, containing within him the firepower of a whole squad of Space Marines.

The rest of the strikeforce advanced in their wake. Shon'tu's own squad, alongside the Choir, swept the avenues of fire with bolter barrels, watching for the glint of Imperial Fists armour. Lysander's men had chosen to face them here, perhaps to force a decisive battle, perhaps because this was sacred ground.

'Brethren!' bellowed the amplified voice of Forge-Chaplain Koultus. Koultus's skull-shaped faceplate had a yawning mouth framing a speaker which boomed his voice in all directions. 'Behold you all the enemy! They cower from us! They pray that death might come before their weak hearts compel them to flee! Grant their wishes, and by iron seal their fates!'

The Choir rushed forwards around him, leaping through the wreckage left by the Obliterators. Their gunmetal armour burned from the inside, blue and red flames flickering where the plasteel plates met. The fires were barely contained, for they formed the haloes of daemons caged within them, desperate to break free through the sacrament of combat.

The first of the Obliterators clambered into the lip of the sarcophagus. Its limbs reformed into twin assault cannons, bundles of revolving barrels which span as they hammered out a rain of fire towards the Imperial Fists at the other end of the tomb. A few return shots snapped up at it, but the Obliterator stood proud as its brothers of the Coven took up position beside it. Steelwatcher Mhul was directing their fire, crouched beside the huge sarcophagus, the enlarged lens of his bionic eye sending greenish light beams playing across the statuary ahead.

Shon'tu's own veteran squad were the backbone of this force, advancing patiently with bolters levelled. Soon their fire would chew through the few Imperial Fists that weathered the storm of the Obliterators. Shon'tu was a patient creature, but even his soul seemed to drag him forwards a pace, eager to kill.

Shon'tu backed against a half-collapsed statue that had once depicted one of the honour guard of the hero buried here. He peered through the dust kicked up by the gunfire and saw the shape of an Imperial Fist in Terminator armour, sheltering behind a pile of fallen rubble as he gave orders to the Space Marines around him. He was huge, shaven-headed, with a massive storm shield in one hand. In the other was a weapon that Shon'tu recognised – a thunder hammer with its end forged into the shape of a fist. The Fist of Dorn.

Captain Lysander.

Shon'tu's spirit won the battle, and Shon'tu rushed forwards for the kill.

'HOLD THEM AT the sarcophagus!' yelled Lysander over the gunfire. 'Advance! Imperial Fists, advance!'

Lysander could see one Scout fallen, a leg blown off by the storm of fire that had come from the Obliterators. Lysander knew of the Obliterators – he had fought them – and he knew well how deadly they could be. There was nothing in the Imperial Fists' armoury that could kill as swiftly, man for man, as those infected by the tech-virus.

Lysander held his shield in front of him as he led the way forwards. Gunfire hammered against it, jarring his arm. His command squad advanced behind him, with Squad Rigalto to the right. Lysander could hear Rigalto yelling his own orders and bolter fire was streaking up towards the sarcophagus in return now. The sound was deafening – literally so, for anyone other than a Space Marine, with his enhanced and protected senses, would have been robbed of hearing by the din.

Something screeched among the bedlam. Some old soldier's instinct took over in Lysander and he brought his shield down just in time to take the charge of an Iron Warrior who crashed through the statue forest right into him. Lysander kept his footing and slammed the shield down, trapping the leg of the Iron Warrior and pinning it to the ground.

The Iron Warrior was the colours of his Legion, oily gunmetal with yellow and black warning strips. But he was not a Space Marine. He had given up that label when he had allowed himself to be possessed by the thing squirming out of the eyepieces of his faceplate. Its twin wriggling pseudopods lashed from holes in his face and one of its gauntlets burst apart, more fleshy tendrils snaking out to wrap around the edges of Lysander's shield.

Lysander's stomachs turned at the sight of the possessed Iron Warrior. He raised the Fist of Dorn over his head and slammed the butt end down, impaling the Iron Warrior through the chest. He ripped it free and lifted his shield, carrying the enemy up on it and slamming it into the pedestal of a statue. Lysander brought the Fist of Dorn down again, the head falling in an arc, crunching into the Iron Warrior's deformed face.

'Possessed!' yelled Sergeant Laocos. 'Brothers, the enemy wears the face of his corruption!'

'Not for long!' came the voice of Brother-Scholar Demosthor. A volley of assault cannon fire blew one possessed's head open, revealing a mass of squirming muscle like the bloom of a fleshy flower. The screeching thing kept attacking, but now blind and without coordination. Demosthor drew back his power fist and punched the Iron Warrior with such strength he was thrown clear out of sight by the impact.

Lysander pushed on, throwing another Iron Warrior aside with a swing of his shield. The sarcophagus rose right ahead of him, the shape of the nearest Obliterator illuminated by the blaze of fire roaring from the weapons unfolded from its arms. Lysander planted a foot on the lower edge of the sarcophagus and powered up onto the top.

The Obliterator turned to face him. Its face was a mass of muscle and machinery, gun barrels emerging from its eye-sockets and its mouth lolling open, glowing with the fire of its internal forges. Smoke and steam rose from it, spurting from between the armour plates fused with its flesh. The multi-barrelled cannon on one of its arms folded back into the mass of muscle and steel, and iron-sheathed claws emerged in its place, forming a bunched fist crackling under a power field.

Lysander braced himself into a stance his body knew from decades sparring in the duelling rings of the *Phalanx* and the battlefields of the Imperium. His shoulder dropped, shield held low and firm to take the charge. The floor under his feet was uneven, for he was standing on the carved face of Ionis, whose body lay in the sarcophagus below.

The Obliterator roared a wordless war-cry, loud and braying, the sound of an angry machine. Its bulk loped forwards, fist drawn back to club down and crush.

Lysander sidestepped with speed that should have been impossible for his Terminator-armoured form. He spun, cracking the front of his shield into the side of the Obliterator, using its own momentum to knock it forwards off-balance. He swung the Fist of Dorn around into the Obliterator's back, smashing into its spine. Bone and iron cracked. The Obliterator slumped to one knee and Lysander slammed the lower edge of his shield down onto the back of its calf, splintering the stone beneath and trapping the Iron Warrior in place.

The second swipe of Lysander's hammer crunched through the Obliterator's upper back. The head of the hammer ripped right through the Iron Warrior's bulk, tearing its upper chest and head off in a fountain of shredded meat and gore. Sparks sprayed from its ruined body as it toppled over.

'Menander!' said Lysander into the vox-net as he turned to scan for more targets. 'What is your situation?'

'Almost in position,' came the reply.

'We hold the sarcophagus,' said Lysander. 'Act now!'

'It will be done,' said Menander.

Rigalto's squad were embattled at the other end of the sarcophagus, pinned down by volleys of bolter fire from the advancing Iron Warriors. The Imperial Fists were outnumbered and outgunned. They could not hold. Not for more than a few moments.

Lysander's thoughts were broken as he saw the black and yellow heraldry, like a warning sign. He saw the brass superstructure around the armour, the nightmare in clockwork striding through the wreckage.

This Iron Warrior's armour was bulkier and more elaborate, the ornate plates supported by a framework of brass struts and powered by a shuddering back-mounted generator with spinning cogs and pumping pistons, wreathing the traitor's form in greasy smoke. One hand was a monstrous claw, and the other was encased in a triple-barrelled bolt cannon from which hung chains of ammunition rattling as it blasted volleys of fire into Squad Rigalto.

The Iron Warrior's face was bare, but it was a face as much of steel as of flesh. Twin rebreathers were implanted in his throat and his mouth was articulated like a hunter's trap with teeth of iron. The eyes were human, and it seemed that into them was poured all the hatred and anger that had been replaced by steel throughout the rest of the traitor's body.

'Warsmith!' bellowed Lysander. 'Shon'tu! I see you!

Before the Emperor's sight shall you fall!'

Shon'tu looked up at Lysander and, somehow, that mechanical nightmare of a face smiled. 'Commander Lysander!' he replied. 'Such kind fates the warp has woven, to give your death to me!'

Shon'tu laughed and kicked through a ruined statue, where an Imperial Fist of Squad Rigalto lay trying to get back to his feet with a bolter shell through his thigh. Shon'tu's claw clamped around the Imperial Fists warrior's torso and he held him up for Lysander to see. The talons of the claws sheared closed, pneumatic pistons slamming shut, and the Imperial Fist's body was sliced into three. The parts flopped to the ground, blood already pumping from between the sheared ceramite. The blood spattered across Shon'tu and hissed as it touched the warsmith's hot armour, turning to black smoke.

'In position,' came Menander's vox.

'Fall back!' ordered Lysander, not taking his eyes from the sight of Shon'tu driving on through the gunfire. 'Imperial Fists, stay tight and fall back!'

The sound that reached Lysander's hearing through the gunfire was Shon'tu laughing, an awful mechanical noise like tearing metal. One of the surviving Obliterators turned its guns on Lysander and he ducked back behind the plasteel slab of his shield. The weight of fire hitting it was like an avalanche, almost throwing Lysander onto his back.

Lysander jumped down from the sarcophagus. His command squad were back to back, surrounded by shattered statuary and the bodies of the possessed Iron Warriors who had charged into the range of their guns and power fists. Down at the base of the sarcophagus Lysander could see one of Menander's Scouts crouched down, attaching a large, thick metal disc to the stone. Lysander recognised it as a demolition charge

Bolter fire slammed into the Scout. The Imperial Fist slumped against the sarcophagus, mouth gaping dumbly, eyes glassy.

The charge was set. His duty was done.

Lysander led the way back towards the edge of the tomb. The Terminators' storm bolters gave Rigalto's squad enough covering fire to make it out from under the guns of the Iron Warriors. Sergeant Rigalto himself was firing his bolter one-handed, his other hand a mess of torn skin and gore.

The Imperial Fists passed through the corridors leading away from the tomb. Menander and the surviving three Scouts were last out, Menander slamming his hand against a control plate mounted on the wall. Pneumatic pistons hissed and warnings sounded, and reinforced twin blast doors slid down, closing off the tomb with a biological seal.

It wouldn't stand up to a concerted blast of fire from the Iron Warriors' Obliterators. It wouldn't have to.

Lysander focused on the detonator rune on his retina.

'THE IMPERIAL FISTS do not retreat,' said Shon'tu, more to himself than to anyone else. The dead Space Marine lay just behind him, oozing vermilion blood, and even as they witnessed their battle-brother dying Lysander and his force were falling back.

Shon'tu opened up a vox-link to the *Ferrous Malice*. 'Velthinar!' he demanded.

'Could the warsmith deign to speak with us?' came the reply from the daemon that squatted in the bowels of the Iron Warriors ship. 'We who have failed him so?'

'I have not the time,' said Shon'tu. 'Scour the memories taken from the *Bastion Inviolate*. Seek out knowledge of Ionis, a hero of the Imperial Fists, entombed on the *Endeavour of Will*. Now!'

The Iron Warriors around Shon'tu were pursuing the Imperial Fists squad in front of them through the ruins that remained of the tomb's decoration. Shon'tu could see Lysander and his Terminator-armoured cohorts also moving towards the exits.

They could be cut off and trapped like rats. The Choir, those Iron Warriors blessed enough to harbour daemons sent to possess them, could move rapidly, like hunting animals. The Obliterators could blast and melt through bulkhead walls. The Iron Warriors had superior numbers and firepower. Lysander would never commit his force to a retreat into the tangle of maintenance and crew decks, never. It was as wrong as could be.

'Warsmith,' came Velthinar's chittering buzz of a voice. 'Ionis was a Castellan of the *Phalanx*, millennia ago. For three hundred years he served, until caught in the virus-bombing of Golgothix Superior and slain.'

'Virus-bombing,' spat Shon'tu. 'Lysander! I owe you a betrayal! I owe you a death by deceit! Iron Warriors, retreat! Back to the Dreadclaws!'

The order did not have time to register in the minds of the Iron Warriors before the detonation charge mounted on the sarcophagus exploded. The detonation threw members of the possessed Choir off their feet, throwing chunks of statue everywhere. Normal troops would have been killed and thrown into disarray, but not the Iron Warriors. That wasn't the aim.

Shon'tu could see, through the billowing dust and smoke, the side of the sarcophagus blasted open. The grinning skull of Ionis, resting on a bed of golden silks now tattered and blackened, rolled onto its side as if fixing Shon'tu with its eye sockets. Super-cooled air misted and rolled from the ruptured sarcophagus.

One of the Choir was loping through the ruins, falling behind his fellow possessed. He slipped to one knee, face-plate breaking open into a tangle of gnarled mandibles like a fist opening and closing. The possessed's body convulsed and a yawning mouth opened up in its chest, a fat purple tongue lolling out and coughing out stringy red gore.

The Iron Warrior's joints were eroding, some corrosive substance finding purchase in the joints of the armour. One of his arms fell off, crumbling bone and flaking muscle pouring from the exposed socket. The ceramite was becoming pitted and discoloured, the exposed flesh drying and flaking off as if ageing centuries in a few moments.

The possessed toppled to the ground and came apart, armour cracking like dropped pottery.

'Virus attack!' yelled Shon'tu. 'Mhul! Koultus! Get them back to the Dreadclaws in good order! Move!'

One of the Obliterators had been caught in the invisible tide. The virus leaking from the ruptured sarcophagus had infected the thick bands of muscle wrapping around its deformed armour. The muscles contracted, the armour plates warping and splitting under the pressure, spiny growths bursting from exposed flesh. Malformed gun barrels cycled, lumps of fused ammunition thunking to the floor. The Obliterator's face burst into a clutch of eyeballs, each one swelling and bursting to dribble red-white gore down the torn armour. It took a long few moments to die, its body deforming until it was turned almost completely inside out, metallic organs split into fans of bloody steel and loops of articulated entrails clattering around its feet.

The warning systems built into Shon'tu's cranial augmentations were sending pulses of alert hormones through him, and setting off microscopic klaxons and strobes in his ears and eyes. Every bio-alert was going off, his armour detecting the presence of pathogens, his augmetic organs fending off the voracious strains of virus which mutated into new forms with every moment.

Shon'tu made it to the rear of the tomb. Twin blast doors had descended, cutting off the Tomb of Ionis and turning it into a biological containment zone. Shon'tu ripped through the first door with his power claw, punching through the front and ripping the door off its mountings. The second lasted no longer, and he was through, the cavernous outer hull voids reaching ahead of him. Steelwatcher Mhul and the remaining possessed had made it through too, and Shon'tu could feel the impacts of the Obliterators stomping behind him.

The virus incubated in Ionis's ancient corpse was voracious enough to kill a Space Marine, but not a warsmith of the Iron Warriors. Most of the Iron Warriors of Shon'tu's own unit, veterans with multiple augmetics and enhanced physiologies, had also made it, their altered immune systems rapidly adapting to the virus's assaults. Most of the possessed were gone, left behind among the ruined statuary to writhe and deform as they died.

Shon'tu cast a glance back towards the Tomb of Ionis, now a smoking ruin blanketed in an invisible layer of bio-predator. The emotions in him were not human, but might have most closely resembled a mix of anger, shame and hate.

'A trick worthy of victory,' said Shon'tu. 'But it is no victory you have won here. All my brothers wait for you. The *Ferrous Malice* waits for you. You have bought yourself a far worse death, Lysander, and I will still be the one to deliver it.'

The remains of the Iron Warriors strike force headed for the waiting Dreadclaws as maintenance servitors were already trundling to erect replacement bio-seals to cut off the Tomb of Ionis.

It did not matter, this defeat, any more than the failure of Velthinar to destroy the *Endeavour of Will's* machine-spirit truly mattered. Shon'tu had not reached the position of warsmith without thinking many steps ahead. The next stage of the star fort's death was already laid out, ready to be enacted with an order. The Imperial Fists had achieved nothing here but to listen to the ticking of the clock counting down their final moments.

LYSANDER KNEW THERE would be little time before he would have to act again in the star fort's defence. The Iron Warriors were the masters of the siege, just as the Imperial Fists were the masters of defence – Shon'tu would not have thrown his entire force against one weak spot. He would have more in reserve, ready to storm in when the first breaches were opened. They would attack soon enough. Shon'tu would not let the ignominy of defeat last for long.

Lysander was alone as he ascended the chill spiral staircase towards the belfry, a place lined in marble and silver plate, kept isolated from the rest of the star fort. Above him the lofty reaches of the belfry's rafters were hung with huge bronze bells. The belfry's single occupant knelt on the floor, a small desk in front of him with an array of inkwells, quill stands, pots of sealing wax and reams of parchment. His head was bent as if in prayer and he did not turn to look at Lysander – not because he did not care that the captain had approached, but because the eyes hidden under the heavy bottle-green hood could not see at all.

'News must be grave,' said Astropath Vaynce. 'It is rare anyone comes up here when there is not some crisis to be transmitted to the galaxy.'

'I am sorry to break your silence,' said Lysander.

'It is in silence that I take solace,' replied Vaynce. 'But I have my duty. What do you wish of me, Captain Lysander?'

'I have a message I need you to send,' said Lysander. He could see now that the shadowy walls of the belfry were lined with intricate cages, each with several tiny, silent birds, their bright plumage hidden in the gloom, hopping between their perches. Vaynce had the company of several hundred birds in total.

'I understand the Tomb of Ionis was violated,' said Vaynce.

Lysander was silent for a moment. 'It is no concern of yours, astropath. Damage was inflicted to the star fort, as would be the case in any battle.'

'Ionis had lain here for thousands of years,' said Vaynce. 'So few knew what his sarcophagus really contained. A stroke of cunning, do you not think? To contain a sample of such a dangerous bio-predator within the body of the last man it killed, and disguise it as his resting place? How many men and women who served here knew it was beneath their feet? I would imagine it was sealed there so it could be recovered and employed as a weapon by the Imperial Fists. Perhaps that purpose was forgotten. In any case, it will not be fulfilled now.'

'Ionis decreed with his last breaths that he be used as such a weapon,' replied Lysander.

'Some would call it a violation,' said Vaynce, 'of the venerated dead.'

'Then let them say it,' said Lysander. 'I have answers for them.'

Vaynce smiled and turned. His eyes were bound with a strip of embroidered cloth which could not quite hide the enlarged, scorched pits beneath. He smiled. His teeth were black, carved from ebony and inscribed with prayers of humility and perseverance. 'Mere words, captain,' he said. 'Forgive me. I spend much time alone. Proper etiquette has rather… passed me by.'

'Can you encode my message now?' said Lysander.

'Indeed,' replied Vaynce. He took a book from beneath the pile of parchment in front of him and opened it. Its pages were crammed with symbols, some pictures of animals or objects, others completely abstract. Each had a meaning that changed with its proximity to other symbols, forming an infinitely complicated language of symbols that those strange, blessed individuals known as astropaths had to master before they could serve the Imperium. Vaynce ran his fingers along the page, reading the symbols through the feel of the ink on the paper. 'Commence, if you will.'

Captain Lysander dictated his message to Astropath Vaynce. He kept it succinct, leaving out all but that which was necessary, knowing that an astropath's art became more difficult, the message more prone to mistranslation at the other end, the longer it was.

Vaynce did not flinch as he heard it. One hand flicked through the book with a speed born of decades of practice, the other scratching down symbols on a strip of parchment that unrolled from a tiny motorised reel. He used a quill and reddish ink.

When Lysander was done, Vaynce lit a stick of incense and took a fingertip of ash, smearing it in a circular symbol onto the floor in front of him. He spat into the circle, mumbled a prayer, and wiped off the ash and spittle with his sleeve. The ritual done with, he rolled up the parchment into a tight tube and sealed it with a blob of wax and the ring that hung on a chain around his neck.

'And the recipient?' asked Vaynce, although it was obvious to whom the message was addressed.

Lysander told him the identity of the recipient. Vaynce scrawled a corresponding symbol on the outside of the rolled parchment, then climbed unsteadily to his feet. He tottered over to one of the bird cages, opened the door, and took out a bird with blue and red plumage that glittered under the light of the belfry's glow-globes. The bird sat calmly on Vaynce's finger, tiny black eyes flitting from Lysander to the astropath, making no effort to fly away.

'We all have our ways,' said Vaynce. 'Every one of us is different. Some make sculptures, some paint pictures. Some even make music. But in the end we are the same. Whatever we create, we must destroy.'

The astropath tied the rolled-up message to the bird's leg with a piece of scarlet ribbon. 'Go, go,' he whispered, and the bird flitted off his finger and skipped up towards the bells hanging from the rafters.

'It is the trauma of destruction,' said Vaynce, 'that gives it form in the warp. To see our creations die gives us the focus to do what we must.'

A grid of needle-thin lasers glittered into existence, strung between the bells like a driftnet. The tiny bird flew through the grid and disappeared in a flash of flame.

Vaynce closed his eyes. The embroidery around his eyes glowed and the empty sockets smouldered beneath them. Flickers of blue-white power played around Vaynce's skull, earthing through his fingers to the belfry floor.

Lysander, though he possessed no psychic ability, could feel the fabric of reality shifting, as if a wrinkle was being pulled out or the galaxy had moved along some infinitely distant fault line.

Vaynce coughed and his shoulders slumped. Smoke coiled off him.

'It is done,' he said.

'Was it received?'

'Impossible to tell,' replied Vaynce. 'It would be futile, I believe, to expect a confirmation, given the recipient.'

'Then we are finished here,' said Lysander.

'I understand.'

'No,' said Lysander. 'Perhaps you do not.'

Vaynce sighed and sat back down next to his writing desk. 'What I have sent for you is… toxic. The information contained therein is dangerous.'

'Not least,' said Lysander, 'to our enemies. And I have no doubt that Shon'tu has the means at his disposal to tear memories from even the mind of an astropath. Ours would not be the first Imperial force to be undone by just such a breach.'

'Some astropaths possess compartmentalised minds,' said Vaynce. 'Dangerous knowledge can be isolated and burned away, and the memory wiped clean. But not I.'

'Then you know what must be done.'

'Of course.' Vaynce pulled down the hood of his robe, exposing a shaven skull criss-crossed with burn marks.

Lysander levelled his storm bolter at the back of Vaynce's head. The selector was set to single shot – even so, it would be massive overkill.

'If there was another way,' he said, 'I would take it.'

'I have always known that it would end this way,' replied Vaynce, his voice unwavering. 'Some of us can see… echoes, of what might be. I saw this place many times before I was assigned to this star fort. I knew that I would die here. Whatever form our duty takes, we must welcome it, must we not? We must give thanks that we know what must be done.'

Lysander did not answer. The report of the storm bolter shot echoed around the belfry, ringing off the bells overhead. Vaynce's headless body slumped onto its front, the astropath's skull vaporised by the bolter shell's detonation.

Lysander lowered the gun. He left the body where it was, and descended the stairs to join his fellow Imperial Fists.

PART 3

THE RITUAL CHAMBER, when stripped of the battlefield trophies the Iron Warriors had set up there, served as a passable fighting pit. Two huge doorways were revealed when captured banners and tapestries were removed, and the sacrificial stone was strewn with a handful of shell casings and a sprinkling of blood to ready it for battle.

One door rumbled open. The holding pen beyond was full of the seething, coiled flesh of the first combatant, a serpentine monster composed of dozens of torsos fixed end to end. Its hundred limbs were fused from the claws and talons of executed xenos creatures, and they skittered along the floor drawing sparks as the serpent raised a head hung with grasping hands around a crocodilian maw. The serpent whipped around the chamber, every movement revealing another way in which human and xenos had been fused into a single horror. Here and there faces remained and they were alive, conscious and full of terror, features deformed in pain. A stinger on the serpent's tail was held in place by a fusion of human and alien heads, half-flensed skulls and drooling jaws screaming silently.

The second door opened. The creature revealed was enormous and apelike, its massive shoulders supporting club-like arms that dragged along the ground, leaving a trail of blood from its torn skin. Skinless muscle wrapped a framework of fused skeletons, the bones inscribed with runes that glowed with the creature's fury. Steam hissed between its vertebrae and from the vertical mouths of its two heads, wreathing around the tiny red eyes set deep into each deformed mass.

The serpent reeled around the wall opposite the new-comer, hissing and spitting as it reacted to its rival. The beast roared, its two voices combining to a storm of atonal noise, and slammed its fists into the floor. The serpent made to cower and the beast took a step forwards, before the serpent bunched its muscles and struck.

The beast was far too quick for anything of its size. One fist whipped up and caught the serpent around the throat, holding it down pinned against the floor as the length of its body thrashed. The beast's other fist came up and hammered down onto the top of the serpent's head, again and again. Bone crunched and gore spattered across the chamber's walls.

But the beast had not paid attention to the serpent's stinger. The slender point of curved bone hissed with acidic venom as it arched over the beast's shoulder, the human and xenos heads embedded around it twisting as the muscle beneath tensed.

The beast slammed the serpent into the ground again. Its mouths split wide as it made to bite into the serpent's head, and bloody saliva ran between the rows of fangs lining its mouths and throats.

The stinger punched down through the flesh of the beast's shoulder. The beast let out a twin howl as the poison sacs along the serpent's underside emptied themselves into its torso. Flesh and skin blistered along the beast's back, and greenish boils welled up and burst. The beast clutched at its shoulder, and chunks of corrupted flesh came away by the handful, exposing bone and organ beneath. The serpent, wounded but alive, slithered away to the back of the room and watched the beast stumble blindly. The venom had reached its faces and they were withering away, fangs falling from its jaws and thudding to the floor amid the rain of blood and muscle.

The beast thudded into the wall and slid down it. Its voice was growing weak as its lungs were eaten away. Its upper body was now a semi-liquid mass, only the bones remaining intact as everything between them sluiced away. Finally it was silent, gory skulls lolling senselessly, blood emptying away into the drains in the chamber floor.

Doors opened and crewmen entered the room. Most of the *Ferrous Malice's* crew were mutants, whose deformities had made them reviled and oppressed by the rest of the Imperium, and who eagerly flocked for the chance to serve the Imperium's enemies. In their malformed limbs they carried goads and coils of rope, and they advanced on the wounded serpent coiled in the corner. They jabbed at it, driving it back towards the door it had emerged from as its half-crushed head wavered between them and its coils bunched up as it prepared to strike.

The mutants yelled to one another in the short, barking language of the ship's crew, herding the serpent back. The serpent snatched a goading pike off one of the mutants and splintered it between its jaws, and threw another off his feet with a lash of its tail. But metre by metre the crew forced it through the doorway, and one of their number hauled on a lever that slammed the door shut behind it.

'Leave us,' came an order from vox-casters mounted in the chamber. The mutants cowered at the artificial voice and hurried out of the chamber, dragging their wounded crewmate along the floor.

In their place, Warsmith Shon'tu entered. When the last of the crewmen were gone and the door shut behind him, he walked over to the dead beast and examined its ruined corpse. He knelt down and magnification lenses unfolded over his eye, bringing out the detail of the beast's strange physiology. With much of its flesh liquefied it was clear from the skeleton the number of creatures that had been fused together to make it.

'You have your sacrifice,' said Shon'tu, though the beast could surely not hear him. 'A hundred victims made it, and a hundred more made its conqueror. Once they died by the knives of our priests, and again they died by violence. This is what was written. This was what you demanded.'

'To show ourselves,' came a reply, a high, grating hiss from somewhere near the chamber's sacrificial stone. 'Nothing more.'

'Then show yourself, as you are bound,' said Shon'tu.

The blood and shadows around the sacrificial stone flowed up into the air, as if filling an invisible vessel. They formed a spindly, roughly humanoid shape, with a head hung low between its shoulders and a long, equine face. It was somewhat taller than a man, and when half formed it drew the shadows around it like a cloak or furled wings, the spindly construct of blood obscured by the darkness that clung to it.

Behind it several more were forming in the same way, figures that seemed barely sketched on the surface of reality, stylised daemons scratched in blood onto the canvas of the air.

Shon'tu took a scroll case that hung on the waist of his armour. He opened it and unravelled the long sheet of lizard-like hide within. It was covered in cramped writing and symbols, and at the end was the seal, in black wax, of the steel helm emblem of the Iron Warriors Legion.

The leader of the daemons skittered forwards, its limbs seemingly jointed at random. Its head, which had now formed three eyes of bluish fire, was held low as it perused the writing on the hide.

'The contract is as it was made,' said the daemon. 'All parties are thus bound.'

'Then you must bargain,' said Shon'tu. 'The terms of our agreement state that you must enter into an agreement for services we demand of you.'

'And you must give us what we want,' said the dae-mon. 'The Dancers on the Precipice do no man's will for nothing.'

Shon'tu scowled. 'It is always thus,' he said. 'Though our enemies are the same, though the warp's glory relies on our labours, still the spawn of the warp must take their payment.'

'It is written,' said the Dancer. 'So it shall be.'

Shon'tu opened a small compartment in the armour on his chest. Inside was a tiny glass vial of red liquid. 'Shed by Perturabo,' he said, 'upon the fields of Isstvan. Collected even as the Corpse-God's lackeys were butchered beneath our guns. Seasoned in the smoke from their pyres.'

'The blood,' said the Dancer, 'of a primarch.'

Its fingers grew longer as it reached for the vial. Shon'tu snatched it back out of the daemon's reach. 'I have a very specific task,' he said, 'for which this is the payment.'

'Give it unto us,' replied the Dancer, 'and it shall be done.'

'Payment will be granted when the task is complete,' retorted Shon'tu. 'That is also written.'

The Dancer spat in frustration. 'For the blood of Pertur-abo, for the life-stuff of the warp's prophet, we will do as you wish. But break this covenant, delete what was writ-ten, and terrible shall be the warp's vengeance! For ten thousand years you will find no ally in the empyrean, War-smith Shon'tu. Only enemies shall swarm wherever your soul touches the warp, and the gods themselves will learn of it!'

'There will be no reneging on this bargain,' said Shon'tu. 'That is not our way. This is a high price to pay, and it does us ill to part with it; but the victory it will buy us is worth the price, and it will be paid.'

The Dancer turned to its fellows. Just beyond reality shimmered the forms of many more, a whole tribe of these warp-predators. Their silent conversation lasted a few moments and the Dancer turned back to Shon'tu.

'What is it the Iron Warriors desire?'

Shon'tu locked the vial of primarch's blood back into its compartment in his armour. 'Kill Lysander,' he replied.

THE FIRST SIGN that anything was wrong, as was so often the case, was when the bodies were found.

Three of them, all engineers, were found near one of the star fort's primary thruster arrays. The array, which was used to keep the *Endeavour of Will* in a steady orbit around its star, had been one of the many systems to be damaged during the attack on the machine-spirit, and the engineers were attempting to get it back to working order. They wore grey habits emblazoned with the half-cog symbol, showing that they were laymen trained by the magi of the Adeptus Mechanicus; and the body of each had been hollowed out, as if by hungry fingers cracking them open and tearing out the meat inside.

Lysander knelt in that moment beside the corpses lain out on the floor of the barracks, where they had been brought. They were a sorry sight, lopsided and sagging as if deflated. Rigalto stood behind him with a couple of the battle-brothers from his squad, along with the gaggle of crewmen who had found the bodies. Rigalto's wounded hand was bound and bloody.

'What other signs were there?' asked Lysander, not taking his eyes from the bodies.

'Prints,' said one of the crew, a woman, stocky and smeared with machine grease. 'On the floor and the ceiling. In blood.'

'Footprints?'

'I could not tell.'

Lysander stood up. 'They were in blood?'

'They were.'

He pointed at the corpses. 'Their blood?'

'I could not tell.'

'They were eaten,' said another member of the crew. This one was lanky with awful skin, and a deep rash around his mouth and nose where a rebreather mask normally sat.

'Duct spiders. We had an infestation of 'em on the *Executioner's Moon*. They get into the engines and breed, and they'll chew you up just like that.'

'This is daemon-work,' said Lysander.

'Are you certain?' said Rigalto.

'I have rarely been more certain of anything. These souls were their way in. With enough will, enough power, even the mind of a non-psyker can be a gateway for the daemon. We bloodied Shon'tu's nose at the Tomb, my brothers. It is not the way of the Iron Warriors to send warp-spawn to do what they could themselves do face to face. We are forcing their hand.'

'Then let us take what encouragement we can, captain,' said Rigalto. 'But that does not change the fact that these things are running around our star fort.'

'Leave us,' said Lysander. The crew, used to taking their orders from an Imperial Fist, bowed their heads and left the barracks room, leaving the Space Marines with the bodies.

'And you, Rigalto,' added Lysander.

'Captain? If we are to hunt them down we must stick together. We could sweep by sections, drive them towards–'

'Leave,' said Lysander. 'This is not a battle to be fought, because the enemy is not a soldier. Not this daemon. It is an assassin. It will not make itself known until it can move on its target. We could wait forever for it to emerge from whatever shadow it hides in, only for it to strike when our guard eventually falls.'

'Then it is here to kill you,' said Rigalto. 'And you will use yourself as bait?'

'The bait has no say in the kill,' replied Lysander. 'I shall. My orders have kept us alive thus far. Follow them again, Rigalto. Make your brothers ready, for Shon'tu will strike as soon as his daemons have either succeeded or failed. Go.'

'As you command, captain,' said Rigalto with a bow of the head. 'Good luck.'

'Dorn wrote that there is no such thing as luck,' replied

Lysander. 'Fate perhaps, but not luck. To your duties, sergeant.'

'Yes, captain.'

Rigalto saluted and turned away, leading his squadmates out of the barracks. Lysander turned again to the sorry sight of the bodies on the floor.

'If you hear all, as you claim,' he said quietly, 'then hear this. I am the victim you are commanded to kill, but you will find no victim on this star fort. If you can feel anything so human as regret, then you will regret the binding that compels you to seek me out. I am an Imperial Fist, a son of Rogal Dorn, and I do not feel fear. But I know what fear is, because it is my duty to inflict it on creatures such as you.'

Lysander could hear them, their limbs clicking on the walls and ceiling of the corridors around the barracks like so many spiders scuttling around their web. He did not look back as he left the barracks and the corpses, and headed towards the star fort's apothecarion.

THE DANCERS AT the Precipice did not perceive reality at all. Existing partially in the warp, their senses strained to reach across the veil to real space. It was the warp's reflection they saw, the emotional echoes of structures in reality. The corridors and hangars of the *Endeavour of Will* were seen in the shades of old emotions left there. All areas of the star fort were veneered in a thin layer of fear, as suffered by the unaugmented crew in times of battle. Pain was scattered, like blood spatter, around old battle damage scars, and it pooled in glowing stains around triage stations and the way leading to the apothecarion.

Arrogance and a sense of iron-bound duty glowed around the command areas where the Imperial Fists were most often found, details picked out in anger and flavoured with the lust for battle secretly held by so many Space Marines, and acknowledged by only a few. The airlocks, where the dead were traditionally sent on their final voyage, were steeped in sorrow and regret. Trace elements of happiness, even pinpoints of ecstasy in hidden secret places among the star fort's architecture, were swamped by the grim emotions of war, those stains that lasted the longest and brought out every passageway and compartment as the Dancers scampered through them.

They followed the pain. They had tasted Lysander and the train of relentless duty he left, a metallic thread winding through the star fort, and it coincided with the increasing density of pain and desperation encrusting the approaches to the apothecarion.

The Dancers had no leader. They were moved by the currents of the warp that flowed through them, and in that moment it demanded that they kill. Lysander's was a taste they knew well, and nothing would be as delicious as to temper it with pain and anger, and the awful certainty that came with the approach of death. They had already killed, but the deaths of those whose bodies they had usurped was weak and watery. Their deaths were tasteless compared to the banquet that would be Lysander's death. The warp gave them hunger, and they sprang on to sate it.

TECHMARINE HESTION WAS awake. His eyes opened as Lysander boomed hurriedly into the room. The auto-surgeon knitting together the skin of his chest recoiled at the motion, spindly arms folding up and away from the exposed muscle. He still looked shockingly weak, his musculature scorched and wasted away, and it looked impossible for him to ever fill the armour stacked up at his bedside. He sat up as best he could at Lysander's approach.

'Captain!' he said, raw-throated. 'I have heard of battle. The orderlies know little, only that the enemy is upon us and that you have fought them off. Is it so?'

'Thus far,' said Lysander. 'The battle is not done. And forgive me, brother, for I have brought it with me.'

The apothecarion darkened. Spidery shadows flickered over the glow-globes in the ceiling. Half-glimpsed figures of gnarled, blood-red muscle, cloaked in darkness, scampered around the walls. Lysander backed up against Hestion's bed, drawing the Fist of Dorn up into a guard and shouldering his shield so it protected Hestion from the gathering shadows.

Spectral fingers lashed out, congealing into reality as they raked across Lysander's shield. More reached out from the warp and snared Lysander's limbs, trying to haul him off his feet. He wrenched his shield arm around and batted one of the shadows against the far wall, its body like a bundle of spiders' legs bunching up as it slammed into the wall and thrashed to the ground. Lysander raised the hammer and punched its head into a second daemon as it coalesced in front of him – the daemon flitted back, vanishing through the wall as the hammer crunched home a hair's breadth too late.

'I may be laid low, but I am still Adeptus Astartes,' said Hestion, struggling to sit up. 'Hand me my gun, Lysander. My blade.'

'You will fight, my brother, fear not on that score,' said Lysander as he circled, starting at the daemons as they stalked through the half-light around him. 'I must ask more of you than I have ever asked of an Imperial Fist.'

'Then ask, captain. What little I have left to give, I would give in battle.'

'For once, Hestion, do not give so unthinkingly. For I ask of you your death.'

Hestion forced himself into a sitting position and swung his legs over the side of the bed, grimacing as his half-healed skin tore. He wrenched a surgical blade from the autosurgeon above him, wielding it like a dagger. 'I do not understand, captain,' he said, voice strained.

'Your death, Hestion. The one thing I can have no right to demand of you. I must ask for it, freely given.'

'I will die here anyway, captain. The apothecary cogitator has made its prognosis. My organs are too badly damaged. Soon I will be comatose, and death will then be swift.'

Another daemon slashed forwards, aiming for Hestion. Lysander stepped into its path and caught the charge on his shield. He was forced back a pace, before swinging the Fist of Dorn into the daemon and tearing it into a shower of shredded limbs and broken shadows.

'Back!' yelled Lysander. 'Just as Dorn cast the daemon from Terra, so I will cast you from this place! Back to the warp, to burn beneath the wrath of your gods! You will not take Lysander today!'

'I told myself that death is no shame, if it be a warrior's death,' said Hestion. His blade was held in front of him, but his hand wavered, for most of the muscles had been scorched away and his strength was gone.

'It will not be a warrior's death,' said Lysander. 'It will be a wretched one. Will you give this to me, my brother? I ask you as a friend, not a commander. Will you accept?'

Hestion's eyes turned from Lysander to the daemons. They were gathering more thickly now, as if the apothecarion was disappearing to be replaced by a hellish place composed of daemon's flesh.

'When you returned from Malodrax,' the Techmarine said, 'some said that you should not rejoin us. The risk was too great that you had… brought something back with you. That you were corrupted, somewhere deep down.'

'What are you saying, Hestion?' demanded Lysander.

Hestion's voice shook as he forced out the words. 'You ask if I trust you with my death, brother. My reply is that I… I do not know.'

The walls bowed in and the daemons tore through, reality splitting like torn skin. The Dancers at the Precipice roared like a tornado of daemons' flesh centred on Lysander and Hestion, limbs lashing out at the two Imperial Fists. Lysander caught blows on his shield and on the haft of the Fist of Dorn, protecting Hestion as best he could. Hestion fended off a claw that unfolded from a stalk of lashing, knotted flesh, cutting through the unreal muscle with his blade, but other talons caught him and opened up new wounds on his half-formed skin. Hestion slumped off the bed to one knee, a red slash along the side of his throat, exposing spine and sinew.

Hestion coughed out an angry growl. He grabbed one of the Dancers with his free hand, dragging it out of the swirling mass. He stabbed down at its shifting face, the features swimming around the blade as it punched into the place where its head should have been. Limbs split and reformed, squirming under Hestion and pincering around him to hold him fast. Lysander kicked out and shattered the daemon's body with a massive armoured boot, smacking the remains off Hestion with a swing of his hammer.

The Dancers swarmed closer. Hestion was caught by a dozen limbs at once and hauled off his feet, pulled into the mass. Lysander yelled and tried to drag the Techmarine back, even as the Dancers ripped at him too, scoring deep gashes in the ceramite of his armour and shield, clawing at his face and eyes.

'I was there when the black sun rose!'

Lysander's voice cut through the hiss of the daemons' talons.

'Upon the blood-red sands, I laid him low!' continued Lysander. 'I cast his head into the ammonia sea! I stood against you and I defeated you! I am the Gilded Wrath of Malodrax!'

IT WAS UPON the blasted ground of Malodrax that the Dancers at the Precipice coalesced into real space for the first time, dragged out of formlessness and bedlam by a thousand voices raised in terror and pain. Malodrax was one of a million worlds found, conquered and subsequently forgotten by the Imperium, and seized by the powers of the warp who did not forget. From the flint-bladed mountains and ammonia oceans of Malodrax were forged death pits and warrens, carved by the hands of slaves and the sorcery of Chaos's champions. Each one was dedicated to a different form of torment or execution. Artists begged the God of Change to transport them to Malodrax so they might create wonders there that no sane world would permit. Daemons gambolled between the death pits, and among them were the Dancers at the Precipice, who congealed from the stuff of the warp to attend joyfully on the millions of extinguished lives.

Cultists among the shipping lanes of the Imperium diverted passenger liners and pilgrim hulks into the dead, uninhabited space around Malodrax. Their living cargoes were poured into the death pits, and the Dancers at the Precipice took their place among the daemons and madmen welcoming them to their new and final home in the lava chambers or parasite nests, the endless steel-clad tunnels hung with flensed skin, the acid springs and the oubliettes full of razorblades.

The Iron Warriors saw a place of worship and pain, yes, but also one of inefficiency and waste. Space Marines of the Iron Warriors Legion landed there and turned the bands of daemons into armies, the death pits into factories. Daemon-scholars were summoned or created to keep a tally of every death offered up to the warp, and every form of torture discovered among the madness.

Then from the warp arrived a spacecraft accompanied by the heralds of Tzeentch singing in celebration. Every daemon, it is said, stopped their bloody work and watched as it descended from the torn skies of Malodrax. It had been lost in the warp for many years, as evidenced by the blistered hull and its state of disrepair, but there was no mistaking the heraldry of the Imperial Fists it bore. It was the *Shield of Valour*, thought destroyed in a warp collapse decades before, and it had been vomited up by the ether as a gift to the daemons of Malodrax. The Iron Warriors formed a guard to shepherd the passengers off the ship, and even now there was no doubting the pride and deadliness of those men – for they were Imperial Fists. First among them, like an animal kept caged in his armour of gold, was a Space Marine captain who with the merest glance told everyone who saw him what he would do to them when he got free.

All of the Imperial Fists were consigned to the pits. One by one, they died. They held on for a long time, and the unique opportunities offered by a Space Marine's physiology were not wasted by those daemons who fancied themselves surgeons. The Iron Warriors made a particular point of watching the captain, for they knew that he would last the longest. They were disappointed that he died so soon after his battle-brothers, and that the daemons, in their enthusiasm, had heaped upon him so many varying methods of death that it was impossible to tell what had killed him.

The Iron Warriors argued with the daemon torturers. The Dancers at the Precipice were among them, newly-born and already resenting the bonds that compelled them to obey the Iron Warriors or fade from real space. They denied that they had thrown away the Imperial Fist's life, for his soul was now being rent by their fellow daemons of the warp, and indeed the Iron Warriors were the wasteful ones for they denied the warp their kill for too long.

Guns were drawn. Daemons' teeth were bared. The Iron Warriors and the daemons were ready to offer each other's deaths up to the warp; then one of them noticed the Imperial Fists captain's corpse was missing.

What followed was remembered only in scraps of memory. A few details were scraped onto the walls of a fortress in the warp, where details of a billion battles were kept inscribed on the massive lead blocks of its battlements. Others turned up in séances and daemon-haunted nightmares for years afterwards. The Imperial Fist became the Gilded Wrath of Malodrax, and daemons spoke of him as men spoke of daemons. He tore his way through the death pits, and by the time he reached the surface of Malodrax he was accompanied by everyone who could walk and fight that had broken from their chains as he slaughtered every daemon in his way.

Somehow, a message reached the Imperial Fists. A force sent to Malodrax found their battle-brother fending off a tide of horrors at the edge of a chemical ocean. The Dancers at the Precipice fought him there, and from their number he tore the one who had been their primary personality, the thing closest to a leader.

The Imperial Fist tore the daemon's head off and threw it into the sea. Malodrax's sun turned black, the eclipse like an eye closing in response to the challenge. The Space marine cried out that he was Darnath Lysander, and that no daemon could kill him. And the Iron Warriors who had overseen his captivity, if they had a spine between them, would face him there and fight to the death, for no one locked up an Imperial Fist and lived.

The Imperial Fists landed and took their brother back to his Chapter before daemon reinforcements could arrive. Lysander spat on the ground and cursed the Iron Warriors. A daemon was hatred and evil incarnate, but an Iron Warrior had once been a man who had chosen to become what he was. Lysander would never forgive them, not for what they had done to him, but for what they had done to themselves. And he would see them all dead in his lifetime, or he would have failed in his duty to mankind.

THE DANCERS HOVERED around Lysander. They crouched against the ceiling and on the floor, the knotted muscle of their bodies masked in shifting veils of shadow that fluttered like banners in the wind.

'I took one of you,' said Lysander. 'I laid him low. The inquisitors of the Holy Ordos sought out the works of madmen and prophets, and found there the binding laws of the Dancers at the Precipice. I know that when I shed your blood, you are bound to me. You must obey, only once, but absolutely. Is this not so? Is this not written?'

'It is so,' came the hissing reply. 'Upon the hides of the Gravendran Hydra, in the ink from the Tears of Morgedren, it was written. This was the contract that wove us into being from the raw stuff of the warp. This was the form taken by the will of Tzeentch.'

'Then I may command you once.'

'Not to destruction!' came the reply. It seemed all the Dancers spoke at once, but as if through the same throat, so many voices tangled into one torrent of noise. 'Not unto the end of existence! It is written!'

Lysander turned and looked down at Hestion. The Techmarine was breathing heavily, his fused ribs obvious as they moved beneath gelatinous, half-made muscle. He did not look back, his eyes instead fixed on the daemons that formed a wall before him. Lysander looked away from the Techmarine and spoke.

'Take the body of Techmarine Hestion of the Imperial Fists,' he said. 'Into his body I bind you. Let his form be your prison. This is the will of the Gilded Wrath of Malodrax, and you are compelled to obey. So it is written.'

The daemons screamed. They fought. They howled and scratched at reality. But they were bound by fate, a force as certain and relentless in the warp as gravity was in real space. Their forms stretched and deformed as they were drawn by the grasp of fate towards Hestion.

It was impossible to tell if Hestion understood what was happening as he was caught in a cage of painful light, his form merging with that of the Dancers. Their tangled limbs rippled through his skin and muscle, their glowing eyes bulged from his body and his features distorted with theirs.

Hestion's body contracted again, forcing the Dancers into his own form. He writhed on the apothecarion floor, and joints cracked and popped as his body was forced out of its proper shape. The faces of the Dancers, red eyes and indistinct folds of features, shifted under his skin. Hestion's face was as distorted as the rest of him, jaw locked open, eyes screwed shut, blood trickling from his nose and eyes.

'Now you have a body, an honest human body,' said Lysander, bringing the Fist of Dorn over his head. 'And now you can die.'

The Dancers screamed in denial, but as was written, the Gilded Wrath who had defeated them had bound them to his will and they could not escape the bonds of fate that held them in Hestion's body. Hestion was in there with them too, and perhaps some of the screams that issued from his raw throat were his. But they were lost among the inhuman sound that issued from Hestion, a howl like a gale roaring straight from the warp.

Lysander yelled and brought the Fist of Dorn down. Hestion, his body commanded by the Dancers at the Precipice, tried to rise to face him, but Hestion's body was broken and Lysander was too quick. The head of the hammer slammed into Hestion's chest and drove him against the wall of the apothecarion. Ribs crunched and splayed, painting the wall with the Techmarine's blood. From his ruptured body the broken limbs of the Dancers reached, waving feebly at Lysander as if trying to fend him off.

Lysander's second strike knocked Hestion's head from his shoulders. His body toppled to the side, and the cries of the daemons were replaced with the awful high-pitched squealing and gibbering that was their death rattle. As Hestion's blood pooled on the floor, the Dancers at the Precipice discorporated and became once again the formless stuff of the warp.

The silence seemed to take a long time to return. The air rang with the din that had died down, as if the apothecarion was reluctant to let go of the battle it had seen. Moment by moment the echoes faded, until the only sound was the dripping of Hestion's blood from the ceiling and the autosurgeon bed.

Lysander knelt beside the body of the Techmarine. Hestion's body was a wreck, intact only below the waist, the torso broken open and the head gone.

'I am...' said Lysander. The rest of the sentence caught in his throat.

I am sorry, brother. There was no one to hear it.

He switched on his vox-link. 'Rigalto, Menander. Lysander here. The daemons have been cast out, but Techmarine Hestion is dead. Attend upon the apothecarion for his honour guard. Though we are at war, we will give him the rites that are his due.'

Acknowledgement runes flickered. Lysander stood back up, and looked down at himself. Hestion's blood was spattered over him, already congealing into rust-red crystals, for a Space Marine's blood did so almost instantly to seal the wounds of battle.

Lysander leaned the Fist of Dorn against the wall and, pulling the sheets from a nearby bed, began to wipe Hestion's blood from his armour.

THE MUSTER DECK of the *Ferrous Malice* was hung with captive banners, from the delicate silks of an eldar pirate lord to the bullet-shredded standards of Imperial Guard regiments. The siege masters of the Iron Warriors had taken them from the most secure fortresses in the galaxy, or from the corpses of the enemies who had dared to besiege their own strongholds.

Shon'tu looked up at them, and knew that added to them would be a standard torn from the hallways of the *Endeavour of Will*. It was not a vow, it was not an ambition. It was a simple fact. The gods of the warp had decided it would be so. Fate would take care of the rest. Fate, and the guns of the Iron Warriors.

Shon'tu turned to the Iron Warriors gathered on the muster deck. Beneath the blood-coloured light from above, the steel of their armour shone grimly, punctuated by the glow of the eye lenses beneath the visors of their helmets. Well over fifty Iron Warriors stood ranked up, the entire warband sworn to Warsmith Shon'tu. Four squads of Space Marines, along with the surviving Obliterators of the Coven and the possessed of the Choir. Forge-Chaplain Koultus, priest of the dark gods who brought the favour of the warp with him. Steelwatcher Mhul, Shon'tu's weaponsmith. Shon'tu's own veterans. Even with the losses at the Tomb of Ionis, the Iron Warriors outnumbered the Imperial Fists by three to one at least.

And every one of them wore iron within just as he wore the iron of his armour without. Every one had taken the steps on the path that Shon'tu himself had almost finished – the conversion from man into machine, from a weak thing of fallible flesh to a weapon in the image of the primarch Perturabo. The forges of the Iron Warriors created bionics with technology long forgotten by the Adeptus Mechanicus of the Imperium, and every one of Shon'tu's warband carried within him a relentless steel heart or a bionic limb, cranial implants loaded with battle-routines or inhuman artificial senses.

'Fate has seen fit,' said Shon'tu, 'to place before us a test. A puzzle box hangs in the void before us to be unlocked. The prize inside is the head of Captain Lysander of the Imperial Fists. The daemon could not tear its machine-spirit from its shell. We have sought to pick its lock with a surgical assault. We have sought to bypass its defences and strike at the prize directly.' Shon'tu drove a fist into the palm of his gauntlet. 'The only tactic that remains is to smash it!'

The Iron Warriors raised their left fists. 'Iron within!' they yelled. 'Iron without!'

'Brother Malikos!' ordered Shon'tu. 'To your squad falls the task of securing the western lance battery. The assault on the machine-spirit left it dormant, and it has no defences against our Dreadclaws. Brother Veyrin, you will accompany Steelwatcher Mhul to the spur. Brother Tektos, Brother Skast, with me you will secure the rest of the western defence spur.'

The hullward edge of the muster deck was dominated by enormous cradles holding a dozen Dreadclaw assault-pods. Vapour hissed as pneumatic arms lowered the pods into boarding positions, warning lanterns flashing. Mutant crewmen scrambled across the machinery, tightening valves and operating controls, as the Iron Warriors lined up with parade ground efficiency to board.

Shon'tu's mind had long been given over to the seething stuff of a devotee of Chaos, but fragments of human emotions could still surface, an echo of the man he had presumably been several lifetimes ago. He was angry. He was humiliated. The Imperial Fists had him – Lysander had bested him, with a cunning that should have been the province of an Iron Warrior. Lysander's death would burn that away. The human side of Shon'tu would be forced down again, buried under the steel of an Iron Warrior, not to emerge again for another ten thousand years.

He would have to send his whole warband onto the *Endeavour of Will*. It was the only way he could be sure that no trickery of Lysander's could withstand an attack. He had held back his force to test the Imperial Fists' defences, and to claim the prize of the star fort and Lysander's head without risking his entire strength. But risking it now was worth it. To silence that weak human, the final part of him not yet replaced with iron, it was worth it.

The Iron Warriors embarked into their assault-pods. The sergeants spoke words of prayer to the Iron Warriors they led. The crew hauled the Dreadclaws closed after them, sealing the embarkation doors with sigils of warding that called on the powers of the warp to deliver them to their enemies.

Shon'tu's own veterans lined up with him at the final Dreadclaw. 'I shall cast the head of Lysander into the warp,' he told them. 'It matters not who kills him. To us all the glory will belong. But I shall stand upon the threshold and give his head to the gods. That is all that matters.'

'For such an offering,' said Brother Ku'Van, 'daemonhood will surely be granted.'

'Then if it is so,' said Shon'tu, 'I shall take the wings of the daemon and let their shadow fall across the Imperium. No Imperial Fist will be spared my wrath. And then, no Space Marine. And then, no man. It is here that it will begin; with the death of Lysander, and with the boon of daemonhood, it will never end.'

Shon'tu's squad climbed into the Dreadclaw. Gravrestraints locked around them as the door was hauled closed, and the only light was the winking of the status display that told Shon'tu the Dreadclaw was ready to launch.

'Iron within!' ordered Shon'tu. 'Iron without! To the fray, my brothers! Launch!'

'HE WAS A Space Marine,' said Lysander, his head bowed. 'He was a son of Dorn. A defender of the Imperium. A golden light in the darkness. But above all things, he was a brother.'

Lined up in the airlock corridor stood the seven surviving members of Squad Rigalto, Scout-Sergeant Menander and his two remaining Scouts, and Lysander's First Company command squad. In front of them, held above the ground by a suspensor unit, was Techmarine Hestion's coffin. It was a functional box for transporting bodies from the apothecarion – a Space Marine required better, according to the law of the Chapter, but on a war footing there had not been the time to organise full funeral rites for Hestion. As commanding officer it was Lysander's duty to say the eulogy, a duty he had fulfilled many dozens of times. The circular airlock portal was ready to receive the coffin and send it on its way into the void, as was traditional for those who died on a spacecraft or space station. Hestion's gene-seed had been extracted by the star fort's apothecary staff as best it could from what remained of his head and neck, and all that remained for the Techmarine was this final journey.

'Victory,' said Lysander, 'is sacrifice. Rogal Dorn teaches us this. He learned it in turn from the Emperor Most High, who willingly sacrificed everything he was to defeat the arch-traitor, Horus. One day the sacrifice will be ours to make, just as it was our battle-brother Hestion's, and it is the greatest honour we can bestow upon him to make that sacrifice as he did before us. Go to Dorn, brother, stand beside the Emperor, and at His side may you fight on.'

'May you fight on,' echoed the assembled Imperial Fists. Their heads were bowed in prayer, too. They had performed this scene already for the Space Marines lost at the Tomb of Ionis, and sent five such coffins into space with the same sentiments. It never became routine, this farewell to a brother, because every Imperial Fist knew that one day it would be him in the coffin, be it a wooden box cast from an airlock or a gilded sarcophagus interred in a memorial on the *Phalanx*.

But this time was different. Hestion had died from a head

wound that every Imperial Fist who saw the corpse knew was from a thunder hammer strike. The only such weapon on the *Endeavour of Will* now hung across the back of Captain Lysander. Even if Hestion's body had been a host to daemons, Hestion himself dead, it had still been the hand of a fellow Imperial Fist that struck the final blow. It was not the first time a brother had killed a brother, nor would it be the last, but such an event was always toxic. It could only happen through treachery, as one brother turned on another, or the collapse of an Imperial Fist's vaunted mental defences, as when a mind was driven from its body and replaced with the daemon. For Lysander to have killed Hestion, no matter how justified in the moment, must have been the result of some appalling violation of everything a Space Marine should be.

Two of Squad Rigalto pushed the coffin towards the airlock. One of the star fort's crew operated the controls that slid open the portal, and the coffin passed through the first airlock door. The inner door closed again, the airlock depressurised, and the outer door opened.

The coffin slid out into the void, accompanied only by silence and a shoal of icy slivers that flaked off in the sudden cold of space. Hestion's coffin got smaller and smaller, lit into a hard-edged lozenge of red light from the star Kholestus, until it became impossible to distinguish from the scattering of stars and the billows of the nebulae marking the edge of the Eye of Terror.

Lysander's vox chirped. 'Sensorium helm here,' came the voice of one of the star fort's bridge crew. 'Multiple contacts coming in, looks like boarding craft. They're moving in on the western spur.'

'What defences are active there?' said Lysander.

'None,' came the reply. 'All were lost to the machine-spirit.'

Lysander looked up at the Imperial Fists who were now waiting for his orders. They knew from the tone of his voice that the time for reflection was gone, and that they were back at war.

'Shon'tu has launched his final attack,' said Lysander.

'We have humiliated him and he is sending everything he has to destroy us. But that also means he is risking everything he has. Take comfort from the examples of the brothers we have lost. Through sacrifice, they have defied Shon'tu this far. Through sacrifice, if needs be, we shall defy him again. You have your orders. You know what is expected of you. To your stations, sons of Dorn.'

As the Imperial Fists split up to man the positions Lysander had dictated, Lysander took a final look through the airlock porthole. Hestion's coffin was invisible against the backdrop of stars. The Techmarine had gone to join Dorn and the Emperor at the end of time, to fight the final battle for mankind's soul. Lysander had at least one more battle to fight before he could take his place there too.

It was worth it. There was no doubt about that. Everything could be gambled and lost, if that was what it took to achieve victory.

Everything.

Though the Obliterators could no longer speak – their vocal cords having long ago been sacrificed for yet another gun barrel – there was never any doubt about their mood. They existed in a permanent state of anger, for the tech-virus that had altered their bodies also took a hold of their minds and filled them with the desire to destroy everything around them. Commanding such troops was as much a matter of reining them in as letting them loose.

Steelwatcher Mhul had the task of commanding the coven of Obliterators that belonged to Shon'tu's warband. Only two such creatures remained, the other having fallen to Lysander and the Fist of Dorn or to the virus in the Tomb of Ionis. Two was more than enough.

Mhul watched the Obliterators tear through the layers of steel and circuitry surrounding the massive cylindrical base of the defence laser. The laser was the largest weapon in the western spur of the star fort, a titanic weapon which focused enough power to punch a torrent of las-fire straight through the hull of a spaceship the size of the

Ferrous Malice. The Obliterators could not fit through the narrow passages designed for the unaugmented crew of the *Endeavour of Will*, so they made their own path. Mhul followed, prodding the Obliterators in the right direction with bursts of pain from the mind impulse unit that surrounded his head like a steel halo.

The Obliterators' hands reformed into steel claws that ripped away the metal of the weapon's housing, revealing stacks of datamedium amid the destruction.

'Stop,' said Mhul, his words accompanied by a burst of psychic code that seized the Obliterators' muscles. 'There. You. Infect it.'

One of the Obliterators took a step back and reeled as if struck. His face split open and cycled through various calibres of gun barrels, melding from one to the other from the flesh and steel inside its skull. Finally something other than a weapon emerged – a nest of tendrils, fleshy and red, that probed in front of them accompanied by a wet hissing sound. The tendrils found the crystalline datamedium and wrapped around it, slithering across its surface to find a way in.

The Obliterators were created when an Iron Warrior, already as much machine as Space Marine, became host to a tech-virus. The virus itself had its origin in the warp. Perhaps it was a gift from one of the dark gods that reigned there, or was a curse on the Traitor Legions. Perhaps it was a natural predator (as natural as anything could be in the warp), or it was a daemon itself, one that existed entirely in information form. Whatever its reason for being, it took the substance of a Space Marine and turned it into a biomechanical weapon, every muscle and bone adapted to form part of the hundreds of weapon systems an Obliterator could form from his mutating body. And the tech-virus had another property even more dangerous than its capacity to turn flesh into a weapon. It was infectious, and could be transmitted.

The tendrils wormed their way under the surface of the datamedium. The crystal became blotchy and discoloured as the virus found a new place to live and thrive, forming mottled blooms like bacteria on a culture plate.

The air was filled with the sound of grinding metal as the whole defence laser shuddered. It rotated in its mountings, the building-sized laser barrel turning towards the main structure of the *Endeavour of Will*. Flakes of rust fell like a dark rain around Steelwatcher Mhul, and loose components clattered to the deck around him. The Obliterators extracted themselves from the tangle of metal as it churned with the movement. The one who had infected the gun stumbled out of the wreckage as its face reformed into the scowl it always carried, one eye narrow and hateful, the other replaced with a gun barrel.

The Obliterators crouched down beside Steelwatcher Mhul like attack dogs deprived of prey, scanning for targets.

'Good,' said Mhul, sending a wave of pacifying code through the coven. He switched to the command vox-channel. 'Warsmith,' he said. 'It is done.'

SHON'TU AND THE Iron Warriors under his command stood lined up ready to advance, in the primary arterial corridor that led to the main structure of the *Endeavour of Will*. The top half of the corridor was transparent and so Shon'tu could see the mass of the star fort looming over him, covered with soaring battlements and arched portholes, studded with weaponry. The banners of the Imperial Fists, articulated sheets of steel half a kilometre long, hung to display the gold colours and red fist of the Chapter.

'See?' said Shon'tu, pointing up at the colours that hung from the star fort. 'We shall tear them down. There shall hang the heraldry of Olympia.'

'Warsmith,' came Mhul's voice over the vox. 'It is done.'

'Good,' replied Shon'tu. 'Ensure that the targeting is sound, and then open fire.'

The *Endeavour of Will* had one massive advantage over the Iron Warriors. Even with its weapons mostly dead and its garrison outnumbered, its sheer size made it a difficult fortress to break down. Between the Iron Warriors and the command centres at the heart of the star fort, the machine-spirit housing and datamedium vault, the bridge from which the whole star fort was controlled, were hundreds of kilometres of corridors, thousands of bulkheads and blast doors. Forcing a way through them would take time the Imperial Fists could use to set ambushes or outflank the Iron Warriors, cut them off from one another and channel them into battles they fought on their terms. The Iron Warriors would still be victorious, but only at the expense of many of Shon'tu's warband, and that was not an acceptable way for an Iron Warrior to fight a battle.

There was no easy way into the heart of the *Endeavour of Will*. So Shon'tu would make one.

There need be no risk at all, said a familiar but unwelcome voice in Shon'tu's head, buzzing around his cranial implants and hijacking the logic circuits wired into his brain. *There is another way.*

'Silence,' said Shon'tu, quietly enough for only him to hear.

Release me.

'I said silence.'

The whole western spire shuddered and thrummed with power. Behind Shon'tu's position the titanic defence laser was powering up, the energy coils along its length glowing at first a dull burnt orange, then blue, then white, as enormous amounts of power were pooled. The barrel completed its traverse to point straight at the centre of the star fort. Safety circuits that would normally prevent the laser from being aimed at the star fort itself had been burned out by the Obliterator virus, while the control circuits destroyed by the initial attack on the machine-spirit had been repaired. The defence laser was in Iron Warriors hands now, and there was nothing the star fort or anyone on board could do to stop it.

The laser fired, and it seemed that the void itself was torn open, a gash through reality that opened up to an ocean of burning light. The augmetic vision of the Iron Warriors kept them from being blinded. The heat and magnetic shielding of the star fort's structure kept them from being incinerated and irradiated. For that split second, a lance of energy hotter than a star transfixed the star fort like an arrow through the heart.

When the glare died, the star fort was laid open, a massive wound revealing the tangled steel entrails surrounding the machine-spirit core and the command decks. Torrents of wreckage spilled out, spinning off into the void in all directions. Severed power lines spat energy at random and explosions burst silently, instantly snuffed out by the vacuum.

'Onwards,' voxed Shon'tu. 'They are dead, they merely do not know it. Let us educate them. Onwards!'

The Iron Warriors followed Shon'tu as he led them down the arterial tunnel towards the ruptured heart of the *Endeavour of Will*, feet tramping in time, as the wreckage from the blast pattered against the transparent ceiling overhead.

LYSANDER FORGED THROUGH the dense smoke, the heavy chemical taste of it distinct even through his armour's filter, which had folded up over his mouth and nose.

He had been on his way to the command deck when the explosion had hit. He had known instantly that something huge had impacted upon the *Endeavour of Will* – the din echoed from every corner of the star fort, the floor shaking in a manner that told of the whole station shuddering, the sudden kaleidoscope of warning icons on his retina signifying a massive strike.

Around him, sections of ceiling had fallen in, and slabs of flooring had collapsed into the decks below. A fire had caught light somewhere very near and within seconds had filled the corridor with toxic smoke. Lysander found his footing, bracing himself against a buttress in the wall.

'Rigalto!' yelled Lysander into the vox. 'Where are you?'

'Command deck, captain,' came the reply.

'Casualties?'

'None of my squad or Menander's. I can't tell if any of the crew is hurt, but I can scarcely believe there are no casualties. One of the defence lasers hit us. Shon'tu must have taken control of it.'

'He has,' said Lysander. 'He had four choices for his final assault. That was one of them.'

'Commander?'

'Shon'tu's way of war is much like ours,' replied Lysander. His augmetic senses had adapted to the smoke and fire, and he could see several bodies in the corridor ahead of him, knocked unconscious or killed outright by the explosion and now aflame. The crew uniforms, with the heraldry of the Imperial Fists, were being consumed by the fire. 'According to our ways, only a few possibilities for capturing the fort presented themselves. This was one of them. Shon'tu has gone through the same process of thought.'

'Then what are your orders?'

'Take your squad and Menander's to the datamedium vault,' replied Lysander.

'The vault? There are more defensible areas of–'

'Those are your orders,' repeated Lysander. 'Shon'tu relies on speed and shock. Do not give him those advantages. Go now, I will meet you there.'

Lysander ignored Rigalto's acknowledgement, as through the smoke and flames charged the shape of a Space Marine.

Lysander knew it was an Iron Warrior by its unnatural silhouette, broken by ungainly bionics which looked more like industrial tools than replacement limbs. A steam hammer was attached by pistons and cables to the stump of one arm, and it crashed through a sheet of fallen ceiling as it swung at Lysander.

Lysander ducked the blow and brought the Fist of Dorn around for a reverse strike. But the floor shifted beneath him and he was falling head over toe, metal twisting around him.

Lysander hit the deck below at an awkward angle, almost head-first. Flames were everywhere around him, scorching his unprotected face, rippling up the walls and along what remained of the ceiling. He forced his way back to his feet but already the Iron Warrior was falling after him, hammer-first, steam spraying as the pistons drove the weapon forwards.

The hammer crunched into Lysander's chest. Lysander sprawled onto his back under the weight, rolling onto his shield side to get out from under the enemy. The Iron Warrior stayed with him, his human hand holding on as the hammer was brought up to slam down again, this time into Lysander's face.

Lysander smacked the edge of his shield into the Iron Warrior's visor. The visor was sheared away and for a moment Lysander could see his assailant's face. The skin was grey and withered, as if it had been drained of all vital fluids and filled up with colourless sludge. The eyes were silver orbs without pupils. The nose was gone completely, leaving two slits leading to implanted filters. The face ended just above where the mouth should be, everything from that point to the collarbone a tangle of cables, gauges and valves, spurting steam.

Lysander and the Iron Warrior were bathed in flames. Lysander wrestled with his attacker as the fire rippled over him, submerging him as if in water. He could feel the skin of his face blistering, the inside of his armour heating up, as he kicked and thrashed to throw the Iron Warrior off him.

Lysander caught the Iron Warrior's hammer with the haft of his own, forcing the traitor to one side. His shield arm was free again and he forced the shield under the Iron Warrior's body, levering the traitor off of him. With a yell of effort and anger he threw the Iron Warrior back into the flames.

Lysander lost sight of his attacker. The flames and the choking smoke masked everything. Even the ceramite of Lysander's armour was faltering in the fire, scorching him at the joints. He had to get out, but if he turned and ran the enemy would have a free shot at his back – and even

Terminator armour could not be trusted to save him then.

The Iron Warrior leaped through the flames, the exposed skin of his face crackling and bubbling. Lysander stepped back, raising his shield to take the charge.

The side of the Iron Warrior's head burst in a spray of dark blood and torn wires. He skidded onto the ground, sliding through the flames and coming to a halt at Lysander's feet. He twitched a little and the flames rolled over him.

Sergeant Laocos strode out of the smoke. Lysander recognised the leader of his command squad, and the glowing of the barrels of his storm bolter, the gun which had just fired the fatal shot.

'Captain!' shouted Laocos over the din of the fire. 'The enemy seeks to surround and flank us! We must move!'

Brother-Scholar Demosthor was behind Laocos, tracking for targets with his assault cannon. The deck behind him was in a similar state of destruction, and while no unaugmented crew could have survived down here, the Iron Warriors could use it as a way through the star fort if they moved fast enough.

'To the datamedium vault!' shouted Lysander. 'That is where our stand will be!'

Laocos nodded. 'My brothers! Forge on!'

The five-strong squad gathered on Laocos and followed Lysander as he kicked his way through the burning wreckage and headed for the nearest stairwell leading upwards. The pain was great, with the burns on his face and joints just now flaring up, but a Space Marine could ignore pain for as long as he had to.

'I suspect I know what you are planning,' said Laocos. His voice came over an individual vox-channel – the rest of the squad could not hear. 'As your sergeant, it is my duty to speak.'

'Then do so,' replied Lysander. He shouldered open a buckled door and revealed a stairwell. The deck above was smothered in smoke but there were no flames, and the way towards the vault looked clear.

'I am compelled to ask if you truly understand the consequences of this plan,' said Laocos.

'I am more aware of them than anyone,' replied Lysander. 'Shon'tu must fall, that is certain. And we have all heard of what his kind did to you on Malodrax. Any one of us would–'

'I am not fighting for revenge,' said Lysander sharply. 'On Malodrax I saw what the Iron Warriors truly are, and that they cannot be permitted to live on. That is the sole relevance of the events on Malodrax to this battle. Shon'tu will not die to satisfy my bloodlust. He will die to ensure mankind never suffers from his depredations again. Does that answer your concerns, sergeant?'

'My apologies, captain,' said Laocos. 'I felt I had to say something.'

'And it is said,' replied Lysander. He climbed the stairs and headed towards the central spire of the star fort, where the heavily armoured vault of datamedium lay, and where the machine-spirit of the *Endeavour of Will* now held court.

RARELY DID ANYONE enter through the airlocked doors of the datamedium vault. The air was recycled from the same atmosphere that had been sealed inside the last time the datamedium stacks had been maintained, more than six hundred years ago. The stacks themselves formed rows of columns reaching up to the ceiling, like the pipes of an infernally complicated pipe organ taking up the entirety of the huge chamber. The stacks of black crystal were banded with gold and brass, and thick bundles of cables hung down between them like the viny foliage of a jungle. Freezing mist clung to the floor, generated by the coolant flowing through the pipes that criss-crossed the floor, and the air was as chill.

In those stacks of black crystal cylinders resided vast amounts of information, more than a planet's worth of human minds could contain: all the memories, wisdom and personality that made up the machine-spirit of the *Endeavour of Will*. It was the most sacred place on the whole star fort, and a follower of the Adeptus Mechanicus would fall to his knees in the presence of such knowledge, such closeness to the infinite wisdom of the Omnissiah.

Freezing air hissed and vapour billowed as one of the doors slid open. Rigalto and Menander's squads entered, spreading out rapidly as they scouted out the best firing zones and defensive positions.

'It is a fine place to fight,' said Menander. 'Cover from every direction. Limited entrances. Very fine.'

'But a bad place to be trapped,' replied Rigalto. 'And any damage here could lose a hundred years of knowledge. I would say it is an ill place for a battle. Better that we should sabotage the command circuits and hold one of the spurs, and attempt to get its weapons back on-line.'

'But then we would relinquish this vault,' said Menander, 'and the enemy would have the machine-spirit at their mercy. They would succeed where they failed before, to do to it what they did to the *Bastion Inviolate*.'

'Perhaps you are right, Brother Menander. And Lysander has chosen this place for the battle. He knows more of such things than I.'

'Than any of us,' agreed Menander.

Menander joined his Scouts near the only other way into the vault, among a bank of brass-cased cogitators around the door set into the far wall. The three Scouts and their sergeant were armed with sniper rifles from the star fort's armoury and they concealed themselves among the knurled valve wheels and steam pipes that connected the various cogitator sections, giving themselves lanes of fire right down the length of the vault.

Rigalto formed a firing line across the vault, his men's bolters levelled like an execution squad. The squad's tattered banner was planted in the middle of the line, the bullet-riddled fist symbol, on a field of red, surrounded by silver lightning bolts. To the battle honours embroidered beneath the symbol would be added the *Endeavour of Will*, if anyone from the squad survived.

The sound of gunfire and thumping explosions reached

the vault. Loose components fell as the vault shuddered and distant warnings blared. The damage control signals reaching the sergeants told them that the star fort's central spire was massively compromised, with many decks completely depressurised and the crew fighting countless fires. Crew were still dying out there, both to fire and vacuum, and to the guns of the invaders as they stormed through the ruined star fort.

The doors boomed open again and Lysander's squad stomped through, trailing smoke as they went. Lysander himself was the most badly scorched of them, his face red and raw, one side of his golden yellow armour black with soot.

'They are on our tail!' yelled Lysander. 'Stand fast, Imperial Fists! They have the numbers, but we have the will!'

A burst of fire ripped through the wall beside Lysander, throwing two of his command squad to the ground. Through the wreckage crunched the two Obliterators, the vanguard of Shon'tu's force, blazing fire in every direction. Their flesh was seething and sheened with blood, black tendrils of corruption writhing from their skin. The steel of the wall they burst through became blackened and veined, the tech-virus they carried bleeding out from them into everything around them.

Lysander grabbed one of the fallen command squad and dragged him into the cover of a datamedium column. The rest of the command squad followed, Brother-Scholar Demosthor carrying Brother Tingelis over one shoulder as he turned to bring the assault cannon in his other hand to bear. Shrapnel rained off Demosthor as he returned fire, and the Obliterators disappeared in a storm of flame and debris.

'Rigalto! Watch our flank! My brothers, bring them down!'

Demosthor shrugged Tingelis off his shoulder and braced beside one of the columns, keeping up the storm of fire as his assault cannon's barrels span. Lysander looked down to see that he had dragged Sergeant Laocos from the fray – Laocos's armour was smoking and battered but he did not look badly hurt. Laocos rolled to one knee and hammered out fire in the same direction as Demosthor with his storm bolter.

The attack was a diversion. The Obliterators' task was to draw the attention of the Imperial Fists' gun-line. The real attack ripped through the opposite wall, explosive charges blasting out a section of the wall and sending shards of datamedium crystal showering down. An Iron Warriors champion was first through the breach, surrounded by the baying remnants of the possessed who had been mauled so badly at the Tomb of Ionis. He wore a debased echo of a Chaplain's garb, his face an iron skull, a mace in his hand with a head in the shape of an eight-pointed star.

The possessed charged right into the teeth of Rigalto's guns. The bolter drill that Rigalto had taught them with such discipline sent chains of fire rattling through the bodies of the possessed. Eyes and mouths, clawed and taloned limbs, burst from the shredded flesh of the possessed. They fell and mutated where they lay, forms liquefying into piles of quivering, warp-tainted gore.

The Chaplain was struck in the chest and thrown against one of the columns. He rolled into the cover, the last of the possessed loping through the carnage towards the gun-line. One of them vaulted over a bundle of pipes behind which two of the Imperial Fists were sheltering – Rigalto stepped forwards and impaled the possessed Iron Warrior with a thrust of his chainsword. The blade carved out through the Iron Warrior's lower back and Rigalto twisted it, pulling it out and bringing the contents of the Iron Warrior's abdomen with it. Rigalto plunged the blade over and over again into the possessed, each withdrawal bringing out a fouler knot of squirming flesh, until there was not enough structure left in the Iron Warrior's body to contain its corruption and its armour clattered to the deck, liquid gore spilling out.

But the Iron Warriors had their foothold. Shon'tu's hulking form was just visible through the mist of bolter smoke, surrounded by perhaps forty Iron Warriors taking advantage of the possessed's charge to sprint through the wreckage and into cover of their own. Lysander could see Shon'tu's battle plan unfolding even as Rigalto's squad returned fire and the first Iron Warriors fire fell among them. He had his beachhead, his breach had been secured. And he had more guns than the Imperial Fists.

He would win. There was no doubt about that. It was a fine piece of strike warfare, a besieger's gambit to force the beseiged into fighting a final battle that he could not win.

'Shon'tu!' bellowed Lysander, knowing that the Iron Warrior could hear him. 'Here is the head of Lysander! Here is a trophy for the halls of your Legion! Take it and become a god!'

In spite of what he had become, of all the inhuman filth in which his soul was steeped, warsmith Shon'tu was still a Space Marine, and he still suffered from a weakness that was so definingly theirs. He still had the pride which had seen Chapters, and Legions before them, refuse to quit the field when all was lost; which had created animosity when there should have been brotherhood. It was the pride from which the Horus Heresy itself had taken root.

Shon'tu's augmetic eyes focused on Lysander. Bolter fire punched through the datamedium around him but Lysander stood proud of the cover, impossible to mistake even through the grime and chaos of the battle. Shon'tu shoved aside the Iron Warrior in front of him and broke into a run, gunfire sparking against his armour.

Lysander's command squad drew in around him, but they too recognised a warrior's pride when it was brought into play. Their efforts were focused on keeping their commander safe from the advancing Obliterators. Lysander alone would face Shon'tu.

Shon'tu seemed to cover the breadth of the datamedium vault in a few huge strides. In a cloud of steam and smoke he fell upon Lysander like a comet from the sky. His claw sliced forwards, talons snapping shut towards Lysander's face. Lysander ducked and took as much of the impact as he could on his shield. He was thrown back, bowling Sergeant Laocos aside, and rolled as he landed to bring him out of the way of the claw, which ripped into the deck beneath him.

Lysander and Shon'tu were face to face for half a second, more than long enough for Lysander to learn that there was nothing human in what remained of the warsmith's face.

Lysander batted aside Shon'tu's next attack with his shield, knowing it was a feint. The real attack was from Shon'tu's triple-barrelled boltgun, which he tried to ram up into Lysander's midriff so he could unload half its ammo chain into the Imperial Fist's body. Lysander spun, knocked the gun aside with the haft of the Fist of Dorn, and kicked out hard enough to shatter the bronze struts lending strength to Shon'tu's right leg.

Shon'tu stumbled back and Lysander had a moment to seize the advantage. It had to be enough. He placed his hand against the nearest datamedium column and let his armour's interface connect with it, a probe in his gauntlet extending to dip into the ocean of knowledge inside.

'I am ready,' said the artificial voice that tapped into his vox-unit. It was the voice of the *Endeavour of Will* – the machine-spirit, the intelligence that had inhabited this place since its forging in the days when the Emperor still walked the galaxy.

'You have one more battle to fight,' said Lysander. He knew that his battle-brothers could only hear his side of the conversation. 'One blow to strike.'

'It must be done.'

'Forgive me, machine-spirit, that I command this of you.'

'Then redeem yourself, Imperial Fist, by avenging what I have lost.'

Lysander gave the order, a thought that triggered a sequence of commands in the machine-spirit. They in turn triggered more, the effect spreading out like ripples in a pond or the multiplication of an epidemic. Torrents of information were retrieved and released, centuries of battle-lore, millions of hours of battleground data, endless waterfalls of stellar cartography, earthquakes of raw mathematics coursing through every remaining stack of datamedium.

Some of the Iron Warriors might have understood what was happening. Shon'tu certainly did. As the green glow from the datamedium bathed the vault, he stepped back from the duel with Lysander. As power arced against the floor and ceiling, he ducked down, claw brought up to guard instead of attack.

'I want to look into your eyes,' said Lysander, 'and see the moment you know defeat.'

'You dare?' yelled Shon'tu. 'You think this is a victory?'

'What else is it?' Around Lysander, green-white bolts of power, like lightning, were earthing against the floor. The columns were glowing so bright now that the whole vault shone with them, and they were bulging, cracking as the volume of information multiplied beyond their capacity to store it.

'You will learn,' retorted Shon'tu. 'When your soul goes dark! When this galaxy burns! You will learn!'

The columns shattered. Shards of crystal flew, spearing into the armour of Imperial Fist and Iron Warrior alike. They were not deadly enough to lay a Space Marine low, but they were not the true danger.

Every digit of information ever assembled or contemplated by the *Endeavour of Will* erupted into the vault, pure and raw.

Lysander's armour seized and shorted around him, suddenly heavy as the nerve-fibre bundles and servos were overloaded. Shots of pain punched through him as the many implants he possessed, interfaces drilled into his fused ribcage and cranial jacks that allowed input to his augmented eyes, sparked and died.

But the Iron Warriors suffered much worse. Shon'tu tried to continue with his retort, but his brass-cased form contorted and spurted jets of burning fuel. Components burst from the little flesh he had, panels of his armour falling open and bundles of bionics tumbling out. The other Iron Warriors were falling and spasming, losing control of their half-mechanical bodies.

The torrent of information released by the machine-spirit had flooded into them, and into the machinery with which they had replaced their weak, untrustworthy flesh. As one, every single bionic in the Iron Warriors of Shon'tu's warband overloaded and destroyed itself.

THE RETREAT HAD been ragged. Almost half the warband were dead, shot down as they limped or crawled away from the datamedium vault. The Imperial Fists had been mauled, too, and some of the hated enemy had fallen. But it had been an appalling loss. Shon'tu felt what a human might call shame, if such a word could encompass the volcanic hate that it ignited; the emptiness within him, as vast and cold as the void, which could only be filled with thoughts of revenge.

Release me, came the voice again. It struck as Shon'tu was leading the retreat back towards the defence laser spur, dragging his heavy inert mechanical form along with the few motor systems that still functioned inside him. Around him the Iron Warriors were trying to maintain decent order, many unable to fight, their arms useless and their weapons seized up; some barely able to move.

Release me. It must be done.

'I cannot. You know that...'

In defeat all bonds break. In desperation, in the face of shame and catastrophe, the only rule is revenge. Release me. It is the only way. You know this to be true.

Shon'tu looked back along the route he had taken to the datamedium vault. It was burnt out and wrecked, scattered with the bodies of the star fort's crew who had fallen to the laser strike or the Iron Warriors' guns. Now he saw Forge-Chaplain Kourtos being carried by two of his Iron Warriors, his bullet-scarred body spasming as his spinal implants refused to obey the orders coming from his cortex.

Gunfire streaked from the Imperial Fists, who were pursuing in tight order, moving from cover to cover and taking only what shots could not be returned. One of the Iron Warriors fell and Kourtos clattered to the deck. Silhouetted against a bank of flames, one of the Imperial Fists Terminators stood out from cover and levelled his assault cannon. A volley of fire thudded into Kourtos's body and the Forge-Chaplain, unable to move, was torn apart. Chunks of his flesh spattered across the ceiling and walls, and over the Iron Warriors trying to drag themselves into cover.

'Then I release you!' yelled Shon'tu. 'In the name of vengeance! To see the corpse of this star fort tumbling through the void, as dead as the Imperial Fists for whom it has become a tomb! I release you from your bonds of servitude, from imprisonment in the *Ferrous Malice*! Lord Velthinar, I release you!'

SEEN FROM SPACE, the *Endeavour of Will* was clearly wounded, still bleeding wreckage from the crater left by the defence laser's strike. A halo of debris surrounded it and flashes of explosions sparked as the fires in its central spire continued to burn, and fuel and ammunition stores cooked off. Much of it was completely dark, lights extinguished by the loss of power. It was a stricken animal, lame and vulnerable.

The *Ferrous Malice* was the predator. Far smaller, but unwounded and swift, it bore down upon the *Endeavour of Will*. Its hull split open and it seemed for a moment that it would try to grapple the star fort as it had the *Siege of Malebruk*. But forward thrusters fired and the grand cruiser slowed, pointing its slit belly towards the *Endeavour of Will*.

Light bled out. Multicoloured fire bathed the ship as the first limbs unfolded from its interior, followed by the chitinous bulk of a creature that had spent an aeon confined.

The daemon Velthinar forced its way out of the ship. Its abdomen was a long, slithering white-fleshed mass that pulsed with veins, its thorax armoured in gilt and jewels.

Hundreds of limbs opened up, tipped in golden claws. Finally its wings unfurled, a tremendous mass of iridescent sails uncoiling. With a single beat the dozen wings thrust Velthinar towards the *Endeavour of Will*.

Lightning crackled around it in every colour. The red giant star dulled as Velthinar drew off its light, surrounding itself in the star's fire so that every edge and tip of its armoured form glowed painfully bright. White-hot and trailing flame lightning like a comet, Velthinar accelerated, arrowing straight for the *Endeavour of Will*, shining with enough power to punch through the star fort and rip out its innards.

'Velthinar rises!' came the screaming voice of Shon'tu. 'You think you have defeated us, Imperial Fist? You do not even know what defeat means! But fear not! Velthinar will show you!'

Lysander and his squad heard Shon'tu's words as they pursued the Iron Warriors through the arterial corridor leading towards the defence spur. The corridor was dense with smoke but even so the aim of his command squad had despatched half a dozen Iron Warriors during their retreat, and they had almost reached the foothold the Iron Warriors had established with their Dreadclaw assault-pods. Lysander peered through the smoke, unable to make out any detail among the darkness. Gunfire could be heard from elsewhere in the spur as Rigalto's squad moved swiftly to recapture the defence laser itself.

'Warsmith!' yelled Lysander in reply. 'I hear only the words of one fleeing for his life! I hear the squeals of a coward! Stand forward and face me, as you were so eager to a few moments ago! Or do the Iron Warriors do all their fighting with words?'

The squad spread out around Lysander, covering every angle of fire. The shapes of giant capacitors loomed from the smoke, empty now of the energy they had stored for the defence laser. Lysander made out one of the Dreadclaw pods, its serrated jaws protruding through the hull into the space between two capacitors.

Above Lysander, the transparent roof of the corridor cleared for a moment as the smoke coiled out of the way. The light breaking through shone from a vast insectoid daemon streaking through space, aiming for the centre of the star fort. It was an abomination, half titanic maggot and half bejewelled predatory insect, and the power streaming off it burned brighter than the nearest star.

Lysander took a few steps forwards and saw Shon'tu. The warsmith had made it to one of the Dreadclaws and was in the process of hauling its jaws shut.

'See, Lysander!' yelled Shon'tu. 'See the herald of your deaths! Every move you made, I had a counter! For every thrust, I had a feint! Our victory was decided before the first shot was fired, Imperial Fist!'

Lysander charged through the smoke. He slammed into the jaw of the Dreadclaw just as it was closing, reducing his view of Shon'tu to a sliver. The warsmith's face was lit red by the warning lights inside the assault-pod, just a few centimetres from Lysander's.

'My brothers on Malodrax were weak,' said Shon'tu. 'They were the dregs of our Legion. You think you have stared into the soul of the Iron Warriors. You have no idea.' Shon'tu smiled as he saw Lysander trying to force the Dreadclaw's jaws open, and failing.

'I know what you left behind on Malodrax,' said Shon'tu, with a smirk on the remains of his half-mechanical face. 'And I know what you took from there, too. What you still carry. It is what drives you to kill me, Lysander. It will be the death of every battle-brother who ever stands at your side, and it will not let you go until you have killed everything you fight for!'

'I didn't fight you here to defeat you,' said Lysander as the jaw ground closed. 'I fought you here to bring out Velthinar.'

The faintest trace of confusion passed over Shon'tu's face. Then the Dreadclaw was closed and in a hiss of steam the clamps holding it in place disengaged.

'Breach!' yelled Lysander. 'Back! Fall back and seal us off!'

The Dreadclaw's thrusters roared and the assault-pod was ripped back out of the star fort's hull. Air whistled out behind it. Lysander pulled his helmet from the waist of his armour and jammed it over his head as warning runes flickered telling him the air pressure had suddenly dropped to little over nothing.

Smoke swirled out, the air suddenly clear. The area was strewn with the bodies of Iron Warriors, and Lysander's squad shot down a couple who were still moving even as the air dissipated and silence fell.

'Missed him,' voxed Brother-Scholar Demosthor. 'Damnation and filth.'

Lysander did not answer. He looked back up through the ceiling of the arterial corridor, the view no longer obscured. But he was not looking at the burning mass of Velthinar. He was looking at the storm of purplish lightning that was swelling into real space just behind the daemon, the sign of a spacecraft ripping its way from the warp.

'Throne of Gold,' said Sergeant Laocos, standing just behind Lysander and following his gaze. 'What is that?'

'A friend,' replied Lysander.

VELTHINAR KNEW THAT something was wrong. It paused in its path towards the *Endeavour of Will* and turned to see what was causing the disturbance in the warp behind it.

What it saw was reality splitting and the stuff of the warp pouring through. A billowing tide of sorcery crashed into the vacuum, carrying upon it a vast shape, like a ghost hulk carried on a stormy ocean. Its hull was pitted and scored with the punishment of the warp, and every surface was blistered with pustules and veins. Eyes opened everywhere there was space for them, clustering like buboes, rolling madly and bloodshot. The shape trailed ragged tentacles and arteries that spilled blackish blood into the void.

It was deformed and horrible, all symmetry destroyed, but it still carried enough of its original form to be identified as a star fort, much the same shape and size as the

Endeavour of Will. A few tattered banners still hung from it, carrying the colours of the Imperial Fists.

'I cannot be redeemed,' bellowed an artificial voice, transmitted through the substance of reality. It was heard by everyone for light years around, but it was directed at the daemon Velthinar. 'I cannot be saved. I cannot know peace.'

Tentacles burst from beneath the corrupted mass of the star fort, snaking around Velthinar's primary limbs. Velthinar thrashed, but the star fort was bigger and stronger.

'But I can have revenge,' the voice continued.

Velthinar fought. The energy it had siphoned from the star Kholestus raked across the corrupted star fort, blasting off battlements and defence spurs, but it was no good. The grip was tight and not even Velthinar Silverspine could break free.

Velthinar was looking into the million eyes of the *Bastion Inviolate*.

'My god will shred your soul!' spat the daemon.

'I have no soul,' came the reply. 'I was a machine. Now I am a disease. You did this to me.'

'Serve Him!' countered Velthinar. 'Untold power will be yours!'

'I do not want power,' said the *Bastion Inviolate*, 'save the power to break you upon the anvil of my hate.'

A tentacle wrapped around the head and mouthparts of Velthinar, silencing the daemon for the moment. The eyes of the *Bastion Inviolate* turned towards the *Endeavour of Will*, the star fort which had until recently been its brother.

'Lysander,' it said.

ON THE ENDEAVOUR *of Will*, Lysander heard the voice, and he knew that it could hear him too. He had watched the corrupted star fort and the daemon struggling, and it had been clear from the outset that the *Bastion Inviolate* would win. Velthinar Silverspine had not destroyed it, for a being with the tenacity and willpower of the *Bastion Inviolate's* machine-spirit would not simply be wiped out by corruption. It would become something else, something awful, and it would thrive.

'Your astropath called for me,' the machine-spirit said. 'He told I could have revenge on the being that did this to me.'

'And you have it,' said Lysander. 'Now depart. This reality has no place for you now.'

'I know what I am,' said the *Bastion Inviolate*. 'And I know the oaths that you swear. I am an abomination. Your kind must hunt me down.'

'And we shall,' said Lysander. 'When we meet again, it will be as enemies.'

'That will not be for a long time.' The *Bastion Inviolate* held up the squirming daemon like a hunter displaying the body of a kill. 'For many thousands of years I feel my enthusiasm shall remain. I am a newcomer to the warp. I have much to learn of what pain a daemon can feel. It will be a long time in the learning.'

'We will find you,' said Lysander.

'And when you do, the sundered corpse of this creature will be impaled upon my battlements, and its flayed skin shall be my standard. Farewell, Captain Lysander of the Imperial Fists. What remains of me with the capacity to honour you will soon be lost to the warp, but for now, it salutes you.'

Lysander could hear Velthinar screaming as the warp tore open again and the *Bastion Inviolate* sank out of real space. The daemon struggled and thrashed but the star fort held it fast in its hundreds of spiny tentacles. The vacuum boomed shut behind it, and when the afterglow died down, Velthinar Silverspine and the *Bastion Inviolate* were gone.

THE DANCER WAS a messenger, neutered of its deadliness and malice, a barely perceptible shadow within a shadow. The destruction of its kind had left only this shade, the ghost of a daemon. Only its eyes were obvious, flickering red-black orbs that darted in every direction as if watching for enemies.

Lysander knew it was there before he saw it. It had been nine days since the *Ferrous Malice*, shorn of the daemon that commanded it, had limped away from the *Endeavour of Will* with Shon'tu and the surviving Iron Warriors on board, and the star fort was still a wreck. More than half its crew were dead and large areas were ruined, amongst them the shattered expanse of map rooms and tactical libraries that Lysander was searching for dead crew or Iron Warriors.

Lysander froze, hand hovering over the shaft of the Fist of Dorn.

'I have not come to fight,' hissed the Dancer.

'The last time I met your kind, I tore you all to shreds. And the time before that. So for your sake, be speaking the truth.'

The Dancer slithered out of the darkness where it had been lurking, beneath the charred remains of a map table surrounded by scrolls and books. 'I come to give thanks.'

Lysander spat on the floor. 'Thanks from the warp are a curse. Begone or I will throw you back to your god in pieces.'

'But what else can the gods of the warp give to Captain Lysander of the Imperial Fists, when he has given to them a victory their servants could not win? The violation of Ionis's tomb. The death of Astropath Vaynce. The soul of Techmarine Hestion, upon which we still feast. The loss of a billion minds' worth of battle-lore. And the pact with the *Bastion Inviolate*, a pact to which no god could force a spirit such as yours and yet one of which you were the author! How could any servant of the warp win such victories from the Imperial Fists? Shon'tu sought only your deaths. He could never have won such triumph as we gained, but you have given it to us of your own will.'

Lysander hefted the Fist of Dorn and took a stride towards the Dancer. The daemon did not move, holding out its arms as if about to embrace the Imperial Fist.

'The warp thanks you, Lysander! The greatest champion of the gods could not have done more!'

Lysander swatted the daemon aside with the Fist of Dorn. The hammer's head tore right through the creature and its shadow dissipated into a thousand wisps that vanished like smoke into the air. There was no impact, no satisfying crunch of bone. The daemon was simply gone, for it had been sketched so lightly on reality its destruction had no meaning.

Lysander stood there for a long time. The words of a daemon would not sway him. They might worm into a lesser man's head, to discourage and corrupt, but not the mind of an Imperial Fist.

Nothing had changed. If anything, the events aboard the *Endeavour of Will* had proven to him what he already knew.

Everything could be sacrificed. It took a man of Lysander's will to know that. Everything was secondary to victory.

Everything.

FATEWEAVER

JOHN FRENCH

'We know no fear. It was cut from our souls at birth. We can feel it only as an absence, as an empty shadow cast by the light of annihilation. In the face of a future of atrocity I stand mute, numb to the only feeling that would make me human. But I remember what fear was: its cold pulse in my veins; its echo in my ears. I remember fear, and remember that I was once human. I look towards what must come to pass and I wish that I could meet it as my ancestors did, with fear. The future deserves that, it deserves fear.'

– Epistolary Cyrus Aurelius, unheard confession

I

SUMMONED

THE VISION UNFOLDED into the present in a cascade of sensations.

The sword is hot in his hand, the fury at its core bright with his rage. He cuts, feeling his armour move with the surge of his muscles. The edge meets deformed flesh, the sword shuddering in his grip as power flows through it. A bloated creature with a face like a flayed skull dissolves into smoke. Threat runes spin across his vision, pulsing red, swarming. A taste like burnt sugar and ruined meat fills his mouth.

He is a figure in blue armour the shade of a clear sky, standing at the centre of a turning circle of countless twisted creatures. They close on him, pacing forwards, claws clicking on the stone floor. He can feel the creatures' raw power, feel them thirsting for his soul. A death light fills their eyes. He stands alone and knows that he has failed.

A shape with a wide mouth of glittering needle teeth comes at him, its limbs flowing into new shapes as it moves. The storm bolter roars in his fist, muscle fibres swallowing its kick. Detonations turn warp bloated flesh to red pulp. A threat rune blinks out. He turns, finger still squeezing the trigger, watching the ammunition count fall as the weapon trails a line of fire.

I have failed, *he thinks*, and there will be nothing after this moment.

The gun clatters silent. He raises his sword. A clawed hand bites through a leg joint. He feels the warm fluid pooling inside his armour. He steps forward, ramming the sword into the open mouth of a bird-shaped creature until its blade disappears in flesh. The power flows through him like a storm rush. The half-feathered body explodes in a blaze of light. He realises he is screaming. Lightning gathers around his body in a crackling spiral. The creatures fall back for a brief moment, turning their lidless eyes from the light. He raises the sword. His limbs are shuddering. Inside his helmet he is weeping blood.

They come for him again, a tide of teeth and claws. He is striking, each blow a thunderclap. Many of the creatures fall, their distorted forms sliding back into shadow and smoke. But they are many and he is alone.

This has not come to pass yet, *he thinks*, this is not happening. I am not dying. This is my fate, what shall be. This is the future, it has not happened yet. *But the thought dies.*

The creatures around him howl and he feels the psychic crystals haloing his head shatter. He is blind.

The world goes quiet and warm.

I am dying, *he thinks*, I have failed and there will be nothing left, nothing but ash and hungering darkness.

Something within him dims, fluttering to nothing like a flame fading to cold embers.

He tries to raise his sword.

He is falling…

He was…

… running the ashes of a dead world through his fingers. The vision faded, bleeding away into the grey present. He blinked, pushing away the sensations that remained coiled in his mind like a fever's touch. He had seen echoes of possible futures before, but this had felt different; stronger, more instant, like a memory of something that had already happened.

'Epistolary?' said a voice, its sound flat inside his helmet.

Cyrus looked up from the grey dust falling from his armoured fingers.

He flicked his eyes across the green runes at the edge of his sight; the four green cruciform marks of Phobos's squad winked back at him. He turned to look back at his escort spread behind him in a loose diamond. The white of their armour was bright beneath the shroud grey sky.

Like him they were clad in monstrous Terminator armour. Their genetically enhanced physiques wrapped in layer upon layer of adamantium, their movements augmented by sheathes of fibre bundles that ran through the armour like a second set of muscles. The suits were relics of a lost time, their components replaced and repaired so many times that they were like walking scar tissue. To wear such armour was to feel the past as a cold shroud against one's skin. Hundreds of his Chapter ancestors had worn Cyrus's suit before it had passed to him. Most of those ancestors had died wearing it, he recalled.

'Is everything well, brother?' said the red-helmed sergeant.

'Yes, brother. An errant thought, nothing more.'

'As you say, Epistolary.' Phobos's tone was clipped and respectful, but Cyrus could feel the sergeant's questions unspoken behind the blunt snout of his helm: why had they come down to the surface of this planet?

A flat, grey plain extended away from them, its surface undisturbed by wind, rain or the tread of feet. Runes flowed across Cyrus's vision, his sensorium searching for movement, heat, life, and finding nothing. Two hundred and thirty million people had died here. He blink-clicked away the questing runes; this world was dead, and it had died at its protector's hand.

It was called Kataris, an agri-world of processing cities and endless plains of crops, ripening under a bright sun. It had died in less time than it took that sun to circle the sky. Something had drawn the eyes of the daemons to it, and they had come from beyond reality. Millions had died in the first assault. Their deaths had prepared the world for the arrival of more of their kind. More and more had slipped across the shadow divide between reality and the warp. The few, the very few people who had not died then became a defiant clutch of humanity clinging to the planet's last fortifications. There they had muttered prayers, tears rolling down their ash-dusted cheeks, and waited for the end.

An astropath had sent a desperate call out through the warp. It had called for help, for the protection promised by the priests of the Imperial Creed. 'The Emperor protects' had been the last words of the message. And a single word of execution had answered that message: Exterminatus. The death sentence of a world and all who lived on it. Kataris had pleaded for aid and been answered by death falling from the tortured sky. For a moment the wide plains of ruin had been still, the sound of thunder settling with the dust. Then the inferno came, rushing across the world from horizon to horizon, consuming the tainted air in a roar like the war-cries shouted at the end of time.

Cyrus could almost taste the pyre.

'This was no victory,' he murmured to himself.

Decades before, Cyrus and his brothers had fought on Kataris against a raiding force of eldar. They had defeated the aliens and broken their hidden witch-gate. It had been a vicious war, but they had won and the world had lived. This time their answer to the dead world's plea was too late. They had arrived many days after the ships of the Inquisition execution force had departed.

If we had been here, could we have saved this world? The question had no answer, but that did not stop Cyrus asking it to himself. Unlike the rest of his brothers he could feel what had happened here as echoes lingering in the immaterium. He was a psyker, gifted with an ability to channel and manipulate the power of the realm beyond reality. The warp was a nightmare other realm of psychic energy, but the mind of a psyker could tap and shape that energy. To some it was sorcery. To others it was a step in the evolution of humanity. To Cyrus it was a weapon. It was a gift that allowed Cyrus to do things beyond even his brother White Consuls. But the gift also set him apart from the rest of his Chapter; it could not be otherwise. How could it be, when he felt the death of this world resonate over him like dust blowing over bare skin?

That is why I ordered us to come to the surface, he thought. Because someone needed to witness what had happened, someone needed to touch it and remember the price of survival.

'Epistolary,' said a voice washed in static. It came from the bridge of the *Aethon*, the battle-barge that hung above them in high orbit.

'Speak,' said Cyrus.

'We have received a signal. It seems to be another plea for help.' The voice paused. 'It includes the word "Fateweaver".'

Cyrus closed his eyes for a moment. It could only mean one thing.

The world he stood on was only the latest to be subject to a daemonic incursion. World after world had fallen in this crescent of stars that edged the Eye of Terror. Thousands of millions had died as the Inquisition attempted to contain the incursion. And in the wake of this destruction a name followed like whisper made with a dying breath: Fateweaver.

'Where?' asked Cyrus.

'The message is garbled but we have an origin location. An astropathic relay fortress in the Claros system.' The vision of the future resurfaced in Cyrus's mind. 'What are your orders?'

THE ASTROPATH'S VOICE sounded like the rasp of a dying man. '...report... Claros... the enemy beyond...' The robed figure turned in a cone of cold green light, mouth flapping in a thin face as it spoke words which were not its own. '...lies... Fateweaver, we... blinded... failing...' The man's lips twisted, breath wheezing as he tried to say incomplete thoughts. '...soul... that hear this... send... help... accursed eternity.'

Cyrus sat alone and watched the holo-recording. He wore no armour; his suit of blue Terminator plate was being cleansed and re-blessed after his journey to the surface of Kataris. A cowled robe of white covered his hunched form, its edges woven in blue and with the names of Chapter ancestors. Within the cowl's shadow his gaunt face looked as if it were carved from white marble. Around him the battle council chamber was dark, the pale light of the holo-recording showing the outlines of a wide stone table and chairs. Beyond the circle of light the darkness hummed with the roar of the *Aethon's* engines as it cut through the warp.

As soon as he had stepped back onto the *Aethon*, Cyrus had asked for a recording of the signal. As an Epistolary of the Adeptus Astartes, he was capable of receiving the psychic messages that passed from the mind of one astropath to another. Passing through the warp, these messages crossed the vast distances of space faster than the light of stars. This message, though, had arrived while he was down on the surface of Kataris. Amongst the death echoes surrounding that world his mind had been deaf to such subtle telepathy. The *Aethon's* own astropath had received it and now Cyrus looked at a recording of that moment.

Something about the signal disturbed him. It was garbled, chewed by its transmission from one mind to another, but he felt as if he could almost hear the words that hung unsaid in the gaps.

'It won't change you know.' The voice came out of the gloom towards the chamber's door.

Cyrus looked up. His eyes turned the darkness into monochrome shades of light and shadow. The figure standing at the other end of the deserted council chamber wore a tunic of white fabric. His blunt head was shaved smooth and snaked with scars, and there were two chrome studs above his left eye. Bare forearms, thick with muscle and looped by heavy copper vambraces, hung loose at his side.

'Phobos,' Cyrus said, smiling as the figure walked forwards. 'Come to shake me from my melancholy?' Phobos said nothing but stopped on the other side of the circular stone table. Between them the holographic astropath still turned and spoke in its cone of light.

Phobos stared at the projection. 'You still judge it best to follow this?'

Cyrus frowned: there was something wrong with his old friend. There was no trace of the usual stone dry humour in his words, just a tone that Cyrus could not place.

'Yes, brother,' said Cyrus, standing up from the iron backed chair. 'You did not raise an objection when I ordered the *Aethon* to the Claros system. Is there something you wish to say now?' Phobos was silent, but Cyrus could see emotions playing across the sergeant's blunt features.

Cyrus was commander of the force aboard the *Aethon*; he had no need to listen to the sergeant's misgivings, but he would. As a psyker he had always stood apart from others. It was as true now as it had been when he was a shunned boy on a long forgotten world. But Phobos had never shown the remoteness that was common in his brothers. A sergeant of the First Company, a Proconsul, bearer of the Crux Terminatus, he was a warrior to the bone, and the closest thing to a friend Cyrus had ever known.

'We have been wardens out here for three decades,' said Phobos slowly. 'Three decades of war.'

'That was our oath and our duty,' said Cyrus.

'Yes, and a duty we paid in blood,' said Phobos. Cyrus nodded. It had been paid in blood indeed. The *Aethon* was a battle-barge, a vessel for making war amongst the stars. It could carry three hundred Adeptus Astartes, their vehicles and tools of war. When it had left Sabatine it had been close to its full strength, but three decades of war in the margins of the Eye of Terror had demanded its price. Captains and veterans of hundreds of years of war lay dead on lost worlds, or drifting through the cold void. Silence filled the ship, its crew reduced to servitors, and its systems to the bare essentials necessary to serve the remaining White Consuls.

Yes, and we paid that price many times over, my friend, thought Cyrus. 'Is there any other way for the Adeptus Astartes to fulfil their duty?' he said instead, with a sternness he did not feel.

'We are White Consuls.' Phobos leaned on the table looking at the raptor head emblems carved into the stone surface. 'We are inches away from extinction. The Chapter calls and...' His words fell away.

'And what?' Cyrus watched his friend swallow.

'The Chapter calls, but we linger.'

'You think that is what we do? Linger?'

'I think that our Chapter needs us,' said Phobos.

Cyrus felt ice run through him at the words. It was true. The Chapter had gathered in great numbers to face a terrible foe, and it had been wounded to the point that its future hung by a thread. The call had come, drawing all the sons of Sabatine back to their home.

'And what of the purpose of our Chapter, Sergeant Phobos?' said Cyrus, and Phobos looked up at the coldness in his voice. 'We are White Consuls, Primogenitors of Guilliman. We shepherd and guard mankind. That is what we were created for. That is our duty to our Chapter.'

'And if the Chapter is no more?' growled Phobos. 'If it is destroyed and we are not there?'

'If we forget our purpose, my friend, then there will be nothing but ash blowing across dead worlds.' He thought he saw a flash of sympathy in Phobos's dark eyes, and knew that he had seen the echo of lost Kataris in his words.

'It had fallen,' said Phobos, his voice softening. 'There was nothing that could have been done to save it. Were we there, or ten times our number, there would have been no option but Exterminatus.'

Cyrus thought of the dead world's last scream for help before it burned.

'We could not have saved it, and we will not be able to save Claros if the daemons come to it,' Phobos added.

'There is always something that should be tried before you step into annihilation.' Cyrus growled. 'Pay for the survival of humanity with atrocity and there will be nothing left.' He shut down the holo-display, and walked away leaving Phobos alone in the dark.

THE AETHON CUT towards the bronze-hulled space station, its auspex nodes filling the void around it with overlapping folds of sensor fields. It was over eight kilometres long, a blunt barb of off-white armour and macro weaponry folded in crackling void shields. The roar of its plasma engines at full burn made the bridge vibrate under Cyrus's feet.

'No signs of enemy activity, or battle residue, my lord,' said the logistician bound into the main sensor dais. The man turned his green bionic eyes to Cyrus. 'The station seems to be intact and unharmed. They are acknowledging our hails and have accepted our request to dock.'

'Very well,' said Cyrus. He had expected to find the station wreathed in the fires of battle and shouting for help with its last breath. But looking at it on a viewscreen it was clear that it was far from falling.

Claros station looked a great wheel turning in starlight. Its armour gleamed as if forged from polished bronze. Five wings extended spoke-like from the station's central hub, each resembling the transept of a cathedral and over two kilometres long. Buttresses and towers tangled the station's surface, light glinting from the faces of vast statues that gazed out on the void with blank eyes. At its centre a tower extended above the central hub, its domed tip a mass of antennae masts. A thick collar of stone ringed the base of the tower, its surface blistered with shield generators and gargoyles the size of hab blocks. To Cyrus's eyes it looked formidable.

Beside him Phobos shifted. Freshly attached purity seals hung from his shoulder guards, and he held his crimson helmet in the crook of his arm. Cyrus had not spoken to him since their words in the command chamber.

'I will prepare an honour guard, if you intend to go aboard,' said Phobos.

Cyrus could feel the question held in check behind Phobos's words: if we came here to save this place and it does not need saving, why waste more time?

The memory of the vision he had seen on Kataris slid into Cyrus's mind: the stink of warp, the wet warmth of his blood. The memory was as fresh and raw as an unhealed wound. He was a haruspex, trained in his Chapter's tradition as a diviner of meaning in visions and omens. To an oracle there was no such thing as blind chance. The arrival of the signal and his vision were linked. Fate was pulling him to this place, he was sure.

'Yes,' Cyrus said. 'Prepare the battle force to stand in armour. There is more here than meets the eye.'

THE DOCKING BAY rumbled. Beyond the bay's blast doors, the hull of the *Aethon* met the armoured dock of Claros with a sound like the tolling of an iron bell.

Before the doors the White Consuls stood in ranks, their armour bright under the light that filled the docking bay. Cyrus stood at their head, his force sword resting point down, its psy-active core quiet without his will to give it life. Parchments hung from his shoulders and greaves, and white cloth fell to the deck from his torso. In deference to the occasion his helmet hung from his waist so that his pale face looked out uncovered from its collar of crystal nodes.

Phobos and his Terminators stood a step behind Cyrus, and behind them were the Devastators of Valerian alongside the Vanguard and Tactical squads under Galba and Vetranio. All stood below the strength demanded by the *Codex*. But they were still a battle force of the Adeptus Astartes, an assemblage great enough to break armies.

The blast doors split open with a hiss of pressure. A void-cold wind spilled into the docking bay, stirring the parchments on Cyrus's armour. Two figures waited in the growing breach at the head of a sea of kneeling figures. One was a man with a hawk-thin face and a wash of gloss black hair pulled back into a braided tail. The burnished gold of his chest armour – worked with laurels and eagle wings – caught the light as he bowed. Beside the man was a tall woman with a wrinkled, withered face, the bald skin of her scalp tattooed with swirls of faded text. A high-collared blue coat covered her thin form, and she held a staff in her right hand. An eagle topped its black shaft, a blue crystal eye clutched in its claws. She looked at Cyrus with an expression of rank dislike, a sneer edging her mouth.

'Hail in the name of the Emperor.' The man's voice trembled in the cold air. Behind the man the kneeling ranks echoed the words.

Cyrus bowed his head briefly; he disliked such moments. To most people of the Imperium the Space Marines were a breed apart: terrifying beings of protection and destruction made at the dawn of history by an Emperor they called a god. Such crawling deference was to be expected, but to Cyrus it ignored the reason for his existence: to protect these people and the realm of which they were a part.

'Rise,' he said, stepping forwards and offering the pair a smile. 'I am Cyrus Aurelius, Epistolary of the White Consuls, and we come in might as we were called.' The man looked up and Cyrus saw curiosity mingled with anxiety.

'Rihat, colonel commander of the Helicon Guard.' There was a tremor of fear in the man's voice. Rihat gestured to the woman at his side. 'And this is Hekate, Savant Imma–'

'*This* can speak for herself.' The woman's voice cut through Rihat's words like a knife.

She looked straight at Cyrus; there was no fear or awe in her eyes. He could feel the strength of the woman's mind, the tamed and tethered psychic power held within her.

'You see the confusion in his eyes, Space Marine?' she said. 'The fear he feels at the presence of the Emperor's angels of death?'

'My lord, we are honoured by your presence...' blustered Rihat, his face paling.

Cyrus kept his gaze locked with Hekate's. He felt the contest in that look, the challenge.

'Why are you here, Space Marine?' she asked, tilting her

head, and Cyrus knew that she had seen his kind before, had perhaps seen and survived more than most humans could imagine. She was a primaris psyker, a battle psyker and occult savant who might be his equal or superior in power. He wondered at the dislike and anger that radiated from her like an icy cloud.

'We were summoned, lady,' said Cyrus calmly. 'We intercepted a call for aid that indicated that this station was under threat. We came to answer that call.'

Rihat flicked a puzzled look at Hekate who broke Cyrus's gaze to return it. Rihat shook his head, frowning. 'My lord, no signal was sent.'

CYRUS FLICKED THE bone cards over one at a time. His eyes took in images while his mind danced with inferences and possibilities. He did not like any of them.

The chamber around him was echoing and bright. Pillars of white marble rose from a floor of pale green stone. Light shone from clusters of glow-globes which hung by chains from the arched roof. Sentences of High Gothic covered every inch of the chamber. Rihat had said that they were the words of lost messages heard by astropaths over the thousands of years the station had existed. The lost words filled many rooms. Some, he had been told, believed that they formed a kind of oracle, that fate could be divined in their broken fragments of meaning. That belief had seemed fitting to Cyrus.

On the brass-topped table, beside the pile of bone cards, the holo-recording of the astropathic message turned and spoke. Cyrus had been listening to it again and again since his arrival. He believed that the signal had come from the station he stood in, but it was also clear that the station had not called for help. He would not leave, though, not yet; there were too many unanswered questions.

Phobos had nodded at the order to remain, but Cyrus had felt the sergeant's dissent in his dutiful response: why waste more time? Because of a vision and a feeling that I cannot share with you, was the answer that had gone unsaid. The sergeant had withdrawn with Rihat to review the station's tactical readiness, while Cyrus had asked for a place of solitude. They had brought him to the pillared chamber and there he had stayed, shuffling through his brooding thoughts for several hours.

A blind man reaching into oblivion, that is what I am, he thought.

The bone cards were slivers of polished ivory the length of a human hand. An intricate picture painted with subtle skill in fading colours looked up from one side of each card. Some showed figures from myth, others patterns of lines and numbers. Words in High Gothic wove through each design. In the hands of a psyker sensitive to how the future echoed through the tides of the warp they could reveal hidden truths about what was and what might be. It was an old form of divination, one that had persisted with variations for millennia. The designs of the cards came from a time before the great darkness of the Age of Strife, an age of lost history and forgotten lore. The bone cards that flicked through Cyrus's armoured fingers had been crafted on Sabatine, the home world of the White Consuls. Cyrus had used this set for over two centuries, and they felt as much a part of him as the armour that wrapped his body.

He turned another card. The Blind Oracle sat over the Nine Blades: confused ends, paradox and lies.

'...Fateweaver...' the voice recording crackled next to him. He lifted his hand to turn the last bone card.

The vision pierced his thoughts like a knife.

The sword in his hand, blood sizzling as it drips down his arm to meet the weapon's caged fire. The sword twisting in his grip, pinning feathered flesh to the floor. A carrion scream, echoing through him, blotting out the shouts of his brothers around him. Light flowing like water from a face like a flayed bird, flowing into the floor, twisting through metal, changing it, becoming it. Its mouth is opening to say...

'You are adept at divination, I see,' said a voice close by. Reality snapped back into place around Cyrus, leaving him with a dull ache behind his eyes. He looked up from the unturned card to the speaker. It was a man, thin and bent by time, the green silk of his robes falling from hunched shoulders. A stole of black and gold thread circled his thin neck and a skull cap of blue velvet topped a wizened and bearded face. He had no eyes but the empty sockets seemed to be watching Cyrus. In his mind Cyrus could feel the ghost touch of the man's psychic senses play across his skin. The man smiled, showing Cyrus a mouth of crooked teeth.

'Never been much interested in it myself,' the man said. He raised a hand and shrugged. 'I know. Astropaths are supposed to be concerned with such things: the deeper resonances of the universe, insights into eternal mysteries. But, I must admit I find it tedious, and liable to lose me too much sleep.' Cyrus found that he was smiling. The man shuffled closer, the tip of a silver cane tapping as it took his weight with each step. 'I am sorry to disturb you, but I thought I should apologise for not greeting you when you arrived.' The old man dipped his head, making him briefly even more hunched. 'My name is Colophon; I am the senior astropath of this station.'

'Epistolary Cyrus Aurelius of the White Consuls,' said Cyrus, returning the bow without thinking.

Colophon grinned broadly. 'Hmm, a Librarian of the Adeptus Astartes. No wonder Hekate is so put out. Can't stand a rival that one.'

Cyrus remembered the primaris psyker's challenging gaze when they had met at the docking gate. 'I am sure that she is a worthy servant of the Imperium,' he replied carefully.

'You must have Emperor-given patience. I can't stand her myself.'

Colophon stepped closer, leaning in to where the recording of the signal still turned on the brass table top. The naturalness of Colophon's movements struck Cyrus. Astropaths often possessed psychic senses that allowed them to see the world through a veil of telepathic resonance. But if it were not for his empty eye sockets, Cyrus would have said that the old man could see perfectly.

Colophon cocked his head to one side, listening. The recording rasped through the last syllables of its cycle and began again.

'So this is the signal that brought you here, the one that has everyone so puzzled?'

Cyrus nodded. 'Yes, it is what brought us here. It is distorted but it appeared to be a call for help.' Colophon did not reply but waited while the message finished.

'Yes, yes. I see what you mean,' he said finally. 'But as Rihat and Hekate told you, no signal has been sent from here. Certainly not one of this nature.' He gave a chuckle. 'I should know.' He turned away from the projection, sucking his teeth. 'Librarians are versed in the basics of astropathic transmission; had you not considered the possibility of temporal distortion?'

The possibility *had* occurred to Cyrus. Astropathic messages passed through the warp, and were subject to that realm's inconsistent flow of time. A message might arrive millennia after it was sent, or be broken into incomprehensible pieces, or even arrive before it was sent. The message might be a plea from a future waiting just beyond the horizon of the present. It was that possibility of an unknown future that had made Cyrus linger.

'It had occurred to me,' Cyrus said. 'Do you think it likely?'

Colophon shrugged. 'The possibility alarms you?'

Cyrus thought of the ash of the dead world running through his fingers. 'Yes, particularly given recent events.'

Colophon's eyebrows rose. 'Recent events?'

Cyrus frowned. The incursions were only fragments of a sudden flaring of conflict around the Eye of Terror. Never a place of peace, in recent times it had become a place of all out war, a war that the Imperium might lose. Forces from several Chapters were involved, and the front was spreading.

'The incursion from the Eye,' he said, 'the manifestation

of the *Accursed Eternity*. This is a strategic station; word of these things must have passed through here?'

Colophon shook his head. 'This is a relay station: a hundred of my kind sifting the void for messages, absorbing them and echoing them on far beyond the reach of the original sender. We do not hear the messages that pass through us, any more than a pipe drinks the water that passes through it.'

'I thought that as senior astropath you might have received word of the war…'

A frown spread wrinkles across Colophon's face. 'No, I am simply concerned with the flow of messages, not their content. If anyone knows it will be Hekate. She must have thought it unnecessary to tell me. She is our chief watchdog, our "Savant Immaterium". An honourable position, though she loathes the fact that a primaris must sit here and look after us less gifted souls.' He gave a snort. 'You would never have guessed would you?'

There was a pause and Cyrus was about to speak again when the old man seemed to shake himself of worry. He gave a smile that only looked a little forced and tapped his cane on the floor. 'Come, let us walk, Cyrus Aurelius of the White Consuls. It will do my bones good and might ease whatever is worrying you.' He began to walk off, cane tip clicking. Cyrus followed, wondering about echoes and messages from an unknown future.

COLONEL RIHAT HAD never seen an angel of death before. He had been a soldier for most of his life – had seen people die: a few pirates during the scouring of the margin worlds, a few deserters – but he had never been in a fight larger than a skirmish.

In his old regiment he had been a platoon officer, though after a few decades he had known that he would never rise any higher. One day the regiment had been shipped to the Cadian Gate. He had been in transit from a garrison duty on a backwater mining world and missed the redeployment. There was nowhere for him to go, so they had sent him to join the Helicon Guard.

The Helicon Guard was a regiment of veterans pulled together from units that had suffered such high casualties that they were no longer viable as a combat force. Recruits took its ochre and red fatigues and bronze battle armour when they joined, casting off their former allegiances. Most were from regiments raised in systems around the Eye: hard people from hives or population sinks on worlds where you could look up and see the Eye glaring back out of the night sky.

Rihat knew that he had no right to the respect of the men and women under him. Command had fallen to him by a technicality: he had been the most senior officer when he joined and had thus been promoted to the role. He was not a hero, he knew that. He did his best, and tried to lean on what experience he did have. But that experience did not include a detailed knowledge of the Adeptus Astartes.

His first reaction was fear. When the blast doors of the station dock opened, he had felt a cold knot tighten in his guts. It was not just the warriors' size – that they were taller than any of the troopers ranked behind him – it was something about how they moved and looked at you. He remembered as a child seeing one of the ice lions of his home world. The beast had padded out onto the tundra road in front of their vehicle, its movements slow, muscle shifting under its patterned pelt. It had stopped and looked at them. Rihat had looked back into the animal's yellow eyes. For a second he had known that he was looking into the soul of something utterly indifferent to him, something whose nature was to kill or not as it chose. Looking into the eyes of the one called Cyrus he had felt an echo of that memory.

His second reaction was curiosity. The one called Phobos had asked to appraise the station, and so Rihat found himself walking beside the angel of death down the station's passages and colonnades. As they walked he could not help but glance at the Space Marine's blunt face. There was a compact ferocity to it, a predator cast to the set of the eyes and brow. He wondered what kind of soul moved behind that face.

'Something worrying you, colonel?' said Phobos, his voice a stony growl.

'No, my lord,' said Rihat, trying carefully to hide his unease.

The Space Marine grunted. 'Phobos, colonel. I am no lord, and you are a commander of men, an officer.' He turned an emotionless gaze on Rihat. 'My given name will suffice.'

Rihat gave a small nod that Phobos did not seem to notice.

They turned into a wide passage which ran around the inside of the kilometre-wide central hub of the station. Walls of verdigris bronze arched up to a central spine hung with glow-globes clasped in eagle claw fittings. This was the largest and greatest of the central passages. Any part of the station could be reached from its circle.

'You have not seen a warrior of the Adeptus Astartes before.'

It was a flat statement, Rihat realised. It was difficult to judge what Phobos intended. There was no emotion in his words, at least none that Rihat could sense. He watched as a woman in the robe of a Cipher looked at Phobos, the mnemonics she was muttering fading to nothing as she stared.

'No, I don't think many here have.'

'The primaris psyker, the one called Hekate; she has,' said Phobos in the same flat growl.

Rihat frowned. Hekate seemed to know a lot more than anyone else around her and was never shy of saying so. How she had talked to the Space Marines in the docking bay had shocked Rihat. It was almost as if she held them in contempt. 'Perhaps,' he said, shaking his head at how anyone could face one of these creatures and speak to them as if they were ignorant children. But Hekate had done just that.

'Are we so strange to your eyes?'

The question made Rihat blink with surprise for a moment. He almost wanted to smile. 'Yes. To be honest, yes, you are.'

Phobos gave a thoughtful grunt, head nodding slightly in its armoured setting. 'The angels of death walking amongst mortals.'

'Yes, something like that,' said Rihat, frowning. For a moment he had heard a hint of something he could not quite place in the Space Marine's voice.

Phobos stopped and turned to Rihat. Behind them the honour guard clattered to a halt. The Space Marine looked steadily at Rihat, his storm-grey eyes unblinking amongst ridges of glossy scar tissue. His armour was white, but Rihat could see gouges and score marks under the paint. The crux on Phobos's left shoulder was a death's head of dull stone. There were patches where damage had been ground smooth. A sword hung in a bronze-worked scabbard at his waist, its grip bound with hide, its pommel a silver skull. Rihat doubted he could easily lift it.

Phobos's armour clicked and whined as he shifted his posture, leaning closer. A smell of machine oil filled Rihat's nose. He raised an eyebrow. 'Tell me, do I look like an angel?'

'No... No, you don't. You look like the most terrifying thing I have ever seen.'

A ghost of a smile twitched across Phobos's face. 'Very good, colonel,' he said, and turned to walk on, seeming to growl as he moved.

After a few steps, Rihat realised that the Space Marine was chuckling.

'How long have you been an oracle?'

The question had come after they had walked the corridors and chambers of Claros station for several hours, Cyrus striding alongside the shuffling old man. They had talked and Cyrus found himself warming to Colophon's wry remarks and sharp questions.

'For as long as I can remember,' Cyrus said. The brief years of his youth opened in his mind. The fear of his parents at their child's strangeness, the shuddering terror of his dreams: all long ago on a world that existed now only in his memory. 'It was the first sign of my talent. I would see snatches of things that would later happen.'

Colophon nodded. 'The first awakenings of psychic talent are always the worst,' said the old man softly.

'Yes,' said Cyrus. The Librarian found himself wondering at what might have happened to him if he had not proved strong enough in mind and body to be sent from the Black Ships to the White Consuls. Would he have been shuffling along these corridors, blind to everything beyond his mind's eyes?

They turned to walk down a central chamber of one of the five wings of the station. It was wide and tall enough that a Titan could have strode between its stone pillars. People crowded its black stone floor. Administratum Ciphers hurried past, muttering mnemonic rhyme as they carried information from one part of the station to another. Hooded adepts talked in small groups, their mouths hidden by wide grey hoods. Menials in drab grey carried stacks of brass data sceptres, the tattooed marks of their service bright on their shaved heads. Wide eyes followed Cyrus from the crowd, fear and awe mingling on their faces. Some had knelt until he passed. It made him uncomfortable. He was a warrior used to the company of his brothers, not the grovelling fear of those he tried to protect.

'It must be a burden,' said Colophon, breaking Cyrus's thoughts. 'To see the future, to know what must happen.'

Cyrus shrugged, the gesture magnified through his armour into a massive shifting of armour plates. 'It is a tool, that is all. A weapon that I wield for my Chapter and the Imperium.'

Colophon turned his blind eyes towards Cyrus, and the Librarian felt the old man's psychic senses focus on him. 'Is it a vision of what will happen that makes you wait and worry so, my friend? Do you know that something will happen here?'

Cyrus thought of the omens in the bone slivers, of the snatches of sensation and vision: snarling faces, bird-like cries, his life pulsing away. 'Sometimes an omen is wrong, or open to interpretation,' he said carefully. 'Even if it appears clear, by knowing it and acting the oracle may change that future.'

'A very clear answer to a different question,' chuckled Colophon, turning to point them towards an arched door which led out of the pillared chamber. Beyond the door a spiral of wide iron steps led downwards. At the bottom was a tangle of narrow corridors, and cramped chambers. Most were closed by brass bound doors. Through the unsealed doors Cyrus could see figures polishing data sceptres by candlelight. In other chambers bent-backed curators shifted piles of parchment scrolls between dusty shelves. They looked up and watched as Cyrus and Colophon passed.

This place exists for the hundred astropaths that sit at its centre, he thought, but here is the blood and muscle of the station, never resting, always moving on the edge of others' shadows.

'Tell me,' said Colophon, and Cyrus heard the shift in his voice, the edge of worry. Cyrus stopped and Colophon turned to face him, flickering candlelight from a side chamber turning the old man's face into a twitching mask of shadow. 'What is it that you see coming?'

'Blood, Colophon. I see blood and ruin.'

THE ASTROPATHIC CHAMBER was a place of whispers. A circular bowl over five hundred paces wide, it sides rose in tiers of grey stone seats to a domed ceiling of black glass. Green-robed astropaths sat on every tier. There were hundreds of them, their minds open to the immaterium like nets cast into the currents of a deep ocean. Gathered in these numbers they could send messages over vast distances. They were a choir of minds acting in concert, but each reacted to their task differently. Some mumbled strings of words, or twitched as if stirring in a fitful dream. Others sat as still as statues, chests hardly moving as they breathed. The air was heavy, filled with the smell of sweat, incense and the static tang of psychic power. Ether-sensors hung from the ceiling above, feeling the flow of power within the chamber, alert for anything abnormal. Even psykers soul-bound to the Emperor were a risk when gathered together in large numbers. Out in the shadow tides of the warp such a gathering shone bright to the predators that swarmed there. The sensors were there to warn of any dangerous levels of psychic activity.

The hush broke without warning as an astropath on the third tier moaned and shivered in her trance. Supervisory adepts looked up from their screens and moved towards her. When the adepts were a pace away she arched her back and screamed. There was a sound of bones cracking as she convulsed. Above them the ether-sensors shattered. A mist coiled from the woman's mouth spreading into the air. It touched another green-robed figure and a new voice began to scream. The adepts froze for an instant and then began to run to the containment system.

More astropaths began to howl. Sparks rained down onto the tiered seats as the sensor arrays exploded. On every tier green-robed bodies spasmed, fingers clawing at the stone armrests of their chairs, pus running from empty eyes. A heavy stench of iron and raw meat spread through the air. Voice after voice rose into a storm of noise like the call of a choir of the damned. Frost began running across the domed ceiling. At the centre of the chamber adepts and guards fell to their knees. Some of the guards vomited as they felt voices rush through their minds, voices that moaned and pleaded for mercy. Alarms began to sound, but their shrills were swallowed in the chorus of screams.

They began to die. One man opened his mouth and liquid fire poured down his body, his flesh powdering from his bones. Another tried to stand, cables ripping from his scalp. He stumbled and exploded in a wet cloud of skin and bone fragments. Others rose screaming into the air before dissolving into smoke and black dust.

The sound grew louder, screams rolling over each other until a single voice shrieked from a hundred throats.

Beyond the chamber panic spread through the station in the blare of alarms, the clang of sealing blast doors and the shouts of running guards.

In the astropathic chamber the screams became a single word.

Then all was still, except for the drip of blood and softly falling ash.

CYRUS CHARGED THROUGH the doors at a run, his strides shaking the floor. Behind him Rihat did his best to match the White Consul's pace. Helicon Guard followed in their wake. Cyrus had been in the station's command chamber when the alarms had sounded and the servitors slaved to the sensors systems began to babble. Rihat had gone pale and then started to run, ordering troops to follow. Cyrus had overtaken him after only ten paces.

The psychic aftershock hit Cyrus as he entered the astropathic chamber, forcing him to stagger. The crystal matrix of his psychic hood was blazing with sickly light as it compensated for the wild power surging around him. A psychic event of huge magnitude had occurred in the chamber and a powerful echo of its fury still lingered. Dark liquid pooled on the floor; crumpled bodies lay in their stone thrones. Behind him, Cyrus heard some of the Helicon Guard vomiting onto the deck. The stink of sorcery was thick in the air: a sharp ozone tang that brought the twisted faces from his vision back into his mind. He scanned the chamber, its devastation lit by sparking glow-globes.

'Spread out,' he called. 'Look for survivors, be alert for any hostile action.' The Guardsmen moved around him, fanning out into the shadows. His storm bolter in hand, Cyrus moved deeper into the chamber.

There were bodies draping the stone tiers in piles of tangled limbs. A powdered layer covered everything, coating the dead so that they looked like grotesque sculptures. Scraps of debris still fell slowly through the air. Cyrus saw a severed hand on the snow-like covering, its fingers twisted into claws. There were lines in the dust, trail marks where people had crawled towards the doors. Dark stains had soaked into the ash in places, and Cyrus's steps left red prints as he moved across the chamber.

A figure staggered towards him, its eyes wide in a face smeared red. Dust spilled from the man as he moved. Cyrus recognised the marks of a senior adept on the man's robes. He mouthed something at Cyrus, his lips moving but his words muffled. Cyrus kept the muzzle of his bolter steady.

'What did you say?' asked Cyrus. The adept's mouth spoke the half sounds again. 'What did you say?' repeated Cyrus.

'He said that they screamed the same thing,' came a cracked voice from behind him.

Cyrus turned to see Colophon limping into the chamber. He looked into the old astropath's eyes, seeing an expression he could not read on the man's face.

Colophon walked over to the adept, who was swaying where he stood. 'I can see it in his thoughts,' he added. 'It is the only thing he is thinking. They screamed the same word at the end.'

Cyrus looked at the adept and saw the silent word in the shape of his moving lips. He felt a cold pulse run through him as he spoke the word out loud: 'Fateweaver.'

The adept nodded, his eyes wide with fear. Cyrus thought of the recorded signal and of the visions that would not leave him. It was all happening as he had feared it must. The daemon came to consume this place, as it had so many others.

Will I fail, he thought, will I be able to defy that part of fate?

'Not all of them are dead,' called Rihat, bent down next to a green-robed figure that lay sprawled on the floor. 'Some survived whatever this was.'

Cyrus saw that a few of the bodies scattered around the chamber were stirring, their movements feeble but signs of life none the less. 'Something is coming,' he said, glancing at the hunched man by his side. 'Colophon, a message must be sent now.' But the old astropath was shaking his head.

'Can't you feel it? The warp around us is...' Colophon closed his eyes briefly, a shiver running through his hunched form. 'The warp around us is a curtain of pain. No message will be able to break through. Even if any of my brothers and sisters recover, it would not be possible.'

Cyrus reached out with his psychic senses and tasted the veil of agony surrounding the station. It was as if a barbed web lay all around them, a shadow's width away. The old man was right; no telepathic message could leave.

Colophon trembled, almost falling, before Rihat caught him and lowered him to sit on the edge of the first stone tier. 'We are alone,' the astropath said. The old man looked up, and Cyrus saw the panic overcoming him. 'An evacuation?' A tremor of fear edged his voice. 'Your ship can hold many. We could–'

'No.' Cyrus cut the old man off. 'It could carry some, but what of the rest, Colophon? What of those we left behind?'

Colophon looked into Cyrus's eyes for an instant and then looked down, his hand trembling on his cane top.

'Your orders, Epistolary?' said Rihat.

Cyrus turned, looking at the tiered chamber and the motionless figures that would never rise from their seats. A few survivors were beginning to call out from the shadows. 'Prepare the defences. We are alone, and so we must hold alone.'

'How long do we have until an attack begins?' asked Rihat. His face was pale and Cyrus could see fear in his wide eyes.

Cyrus looked at the colonel, and then at the blood congealing at their feet. 'It has already begun.'

II

BLOODED

'FLESH WILL FAIL, Space Marine,' said Hekate, and Phobos
had to bite back his anger at the contempt in her voice.
'Against the enemy that comes, this is our true defence.'
Hekate raised her staff to point at the black pillar that
rose above them. Bundles of humming cables snaked
around it, and purity seals covered almost every inch of
its surface. Phobos could see a delicate pattern of marks
etched into the obsidian beneath the fluttering strips of
parchment. The chamber was a narrow armoured cylinder
that followed the pillar into blackness above. The air held
a greasy static charge that played over his armour in small
arcs.

Phobos had been reviewing the station's defences for
hours. His eyes had taken in every readied gun and choke-
point, his mind sifting through possible weaknesses.
Helicon Guard units waited in each of the five wings of
the station. The White Consuls under his and Cyrus's
command formed a force of small units, ready to respond
should the enemy break through. The *Aethon* would
remain docked to the station, its guns ready if necessary. It

was Cyrus's plan and Phobos could not fault it given their resources, but the key to the defence was in front of him.

The pillar was a Geller field generator. The field it projected was a product of techno-arcana of the powerful kind. Normally used to shield ships as they passed through the warp, here it existed to shield the station from daemonic assault.

Phobos disliked Hekate but knew that she spoke truth. Besides his brothers, there were Rihat's regiment of Helicon Guard, batteries of macro cannons trained on the void, and layers of void shields that could keep a battlefleet at bay. But, as Hekate had pointed out, they were not facing a battlefleet. She was a primaris psyker, a savant immaterium who knew secrets that Phobos would never learn. She had shared her thoughts with them over the past hours, and each comment was as accurate as it was barbed. Her latest observation was no less so. The Geller field was the station's true defence.

The field would envelop the central section of the station, closing it off from daemonic assault. There would be sections that would be unshielded, flaws in the invisible wall where a daemon could pass through. These would be the points where flesh and bone would have to stand against the enemy. Should the daemons force a way inside the field envelope then there would be slaughter. Phobos thought of the thousands of non-military personnel crammed into chambers of the central hub, running prayer beads through their fingers, muttering implorations to the Emperor to protect them from their fears.

'Are they at full power?' asked Phobos.

'They are bringing the generator on-line now,' said Rihat, consulting a brass-framed data-slate in his hand. As he finished, the deck began to shake. Bright chains of electricity played up and down the pillar. The purity seals rustled as if in a rising wind. A warning chime sounded in Phobos's ear as his armour detected a growing power spike.

The pillar shivered and issued a sound like a bell tolling underwater. A skin of heat haze formed on its surface.

Phobos could hear a high hum like vibrating glass.

'Fields are at maximum strength,' said Rihat, looking up and running a hand nervously across his head. 'I have commanded the Guard here for a decade and the full field mantle has never been activated.'

Phobos heard unspoken fears in the colonel's voice. Rihat was a commander of men, chosen for that duty because of his quality. But he had never faced the kind of enemy that now came for them. A thought came unbidden to Phobos's mind as he placed a hand upon the man's shoulder: maybe you are another weakness in our armour, Rihat.

'These are not our only defences,' Phobos said. The colonel looked up at the scar-twisted face of the White Consul, and Phobos saw the uncertainty in his eyes. 'We must stand whether these fields fail or not. Should they fail, flesh and spirit will have to suffice.'

Beside him Hekate gave a derisive snort. 'That is true, Space Marine,' said the psyker with a grim smile, 'but if it comes to that, the station will fall.'

A PRE-STORM QUIET permeated the pillared chamber where the White Consuls armed themselves. They gathered in squads, talking in low voices as servitors attached oath parchments to their shoulder guards. The clink of weapons and the smell of incense hung in the air.

Cyrus stood apart, his thoughts drifting back into the past. He was not supposed to have memories from before he became a White Consul. Years of psychic conditioning, and the indoctrinations of the Adeptus Astartes, should have removed any remnants of what he had been. But he did remember. Sometimes Cyrus wondered if it was the shadow of his oracular gift.

He could not recall much from before he became a Space Marine, but he could remember the day the Black Ships came. They had appeared out of the noon sun and had hung in the blue sky like impossible castles. On the mountain sides and on the plains, people looked up from the shadows they cast over the ground. He had not understood what it meant but the old men of the village had. They glanced at him with fear as they clustered around the fire in the meeting hall that night. They said that the shapes in the sky were the Sky God's witch-seekers, and that they had come to take the god's due.

There were many witches on their world. Most were killed or hounded into the wild, but more were born every year. When the emissaries of the Sky God came they took all the witches they could find up to the stars. If they found witches had been hidden their anger would be terrible. Cyrus had heard them talk and knew what would happen.

His mother had kept his abilities secret for several years, but it had not lasted; there was too much strangeness about him. Sometimes he yelled strange things in his sleep, or knew what someone was about to do before it happened. People noticed and people talked.

That night his father had sat amongst the men looking pale, saying little, not looking at his son. His mother had tried to hide him, had argued with his father, raging through falling tears. It had made no difference. The village had waited outside the house until his father led him out. They took him down to the plains where the temples that fell from the sky waited, swallowing long lines of people: confused old men, wild-eyed hermits and weeping children. Cyrus had not cried; there was no point. He knew what was going to happen.

The world had given up its witches, but it had ultimately made no difference. A clutch of uncontrollably powerful alpha plus psykers had been born there a decade later. The Imperium had burned the world from orbit, reducing it to cinders. Far away in his cell on Sabatine, Cyrus had woken with the taste of ash in his mouth.

Cyrus blinked and ran his tongue through his mouth. The memory of the gritty taste was a ghost sensation on his palate. The servitors pulled away, smoke coiling from where the wax cooled on his newly attached parchments. He nodded, flexing his hand inside his gauntlet. His storm bolter cycled to readiness with a metallic snarl. Another servitor clanked forwards on chained tracks, his helmet held in callipered hands. The helmet locked over his head with a hiss. For an instant, blind darkness wrapped him before his vision flickered with luminous readouts.

Now we wait for the storm to come, he thought.

IN THE GULF beyond the station's hull, the void split like skin slit with a knife. A luminous miasma poured out of the wound, staining the light of the stars as it spread. It coiled in the vacuum, forming folds and tendrils like milk curdling in dark wine. Half-formed shapes moved through the spreading cloud as thousands of hungering eyes turned towards the station. The wound stretched wider and the cloud grew.

Claros station shook with the metal-voiced fury of cannon fire. Beams of energy and lines of shells streamed across the black expanse. They struck the oncoming tide and sliced through it like claws raking through fat. Chunks of solidifying matter cooked to charred fragments. Explosions scooped holes in ethereal flesh. Vast mouths opened in the cloud's surface crying out in silent pain. And the guns kept firing. Auto loaders rammed macro shells into smoking breeches. Las-capacitors shrieked as they built up charge, and plasma generators boiled with overheating ferocity. Behind blast doors and barricades the defenders felt the station quake and prayed for hope, for salvation, for fate to favour them.

The first salvoes cut into the sickly pall, but it swelled without pausing. When it reached the station's hull it writhed across it, searching for weakness. Where it found that weakness it poured through in an ethereal wave of extending talons and bared teeth.

CYRUS CLOSED HIS eyes. Sounds and images faded until he was conscious of only a few sensations: the familiar feeling of his Terminator armour against his skin, the heft of his sword in his hand, and the worn segments of his gauntlets, flexing as he shifted his grip on the hide-wound hilt. The blade was keening, its edge shivering.

He opened his eyes. The dark metal walls of the lift shaft slid past, the red glow of his brothers' eyes diluting the darkness. Galba and his squad stood beside him. Six figures in ghost white, the blue of their helmets lost in the low light. The top of the lift shaft receded above them. Numbers flickered across Cyrus's vision, counting down the estimated time to engagement.

The enemy had broken through into a tunnel under the fifth station wing. The Helicon Guard defending the unshielded tunnel were on the edge of breaking. Panicked voices washed through Cyrus's vox, and tactical assessments filled his helmet display. It was the sound and measure of a massacre.

This is what we exist for, he thought. This is what we were made for: to step into certain defeat and undo that fate.

The lift platform halted with a metallic clang. In front of Cyrus the blast doors waited. He could almost feel what was beyond those closed metal teeth.

'The Emperor wills it, and we are His weapon,' growled Galba from behind Cyrus.

'The Emperor wills it, and His will is fury,' said Cyrus. Cold power blazed down the sword in his hand, its edge singing in tune with his mind. Chainblades snarled to life. A crackling field enveloped Galba's fist, casting the White Consuls in flickering shadows.

'By His will,' spoke the White Consuls.

The blast doors ground open. A broad, circular passage extended away in front of Cyrus. The pipes and support ribs lining its side made it look like the inside of a vast animal. A shoulder-high barrier of welded plasteel ran across the tunnel's mouth. Behind it, the remains of a company of Helicon Guard were dying.

A wall of sound washed over Cyrus: human shrieks, the crack-fizz of lasguns, and inhuman sounds cried from the throats of daemons. Some of the Helicons were falling back, firing ragged bursts into a glittering fog that rolled across the barricade. Shifting shapes moved like shadows cast by a flickering fire.

Cyrus began to run. He was fifty paces from the barrier, armour shaking with each step. Las-bolts whipped past him, sparkling as they vanished into the boiling fog in front of him. The troops who had not fled the barricade were dying. Distorted shapes with many limbs spun amongst the Guardsmen. Blue flames ate through armour and flesh where the shapes touched. Single-eyed creatures pulled at the barrier with rotting hands. A thick sweet scent reached Cyrus's nose, mocking his sealed armour.

He was thirty paces away. He began firing, his storm bolter stitching fire through threat markers, explosions blooming amongst the coiling fog. A Guardsman staggered away from the barricade and took a trembling step towards Cyrus. His face was pale and streaked with blood, his lasgun loose in his hands. A shape flowed out of the fog behind the man. He took another step. The shape snapped into sharp focus. It stood poised on the top of the barrier. Its body was a lithe sculpture of taut muscle and glittering skin. Eyes that were circles of reflective darkness looked at Cyrus and it hissed like a snake. Cyrus drew his sword back.

The figure leaped, its claws closing over the fleeing Guardsman's head as it turned in the air. It landed in a whip spray of blood as the Guardsman crumpled to the floor. For an instant the creature stood, quivering as if in pleasure. It looked at Cyrus, and smiled with a mouth of hooked teeth.

Cyrus charged. The creature pounced, its teeth wide in its beautiful skull, its eyes glinting like moonlight on frost. Cyrus dropped into a half crouch and rammed his sword forwards. The sword tip punched into the creature's slender neck. Glowing blood flowed down its length as the creature's momentum rammed it onto the blade. Cyrus felt the creature's essence dissolve into black vapour. He ripped the sword back. The creature's death in his mind was like the taste of honey and bile.

Another creature blurred towards him, claws clicking, movements coiling. Cyrus cut, armour and muscles flowing. The figure swayed, and Cyrus's sword struck the deck in a shower of sparks. The creature flipped through the air faster than Cyrus could turn his sword, its claws reaching for his face as it spun. He could see the death in its eyes, felt it call him to oblivion.

An armoured fist closed on the creature's body with a crack of bound thunder. Galba lifted the broken creature from the ground and threw it down. The sergeant brought his foot down on its skull, grinding it to fragments.

'They come,' shouted the sergeant to Cyrus. Bolt shells roared from Galba's pistol as he turned towards the tunnel mouth.

The barricade had given way. Rotting figures scrambled through the breach, rusted blades scraping on the decking, their mouths drooling pus. The Helicon Guard who had clung to the barricades fell back. Cyrus felt a buzzing inside his head, an insect touch on his skin. Shells flew from his storm bolter. He kept the trigger squeezed, the gun sucking rounds from its drum feed. Targets vanished and pulsed back into sight. He stepped forwards into the space gouged by the storm bolter.

Cyrus glanced over at Galba. The sergeant was at the centre of a closing circle of leering faces, slime thick blades hacking at his armour. The four other members of his squad were cutting towards him with their chainblades. Galba punched forwards and gripped a horned head in his lightning-sheathed fist. He lifted the creature and fired his pistol into its eye. The head exploded like an overripe fruit. Cyrus saw Galba back-fist three creatures to pulp before the cage of hacking blades closed over him.

Claws and blades scraped across Cyrus's armour. Rotting bodies surrounded him, their yellow eyes pressed against his helmet lenses. He tried to move his sword arm, felt the press of bodies weighing it down. Something sharp found a join in his armour. He could feel pathogens trying to find purchase in his immune system, radiating pain through his body. Their daemon's reek reached inside his mind. He could feel their hunger. He remembered the vision: the circling creatures, the sword slipping from his hand. Was this the fate he had seen? The thought sunk into him and for an instant he teetered on the edge of doubt.

Anger flared through him, overwhelming his pain and doubt. He would not fall, not here. He would deny that fate.

A pattern of thought and feeling formed in his mind. It burned like a sun trapped in his skull. He held on to it for a moment, feeling it feed on his rage, growing wilder and hotter. He released the thought. Flames burst from him. The creatures around him wailed as their flesh cooked. He poured his anger into the fire, feeling power mirror his rage. It quickened and grew until he was a still figure, at the heart of a white-hot storm. The display inside his helmet dimmed against the brightness. In the inferno the daemons shrieked as he tore their essence apart.

His body sang with the power running through him, and his psychic hood was ice-cold against his scalp. He did not want to let go. He could hear something whispering, calling to him to never let this end, to give himself to it, to hold on to this power forever. It would be right, it would be...

He released the fury in his mind, the burning power collapsing into a dull ember ache in his skull.

Sudden silence and stillness surrounded him. He was breathing hard, his skin clammy and cold in his armour. Around him the floor and walls of the passage glowed. The barricade was a twisted mound of blackened metal, like a crumpled cloth. He turned, meeting the staring eyes of the Helicon Guard who looked up from where they cowered by the lift entrance. Sheathing his sword he reached up and released his helmet. The air smelt of cooked meat and sulphur.

Four members of Galba's squad stood amongst the wreck of the barricade. The teeth of their chainblades were thick with oozing flesh. Galba lay between them. Congealing blood and yellow mucus caked his splintered armour. His helmet was a ruin of squashed bone and torn ceramite.

Galba's four squad brothers lifted their sergeant onto their shoulders. They murmured the death lament of Sabatine as they moved. They would carry him back to the *Aethon* where he would wait in cold stasis until he returned to his birth planet for the last time. Hearing the old words from a planet that was home but which had not borne him, Cyrus found that there was nothing he could say.

ITS NEW FACE was dull and uninteresting. It had worn more faces than it could recall, and it would forget this one as soon as it had taken another. The weaker flesh-born moved around it. They were those that they called soldiers. It found the idea of such a title laughable: as if a name could change their herd animal nature into something greater. It had many names, both granted and stolen. *Changeling* some called it, but that was not its name and the description barely touched the essence of its nature. It knew how little a name was worth.

It breathed, feeling the world as the flesh-born felt it, dulled to simple stimuli and base sensations. A giant warrior in blue stood close by. Space Marines: that was what the flesh-born called them. It could taste this one's thoughts, feel their nuances, the characteristics and temperament they implied. Interesting. So much more interesting than the role it played now. There were subtleties and depths of self-deception at play that would make such an identity a delight to play. But it had a bargain to fulfil, and for that bargain the drab face that it wore was what it needed.

During the battle it had worn the form of lesser children of decadence, passing amongst its supposed kind with flawless ease. Isolated and forgotten on the edge of the violence it had found what it needed. The man had been hugging his legs to his chest and weeping silently. An ideal face to wear, it had thought. It had destroyed the original, reducing the flesh-born's body to dust with a touch. Now it wore the flesh-born's shape.

'Harlik,' said a voice close by.

For a moment it stayed where it was, staring at the scorched plating of the deck.

'Harlik, come on, they're pulling us out.'

Harlik. Yes, that would be the name that went with the face, a dull name for a dull entity. It turned to look at the speaker. A heavy-faced man, smeared with soot, the ochre and red of his uniform stained by blood and vomit.

'Yeah, I'm coming,' it said, its voice perfect, the layer of shocked slowness consistent with what Harlik would have sounded like had he survived the assault. 'I'm coming.'

It followed the flesh-born, tasting their thoughts as it moved amongst them. Most were struggling with emotions and thoughts it could not comprehend: shock, terror, guilt, anger, hope. It could not understand these feelings, but it could imitate their effects flawlessly.

Shoulders hunched, eyes vacant, it trudged on with the rest. It would need a new face as it moved towards its goal. Yes, it would wear another face soon.

THE BLIND FIGURE talked to Cyrus in his dreams.

'There is no way out. Your fate is written,' says the astropath, turning in the cone of hololight, its voice a dry croak. He reaches out but the figure turns, and he sees that it has two faces: one grinning, the other snarling; both blind. He reaches for his sword but feels his hand close on nothing. The two-faced figure laughs.

He is falling through fading shadow, tumbling past stars and moons, drifting through eternity, his body a lie, time a lie.

He stands at the bottom of stone tiers that ascended into darkness. He looks up. Eyes blaze back at him.

His brothers are shouting at him, close by servitors are blurting code in frantic streams. He is raising his sword.

He is standing on the bridge of a ship as it falls through winds that howl with laughter.

Darkness folds over him.

*There are Space Marines in blue armour. He can see drag-
ons coiling on their shoulder guards. A figure in black armour
moves amongst them, a reptilian cloak hanging from his back in
folds of iridescent scales. They are walking through ghost-quiet
corridors. Dark liquid seeps out of the walls in their wake. He
calls to them, but they are wraiths hovering beyond an impenetrable veil.*

*He brings his sword down and the two heads of the astropath
scream with the sound of a murder of dying crows.*

This has not happened. This is the future, *he thinks.*

*The blind figure turns in its cone of cold light, its two faces
grinning, laughing from both of its mouths.*

'No, this is the past,' says the blind figure.

Cyrus opened his eyes with a snarl of pain. A servitor
with a skull of polished chrome cocked its head, looking
at him with cold blue eye lenses, a piston hand poised
above his shoulder armour. He took a ragged breath.

Shadows surrounding pools of harsh light filled the
armoury. He was standing at the centre of a clutch of
white-robed servitors, limbs splayed on a cruciform frame
that supported the dead weight of his armour. The armour
was silent, its machine spirit slumbering while the servitors peeled it from his body.

It had been some hours since the first attempts by the
daemons to break through the gaps in the Geller field. The
warp still enclosed the station but after the first attacks
there had been quiet. It was not peace, though, just an in-
breath before the next onslaught.

Scorched and stained by battle, Cyrus had returned to
the *Aethon* to have his armour stripped and cleansed. He
had hoped that the act would be mirrored in his body
and mind, but his temples still throbbed with the psychic
exertion of the battle. He had not been able to stop thinking about the signal that had called them here. The more
he thought about it the more he was sure he was missing
something about it, something just out of hearing waiting
beneath the surface. Then the vision had taken him again.

He nodded to the servitors and they continued to unpick

the Terminator armour, pulling away plates, and uncoupling system links with cold, mechanical fingers.

'A hard fight,' said a voice beyond the stab lights of the hovering servo-skulls.

Cyrus squinted, his eyes cutting into the darkness. Phobos stood in his own armour, the white Terminator plate making him look a marble statue.

'You look weary,' he said. There was a hint of a smile on his lips.

Cyrus nodded grimly. 'We held the breach. It cost us Galba.'

The first cost we must pay, he thought, a cost I have said we must bear.

'He goes to the ancestors,' said Phobos, nodding. 'As must we all.'

Cyrus did not reply but watched as two servitors disconnected a series of bio-readout cables from plugs in his side. They burbled to each other in machine code as they worked. In over two centuries of war he had seen thousands die. Brothers had fallen at his side, and he had made decisions that had both cost and saved lives. But the first tangible price of coming to Claros troubled him. He felt as if he had sleepwalked into a cobweb that bound tighter around him with every move he made.

'Does it still trouble you?'

Cyrus looked up at Phobos, seeing the look of friendly concern on his brother's face.

'This?' Cyrus winced as the servitors pulled the blood-streaked greave from his leg. 'It will not slow me.' The flesh underneath was livid, black veins crawling out from a suppurating wound.

'No, not that.' The sergeant frowned. 'You are brooding on something; you have been since you decided to come here.'

A servo-skull drifted close to Cyrus's wounded leg, extending a red-hot cauterising blade. Cyrus nodded and the blade lanced into his flesh. He did not make any expression as the smell of burnt flesh sizzled into the air.

'You said before that there was nothing we could do even if this place was attacked. That it would burn anyway.'

Phobos shook his head gently. 'I misspoke. I spoke as I felt I must, but you lead us and you led us here, and here we have an enemy to stand against.'

Cyrus was suddenly aware of how worn his friend looked, his face weathered by war and framed by white armour older than memory.

'You were right, old friend,' breathed Phobos heavily. 'You were right. Don't let my words weaken you for what we must do now.'

Cyrus shook his head. Beside his temple a servo-skull buzzed as it unlinked the crystalline mesh of his psychic hood from his scalp. There were blisters and lesions in places where it rested on his skin.

'The signal and the omens worry me. They are why we are here and I still understand neither fully. That…' He paused sifting through words to sum up his worry. 'That makes me wonder if it was not bait, if I have not led us into a trap, if I should not have chosen differently.'

It was Phobos's turn to shake his head, armoured shoulders turning his chuckle into a ripple of armour. 'The enemy did not come here for us; they came here for the light of the astropaths and the souls on the station. If we weren't here they would already have fallen. And we are not here for omens, brother. We are here to fight and to win.'

Cyrus frowned. 'And we bear the price of that chance for survival?'

Phobos grinned, his scarred face splitting with grim humour. 'That, brother, is why we were made.'

IT BEGAN WITH one man.

Guardsmen crowded the vaulted chamber that ran down the centre of the fourth wing of the station. They had been there for several rotations, not sleeping, just looking nervously into the shadows. No one had explained what was happening. Station command had said only that the station was under attack, and that they were a primary reserve if the enemy broke through from other sections. No one had said who the enemy was, and that only made things worse. Rumours of attacks in other areas had come some hours earlier, but the lack of details created spaces filled by fears and rumour. No two rumours agreed on anything other than a single fact: it was bad. The lack of any solid information only confirmed it.

Private first class Ramiel straightened up from his crouched position and flexed his shoulders under his bronze-plated armour, trying to work the tightness from his back. Over a decade ago he had been a gang boss, lording it over his own chunk of the Vortis underhive in the distant Mandragora sector. He had killed how he liked, and who he liked. It had been a good life. Bad luck had seen him lose that life and gain a rank of flat nothing in an Imperial Guard regiment that went on to lose ninety per cent of its numbers in its first campaign. Ramiel had survived though, he always did.

He had been watching a sealed door that led off the broad colonnade for over four hours. It was supposed to lead to an unshielded section, whatever that meant. Nothing had happened and nothing was going to, just another waste of time. Sure, he had been jumpy when the alarm had come through and they were deployed on maximum alert. They said there were Space Marines on the station, that the station had already been attacked. With every hour spent crouched watching the unmoving door he had believed it less and less. There was no attack, no Space Marines. It was just a drill, a waste of time, and the more he thought about it the more it had started to irritate him.

'Get back on post, Ramiel,' the sour voice of the sergeant spat from a few yards behind him.

Ramiel ignored it; the sergeant was a straight-backed son of a bitch who scared most of the squad. Not Ramiel, though. He knew that the sergeant was a nothing, no real fight in him. Let him shout, he thought, let him try whatever he liked. He pulled his helmet off and dropped it next to his lasgun. He rotated his neck stretching out his muscles as he reached into a pouch and pulled out a lho-stick. He heard the sergeant marching up behind him as he lit the tip of the stick.

'Pick up your gun and get back into position, soldier,' growled the sergeant next to Ramiel's ear.

Ramiel turned and looked the sergeant in the eye. A reckless anger was coursing through him now. He did not know where it had come from: he just knew it felt good. He took a long draw of the lho-stick and grinned at the sergeant.

'Pick it up or–'

Ramiel's fist slammed into the sergeant's guts and he brought his knee up hard as the man doubled over. The sergeant went down with a wet noise and lay on the floor, blood pooling around his mashed face. There was a soundless pause; men were staring from other positions across the colonnade.

'Well you're down there now, sergeant. Why don't you pick it up?' He smiled and took another drag of his lho-stick.

The sergeant came to his feet faster than Ramiel could blink. There was the polished glitter of a knife in his hand. Ramiel jumped back but the tip of the blade stabbed up under the edge of his armour. Suddenly there was blood splattering the floor. Ramiel lashed a kick at the sergeant, ignoring the pain flaring in his guts. People were running towards them. Suddenly all Ramiel wanted was to see the sergeant's blood pulse away, to see his head become a skinless skull. He came forwards fast and the sergeant lunged, the point of the knife scoring across Ramiel's breastplate. His hand went to the sergeant's face, fingers finding the softness of the eyes. The sergeant screamed. There were others around Ramiel, other people shouting, but he did not care. He pulled the knife from the sergeant's fingers and rammed it up under the man's chin. Blood gushed over him. He was laughing. There was a hand on his shoulder, pulling him. He turned and sliced a face from eye to chin.

A red haze formed in the air. Angry cries spread around Ramiel, figures bunching into knots of sudden violence. Someone opened up with a heavy weapon, hard rounds pulping through the growing crowd. The stone-tiled floor was slippery with dark fluid. There was a stink of offal in the air.

Ramiel kept moving, kept cutting and stabbing. His skin and armour glistened crimson. Around him fallen bodies began to twitch, dead fingers spasming, muscles bunching. Flesh twisted, bursting skin and venting fresh, bright blood. Ramiel could feel the murder hunger inside him like a beast. He raised his hand to cut again, to feed the beast.

Something sharp rammed through Ramiel's chest. He looked down at the black blade tip projecting from his ribs. He grinned a dead man's grin, swaying where he stood. Ramiel's mouth began to open wider and wider. With a sound of ripping sinew the form of an impossible thing pulled itself from Ramiel's skin. The creature sloughed off the sleeve of loose flesh. It was slick with blood, its tongue flicking out to taste the air. Its eyes were pits of reflective darkness in a long skull. It stepped forwards, its black jointed legs shaking with the freshness of its birth, its flesh a raw meat red.

A man who had been firing his lasgun into the fight looked at the newly born daemon and opened his mouth. The daemon bounded forwards, the black blade in its hands leaving a trail of smoke as it cut. The man never had a chance to scream.

The daemon looked around seeing more waiting kills, hearing the pulse of the living calling to it. More of its kin came, pulling themselves from the bodies of the dead and the pools of blood. Lifting the severed head of its first kill the daemon raised its flayed skull face and howled.

IT HAD BEEN the wrong way to clear his mind, thought Cyrus. Walking the station had seemed like a good way to work out troubling thoughts. Armoured in cleaned plate he had paced through the silent halls and the service tunnels where the station's population sheltered as far from the outer areas as possible. They looked at him and he could feel the fear in their eyes. People crowded the service tunnels: menials, prefects, techno-mats, and their families. They formed tight clusters, huddled around a few possessions, talking in low voices as if the sound of raised voices were indecent.

There was a tension in the close atmosphere, panic held just below the surface. He had hoped to gain some clarity of thought, but the atmosphere seemed to infect him with a mixture of fear and caution. He tried to let his thoughts unknot, tried to focus on presenting a soothing presence to the people that looked at him. It was not working. In no small part that was the fault of Hekate.

'It was only the first, and the weakest, attack that we will see.' Hekate's harsh voice rang out. She had chosen this time to impart her thoughts on the situation, following him as he walked the station, staff clicking on the deck in time with her steps.

Hekate had not been present at any of the two assaults on the station. She had been noticeably absent, only appearing afterwards to question survivors and make dire predictions. Cyrus pursed his lips. He could almost hear the look of superiority on her face.

'We held the breach,' growled Cyrus.

'No, we did not,' she spat. 'You held the breach. If it had not been for you and your brothers the enemy would have forced through our defences.'

People were looking up at the raised voices, the air tightening. Cyrus had nearly reached the end of his patience. A thick ache had begun to spread across his head. All he could think about was the holographic image of a blind face repeating a single word just beyond hearing again and again.

He stopped and turned, looking down at the woman, catching the surprised look in her eyes, anger slipping his control.

'Are you not a primaris? What is it that you fear? You have lent no aid to the defences apart from your observations. Is there something that keeps you in the shadows?'

'I–' she began, but Cyrus was in no mood for what she might have said. He leant forwards.

'You may speak the truth and know much, but you seem blind to the fact that we either stand together or we die. The enemy we face will destroy us from within as easily as it will from without.' He looked around at the people huddled and silent at the edge of the passage. 'You do not see this? You know much of the enemy that faces us, more than Rihat, more than I. But you do not see this?'

He looked at the marks of the Psykana tattooed on her scalp and woven into the cloth of her storm coat. An expression that he could not place ghosted across her face. 'Is there something you fear, mistress? Something you know of this enemy that makes you afraid?' She held his gaze and a previously unformed question dropped into his mind. 'What is your purpose here?'

'I cannot say.' There was a low almost fearful note in her voice that surprised Cyrus. 'I tell you the truth that I see. That is what I am here to do. That is the help I give.'

Cyrus gazed at the woman, a suspicion forming in his mind. The Inquisition had servants in many places and drew its acolytes from many quarters. Did such a secret servant stand before him now? There was a regal surety about her that made him wonder what she really was. 'How long have you been here, Mistress Hekate?' he said quietly.

'A little over a month, Brother-Librarian,' she replied, her voice brittle.

'And before that?'

'I cannot say.'

Cyrus smiled but it did not reach his eyes. He was thinking of executed worlds, and the hand that wielded that final judgement. What was she?

Hekate looked away, suddenly appearing hunched and tired as she leant on her staff. 'Another attack will come,' she said without looking at him. 'You should know that the varieties of daemons that attacked were of many orders. Such creatures only overcome their own rivalries when great powers turn them to a single purpose.'

The image of an astropath speaking a broken plea for help flashed through his mind, and a word came to Cyrus's lips. 'Fateweaver,' he said.

Hekate shot him a hard look. For a moment he thought he saw surprise and fear in her blue eyes.

'That is a name that should be spoken with care,' said Hekate with careful control.

Cyrus was about to speak but the ache in his head suddenly blossomed to press against the inside of his skull. The crystals of his psychic hood were sparking. He blinked, opening his eyes to find red light flooding the passage. Alarms filled the air. His vox-link was screeching with panicked voices. He heard the word 'incursion' spit from the static and started running. He had ordered Phobos to be ready as a counter-attack force. The sergeant and his Terminators would reach any breach first.

'Phobos,' he shouted into the vox. As the sergeant replied Cyrus thought he could hear a whispered word repeated again and again.

OVERWHELMED. IT WAS not a word Phobos had often needed to contemplate. Layers of ceramite and adamantium, crafted at the birth of the Imperium, and his skill as a warrior made the word as irrelevant to him as a blow from a flint axe. But the word rang in his mind: undeniable, certain.

A lattice of fire overlaid the scene before him, spitting from his storm bolter, interweaving with that of his brothers. Four of them; there were four of them to turn the tide. A killing rage had engulfed the troops in the fourth wing of the station. Hundreds of Helicon Guard had become a churning sea of hate and murder. They stabbed and hacked at anyone in reach, shouting vile words through torn lips. Amongst the men the daemons moved: black iron blades sizzling as they cut through the press of bodies.

Phobos and his three brothers had pushed into the carnage, hurling the mob back with a torrent of explosions. For a few moments the bloody tide had faltered. Then it had enfolded them like closing jaws.

Phobos's shoulders almost brushed those of his brothers, his eyes flicking from target to target, as he aimed, assessed and fired. His mind was focused solely upon the tactical data, which told him that they could not win. But this wing of the station was close to falling, and if it did the murderous tide would spill past all of their defences. He had made an oath that he would stand against this enemy: that he would not let them pass.

'Nevra, firestorm pattern,' said Phobos calmly. He remembered the hundreds of oaths he had made over decades of war. He had never failed to honour a single one and he was not going to do so now.

A clutch of Helicon Guard came towards them, eyes white, screaming in rage. There was no sanity left in them, no perception of what they had been, only a lust for death and blood.

'By His will,' came Nevra's stony voiced reply. The missiles shrieked from the Cyclone launcher on his shoulders. The first missile hit, then the second, then the rest, each overlapping blast growing into a shrapnel-laden fireball. For a moment the murderous tide seemed to ebb. Phobos smiled grimly to the inside of his helmet as a black cloud mushroomed up to spread dirty smoke and yellow tongues across the ceiling far above. The floor shook and his armour whined as it compensated.

They came out of the fire in a wave of serrated blades and howling faces marked with jagged cuts. Men ran amongst the daemons, their flesh charring as they danced in the flames, howling triumph into the torched air.

'Close formation,' said Phobos. His brothers closed on him, shoulder to shoulder, a white armoured diamond amongst the slaughter. 'Fire on all targets,' he shouted, his storm bolter already roaring as the tide closed over them.

* * *

IT WAS CLOSE now. Alarms blared as it walked down the passage through pulsing red light. Clusters of flesh-born in red and ochre uniform rushed past. It could taste the fear in their thoughts. The children of slaughter had begun their work. Perhaps they would succeed, but it doubted they would; they were so unsubtle, only useful in creating terror and spilling blood. It had masqueraded as such beings many times, had mimicked their blink-quick reactions and their death thirst. It understood them from within and without. They would kill and glory in their massacre, but powerful enemies stood against them: the strongest of the flesh-born, the Space Marines. They had the strength to perhaps stand even against the Taker of Skulls' children. But whether their attack succeeded or not was no matter. Within its multi-faceted mind it smiled. Fear and confusion filled the station and that made the fulfilment of its bargain all the easier. As it had intended.

The hurrying flesh-born passed, paying it no attention. It had chosen this face carefully. The person it had stolen it from was a functionary of modest authority, not high enough to draw too much attention, not so lowly that anyone would question that it walked alone against the flow of movement. It was its third face since it had entered the station, and it hoped that it would need no more.

Turning into an arched door off the main passage it raised a cipher talisman to a sensor panel. A heavy blast door pealed back into the oily walls. It had taken the talisman from the owner of the face it wore. Functioning technology was one of the few things it could not imitate. The passage beyond was quiet and bathed in cold light. It could feel the presence of what it sought. It was close, so close now. Behind it, the armoured door ground shut as it walked into the electric twilight.

'PHOBOS?' CYRUS SAID in his ear.

Phobos sent a burst of shells into the face of a creature of glistening muscle. He saw movement out of the corner of his eye as a blow flicked towards his shoulder. He brought his sword around to meet it. The power field crackled and spat sparks as it met a blade of smoking black iron.

'Yes, Brother-Librarian,' said Phobos, voice straining, muscles and armour bunching as he forced against the inhuman strength of the creature. It opened its mouth and its pink tongue tasted the air. He brought the muzzles of this storm bolter up under the creature's face and fired.

'We are almost with you. Hold, brother, for the primarch, hold,' said Cyrus, his voice distorted by static.

Phobos heard his storm bolter dry cycle as the last round spat from its muzzle. At his back there was a pillar of black stone the width of a battle tank. To his left Nevra was firing short bursts, the Cyclone launcher on his back empty, the teeth of his chainfist thick with viscera. To his right Valens stood, blood streaming from the mangled mass of his helmet; the stump of his severed gun arm dribbled blackening liquid onto the floor. It was barely credible that the veteran still stood let alone fought.

They had driven into the horde of daemons and crazed Helicon Guard, they had thrown dozens back into the immaterium, but it was not enough. Out across the vaulted chamber the horde grew, seeming to swell even as they cut it down. They had lost Gratian, his armour split from helm to gut by a shrieking blade. The enemy had forced them back until they were three figures in gore-painted white, their backs against the pillar. They were too few and the enemy too many. The fourth wing of the station was about to fall.

Phobos met a downward cut at his face, let it whistle past him as he flicked his sword around, slicing a figure from shoulder to hip. Another leapt into the space left by the collapsing body. To his right Nevra's gun went silent.

'No, brother,' said Phobos, his voice low and calm. 'The enemy will break through before you reach us. Our oaths will not be kept.'

There was a second of silence, and then Cyrus's voice came back. 'I hear.' There was an edge to his voice.

To Phobos's left Valens staggered, his knee crashing to

the ground, splintering marble, blood seeping from rents in his armour. Valens brought his power fist up to meet a black sword in a fountain of sparks.

'You know what must be done, brother.' said Phobos. 'I have failed and now there is only one price to pay for victory.' There was a pause. Phobos could almost see his brother weighing-up what Phobos meant, the implication of his words. 'It was what we were made to do; it is our fate.'

'As you will it,' said Cyrus.

Phobos felt a sharp impact across his right shoulder as ceramite splintered under warp-forged iron.

'I go to the ancestors,' said Valens from beside Phobos, the words a wet gurgle in his throat. They were the words of lament and passing spoken for the dead who could not speak for themselves. The words reminded Phobos of the smoke of funeral pyres trailing across the blue skies of Sabatine.

Phobos stabbed at a creature in front of him. He smiled grimly.

'I go to the ancestors,' repeated Phobos, and the voices of Valens and Nevra rose in broken chorus.

'As they are the past, so shall I be.'

Phobos dropped his storm bolter, hand lunging forwards to grasp a creature's twisting horns.

'As I am, so shall all be.' The words of the three Terminators echoed across the vox.

Phobos brought the edge of his sword up under the creature's neck in a sawing sweep that scattered drops of burning blood into the air. Throwing the severed daemon's head at its kin, he lunged at them.

'I am the dead and I will pass through the gates of my ancestors.'

Outside the station the macro cannon and lances of the *Aethon* began to rotate. Plasma flushed into reactors and energy wells, the fury of suns snarling in its shackles.

Phobos could see Valens beaten down at the edge of his sight, lifeblood trailing from his arm as he tried to raise it.

A blow struck Phobos's helmet, carving through into his face and eye. Blind, he rammed his weight forwards and brought his sword around like a scythe, feeling it bite through flesh and bone. He reached up and pulled the helmet from the ruin of his face. The daemon tide stood before him.

'I go to the ancestors!' he shouted, and the world suddenly filled with bright light.

The beams of energy from the *Aethon* hit the fourth wing of the station a third of the way down its length. The lance strike cut the section from station like a limb from a corpse. The rest of the station shuddered as if in pain. Venting molten debris and burning air, the wing fell away taking the four lost White Consuls to their ancestors. An instant later macro cannon shells hit the severed section and it became a brief blaze of light smeared against the black void.

THERE WERE FIVE Space Marines between it and its objective. They wore white armour and blank-faced helmets with red eyes. It had anticipated that they might be a last obstacle to it fulfilling its bargain. Having anticipated them, it was ready.

It came round the corner wearing a new face, the face of a tech-adept long dead and reduced to ash in a dark corridor. The five stood around a sealed blast door covered in strips of parchment attached with red seals. The final door.

'Halt,' said a Space Marine with a red helm, and pointed a weapon at it. The rounded muzzle was venting shimmering gas with a rising hum. The other five Space Marines raised their weapons.

'I come to do my duty, honoured warriors.' The face's voice was a plaintive whine filtered through a mechanical throat. 'See, I bear the writ of service and this is the appointed hour.' The weapons aimed at it stayed silent but did not waiver. These were no weak-willed creatures filled with doubt and fear. It was within a few paces now. It could feel the decision to fire forming in their minds.

Vetranio: that was the leader's name. It took a step forwards and changed its shape.

Its new shape was faster, much faster. It was on Vetranio in a single bound, bone claws the size of scythe blades punching through his eye pieces. It changed again, its shape becoming that of the dead Space Marine. It plucked the gun from Vetranio's dead fingers as he fell. It turned, shooting a stream of energy into the heads of two of the Space Marines. Two remained. They fired at the same instant. It felt something that it understood as pain.

It dropped the weapon and changed its form into a boiling mass of flesh and half-formed faces. Blue fire burned from its eyes and along its limbs. Explosive rounds hit it and it felt chunks rip from its unreal flesh. It leapt at the two Space Marines, glittering droplets trailing after it. They tried to fight but its touch cooked them inside their armour.

When the charred armour no longer twitched, it bent down and picked up the weapon it had dropped. Wearing Vetranio's face it turned towards the sealed portal. The layered doors slid open one at a time, and it saw its prize.

CYRUS WATCHED THE fires die and bleed off into the void. The command hub of the station was a circular chamber in the neck below the central astropathic chamber. Light from screens on stone daises diluted the gloom. The crew at each dais stared grimly at their readouts and dials, trying not to look as the remains of the severed part of the station cooled to embers on the viewscreen above them. Cyrus could feel the funereal hush around him, the numb disbelief at what had happened, at what he had ordered done. Beside him Rihat stood at attention, his thin face grey.

Cyrus had come here as soon as he had given the *Aethon* the order to sever the overwhelmed wing from the station. The rest of the White Consuls were in position ready to respond if another attack should come. He, though, had to see it for himself. On the screen the fading explosions were a red-hued ripple in the sickly haze of colour and substance that hung over the station. Looking at the fading after-image he felt empty, unreal, as if he had looked into a mirror and seen someone else looking back at him.

It was the only way, he thought. If he had not ordered the *Aethon* to destroy what was already lost then the rest of the defences would have fallen soon after. It had been necessary, the kind of choice that had angered him when he had seen its results in the ashen wastes of Kataris. He was the executioner this time; his choices had committed his brothers, and hundreds of others, to oblivion.

'Enough,' he said softly. 'Cut the view-feed.' Rihat motioned and the viewscreen flicked to flowing green readouts of the station's systems.

'Do you have any further orders, lord?' said Rihat, looking up at him with stiff formality.

'No, colonel commander. Not at present.' He nodded as Rihat saluted and stalked away, brittle formality overlaying anger and disbelief. Cyrus could not fault his response.

Almost involuntarily Cyrus took the milled disc of the holo-projector out of a pouch. It held the message that had drawn him here, the message that no one had sent. It sat on the palm of his gauntlet for a second, then the cone of green light sprung up from its surface. The ghost-green figure of the astropath rotated again in front of his eyes.

'...report... Claros... the enemy beyond...'

This broken stream of words had brought him here, it had placed him here. He had watched and listened to these words so often that he heard his memory speak them as much as he heard the recording.

'...lies... Fateweaver... we were blinded... failing...'

Something about the signal had troubled him since he first reviewed it. Somehow it felt familiar, almost as if he had heard it long ago.

'Soul... that hear this...'

Should he have followed its call? Was it a trick?

'...send... help...'

But it felt so familiar.

'Colophon…'

His vision snapped into focus, senses suddenly sharp. The image continued to rotate and speak through its familiar loop.

'…accursed eternity.' The image blinked and began its loop again. Cyrus watched it, his ears straining for the word that he was sure he had heard. It did not occur again. He cycled through the signal but it was as it had always been, a broken string of words spaced with patches of distortion. Had his mind filled a space with a stray thought? He clicked off the projection, looking around at the command chamber without seeing. If he had somehow heard an extra portion of the signal that was not there before, what did it mean?

Colophon. He had not seen the senior astropath for hours. The old man was attending to the recovery of the remaining astropaths in his charge. A stray word heard in a signal sent by no one; could it mean that Colophon would send the signal? That it was a plea from a point in time not yet reached?

Face set into a stone-hard expression, Cyrus strode from the command chamber. A new question had begun to coil around his thoughts like a poisonous snake: what else could the word *Colophon* in a signal from the future imply?

IT STOOD AND looked up at the pillar, watching the power crackle over its black surface and stir the strips of parchment. The thing was abhorrent; even being this close made the skin of its stolen flesh crawl. The space around the pillar was filled with eddies of power that tugged at its substance. The pillar projected a veil far out from this chamber, enclosing this place and keeping its kind away from the prey they sought, the prey that they had hunted across worlds and through time. It had seen veils of this kind before, enclosing the ships of the flesh-born as they hurried through the warp. Like riptides woven into a spun glass curtain, they kept those ships safe. That was until they failed. With the veil around this place gone the rest of its kind could reach their prey. There would be much slaughter among the flesh-born.

For a second it considered whether to keep to its bargain. It would gain much, that was true. An endless amount of possibilities and favours would be its to claim, and bargains with the greater kind were difficult to break. But it was a creature of lies and the delight of the unexpected change was delicious. If it left here now the energies sustaining its kin would eventually dissipate in the poisonous nature of the flesh-world. This place would stand. The flesh-kin would endure. The blind prey hiding amongst them would survive and rise from its weakness again. And what then? What possibilities would there be then, what endless unforeseen new permutations and changes to fate?

Slowly, it raised the weapon taken from the warrior whose face it wore, the glowing ribs along the weapon's back brightening as if sensing its intent.

But, it thought, a bargain was a bargain.

The whine from the weapon rose in pitch until it was a shrill of barely restrained power. It grinned with its stolen face and squeezed the trigger. A bolt of sun-bright light speared from the weapon. The bolt of energy struck the pillar and liquefied the workings at its core.

For a second the pillar quivered, the power it had projected around the station snapping, its tethers broken. It cracked with a sound of shearing iron. Balls of lightning formed and collapsed around the pillar's surface. Parchments charred to black scraps that fell amongst a deluge of sparks. Then it exploded in a wave of brilliant light.

By the time the Geller field generator, exploded the being some called the Changeling had long vanished, discarding its last face without a thought.

FOR A FEW minutes no one on Claros station realised what had happened. In the sheltered passages people continued to talk, mumbling worries to each other, stirring food over the flickering heat of chemical burners, and laughing at grim jokes. Behind barricades the Helicon Guard watched and waited as they had for hours, muscles cramping from not moving, wondering when they would be able to sleep. The armour-clad White Consuls stood in a scattered selection of passages, their minds calm, waiting for the next attack to pull them from inaction. In a lightless chamber Colophon sat immobile, the remaining astropaths ringing him in silence.

In the half-lit gloom of the command chamber Colonel Rihat turned away from the disappearing back of the Librarian. For a moment he had thought he had seen a flicker of emotion in Cyrus's eye, a glimmer beneath cold dark water. He had heard stories of the Adeptus Astartes, that they were mankind's final shield, made by the Emperor at the dawn of the Imperium. He had seen the truth of the stories, seen that those words could never approach the truth. He realised he had not understood them, that he could never understand them.

The shout snapped his head around, his thoughts vanishing at the terror in the voice. 'The Geller field!' The officer looked at Rihat, eyes wide. Crimson runes began to flicker across control surfaces, angry red spreading around the chamber, parchment readouts spewing from the fingers of data servitors. 'It's gone!'

Rihat's first thought was to ask why, but as the icy reality filled him he knew it was a useless question. The truth was blaring at him from every corner of the chamber. Their greatest defence had fallen and the enemy would be coming.

'Arm yourselves,' he shouted and drew his pistol. Alarm sirens began to sound a moment later.

THE WARP FOUND the genatorium chamber in the seconds after the field failed. Blackened cylinders the height of hab blocks filled its floor. Each was a low-yield plasma generator that fed power to the station's central hub. The machines had functioned for millennia, beating with a steady pulse, holding at their hearts the power of suns. Servitors and engineers moved through the chamber, murmuring machine code and shaking blessed oil over their beloved machines. The first sign that something was wrong was a blurt of angry code from a monitor servitor. The enginseers moved to see what had troubled the spirits of their machines. Before they could take more than a step warning sirens filled the air. Runes indicating system failures flashed on control panels. Data parchment spooled onto the floor. The enginseers began to run for their control systems.

There was a shriek of shearing metal. Steam poured into the chamber as pipes ruptured. The enginseers and servitors close to the generators vanished in a wash of venting coolant. Across the station lights flickered and dimmed.

A generator burst, glowing fuel breaking through its layered metallic shell. Molten metal flowed like wax onto the chamber floor. Jagged-edged fragments of debris spun through the air. The remains of the broken machine began to judder, its wreckage twisting and writhing. Wires and cables coiled, bonding to mangled plates. Pistons snapped together into gigantic limbs. Warp flame flowed from component to component as something aware and alive pulled itself from the reshaping wreckage. It had a scorpion body of machine parts and a torso of smoking flesh the colour of cooling iron. A long head crowned by spearlike horns pushed itself from its shoulders. It reared up, raising piston-driven arms, roaring at the glory of its birth.

A second generator exploded, the being within it spinning a form from the ruin of its machine womb. The first born did not wait for its kin, but stalked to the chamber's sealed blast door, claws clenching in anticipation. The door was forged of plasteel and layered adamantium, over two metres thick and eight metres tall. The creature paused for a second and then began to gouge through the armoured door, its eyes alight behind a mask of scorched bronze.

CYRUS MOVED DOWN the central passage at a run. Close behind him Valerian's Devastators followed with the remains of Galba's Vanguard squad. All thoughts of the signal and Colophon had passed from his mind. The Geller field was down and warp entities were breaking through into reality across the station. A dozen desperate fights outlined in snatches of panicked vox traffic scrolled across his helmet display.

'Rihat,' he said, the vox chatter dimming as he linked to the colonel commander. 'This is Cyrus, I am showing massive internal damage data from the secondary plasma generator cluster.'

'Yes, Epistolary. Confirmed: we are seeing the same. Significant power loss and multiple bulkhead breaches moving along the primary access passage.'

'We are moving to the blast door junction on the lower mechanical levels. Whatever is coming down that tunnel, we will meet it there. Order all units in the vicinity to that position.'

'So ordered. I will join you.'

The passage they moved along curved to meet the junction following the circle of the central hub. Ahead, Cyrus could see a cruciform of four passage openings, each many times his height. Arched doors filled a single passage opening. The doors' surface was worked in brass relief with images of vast machines. At the doors' centre was the cog-haloed skull of the Adeptus Mechanicus. Beyond the blast door a broad passage spiralled into the centre of the station where the red-robed tech-priests kept the mechanical heart of the station beating. In that heart something had spawned after the Geller field failed.

A wide semi-circular killing ground was forming in front of the closed doors. In the archways of the other doors Helicon Guard were setting up auto cannons, lifting drum feeds of fat rounds to meet the waiting breeches. Some with the black shoulder guards of unit officers were yelling at Guardsmen to form firing lines.

Cyrus reached the junction as the first blow hit the doors from the inside. They rang like a gong. All other sound died. Men and women looked up from their weapons, eyes fixed on the door, listening to the sound of the blow fade. Cyrus turned to face the door. To his side the four brothers of Galba's Vanguard squad spread out, the motors of their chainblades growling. Valerian hurried his squad back amongst the Helicon Guard, their bulky heavy weapons tracking to cover the doors as they moved.

'Epistolary, my command is nearly at your position,' Rihat's breathless voice crackled over the vox. Cyrus could tell that the man was running.

A second blow hit the doors. Dust trickled from the brass reliefs. The doors glowed red, a heat haze shimmering in front of them.

Cyrus had opened his mouth to reply to Rihat when the third blow struck. The doors burst apart. A vast shape pulled itself through the molten breach. Cyrus had an impression of eyes burning with a furnace heat above a taurian form fused with jagged spider legs. He felt dizzy, the presence and power of the beast beating on his mind like a forge hammer.

The beast roared, its breath a burning gush of vapour. Lines of tracer leapt to meet it, biting into its skin, scoring lines in its metal plating. Cyrus could hear Guardsmen shouting as they fired, terror mixed with defiance in a stream of expletives.

The creature stood for an instant as rounds and energy bolts sparked off its hide. Then it ran forward towards Cyrus and the first line of Guardsmen. It was fast – insect fast – its claws sparking on the deck, piston arms raised above its horned head.

Cyrus threw himself sideways. He hit the floor, the deck plates buckling beneath his weight. The Guardsmen in the first line were not so fast. The beast rammed through the line of bodies, its bladed forelimbs punching through meat and bone, iron fists pistoning down to mash and sever.

Cyrus was on his feet in time to see a second beast pull itself from the ruin of the doors. It looked on the scene with black eyes, a circular mouth of translucent teeth pulsing as if in hunger. Its flesh was a mottled red, the muscles of its arms fused with serrated splits of metal the height of a man. It gave a booming cry and followed its kin into the growing circle of slaughter.

The Helicon Guard lines fragmented, some holding, some running to die in the beasts' flesh-stripping breath. Cyrus took the scene in a glance, as he drew his force sword, blue fire licking its edge. This was no planned engagement; it was a bloody scramble against terror. Their opportunities to change the battle were like water spilling through their fingers. The two iron beasts were advancing side by side, vomiting warp fire onto those they did not rip apart. There was no sign of Rihat or his reinforcements.

'We must split them.' Cyrus said across the vox, charging towards the nearest creature. 'Valerian, I will draw one to you. Fire once one is isolated. Brothers of Galba, take the legs.'

'By your will, brother,' Valerian growled in acknowledgement.

Beside him, Cyrus sensed the four remaining Vanguard of Galba's squad follow him. The back of one of the beasts was twenty paces away. He could see the pale cartilage of its spine projecting from the slick sinew of its back. He pulled power into his mind, rolling it around, letting it gather hate from his psyche. He stopped ten paces from the beast. The four Vanguard sprinted past him, their death laments crackling through the vox.

He released a part of the power gathered in his mind, sending it out in front of him in an etheric shout of challenge. The beast paused, ragged blade edges dripping red, and turned to look at him. Cyrus looked into its black eyes as they reflected the light of gunfire, and raised his open palm. The beast charged.

This is not what I have seen, thought Cyrus, the thought a whisper in the cyclone of power in his mind. It will not end now.

Five paces away the beast reared, its back legs driving it on as its arms and forelimbs rose ready to bring its blades down on Cyrus. He let the power go. Power arced from his palm and flowed across the beast's flesh and iron hide. It staggered, forelegs crashing down to scrabble on the floor. Cyrus felt his mind digging into the machinery of the creature's body, hate and spite writhing through its components, fusing joints and stopping gears. The beast staggered. Cyrus could feel its power gathering to push back at him. He would not be able to hold it back.

The four Vanguard came at the beast's legs from the sides, chainblades swinging. Motor driven teeth bit into pistons and translucent tendons. Two legs crumpled. A leg whipped up and down, punching a metre-long blade through a Vanguard's helm and ramming on through his body, pinning it to the floor in a welter of blood.

The beast howled in Cyrus's mind, shrugging off his psychic shackles. The beast's body whipped forwards, its jaws closing on the head of a Vanguard with the noise of cracking armour. It lifted the Space Marine off the floor, chewing on armour and flesh before spitting it out with a gout of flame.

Two more gone to the ancestors, thought Cyrus. Two more gone in as many seconds.

'Valerian! Now!' he shouted. The Devastators fired before he had finished the order.

Valerian's squad carried heavy bolters, suspensor-cradled blocks of oiled machinery that cycled explosive rounds through their breeches in a rolling laugh of thunder. The beast arched back as explosions blistered across it spine, ripping wet shreds from its flesh. Somewhere out in the chaos that filled the junction, a Helicon gunner with more will than fear began to fire. Others followed, sputtering lines of shells and pulses of las-bolts converging on the beast. Armour plates buckled and shredded under the hail of impacts. Yellow ichor bled from the beast's flesh. It tried to turn, its limbs thrashing as if it was trying to fend off a swarm of insects. It screeched, fire spluttering out with the noise as its legs collapsed. Cyrus was close enough to see the thing's black eyes as its pulped torso scrabbled amongst the ruin of its metal hide. It gave a final growl of rage and dissolved into wreckage and oozing flesh.

In the centre of the Helicon lines, the remaining beast sensed the end of its kin. It turned, its gaze sweeping across the scene, looking for the cause of its twin's demise. Its furnace eyes fixed on the seven Space Marines of Valerian's squad. It ran forwards, chewing men to glistening lumps beneath its strides.

Cyrus was already moving, forcing his way through the press of half-panicked Helicon Guard. He could feel the beast's rage drawing power from the warp as it ground a charnel path towards the Devastators. It was shredding reality in its wake. Half-formed daemons coalesced around its legs, like lesser fish drawn to the bloody kill of a shark. They were slug-like things, congealed out of split corpses, eyes wobbling in suppurating flesh. More of the Helicons began to run.

Valerian stood his ground with his brothers beside him. He was bare-headed, his bolter loose in his hands, controlled fury curling his lip. Unlike many of his brothers, he was unscarred by his century of war, his sculptural features of Sabatine nobility unmarked. He raised his bolter, its barrel scorched by firing, smoke still coiling from its mouth. The beast raised its arm. Pipes jutted from its flesh, forming an irregular fist of tubes bound together by muscle. The beast sent a stream of molten rounds at the Devastators. One of the rounds found the helmet of a White Consul and punched him off his feet in puff of blood and liquefied ceramite. The rest of the squad did not flinch. Valerian waited for the target lock tone to steady, for the range to be optimal. The beast took another step.

'Fire,' said Valerian, and beside him the thunder of heavy bolter fire poured out towards the beast. It slowed for a moment, then crossed its arms over its head and torso, thick plates and blades overlapping to create a shield. It strode on into the storm.

Cyrus pushed aside a Guardsman. The space around the beast boiled with daemon kind. Creatures formed of a boiling mass of tentacles and rotting flesh enveloped Guardsmen in acid embraces. The fire from the remaining Guardsmen had dropped to nothing: many were running, more were dead.

Cyrus raised his sword. The price he had paid for the power he wielded was a dull ache in his mind. A daemon creature made of boils and yellow tumours turned a slit eye on him. He stepped forwards.

Would this be it? Was this the moment he had seen?

Flames suddenly gushed through the daemons. Thick, oily fire crawled over rotting flesh, melting fat from rotting bones. Las-bolts punched into the dissolving forms in disciplined volleys.

'Lord Cyrus,' Rihat's voice crackled through the vox. Cyrus looked around to see the colonel commander striding forwards flanked by lines of bronze-armoured figures in black-visored helms. Red smears and soot covered Rihat's face. His right arm hung loose at his side, the sleeve wet and dark. But there was a defiant look in his eye, and in front of him the flamer units burned their way through the daemon spawn. Creatures with too many limbs and eyes tried to pull themselves forwards even as they collapsed into cinders and smoke.

Cyrus realised that the stuttering roar of heavy bolters had vanished. He turned, looking back to where Valerian's squad had stood. Flames filled his vision, spreading across the junction floor. Beyond the fire the beast lifted a ruin of bloody meat and white fragments in an iron claw. Cyrus began to run through the flames, purity seals burning, armour blackening. His helmet vision darkened, compensating for the brightness of the fire, objects and movements becoming a series of coloured runes overlaying shifting shadows. The beast's movements were a bladed blur overlaid with a green grid of lines.

The three remaining Devastators backed off, weapons fire spitting up at the beast as it advanced. Cyrus came out of the flames, the world snapping back to brightness. He saw Valerian twist the priming handle of a melta charge, and duck a scything blade. He reached for the beast's armoured thorax. The beast reached down, piston jaws flicking shut, as it yanked the sergeant from the ground. It brought the dying Space Marine level with its furnace eyes. Valerian's hand closed on the detonator with the last of his strength. A sun-bright sphere swallowed the sergeant and the beast's arm with a shriek of super-heated air. The beast rocked back, a cry like grating steel splitting the air.

Cyrus took his last strides, muscles and armour straining, his mind pulling power through him in a raw rush. He realised he was shouting; the names of his fallen brothers, of the dead worlds and lost wars, pouring from his lips. The beast sensed him, turned, blades scything downwards. Cyrus struck.

The blow buried the sword to the hilt in oil-black flesh. Inky liquid gushed from the wound. It stank of promethium and decay. A soul-born rage poured from Cyrus into the blade. All he could feel was the tide rolling through him, the anger of his soul given form by the warp. He felt…

…*blood dripping from his armour as he walks through a familiar door…*

A thing with the head of a vulture is laughing. The sound is like a murder of crows….

An astropath turns in a cone of green light. The astropath is laughing. It has two faces…

He is fading to nothing…

CYRUS AWOKE TO fading screams and dimming fires. He lay amongst the ruin of his enemy, the warped machinery draped with tatters of oily flesh that were slowly dissolving to a sickly sheen. His hand still clasped his sword, its edge glimmering with a fading echo of power.

Pulling himself to his feet he felt the fever-ache of the psychic power he had channelled. Every movement brought a dull stab of pain. He looked around, his vision filling with threat assessment icons. The dead were thick on the floor and pools of flame cast the scene in a mottled orange light. No threat icons. They had won.

Cyrus saw Rihat approaching. The colonel was limping slightly, his left arm bloody and cradled at his side.

'Victory, colonel,' Cyrus said with a grim smile.

Rihat did not smile back; he looked grey, pain held back by will alone. 'The enemy has broken through in many places. I am not even sure if some of the defences still hold.' He grimaced as pain shot through his face. 'I do not think they have penetrated into the civilian areas. Not yet.'

Cyrus heard the fatalism in the colonel's voice. 'We will hold, colonel. We will hold no matter the cost.' A surprised look passed across Rihat's face, as if he had puzzled out a hidden truth. He opened his mouth to speak. He did not get the chance.

The voice spoke inside their skulls. *'By the power and grace of the God-Emperor of Mankind, and the authority and majesty of His Holy Inquisition, judgement is proclaimed on this place and on all souls within its bounds.'*

It was a single psychic voice made of many telepathic minds all transmitting the same message. It echoed through the warp with such force that it filled the mind of every person on Claros station. It was an announcement of judgement, a herald of intent.

'All are judged lost and the hammer will so fall. Exterminatus is here declared. May the Emperor have mercy on all true souls.'

The voices faded. Rihat looked at Cyrus, fear and confusion playing across his face. Cyrus staggered as a wave of psychic energy hit. It was the bow wave of a fleet punching back from the warp into reality with hammer-blow force.

Around them shocked silence was breaking into blind panic.

No. Cyrus would not let everything be consumed by the Inquisition's judgement. Not again, not after the price they had already paid. He turned to Rihat, ordering the last two of Valerian's squad to his side with a gesture. 'The Inquisition is here. Their ships will take some time to get within firing range. Get as many people as you can to the *Aethon*. We will break dock and outrun the Exterminatus.' He gave a ferocious grin. 'They can try and stop us but we still have teeth.'

Rihat was frowning. 'Colonel?' Cyrus said.

Rihat looked up at him. 'The Inquisition knew that this place was under attack. But how? You and Colophon said that no messages could be sent?'

Cyrus suddenly felt cold. He thought of his visions, of the sensation of a future growing closer, a vision of an astropath turning in green light. An astropath with two faces. 'Where is Colophon?' he growled.

'I do not know, lord,' shrugged Rihat.

Cyrus nodded, his eyes focused on nothing, his mind racing. *Colophon*: the word he had thought he had heard in the signal. He felt as if all the threads of choices and half-glimpsed futures were weaving together, tightening into single strand. He looked back at Rihat and his last two brother Space Marines. 'The station is lost. Evacuate everyone you can, if I do not return you have command.'

Rihat turned and began to shout orders as Cyrus strode away. He knew where he would find what he needed, where fate was leading him.

'Where are you going, lord?' called Rihat.

'For answers,' growled Cyrus to himself.

THERE WERE NINE ships. Five destroyers rode on bright cones of fire ahead of their greater sisters. Behind the destroyers were two Adeptus Astartes strike cruisers, their crenellated hulls coloured and marked with the deep sea blue of the Star Dragons. Beside them the spear-sleek hull of a Dauntless-class cruiser sliced through the void. At the centre of them all was a vast craft of black metal, its hull capped with towers, its prow a golden point of swept eagle wings. At its birth it had been named for a hero of a lost past; reconsecrated in the service of the Inquisition it bore a name more suited to its task. *The Sixth Hammer* was an executioner, a slayer of worlds. One day it might return to the fleet from which it had been drawn, but at that moment it served the will of the man who watched Claros station grow nearer from its bridge.

Inquisitor Lord Xerxes watched the magnified view of Claros station on a vast holoscreen suspended in front of his throne. The view was stripped bare of tactical data and information icons. He did not need them, nor did he trust artificial aids to judgement. Judgement was a matter of clear-sightedness, something to be decided with the simplest tools and senses available to mankind. On the screen the warp-rift was a wound leaking swirling colours and tendrils of coiling energy. The station, or what remained of it, crawled with writhing ghost light. There was no hope for it, there never had been.

Xerxes turned the slot eyes of his iron face to the two figures that stood to his left. One wore segmented armour lacquered in arterial red over a powerful frame, his face hidden by a black cloth hood. The other was a spindle-thin form of clicking brass joints and desiccated flesh held together by bundles of tubes. The spindle figure wore no mask because it had no real face. Both were inquisitors, the only remaining two of the cell Xerxes had drawn around him. They had lost two of their number, one to the *Accursed Eternity*, another to folly, but their resolve had never wavered. They had hunted the creature called Fateweaver across the stars, executing the planets the daemon invaded, seeking for a way to cast it back into the warp for another aeon. Where they found the daemon they burned the ground from under it. They were the left hand of the Emperor and it was their duty as much as it was their right.

'The judgement has been spoken?' asked Xerxes, his flat voice coming from the horizontal slot in his mask.

'Yes,' said the spindle-bodied inquisitor in a mechanical voice. 'The astropathic choir has transmitted it across the void. Any still alive on the station will know that judgement will be done.'

Xerxes nodded. 'When we are in range the rest of the fleet is to begin the attack. Nothing is to be left for the warp.' He looked back to where the station's bronze hull writhed in the warp's grasp. 'Nothing but ashes and silence.'

* * *

'ASTROPATH.'

The word echoed in the empty silence of the astropathic chamber. The hunched figure in green turned his blind face to follow the fading noise as it reflected from the empty stone tiers.

'Cyrus? That is you, isn't it, my friend?' Colophon's voice added its own echoes to the empty gloom. The astropathic chamber lay at the heart of the station, a sanctuary as far from the advancing daemon forces as was possible. It was deserted, quiet, and dark. What need did the blind have for light?

Cyrus moved out of the shadowed arch of the entrance, armour purring with every movement. He had his storm bolter in his right fist, its twin mouths pointed at the hunchbacked old man. The blue surface of his armour was charred and streaked with drying fluids. He looked like a revenant dragged from a death pyre.

'It is Cyrus.' The Librarian's voice was a low growl. Colophon twitched towards him, his liver-spotted hands clutching the top of his cane. Bathed in the monochrome tint of Cyrus's helmet display he looked scared. No, he looked terrified.

'The Inquisition is coming,' Colophon stammered. 'They will hammer this place to nothing and all of us with it. We should g–'

'Why did you deceive me?' Cyrus kept his distance from the old man, walking a slow circle around Colophon's green-robed form. The single targeting rune in his helmet display was an unresolved amber, pulsing over the old man.

'I have not deceived you.' Colophon stayed where he was, speaking to the air rather than following Cyrus's movements. Cyrus carried on, discarding Colophon's reply without thought.

'The signal, it has been puzzling me ever since we got here. How could it be sent when we were cut off as soon as the attack began? I am not as adept as you at astropathic transmission, but I touched the warp and felt that we were isolated as you said.'

Colophon drew his green robes around him as if against a chill wind. 'I don't understand what you are saying.' He shook his head and took a few steps towards the door of the chamber. 'We should go. We could escape on your ship, we–'

'But the signal did get sent. It drew me here, drew the Inquisition here no doubt.' Cyrus gave a humourless laugh. 'Temporal distortion; you suggested it to me, and I did not consider an alternative.' The old man opened his mouth as if to say something, but Cyrus kept speaking, suspicion and anger making his voice a low rumble of restrained threat. 'You sent the signal, Colophon. You brought me here, and you have brought the final execution of the Inquisition down on this place.'

Colophon shook his head, shock and anger on his face.

'You are mad, my friend,' Colophon spluttered. 'You do not–'

'But how could you veil the warp with pain that even I could feel? And why would you lure people here like playing pieces only to destroy them?' Cyrus drew his sword. 'There is one creature that could do such things, that could watch from within while its kin came from beyond...'

Colophon flinched back as the sword kindled with cold light. 'I am–'

'A creature that could seem to be flesh and blood.' Cyrus felt the weight of the sword in his hand, its power icy in echo of his fury. 'Tell me, *astropath*, if I cut you, how will you bleed?'

'I...'

'Fateweaver.' Cyrus said the name and Colophon flinched as if struck. Inside Cyrus's helm the threat rune turned red. He took a step forwards, his voice a low rumble of menace. 'Is that a name you recognise?'

'I am only an astropath,' wailed Colophon.

Cyrus thought of all the worlds that had been dragged down into the mire of the warp, of the pyre smell of dead Kataris. He felt a fool, he had been manipulated. His visions and his ideals had been turned against him. He did not know why a daemon would play such a game; he did not want to know. The creature in front of him was alone and bound in human flesh that he could destroy. His finger began to squeeze on the storm bolter trigger; his sword glowed brighter in his hand.

His finger froze on the trigger. He could not move his limbs, sweat prickled his skin and he could feel the crystals of his psychic hood become ice-cold as they fought against the psychic power that held him. It had enveloped him so quickly that he had not even sensed its touch.

'You truly are a fool, Space Marine.' The voice came from behind him, the contempt in its tone ringing clear in the still air.

'I am sorry,' said Colophon, the lie spread across his face in a smile. Cyrus heard steps and the clicking of a staff draw nearer. He tried to call on his own power, but the influence focused on him was like a flexing coil that shifted and tightened even as he pushed against it.

'He is not the daemon you call Fateweaver, at least not wholly,' said the mocking voice, now just behind his back. The willow-thin form of Hekate stepped out in front of him. Her eyes glittered brightly and the winged jewel in her staff pulsed with cold radiance. She stood beside Colophon, the old man appearing all the more bent and vulture-like by her side. 'The daemon has two heads, Space Marine,' she said, and smiled.

Cyrus felt as if he was falling, assumptions and truths trailing behind him in tatters.

Colophon was shaking his head as if in sorrow, the wrinkled folds of his thin neck trembling. 'It will be all right, friend,' the astropath said, and Cyrus felt the complete falsity in the words.

Hekate blinked slowly and walked closer to Cyrus so that she could look up at him.

'You will die soon, Space Marine.' She nodded carefully. 'But first you must come and see.' She smiled and the world spun into fragments.

* * *

Cyrus was falling, disconnected sensations flicking through him: the taste of spiced wine; the brush of a feather on skin; pain; the face of his father, hollow and broken; the reek of corpses; colours flowing without form or pattern; the sound of the sea throwing stones at a cliff. All surfaced and faded faster than he could grasp. He wanted to cry out but he had no mouth.

The world flickered into being around him.

He sat on the top of a parapet of warm stone under a sky of clear blue. Looking down he saw a tower wall that descended to a settlement. The low dun stone buildings clustered around the tower's base like young suckling at a mother. Smoke rose from chimneys, scented with flavours of cooking meat and spice. Beyond the frayed edges of the settlement a plain stretched to the sky's base, its surface rippling as a warm wind stirred the green sea of crops.

The sun was warm on his face, the fabric of a white and blue tunic soft against his skin. He clenched his fist, felt the muscles and bones bunch.

'Quite real,' said a voice next to him, and he looked up with a start. Ochre robes swathed the figure that sat next to him, its hunched form hidden by the fabric that stirred and twitched in the wind. Within the shadow of the hood Cyrus thought he saw glimmers of blue, like distant stars in a night sky. For a moment he thought of pitching the robed figure from the parapet, of watching it fall to a pulped ruin on the ground below.

He looked at the hooded figure and shook his head. 'Which head speaks? The one that tells the truth or the one that lies?'

The robed figure chuckled. 'Very good, Space Marine. You begin to perceive truly. A little late it is true but—'

'Where have you brought me, daemon? I will not bend my knee to your kind.'

The figure laughed. To Cyrus it sounded like the cry of carrion birds across a dead land.

'I am not here to corrupt you, Space Marine. I have claimed greater souls than yours, and you flatter yourself to think that you could resist if I tried. Corruption is not my intent. I am here to illuminate you, so that you can understand what has *happened and what has led you to where you are.'*

'Why?' he growled.

'Does a friend and fellow traveller need a reason to grant a gift? A last gift.'

Cyrus thought he could hear the tones of Colophon's voice in the words.

The figure raised a wide, yellow sleeve as a limb with too many joints extended to point down into the town with a taloned finger. 'Look,' it said.

Cyrus looked. Amongst the figures moving through the streets, two walked next to each other. One was a tall woman wrapped in dark cloths, a sour expression on her face. Beside her, a man with a bent back limped to keep up, a worn wooden pole clutched in his wrinkled hands.

'You,' said Cyrus.

'Yes, my two faces.'

'Where is this place?'

'When, might be a better question. You know it, though you may not recognise it.' Cyrus felt suddenly cold despite the sun.

'Kataris,' breathed Cyrus.

Beside him the figure gave a clicking laugh. 'Very good.' It pointed to the clear sky. 'Watch.'

A crack opened in the sky. Its edges were silver-white and within it was black. The sky darkened, purple and red clouds spreading like a bruise across pale skin. In the town below, people had begun to look up and the screaming started. Amongst the panic the tall woman and limping man pressed on towards the tower's base. Out on the plains, fires had begun to kindle and, amongst the smoke, shapes slithered and loped towards the settlement. Sirens began to wail.

'You caused this,' Cyrus growled. 'You summoned your kin to this world and killed it.'

'Perhaps I caused its extinction. In a broad sense that might be true.' The figure paused. 'But I did not summon my kin here. Not intentionally at least.' It turned its hooded head, the shadowed face twisting further than a neck should allow. 'See.'

Cyrus turned, realising that it had never occurred to him to look behind them.

It was not a tower they sat on; it was a landing platform. Behind them, the hulls of lighters and heavy lifters baked in the sun. People were already rushing amongst them attaching fuel hoses; the whine of engines was rising to a shriek.

Fights were breaking out amongst those trying to get away. Cyrus saw a man in the robes of a prefect shot in the face when he tried to stop the ramp of a lifter closing. Others were simply battered aside by those that were stronger than them. The man and woman moved amongst the confusion, seemingly unseen by others. Cyrus watched as they ducked into the hold space of a lighter. A moment later it rose into the sky, heading for one of the few ships clustered around the planet. Others followed, the noise of their engines lost amongst the screams of the settlement and the first howls of the daemons.

'You fled?' *Cyrus looked at the figure beside him.*

'Yes, Space Marine. I fled.'

'Why?'

'Because my kin did not come to this pitiful place for the clutch of worthless souls that breathed its air.' *The figure turned its hooded head back to the settlement. Blood was already flowing through its streets.* 'They came for me.'

'For you?'

'Yes, for me. I have many enemies amongst my kind. Some are my enemies because I laid them low or humiliated them. And then of course there is jealousy: jealousy of the power I had, jealousy of my favour in the eternal court of change.' *The figure shrugged.* 'We are daemons, fragments of the will of greater beings made of lies and hate. Our grudges are never simple, merely eternal.' *Cyrus saw the implication of what the thing was saying.*

'You were hiding.'

'Well done, friend,' *said the figure in Colophon's voice.*

'Why?' *said Cyrus. The world around him faded, its dying screams becoming distant murmurs of horror.*

'That question again,' *came the daemon's voice from the fading world.*

Cyrus could see nothing, He was falling again.

'Because I am blind, Space Marine,' *said the daemon, its*

voice becoming faint and distant. Cyrus felt something like feathers brush his skin in the blackness. 'Because I am blind.'

Cyrus opened his eyes and saw the world of his birth. The daemon stood next to him as he watched the Black Ships come to the skies of his childhood. Its yellow robe fluttered in the wind, the cowl hanging down its hunched back. Its hands clutched the fabric around its tall form, the gesture reminding Cyrus of Colophon pulling his green robes closer around him. It had two heads on long, feathered necks. Each was like the skinless skull of a vulture. Azure blue eyes, without iris or pupil, stared at him from each head.

'The past,' said one head in a voice that sounded like Hekate's. The other was looking up at the dark silhouettes of the spacecraft drifting in low orbit. 'Your past, Space Marine. The world that made you before it burned. I can see this because this is the past. These are dead and unchanging moments in the flow of time.'

The daemon shivered and the world changed, moving through images like cards dealt from a pack.

Here the command chamber of the Aethon, Cyrus watching the shape of an astropath turning in cold green light.

Here warships danced amongst lines of fire and spinning debris, their engines roaring as they turned before the ramming prows of spear-shaped warships. They turned too slowly and died, debris dribbling out of their broken hulls.

'The past,' came the daemon's voice as Cyrus blinked from one moment to another. 'All this is past. I am a weaver of fate, an oracle who sees all the paths of the future. That is my power, my advantage over my rivals and the thing that once kept me out of their jealous reach.'

Here Phobos, his sword held above him, the death lament on his lips.

'But now I am blind, the future is lost to me. I cannot see past the present. This dead past is all that I can see.'

And here Space Marines in blue armour moved through rooms covered in rust brown dust. They have rearing dragons on their shoulder plates.

But I have seen this, *he thinks as he watches*. I have seen this and it is not the past. It is the future.

The daemon continued, ignorant to Cyrus's realisation.

'While I am blind I cannot stand against my kin and so they hunt me across your worlds.'

Cyrus saw something move under the soft layer of dust, like a wave pushed across the surface of water by a shark. A shape is rising from the dust. He shouts but the blue armoured Space Marines do not hear. The shape becomes a figure. It rises from the floor slowly, features forming on its powdered surface. It is reaches towards the Space Marines. Cyrus can sense the death hunger of the figure. He shouts again and the mouth of the dust figure moves.

You die now, *he says with a voice like sand blown on a dry wind. The Space Marines turn to look at him. He is reaching for them.*

He looks at his hands.

They are made of dust.

His vision blinked out and Cyrus was falling through swirling starlight and rushing sensation.

They had returned to the astropathic chamber. Colophon and Hekate stood in front of him.

'You, Cyrus Aurelius,' said Hekate as Colophon nodded. 'I cannot see past you. You are a block in my sight, the point I cannot see past. I never saw you coming here and I cannot see your future now, only your past.'

Cyrus tried to move his limbs but found that they were still locked in place.

'I let you live until now,' Hekate continued. 'You had a purpose in keeping my kin at bay. You might even have won here. But now the Inquisition come and the daemons that hunt me are at my heels, and so I must run and hide again.' She stepped back 'So you must die.'

Hekate turned to walk away, but Colophon paused and smiled up at Cyrus.

'Thank you for the ship that you have so helpfully ordered to run before the Inquisition's fury. It was most kind of you.' He patted Cyrus's unmoving armour and limped after Hekate.

On the highest tier of the chamber silent figures in green robes stepped from the shadows. Warp light shone in their blind eyes. There were eighty-one of them: the survivors of the attack on the astropaths. But he understood then that they had not survived. Those that had resisted had died, those who survived had become bound to Fateweaver. Cyrus could hear a low chattering like the cries of birds and the swish of feathers. Frost was forming under their feet with every step they took down the stone tiers.

'There is one thing you should know before the end, my friend,' called Colophon from the doorway.

'I sent no message,' said Hekate, and both figures vanished from sight.

The astropaths closed on him. Skin flayed from their new forms as the power of the warp reshaped them. Claws extended from hands and feet. Bones snapped and reset in twisted positions. Fur and feathers spread across stretched flesh. Cyrus was at the centre of a circle of snarling creatures.

Cyrus felt the force holding him weaken. Straining with all his will he felt his fingers move on the grip of his sword. His limbs trembled with effort, sweat coating him as he felt muscles shift. Threat runes swarmed his sight.

I have failed, he thinks. This is no longer the future, it is the present. I have failed and here I fall.

III

BOUND

THE STRIKE CRUISERS were the first to fire. Linear accelerators mounted along their spines spoke with one voice. Explosions blossomed off the station's void shields, splashing against domes of energy that shimmered as they collapsed. On the strike cruisers' flank the spear shape of the light cruiser turned on its axis, presenting a flank of macro batteries to the station. Bolts of plasma and explosive shells the size of battle tanks streaked across the void.

On board the smaller destroyers officers waited until the station's shield envelope was on the edge of failing. As the blasts rippled over the last layers of shielding they launched torpedoes. Each carried a melta warhead. They were not intended to destroy but to cripple and burn. For the final killing blow they had other more exotic weapons to unleash.

The Sixth Hammer remained silent, like a king of old watching his young knights take the first blood. From his brass throne Inquisitor Lord Xerxes watched as the perfectly timed torpedo volley struck the station at the instant the last void shield collapsed. He nodded in brief satisfaction and raised his sceptre, its golden length worked with High Gothic script, its tip a leering daemon face of jade. He had killed many worlds and he preferred the final blows to fall at the simplest of commands.

'Fire,' he said, and *The Sixth Hammer* shook at his word.

CLAWS RAKED ACROSS Cyrus's armour. Wild psychic energy lashed at him, slithering from clawed hands searching for weaknesses in his armour. Distorted faces filled his vision biting at him with pointed ivory teeth. He could hear them laughing and babbling in death-dry voices. His arm moved, lifting his storm bolter, dragging upwards as if pulling against tangling webs. Something sharp and serrated found a weak join in his armour. He began to bleed.

The deck quaked under his feet, trembling as if in time with distant thunder. The Inquisition had begun its bombardment.

Anger rolled through him, anger at his own stupidity. He knew he must fail: he had seen it. These were not new moments, they were past memories of visions being lived for the first time. A thing with a withered face was eye to eye with him, its clawed fingers cradling his helmet, razor tips alive with warp light as they reached for his eye pieces.

I will not fall to this fate! He bellowed the thought and the fallen astropaths fell back from him. He seized the anger that boiled through his mind and ripped free of the force that held him. Power flowed from him, radiating outwards as lightning spilled from his sword's edge. His storm bolter spat, pumping explosive rounds through the twisted figures.

The sword was hot in his hand, the fury at its core bright with his rage. He cut into bodies with the death lament on his lips.

THE STATION WAS dying. Rihat knew it. Blood red emergency light suffused the trembling docking corridor, and he could hear the low hiss of atmosphere bleeding into the void through cracks. The doors of the *Aethon's* docking bay remained open as the dwindling stream of people swarmed through them. They had got as many as they could, but there were many more that they had left: hundreds trapped in parts of the station that could not be reached, pockets of Guardsmen surrounded and dying to the creatures that swarmed into the station even as it was torn apart. He had spoken to many of them over the vox, listening to their curses and cries over the spilling static. If he survived he knew he would hear those voices again for years to come, ghost voices cursing him from his dreams.

'We must close the dock, colonel,' called one of the last two White Consuls from just beyond the toothed blast doors. 'The station is coming under sustained bombardment. It will begin to break apart soon. If we are to outrun its death we must break dock.'

Rihat shook his head. 'Not yet. There are more who may reach us. Your Librarian ordered me to save all I could. I will honour that order.'

The Space Marine paused for a moment then gave a curt nod.

Rihat looked back to the people passing him. Grey-robed menials hurried beside purple-mantled prefects. Bloodied and pale-faced Guardsmen, some still cradling their weapons, jostled beside tech-adepts and slab-muscled ratings.

'Colonel, we must break dock now.' The harsh voice made his head snap around. Hurrying towards him were Hekate and Colophon, the bent-backed astropath wheezing as he kept up with the psyker's long strides. 'The bombardment will claim the station in moments; you must give the order now.'

Rihat looked from Hekate to Colophon. The old man looked pale, almost shivering with fear.

'What of Cyrus? He went to find you?'

The old man shook his head. 'I have not seen him,' he said.

'Colonel–' began Hekate, but he cut her off.

'We will go at the last possible moment, mistress.' He gestured at the few people that hurried towards the dock,

403

but kept his eyes locked with the psyker's stare 'The last possible moment.' Hekate glanced at the two Space Marines bracketing the open blast doors, and people still passing through. 'I suggest you get on board. There is not much time.'

The psyker curled her lip but walked away towards the *Aethon*, Colophon limping in her wake.

THEY CAME FOR him again, a tide of teeth, and claws. His storm bolter was silent and empty, discarded on the corpse-strewn floor. Lightning arced from his hand, leaping from body to body. Many fell but the rest still came forwards, scrambling over the dead with vulture cries. They reached him, claws scoring through armour, opening its polished innards to shine in the light of their dead eyes. Cyrus could feel strength leaching from him through a dozen wounds. With a grunt of effort he raised his sword above his head, both hands wrapped around the worn grip. A withered creature hissed at him as it lunged forwards. His first cut split it in two. The second cut scythed through another's stomach and spine.

Something struck him from behind, his shoulder armour splitting as pain stabbed through him. His knee buckled to the ground. He could taste his own blood. Around him he could feel the creatures that had been astropaths laugh at him through the warp.

He could feel the worn joints of the armour gauntlet against his fingers, and the dull pressure of his fingers still gripping his sword. He had expended every weapon he had, used every skill he knew, and still he would fall to the fate he had foreseen. The creatures closed on him. He looked up, pulling himself to his feet. There was one thing, one terrible thing that he had not yet dared to do. It was a monstrous thing, a thing warned against and as difficult to survive as it was to control. Inside his helmet he smiled grimly to himself. With the last shred of his focused will he reached out and ripped a hole through reality.

The creatures fell back as Cyrus stood. The air around

him was an accelerating cyclone of flickering power. He ripped the hole wider, his mind holding the vortex in front of him. It opened wider and wider, spinning with distorting shreds of reality. Twisted bodies vanished into the spinning hole, sucked through it with shrieks of anger and fear. For a second Cyrus held the vortex controlled, felt his mind try and grasp the thing he had birthed into being. He began moving a second before he lost control. The vortex broke from his grip with a shriek like shattering glass. Its black maw ripped wider, spinning everything it touched to nothingness.

Cyrus ran for the doors, feeling his wounded body fill with pain as he moved. Behind him the maw of the vortex grew with a hungering shriek.

THE STATION BURNED. Red fire ate through armour plating, sucking the oxygen from its innards, twisting the bones of its structure until they cracked and distorted like the broken spine of a dying leviathan. Warp fire mingled with the blaze, daemonic faces rising and falling through the flames.

The circling ships of the execution fleet silenced their guns for an instant, pausing before the last blow fell. A narrow spread of torpedoes spat from the prow of *The Sixth Hammer*. Black darts running on bright trails, they carried the most esoteric and dangerous of payloads. As they struck the heart of the station the vortex mechanisms created a rippling chain of holes through reality. Black centred spirals opened in an overlapping cyclone that pulled the station into oblivion.

CYRUS RAN THROUGH corridors filled with smoke and wreckage. His helmet display was pulsing with environmental warning icons that told him of sudden pressure changes, spiking toxicity and fatal oxygen levels. His torn armour was bleeding air from multiple rents. Some of the fibre bundles running through the armour had been severed. He could feel his muscles tearing as they hauled the armour's dead weight through a limping run.

He turned a corner and saw the armoured doors of the dock still open, the docking bay of the *Aethon* beyond lit by strobing warning lights. There was a figure slumped over the dock controls, a last soul standing guard over the gates to safety.

Rihat was dying, his skin pale with oxygen debt, but his hand was still clamped over the door controls keeping the doors open to the very last moment. Cyrus paused. Behind him the long passage was beginning to twist and buckle.

'Colonel,' he said. The man did not move. 'Rihat.' His eyelids flickered and his blue lips mouthed something that Cyrus could not hear. Back down the passage a wide tear opened in the wall, spreading across ceiling and floor, sucking flames and air into the blackness beyond. Cyrus reached down to lift the colonel but the man had stopped moving, his eyes staring without seeing. Cyrus thought of saying something, whispering a last word to the man's soul. He thought of the station that was being torn apart at that moment, as many dying within it as might have reached the *Aethon*, and could think of nothing that would give the dead comfort.

Cyrus moved the man's hand from the dock controls. With a sound of hissing pistons the *Aethon's* blast doors began to close. He walked alone between the closing teeth as the ship broke its bond with the station. Behind him the passage came apart with a shriek of rending metal.

THE VORTICES SWALLOWED the last of the station's carcass. On their edge, the white hull of an Adeptus Astartes battle-barge turned, engines straining to claw against the forces pulling it back into the waiting mouths of the growing vortices.

On his throne Inquisitor Xerxes saw the ship slip from the imploding debris of the station and make for open space, noting the heraldry of the White Consuls. A noble Chapter indeed but one laid low in recent times. The loss of such a ship would be a blow to a brotherhood fading into history. But he could not permit any to outrun a decree of Exterminatus. He nodded to one of the bridge officers and watched as the destroyers and light cruiser accelerated into a looping course that would cut the ship off before it could reach the system's edge.

THE CLOSED DOORS to the *Aethon's* bridge waited in front of him. The carved images of Sabatine glinted in the light of braziers on either side. He paused, tasting the breath that flowed in and out of his lungs.

The daemon would have gone to the bridge to be close to the centre of decisions and authority, to ensure it could influence its own escape. He had hurried through the ship, passing servitors and confused knots of refugees from the station. He had felt tremors run through the ship as its engines fought against the pull of the vortices that had taken the station.

He had stopped in front of the bronze doors. Flickers of half-remembered visions poured through his mind. He knew what would happen, what all the fragmentary glimpses would amount to, the price that would have to be paid.

Slowly he reached up, unlocking his helmet from his armour and tossing it onto the deck. He let out a long breath. The suppressed pain of his wounds was a spreading numbness across his body. He brought his sword up, resting his forehead against the flat of the blade. It was cold against his skin. He thought of the ash of a dead world in his fingers, of his brothers shouting their death lament, of Rihat mouthing unheard last words, of looking up to see a Black Ship in a blue sky.

'It is what we were made for,' he muttered to himself and pushed the bronze doors open.

'FATEWEAVER.' HE SAID its name as the doors swung wide. Faces turned to look at him as he strode onto the bridge, his blackened armour grinding with every step. In front of him the command throne of the ship rose at the centre of a long platform. Clusters of servitors sat hunched over system readouts, a few white-robed serfs moving amongst them. Armoured shutters sealed the viewports that lined the walls of the bridge. A spinning holo-display hung in the air before the command throne. Icons moved in the green gridded projection, showing relative positions and trajectories of ships.

Colophon and Hekate stood together next to the empty throne, the two White Consuls beside them. All of them turned as Cyrus walked towards them. Hekate's face twisted with anger, Colophon's with shock and surprise. Cyrus opened his mouth to call to his brothers, the order to fire forming on his tongue. He never got to speak it.

With a sound of bursting skin and laughter the figures of Colophon and Hekate exploded. Their flesh came apart, skin and glistening muscle hanging briefly in the air as if pinned out on an invisible dissection table. A rank smell of exposed organs and sweet incense filled the bridge, making Cyrus gag. The stretched faces of the old man and the psyker grinned from the elongating and distorting curtain of flesh. The lengths of muscle and skin began to wind together like strands of twine spun into a knotted rope. The flesh changed colour and form. Feathers and claws sprouted and grew. Blue light surrounded the growing shape, weaving through it in bright coils. Wings formed on a hunched back. Skin hung loose over long limbs tipped with bird-like claws. Two long, feathered necks shook themselves in the spinning light before turning to look down at Cyrus. Mismatched eyes stared from above hooked beaks. The daemon laughed with both heads, the sound like the cries of a murder of crows.

Cyrus's two brothers brought their bolt pistols up and fired. A rippling shimmer formed around the shells. They turned in their trajectory and began to orbit the daemon like fireflies. Around them the bridge fell to madness. Servitors ripped themselves from their housings, collapsing onto the floor in pools of oil. Serfs and officers doubled over, vomiting yellow bile onto the deck. With a flick of its hand the daemon sent the bolt shells spiralling away to explode amongst the crew. It raised a clawed limb, iridescent fire sheathing its talons as it pointed at Cyrus. The beaked mouths cracked open to speak.

Cyrus charged, his sword raised above his right shoulder. His muscles tore as they drove his armoured form forwards. He felt a calm settle over him; he could see what would happen, his vision of the future riding just ahead of the present. The moment expanded, dragging through instants. It was his purpose to be there, to make the choice that he could sense waiting for him just beyond the horizon of the present. All was happening as it always was going to, as it would always have to.

The sword sheared through the daemon's sheath of energy and bit into feathered flesh. There was a burst of multihued light. The daemon lurched back, screeching in pain, half collapsing to the deck. Cyrus brought his sword up, spinning its long hilt through his hands, and rammed its point down through the daemon's torso, skewering it to the deck.

He paused, looking down at the daemon. The two heads laughed. Its body began to break apart, dissolving into luminous vapour. The glowing daemon essence flowed into the deck of the ship, rooting itself in the *Aethon*, spreading through its bones.

Cyrus let go of the sword hilt. There was nothing he could do about what would happen next, about the fate to which he had condemned the ship and all on board. He had known he could not kill the daemon; not truly. It would always have the power to cling onto existence somehow. But he had broken its psychical form and he knew it would do everything it could not to flee back to the warp. The only way it could now survive was by taking the substance of the ship as its host.

The fabric of the *Aethon* was changing even as he looked at it, distorting as the daemon coiled through its bones. It would change more in the future, becoming something unrecognisable, something accursed. He knew it; he had seen it.

He looked down at the last of the daemon's physical body, its twin vulture heads twitching amongst liquefying flesh and feathers.

'There is something you should know,' he said as the daemon hissed 'You said you are blind, that you cannot see the future. You said you see only the past endlessly repeated. But what you see is your future, daemon. You are blind because the past is your future.' Cyrus smiled at the daemon as it faded into the deck. 'What I see in the future is what you see in the past. You are blind because of this moment, the moment that the future becomes the past. I am the architect of your fate.'

He looked up at the tactical display of the approaching Inquisition fleet, and the slowly collapsing vortices. The spinning holes in reality would take whatever they swallowed into the warp, to ride on wild currents through time and space. Under his feet he could still feel the plasma engines fighting to pull the ship clear of the vortices' embrace.

Slowly he walked to sit on the command throne and spoke his last order.

'Shut down the engines.'

A moment later the ship went silent. It drifted on through the void, carried by its momentum. Then it began to slide back towards the vortices that had consumed the station.

On the bridge Cyrus rested his sword across his knees. The bridge was changing, cancerous blooms of distorted metal expanding before his eyes as the daemon sunk its claws deeper into the structure. He had no illusions about what he did. He was condemning the ship, the crew and those who had fled onto it in hope of escape. He was condemning them to an accursed eternity riding through time, bound to an abomination.

In the depths of his psyker's soul he felt the vortices close over the *Aethon*. The ship had not raised its Geller fields; it was open to the full force of the warp. Raw psychic power washed the through the hull in an invisible wave. Those aboard died a thousand times over, their bodies broken down and remade over and over again before being scattered as dry dust through the halls of the ship.

Cyrus kept his eyes open through it all, holding his body and soul together with the last scrap of his will.

He thought of the signal. The signal that had fixed this fate from the moment he heard it, the signal the daemon had never sent, that no one had ever sent. He closed his eyes and sent his voice out into the warp. His words would become a broken message to trap himself and the daemon, binding their fates together. Somewhere in the bones of the ship the daemon heard his words and howled.

His last unheard confession spoken, he let go and the storm broke his body and soul apart.

The *Aethon* tumbled on, falling back through time, becoming something new, as was fated.

ABOUT THE AUTHORS

Sarah Cawkwell is a north-east England based freelance writer. Married, with a son (who is the grown up in the house) and two intellectually challenged cats, she's been a determined and prolific writer for many years. Her first novel, *The Gildar Rift*, was published in 2011. When not slaving away over a hot keyboard, Sarah's hobbies include reading everything and anything, running around in fields with swords screaming incomprehensibly and having her soul slowly sucked dry by online games.

After a music career so disastrous it landed him in court, **Darius Hinks** decided a job in publishing might be safer. His fiction for the Black Library includes *Sigvald* and *Warrior Priest*. Rumours that he still has a banjo hidden in his loft are fiercely refuted by his lawyers.

Author of the Soul Drinkers and Grey Knights series, freelance writer **Ben Counter** is one of Black Library's most popular SF authors, and has written RPG supplements and comics books as well as novels. He is a fanatical painter of miniatures, a pursuit which has won him his most prized possession: a prestigious Golden Demon award. He lives in Portsmouth, England, where he can sometimes be seen indulging his enthusiasm for amateur dramatics on the local stage.

John French is a writer and freelance games designer from Nottingham. His work can be seen in the *Dark Heresy*, *Rogue Trader* and *Deathwatch* roleplay games and scattered through a number of other books including the award nominated 'Disciples of the Dark Gods'. When he is not thinking of ways that dark and corrupting beings can destroy reality and space, John enjoys talking about why it would be a good idea, and making it so with his own Traitor Legions on the gaming table… that and drinking good wine.

DIGITAL PREMIÈRES

Read these novels first as eBooks

Download them all from
www.blacklibrary.com/ebook